Periodically A_____ at five thousand feet. Fi_____ is time to ascend."

"Yes, Professo_____ and the airship began to rise through the cold prairie air.

Five thousand . . . six thousand . . . seven . . . eight . . . up and up they went, and still they could not see over the Anomaly. At nine thousand feet their rate of ascent slowed, and the Professor, frowning again at the rock gas tank, said, "I believe we will release ballast, Anton. If you would open the tank?

"Yes, Professor." Anton bent down and turned a knob protruding through the floor of the gondola at his feet. The airship lurched, then rose much faster than before.

Ten thousand feet. Eleven thousand. Twelve, and they were slowing again. They were almost to the wall of fog marking the Anomaly, and still it rose above them, an impossible cliff of white, swirling vapor. Was it his imagination, or could he feel the chill from it even through his warm leather flying gear?

The Professor peered up into the fog. "I think we need another two to three thousand feet," he said, his voice grim but determined. "Release the sandbags, please, Anton."

The ropes dropped from the side of the gondola, the sandbags slipping off them to plummet toward the prairie below. Suddenly, it felt like a giant had grabbed them and hurled them, spinning, into the sky. The world whirled through Anton's vision, wall of fog, sunlit prairie, wall of fog, sunlit prairie. The spinning, mercifully, stopped, but hard on its heels came the unmistakable sound of tearing silk. . . .

MAGEBANE

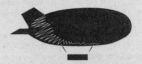

Lee Arthur Chane

DAW BOOKS, INC.
DONALD A. WOLLHEIM, FOUNDER
375 Hudson Street, New York, NY 10014

ELIZABETH R. WOLLHEIM
SHEILA E. GILBERT
PUBLISHERS
www.dawbooks.com

Copyright © 2011 by Edward Willett.

All Rights Reserved.

Cover art by Paul Young.

Cover design by G-Force Design.

DAW Book Collectors No. 1563.

DAW Books are distributed by Penguin Group (USA) Inc.

All characters and events in this book are fictitious.
Any resemblance to persons living or dead is strictly coincidental.

If you purchase this book without a cover you should be aware that this book
may have been stolen property and reported as "unsold and destroyed" to the
publisher. In such case neither the author nor the publisher has received any
payment for this "stripped book."

The scanning, uploading and distribution of this book via the Internet or via any
other means without the permission of the publisher is illegal, and punishable by
law. Please purchase only authorized electronic editions, and do not participate
in or encourage the electronic piracy of copyrighted materials. Your support of
the author's rights is appreciated.

Nearly all the designs and trade names in this book are registered trademarks.
All that are still in commercial use are protected by United States and interna-
tional trademark law.

First Printing, October 2011
1 2 3 4 5 6 7 8 9

DAW TRADEMARK REGISTERED
U.S. PAT. AND TM. OFF. AND FOREIGN COUNTRIES
—MARCA REGISTRADA
HECHO EN U.S.A.

PRINTED IN THE U.S.A.

This book is for my brothers,
Dwight and Jim. They know why.

ACKNOWLEDGMENTS

A large chunk of this book was written at the Banff Centre during a week-long, self-directed residency there in the fall of 2009. My thanks to the Centre for providing such a spectacular place in which to think and work without interruption.

Heartfelt thanks as always go to my editor, Sheila Gilbert, who has the uncanny knack of figuring out both what's right and what's wrong with a novel, and helping the writer make it the best it can be.

Thanks as well to my agent, Ethan Ellenberg, for his knowledgeable advice and hard work on my behalf.

And, finally, the deepest thanks of all to my wife, Margaret Anne, and daughter, Alice, for putting up with the very strange circumstance of having a husband and father who spends all day playing make-believe in his head. I love you both.

PROLOGUE

ALONE ON A HILL, the Healer watched the Minik village burn. Through the smoke, she heard the screams of dying men, violated women, terrified children. Through the smoke, she saw blue-white flashes of magic slashing, burning, mutilating. Through the smoke, she saw the men MageLord Starkind had brought north, murdering the people she had come to help.

In her hand she held her cloth bag of potions for pain, nostrums for nausea, compresses, bandages, sutures, and splints. In her mind, she held her own skills, wisdom, knowledge, and experience . . . and her own measure of power; but the soft magic of which she was a skilled mistress could do nothing against the hard magic of the MageLord.

The Healer had come to help the Minik. Now all she could do was watch them die.

The MageLord's men rode away. The screams had ended long before. The smoke remained, like a funeral shroud drawn mercifully across a ravaged corpse.

The Healer descended the hill and passed through that shroud. As the light faded toward night, she searched the smoldering ruins for anyone left alive. She found nothing but corpses.

All the Minik she had come to help, the Minik she had

come to love, had died—slain by the swords and spears and hard magic of the MageLord and his Mageborn followers.

She climbed the hill to the south of the village once more. The north wind blew the mingled smells of death and smoke into her nostrils. She breathed deep of that acrid stench . . . and breathed deep of hate.

This cannot stand, she thought. *This* will *not stand*.

The MageLords' reign must end.

She turned and stalked away into the night, the north wind at her back.

YEAR 775 OF THE GREAT BARRIER
(YEAR 128 OF THE REVOLUTIONARY CALENDAR)

Anton, bare back cold against wet stone, bare feet colder on wet cobblestones, waited in the rain for the old man to leave the mansion.

He'd waited there the night before, a warmer night than this, but the "Professor," as the storekeepers on Hawser Street had called him, had stayed in, even though for a week before that he had gone out at the same time every night. But tonight, right on schedule, the door to the rented mansion opened and closed, and the Professor descended the front steps, wearing a heavy black coat and gloves, face hidden beneath an umbrella. He climbed into the waiting cab. The driver, dry beneath his own umbrella, clucked to the horse and flicked the reins, and the cab clattered across the cobblestones of the courtyard, turned down an alley, and trundled off toward the glow of gaslights.

The instant it left the yard, Anton pushed away from the wall and dashed across the cobblestones, feet silent, water running down his back and dripping from the ragged bottom of the short pants that were all he wore: he'd left his only half-decent set of clothes tucked away somewhere dry, to warm him when he had finished this night's work. A miasma had descended on the port city of Hexton Down, sickening many, killing a few; if he fell ill, he had no physician to turn to ... hadn't had one since he was twelve, five years gone, before his mother died, his father took to drink, and he fled to the streets to avoid the beatings.

The old house where the Professor had taken up lodgings had been empty for a long time before that ... empty, but not unused. Long since, Anton had discovered a basement window that could be opened despite its lock, if you had the knack of it, and he had spent many a night in the house since, mostly wet, cold nights like this one.

He'd searched the house from top to bottom, several times, and found nothing of value in it; every room was neat and clean and dry, but empty of so much as a whisk broom. At the back, the house connected to a warehouse, and the warehouse, at its far end, opened onto the dock. Obviously it had once belonged to someone with shipping interests. Anton had been very careful, as he'd explored, to leave no trace of his presence, fearing the owners, if they discovered the house had been broken into, would find the loose basement window and seal it up for good.

But tonight he had more in mind than simply sheltering from the rain. The old man had money, lots of it. Box after box, some small, some large, had been delivered to the house since he had rented it: some to the front door, many others to the warehouse. There had to be something of value in there ... maybe even something that could buy him passage on a ship, away from this hellhole and off to the Wild Land. They said anyone could make a new life for himself in Wavehaven or the towns and villages beginning to spring up inland, and Anton desperately needed a new life. If the black cough or the bullyboys didn't get him, the press-gangs would, and Anton didn't fancy spending his next few years, probably his *last* few years, in either a mine or a man-of-war, thank you very much.

The rain might chill him, but at least it also made it unlikely anyone would notice his silent dash across the cobblestones, or when he vanished from sight down the narrow space between the Professor's house and the one next door, also attached to a warehouse on the docks, and also empty. The storekeepers said the Union Republic's economy had taken a turn for the worse and many businesses had gone bankrupt, but since his own economy hardly could *get* any worse, he hadn't personally noticed.

Anton crouched by the basement window and held his breath as he pushed at one corner, then twisted the frame. Had the owners fixed it . . . ?

They hadn't. The window popped from its latch and swung inward. Anton turned around, stuck his legs through and, scraping his belly on the brick, slid over the edge and dropped to the smooth stone floor. The barely gray square of the window did nothing to illuminate the pitch-darkness, but Anton knew where the stairs were, over on the other side above the lamentably empty wine rack.

He crept across the floor, hand outstretched, until he felt the banister. A moment later he was up the stairs and pushing at the door into the kitchen. It swung open with the sound of a cat being strangled, and he froze, listening hard, but the rest of the house remained silent, and so he stepped through.

The three tall windows provided enough light to show that whatever the Professor might be doing in his rented mansion, cooking wasn't part of it. Bowls and vials and mortars and pestles cluttered one table, but when Anton crept over and bent down to take a sniff, he recoiled. It smelled like a brothel's outhouse.

He did find a passable loaf of bread on a sideboard, rather stale, but he'd had worse. Taking it with him to gnaw on, leaving a trail of bread crumbs behind—there was no point in trying to pretend he hadn't been here *this* night—he searched the rest of the house.

The Professor seemed to be camping rather than living there. Whatever had been in the big boxes, it hadn't been furniture. He wasn't even using the bedrooms upstairs. The living room held a folding cot, with a tangled blanket and a rather tortured-looking pillow. A small table bearing a couple of smeared plates, a battered knife and fork, and a half-empty bottle of wine completed the furnishings. Anton picked up the wine bottle and swigged from it to wash down the last of the dry bread, then continued his search.

He grew more and more frustrated as he went from room to room and found nothing . . . nothing of value, anyway. *The warehouse*, he thought. *Everything must have gone in there.*

He knew where the door into the warehouse was. It had always been locked when the house had been empty, and so it was this time.

But this time, a key hung on a peg by the door. Anton inserted it into the lock, turned it . . . and the door swung soundlessly open.

The warehouse's windows, high and narrow beneath the eaves, gave little light. Anton stepped forward, expecting the floor to be at the same level as the house's . . .

. . . but it wasn't. His foot found nothing. He flailed for something to grab hold of, failed to find it, and fell.

His head cracked against the stone, and he plunged from the darkness of the warehouse into the far deeper darkness of unconsciousness.

———

When Anton awoke, he couldn't figure out where he was. He lay, naked beneath a blanket, on something soft. He was warm and dry. Above him, soft yellow light flickered off ceiling beams painted with blue-and-yellow flowers. He stared up at them. They looked familiar . . .

The house. The living room. He was in the living room of the house.

He sat up, but the room swam around him, and he dropped back again with a moan. As he raised a shaking hand to his head, and found a lump on his forehead that felt the size of a horse apple, the door to the kitchen opened. He turned his head and saw the Professor, carrying a steaming mug. "Awake, are you?" the Professor said gruffly. Clean-shaven, with graying hair cut very short, he looked far more formidable up close than Anton had ever thought him to be from a distance. He was very lean, and Anton had assumed that was because he was frail with age, but now that the Professor was wearing only a white undershirt above black trousers, Anton could see the whipcord muscles on his arms, the broad chest, and narrow waist. "Drink this." He lifted Anton with one hand while holding the steaming mug to his lips with the other. Anton, remembering the awful-smelling concoction he'd discovered in the kitchen, hesitated, but the liquid, though bitter, was palatable. The Professor lowered him again, then stood over him, frowning. "What's your name?" he said abruptly.

"Anton," Anton said. "When will the police arrive?"

"Police?" The Professor put the mug on the table beside the bed. "I called no police."

Anton blinked. "But I broke in—"

"I have a proposition for you," the Professor said, and Anton's eyes narrowed. The Professor snorted. "Not that kind of proposition," he said. "How old are you?"

"Seventeen."

"How did you end up on the streets?"

Anton shrugged. "Usual story. Mother dead, father drunk, nightly beatings. What do you care?"

"It's a story I know well," the Professor said. "It was my story, once. But someone changed the ending. A man who found me, beaten, half-dead, in an alley. He took me in, gave me work, gave me food, gave me an education. I went to school. I read. I learned." He crouched beside Anton's bed. "And now, I find myself in the position to help someone else, someone much like I was. I have need of a strong young assistant, Anton. I have planned a great adventure for myself, but I cannot do it on my own. If you are willing to work hard, learn, do everything I tell you, you can share in that adventure." He spread his hands. "I cannot promise any great reward if we succeed. I cannot even promise we will survive. But you will have a place to sleep, food to eat, and important work to do. What do you say?"

Anton's head hurt marginally less since swallowing the Professor's potion, but he still had a hard time taking in what the Professor was saying. "All you know about me is that I broke into your house looking for something to steal," he said slowly. "Why would you offer to help me?"

"I told you: because someone once offered to help me."

"I could still rob you."

The Professor rose, the movement smooth and catlike, and looked down at Anton with his hands on his hips and a sardonic expression. "I'd like to see you try."

Anton closed his eyes for a moment. He had nothing outside this house: one set of worn-out clothes, a pair of shoes with holes in them, and that was it. He lived by stealing from the marketplace, running messages for the bully-boys, picking the occasional pocket. Meals, a place to sleep, escape from Hexton Down, a chance at reward . . . unless the Professor was just blowing smoke about that . . . why not?

He opened his eyes again. "All right," he said. "But what is this great adventure you have planned?"

The Professor smiled for the first time, the candlelight dancing in his eyes. "Tell me, Anton. Have you ever dreamed of flying?"

And Anton, staring up at him, wondered if he had just agreed to help a lunatic.

CHAPTER 1

LIKE A CHICK IN ITS EGG, Jenna lay curled within a bubble of ice half-buried in muck at the bottom of Palace Lake. In her gloved left hand she clutched the frost-covered spellstone that kept the walls of her shelter frozen, teased air from the blue-green water ... and slowed time. After a day and a night, she should have been so cramped from immobility she would not be able to move when the time came, but to her, it had not been a day and a night; to her, it seemed only a few minutes had passed since she had waded into the lake in the early morning darkness. Her thoughts, though flowing normally to her, in fact moved with all the sluggishness of treacle in midwinter.

She had left that cold the day before, passing through the single Gate in the Lesser Barrier into the Palace grounds with a dozen other young women, newly hired to serve as maidservants.

And what happened to those we replaced? she thought bitterly as she waited in her bubble of ice. *Some have grown too old, some have grown too ugly. And some have simply vanished, used, abused, discarded, no questions asked, no investigations launched, no retribution, no recompense ... because those doing the using and abusing and discarding were MageLords.*

The spellstone filled her left hand, but her right held

something else: a tiny crossbow, cocked and loaded, the quarrel white with frost, steaming with cold. Around her neck, she wore a third item of magic: a simple silver circlet, broken in one place, hanging on a cord of leather.

In her time-slowed memory, it had been only a short while since Vinthor had hung that amulet around her neck. "This is the power source," he had said. "Keep it hidden." She had nodded, and pushed it down inside her blouse, so that it lay, cold at first but warming quickly, between her breasts, glad that at least it did not glitter with frost like the spellstone and quarrel.

"The spellstone knows what to do," Vinthor told her. "The moment you are completely submerged, it will form your . . ." he hesitated, searching for the word.

"Blind?" Jenna suggested. "I am going hunting, after all."

Vinthor smiled at that, but it was a smile tinged with sadness. "I wish someone else could do this," he said softly. "But . . ."

"But only a young woman, hired to be a maid, can get inside the Lesser Barrier," Jenna said. "I volunteered, re-member, Vinthor? When you told us what the Patron needed." She remembered the pride she had felt, the excite-ment that at last she could strike a blow for the Commons . . .

. . . for her mother's sister, the aunt she had adored as a small child, until suddenly she wasn't there anymore—vanished, like so many others, in the service of the MageLords.

That memory brought a fresh surge of hatred to her breast. "I want this, Vinthor," she said. "It's the greatest honor I can imagine."

Vinthor nodded, lips pressed tightly together. "Of course. And I have every confidence in you. As does the Patron." He put a hand on her shoulder. "I will be watch-ing," he said. "From outside the Barrier. When you strike your blow . . . I will bear witness to the Patron that you did your part, and did it well."

That had been their farewell. There was nothing else to be said, because they both knew that, whether the attack succeeded or failed, Jenna would almost certainly not survive. It was one thing to get inside the Lesser Barrier: another entirely to get out of it, with the Royal guard in full cry.

And that was why Jenna carried one other small object, not magical at all: a simple glass vial, filled with a fast-acting and fatal poison.

Whatever happened, she must not be taken and questioned by Lord Falk, the Minister of Public Safety. And so, whatever happened, she would not be.

She took another long, slow breath. Subjectively, her wait had not yet been long. But it didn't matter.

Long or short, it would end eventually.

Eventually, the Prince would come.

And then, the Prince would die.

―――――

Not ten strides from where Prince Karl and his bodyguard Teran sat in magical sunlight on soft green grass, a snowstorm raged.

Warm enough with only a wrap around his waist, Karl watched snow slithering across drifts that ended abruptly, flat as knife-sliced slabs of cheese, against the Lesser Barrier, visible only as a slight shimmer in the air like heat waves rising from a fire. Then his eyes narrowed. Something was moving out there.

"Teran, look!" He pointed toward the Barrier. Teran, who had been gazing across the lake at the Palace, twisted his head around to look as a shadow took shape, materializing into a Commoner who was struggling through the snow-choked park on the other side of the Barrier. Swathed in a knee-length coat of black fur, with throat, mouth, and chin wrapped in a dark-green scarf beneath a huge fur hat, the man raised his head as the light of the magesun fell on his face. His eyes met Karl's. For a long moment—a few seconds longer than strictly proper, Karl thought—he stared at the Prince; then he lowered his head and plowed on. Within seconds he faded back into the swirling gloom.

"He didn't look too happy with you, Your Highness," Teran said idly. Being technically on duty, he wore his guard uniform of blue tunic and trousers, silver breastplate and high black boots, but he had set his helmet aside on the grass and his sword next to it. His right hand held a dew-covered bottle of Old Evrenfels Amber. Drinking on duty was definitely against regulations, but the only one who could report him was Karl, and Karl had given him the bottle in the first place, from the magic-cooled chest close at hand.

Karl snorted. "*I* wouldn't be too happy with me, either. But what's he doing wandering through the park in *that* weather?"

"Probably just wanted to get a glimpse of something green and growing," Teran said. He jerked his head in the direction of the Barrier. "It's not easy out there in the winter, you know. Even in the city. That's when the Commoners envy the Mageborn the most. It's a good thing you make a point of going out there once in a while, cutting ribbons, making speeches. Otherwise that envy might turn into hate."

Karl shook his head. "They're fools if they envy me," he said. "Oh, it's a nice enough prison," he looked around at the manicured grass, the flowering bushes, the sparkling blue lake with the sprawling white limestone Palace on its far shore, the many-arched long bridge across the top of the dam that had formed the lake, "but it's still a prison."

"I suspect those held in Falk's dungeon would dispute your definitions," Teran said dryly.

Karl laughed. "True enough." He grinned affectionately at his bodyguard. "So you're saying I should quit bellyaching and enjoy myself."

"Exactly." Teran took another swig of ale. "Like me."

"You're supposed to be protecting me," Karl pointed out.

"From what, exactly?" Teran said. "Out there," he gestured at the snowstorm, "sure, there could be a risk. I could see a Commoner attacking you, since he might not understand how the magic works. But in here?" He looked around. "Unless some goose gets homicidal urges, you're safe as houses. No Mageborn would ever attack the Heir. What would be the point?"

Karl laughed again. "Lucky for you." He took a swallow of his own beer. Teran was quite right, of course. No MageLord or Mageborn *would* attack him, because it would accomplish nothing; he might be the Heir, but if he died, the Keys, the special magic of the King that kept the Great and Lesser Barriers in place, would simply choose a new Heir. No one would know who that Heir was until King Kravon died and the Keys made the leap to their new host. Since the new Heir would be unknown, no one could influence that person ahead of time. Worse, the new Heir might prove to be an enemy of whoever had arranged the assassination—someone who would then be able to act on that enmity with all the resources of the Kingship once the Keys came to him or her.

Outside the Barrier, he supposed it was conceivable, as Teran said, that some deranged Commoner might attack him. He could even imagine—barely—some disgruntled Mageborn attacking him. But all the Mageborn who lived inside the Barrier, southwest of the Palace in the grand houses of the Mageborn Enclave, had sworn fealty to one of the five MageLords who served on the King's Council . . .

. . . well, almost all, he corrected himself. There were three types of mages residing within the Barrier whose fealty was only to the King: a prime example of one type, the Royal guard, currently sat next to him, drinking his beer.

The Healers were another. Though, like all Mageborn, they had some modicum of hard magic, they had an additional skill, rare and valuable. They could use soft magic, useful for healing bodies and minds. Hannik, the First Healer, resided in the Palace like a MageLord, looking after the health (with the help of a handful of lesser-ranked Healers) of everyone inside the Lesser Barrier. It was unthinkable one of *them* would be involved in any kind of violent attack on the Heir.

Finally, there were the mages of the Magecorps, who

served the King under the direction of the First Mage, Tagaza. Made up of the best and the brightest of those who passed through the College of Mages in Berriton, some hundred miles to the north, the Magecorps did everything from making sure the Palace's many magical systems continued operating—"water running, toilets flushing, and lights turned on," as they put it—to researching the theory and practice of magic.

Karl had met First Healer Hannik a few times when he'd suffered a broken bone or nasty cut from some childish misadventure. He met Tagaza almost daily, since Tagaza was his tutor in all things to do with magic and history . . . and, above all, politics.

Karl glanced at the Palace again. It looked pure and white from this distance, almost half a mile away, but he knew better. It seethed with intrigue, everyone jockeying for power and position.

There were twelve hereditary MageLords. Their ancestors had been the most powerful mages of their or any other day. Karl still found it hard to fathom what they had done, transporting themselves and a few hundred followers halfway around the world from the collapsing Old Kingdom. They had established the new kingdom of Evrenfels in the middle of a wilderness and erected the Great and Lesser Barriers to protect the kingdom and themselves. Despite their extraordinary forebears, the current MageLords were not necessarily any more powerful magically than many ordinary Mageborn, but that didn't matter. With the MageLords' titles came vast lands over which they could rule pretty much as they saw fit.

Five of the Twelve held even greater power: they served on the King's Council, which governed the entire land. *In the name of the King, of course*, Karl thought sardonically, though he doubted King Kravon knew about even a tenth of what was done in his name. The King's power lay in being able to appoint the members of the Council, and since even on the Council, some positions were far more powerful—and far more lucrative—than others, every one

of the Twelve was constantly jockeying for the favor of the
King and looking to undercut his or her rivals.

Or would be, Karl thought, *if my father would allow anyone to meet with him except for Lord Athol and Lord Falk.*
And of those two, Prime Adviser and Minister of Public
Safety, respectively, it was common knowledge that only
Falk *truly* had the King's ear . . . which made Falk, who also
commanded the Royal guard *and* the Army of Evrenfels,
the most powerful man in the kingdom.

Karl took another sip of beer as Teran lay back on the
grass, hands behind his head, and closed his eyes. *You'd
think the King might want to see his only son and Heir once
in a while, too,* he thought with a touch of familiar bitterness. *But you'd think wrong.*

He hadn't seen his father since the Confirmation Ceremony on his eighteenth birthday, half a year gone, when
Tagaza had announced that he had tested Karl and that he
was, indeed, the Heir. It had been a very public ceremony,
however, with all of the Twelve, their families, and even the
Commoner Mayor and Council of New Cabora in atten-
dance, and he had not once had an opportunity to speak to
the King.

The last conversation with his father that he could recall
now lay some three years in the past, and had focused entirely on the sad state of the ornamental gardens.

The Confirmation Ceremony had meant that efforts
by the MageLords to curry favor with the Heir, already
intensified by the inaccessibility of the King, had intensified even further. Previous Royal lines had failed, the
Keys shifting to an Heir outside the apparent succession,
which was why the Confirmation Ceremony was a Big
Deal. Now that there was no doubt Karl would one day
be King, those MageLords not on the Council, as well as
those on the Council hoping to keep or improve their current positions, sought to influence him so that the balance
of power would shift their way on that sad day when
death at last claimed King Kravon. And as the MageLords
sought his favor, so, too, did the Mageborn sworn to their

service, seeking to boost their own fortunes alongside their lord's.

Fortunately, Tagaza, who had been First Mage for two decades and tutored Karl for the past twelve years, knew all about Palace intrigue. Thanks to his guidance, Karl assumed an ulterior motive behind every gesture of support, every kind word, every gift, every invitation to a party or play, and kept his own council as to what he thought of the various MageLords.

It sometimes seemed to Karl that, of all the people who dwelled inside the Barrier, only Tagaza and Hannik (and the Commoner servants, of course, but they hardly counted) had not tried, in ways large or small, to win his favor or turn him against rivals.

Then he snorted. Not *quite* true. Falk hadn't tried, either. The Minister of Public Safety didn't *need* Karl's favor, and Karl wasn't fool enough to think he could oust him from that position when he became King, even if he wanted to. In theory, the King could appoint whichever of the Twelve he chose. In practice . . . Karl knew how it would work. Every other member of the Twelve would refuse the position, because they all feared Falk, leaving Karl in the end with no choice but to keep him, and in the meantime, he would have weakened himself in the eyes of everyone else.

Maybe my dear father has the right idea, sequestering himself in the Royal Quarters and never bothering with any actual governing.

He glanced at Teran, and amended his earlier thought once more. Teran hadn't tried to win his favor, either. But he didn't need to: he already had it.

Teran's mother, a theoretical magician, spent her days researching in the Palace archives and writing long, learned papers of which Karl understood one word in ten. He had met her once or twice; she lived in the Mageborn Enclave. Teran's father, though he had died when Teran was very young, had likewise been in the Magecorps, though his duties had been more practical: he had been killed in a cave-in while recharging the magelights in the Commoner-worked coal mine that provided fuel for the MageFurnace that burned day and night beneath the Palace to provide energy for the magic of all the Mageborn within the Lesser Barrier.

Like Karl, Teran had grown up in the Palace, and since they were almost of an age, the two boys had naturally fallen in with each other, roaming freely inside the Barrier, swimming in the lake, buying ice cream in the Enclave, chasing the geese, sneaking into the kitchen ... and one night when they were twelve, sneaking into the maids' bathing room.

That had been memorable not only for the enlightenment and entertainment it had provided, but for revealing to Karl his own peculiar magical ability, an ability he had told no one about because it was too useful as a secret.

As Heir to the Keys, Karl wasn't supposed to *have* any magic of his own. Certainly, he couldn't light fires with a flick of his hand or move small objects without touching them, the way even the lowliest Mageborn could.

But that night, as the boys, passing through the hallways of the servants' quarters after a snack in the kitchens, had passed the bathing rooms, Karl, laughing to Teran about how he'd love to sneak in there, had said, "Too bad they lock the doors with magic." Then he had reached out and tugged on the handle ...

... and the door had opened.

Nobody had seen them that evening, though they'd gotten a delightful eyeful themselves. Teran had said something about how lucky they'd been that the door had been unlocked, and left it at that.

Karl, though, knew very well that the door had *not* been unlocked, but had come unlocked at his touch. After that, he'd started touching other enchanted items just to see what would happen.

He only seemed to be able to deactivate small objects: locks, lights, heating stones. Near the Palace's main entrance stood a famous magical timepiece that showed not only the time but also the positions of the stars and planets, as tiny whirling models inside a crystal dome. One day Karl had casually leaned against it for a while, then walked away. He'd been vaguely disappointed to see it still working . . . but a day later he saw two mages working on it, muttering about it needing adjustment for the first time in half a century. Magecorps mages always seemed to be somewhere near his quarters, trying to fix something that had unexpectedly failed.

Once, when he was about sixteen, he'd even dared to touch the Lesser Barrier, though he'd been warned against it; people who had tried that before had suffered severe frostbite. *No matter how cold it is, a quick touch won't hurt anything,* he'd thought . . . and so he'd reached out, ready to snatch his hand away again in an instant . . .

. . . and hadn't felt any cold at all. In fact, the Barrier had felt almost springy to his touch, like soft rubber. He'd snatched his hand back and never tried again.

His best guess was that his strange power had something to do with his being Heir, but he'd never asked Tagaza about it nor mentioned it to anyone else . . . even Teran. The ability to de-magic small items, unlock locked doors, and turn out magelights seemed much more useful as a secret than something for Tagaza to research . . . and tell Falk about; the First Mage and Minister of Public Safety were close friends.

It was hardly the only secret he held close. He and Teran were still friends, but their relationship was very different now that Teran was in the guard and he was the confirmed Heir. *I have many more secrets than I did as a child,* Karl thought. Then a frown flicked across his face. *I wonder if Teran does, too?*

He shrugged aside that notion, and the whole mass of circling thoughts about Palace life and Kingdom politics that more and more filled his mind these days, put down his beer bottle, and got to his feet. Stretching, he looked around at the wide, tree-studded lawn that sloped up from the lake to the Barrier. This was one of his favorite places, with almost half a mile of water separating him from the Palace.

Few Mageborn visited it, and it was off-limits to Commoners, which gave him the illusion of solitude . . . his bodyguard excepted, of course. On days when the weather inside and out of the Lesser Barrier was the same, he sometimes rested here and pretended that nothing separated him from the rest of the world, that the Barrier didn't even exist.

He couldn't pretend that today, with winter still clawing New Cabora and the "sunlight" within the Barrier cast not by the true sun but by the magesun, an enormous, intensely bright magelight that traversed the interior of the dome-shaped Barrier whenever clouds shrouded the outside world, but at least he could pretend to be a free man, not the near-prisoner his birth had made him.

He nudged the reclining Teran in the side with his bare foot. Teran opened one eye. "You called, Your Highness?"

"I'm going for a swim," he said. "There'd better still be beer left when I come out."

Teran grinned. "I'm sure *most* of it will still be here." He sat up, put on his helmet, then got to his feet, leaned over and picked up his sword belt, and buckled it on. "But first, of course, I have to do my job."

Drawing his sword, he walked down to the edge of the lake. He peered into the water, searched up and down the grassy shore with his hand shading his eyes, and made a show of poking his blade into all the nearby bushes. He came back and saluted. "Guardsmen Teran reporting, sir," he said. "After a hard-fought battle, I have secured the beachhead."

Karl touched his fingers to his forehead. "I salute you, sir. When I am King, you will have your just reward."

"Actually, I'll take it now," Teran said. "If it's all the same to Your Highness." He bent down, took a full bottle of beer from the open chest, pulled out the cork with his teeth, then raised the bottle to Karl. "Enjoy your swim!" he said cheerfully, then took a swig.

Karl laughed, then strolled down to the lake, dropping his clothes as he went. Naked, he stood at the water's edge for a moment, gazing across the lake at the Palace, glad to be here in the *faux* sunshine instead of locked in that den of greed, graft, and politics. Then he stepped forward. His foot touched the lapping waves . . .

. . . and thirty feet offshore, the lake erupted.

A cloud of steam exploded outward, driving a ring of spray across the water. Karl staggered as the blast slammed into him. He glimpsed someone, clad in black, face hidden, standing impossibly on the *surface* of the water. The figure raised its right hand, pointing something at him. Light brighter than the magesun flashed—and a far greater blast than the first hammered him to the ground. Ears ringing, blood running from his nose, acrid fumes burning his throat and eyes, he found himself on his back in the sand, staring up at a sky wreathed in smoke. Coughing and blinking away tears, he heaved himself up on one elbow.

For twenty feet in every direction, the grass around him had burned black. A bush that a moment before had been clothed in small white flowers now stood as naked, shattered, and charred as though struck by lightning. His discarded kilt smoldered where it lay. Water that seconds before had been calm, glittering blue now tossed brown, foam-flecked wavelets against the muddy bank.

A dozen feet from the shore bobbed something black and twisted.

Karl heard Teran's booted feet thudding across the turf toward him, but the sound seemed to come from far away. He found himself standing without really remembering getting up, and then he was wading into the troubled water.

He looked down at what floated there.

Once, it might have been human, but now it was as charred and twisted as the blasted bush. He stared at grinning teeth in a noseless ruin of a face, blind white eyes bulging from sockets whose lids had been burned away. His gaze traveled lower.

The body was female.

When Teran reached him, he was kneeling in the shallow water, his back to the blackened corpse, retching sour beer into the filthy gray waves.

———

Beyond the shimmer of the Lesser Barrier, where falling and blowing snow mingled to conceal all in swirling curtains of white, Vinthor lowered his spyglass. He could no longer see through it anyway: tears had flooded his eyes and frozen on his eyelashes. Lying on a snowdrift, half-covered with snow himself, he would have been invisible to anyone passing within a dozen feet, much less someone blinded by the magical sunshine beyond the Lesser Barrier.

Jenna! The name stabbed his heart like a knife.

Had the invisible Barrier not separated him as completely from the Palace grounds as a wall of steel, he would have rushed the naked Prince and strangled him with his bare hands, bodyguard be damned. That that decadent Mageborn *fool* should continue to live while beautiful Jenna, so young, so full of life, floated in the water as a withered, blackened corpse . . .

He had cursed himself for misjudging his distance and coming unexpectedly onto the very verge of the Barrier fifteen minutes earlier—practically on top of the Prince himself. He'd thought then that it didn't matter, that even if the Prince and his guard, lolling at ease on the other side of the magical wall, did note his face well enough to later identify him, it would mean nothing, with Jenna ready to strike.

But the Prince and the bodyguard both lived, and Jenna, unthinkably, did not.

He scraped the freezing tears from his eyes, then snapped the spyglass closed. Clambering to his feet, he struggled through the snow away from the Barrier, back toward the shadowy, smoky streets of New Cabora. He wanted no one on the other side to see him now, for certain.

He would report what had happened to the Patron.

He did not think the Patron would be pleased.

CHAPTER 2

LORD FALK, MINISTER OF PUBLIC SAFETY, emerged onto the front steps of the Palace after his daily audience with the King. As usual, he had reported on happenings within the Kingdom in extremely vague terms: "some unrest within the Commons . . . Royal Army continues to pursue Minik raiders . . . murmurings from Lord Santhorst's estate of taxes being too high, and a shortage of coal. . . ." If the King had been paying attention, even that should have been enough to alert him to the fact that the state of his Kingdom was not ideal, but of course the King had not been paying attention. He had a new favorite, a boy that looked to Falk to be no more than fifteen, a Commoner, of course, and had spent most of the audience whispering in the boy's ear, the boy sipping wine and eating artfully crafted hors d'oeuvres on silver sticks and generally looking like a cat that had managed to swallow a goose.

Falk had hardly been surprised to see the boy there, since he had been the one to pluck him off the streets of New Cabora for the King's pleasure. He had done it many times before, over the years, but it gave him no small amount of satisfaction to know that he would never have to do it again, if all went according to plan.

Keeping the King entertained, Falk had long since discovered, was the best way to keep him uninvolved in those matters Falk really preferred he remained uninvolved in, such as governing the Kingdom. *I can do that a lot better without his interference*, Falk thought, lips twitching, though not *quite* turning up in a smile: he made it a point to never smile in public.

Had he not had that public image to maintain, though, he would have been grinning from ear to ear. The day was fast approaching when he would no longer have to concern himself with keeping the King happy, for he would be the King.

As I should have been anyway, he thought. He stopped at the top of the broad staircase and looked across the cobblestoned drive to the ceremonial gardens stretching a hundred yards down to the lake. In the middle of the gardens, Queen Castilla on her favorite horse held up her hand in an eternally frozen wave to crowds that had been every bit as imaginary when she was alive as they were now that she was only a not-very-well-executed bronze. Falk's lip curled. *That statue goes first thing*, he thought. It had been Castilla, grandmother of the current King, who had stolen the Kingship from his lineage.

The gardens—a riot of green, red, white, yellow, and blue—stretched beneath the bright light of the magesun to the red-tiled roof of the boathouse and the three sailboats and two rowboats tied to the long pier. Beyond them glittered Palace Lake. On the far side of the lake, half a mile away, a broad green lawn, dotted with trees, ran up until it encountered the Lesser Barrier. Beyond *that*, of course, all was white, wrapped in blizzard.

Falk shaded his eyes with one hand as he glimpsed movement on that lawn. Two men: one naked, walking down to the water, the other in the unmistakable blue of a Royal guard. *Prince Karl*, Falk thought. *Someone else who has almost served his purpose.*

He was about to start down the steps when something flashed. His head shot up, and then he heard a sound like a single clap of thunder . . . but it never thundered inside the Barrier.

And then he saw the cloud of steam and smoke rising from the far side of the lake, and the circle of blackened ground where the Prince had been, and he started running, down the steps, across the drive, sharp left and a dash to the bridge that ran across the top of the dam. "Jansit, to me," Falk snapped to one of the two Royal guards on duty at the Palace end of the bridge. "Perric, summon Captain Fedric and First Mage Tagaza. Tell them Prince Karl has been attacked with magic on the far side of the lake. Go!"

The two guards exchanged startled looks, then Perric raced off toward the Palace and Jansit fell in behind Falk as he ran toward the bridge. To their right was the lake. To their left, halfway across, the river that emptied the lake wound out through the Mageborn Enclave before passing through the Barrier . . . or, this time of year, not passing through, since the river on the other side of the Barrier was frozen solid. Together, they pounded across its cobble-stoned surface. At the far end the road continued another quarter mile to the massive stone arch of the Gate, beneath which was the only opening through the Barrier, kept open by powerful enchantments within the arch. A red banner flying from the tower showed that the Gate was closed, and Falk nodded approvingly. They must have slammed it shut the moment they heard the explosion.

The guards at the Gate were too far away to summon, but there were also two men on duty at the north end of the bridge, staring into the park, where the smoke Falk had seen was now a rapidly dissipating cloud climbing toward the magesun. "Both of you, come with me," Falk snapped. "Prince Karl has been attacked!"

Steps led down from the bridge to the lake's north shore. Falk raced down them, then dashed through the grass. A line of bushes blocked his view of the place where the Prince had been, but when he rounded them, he was relieved to see Karl apparently unharmed, sitting outside a circle of burned grass. His bodyguard's short cape had been flung around his shoulders, though since it hung only as far as the small of his back, it did nothing to hide his nakedness.

Not that Falk cared about that. "Search the shoreline,"

he snapped to the three guards who had followed him.
"Go!" As they hurried off, he went to the Prince's side.
"Your Highness," he said, looking down at the youth. "Are
you unharmed?"

Karl looked up. Blood from his nose had caked his upper lip and chin and run down onto his bare chest. "Yes," he
said. "But I can't say the same for my attacker." He nodded
at the water, and Falk saw for the first time the blackened
corpse bobbing there. He waded two steps into the water,
but all he could tell from a quick look was that it had been
a female. Its clothes had either been blasted away or fused
with its skin, but it wore something around its neck . . .

. . . he peered closer, and felt a shock as though he had
fallen headfirst into the lake's cold water, followed a moment later by a rush of hot rage. He grabbed the amulet
and jerked it free, its scorched leather cord snapping as he
pulled, bits of blackened flesh clinging to it. He shoved the
thing in his pocket, then stepped back from the body.

With his mind, he reached out for magic and energy. The
magic flowed strong all around him, of course; the Palace
was built on—in fact the entire Kingdom was centered
on—a great lode of magic, deep beneath the ground. It had
been that lode that had drawn the First Twelve to this spot,
not to mention allowed them to transport hundreds of people here, almost eight centuries before. This far from the
MageFurnace, he had to draw energy from the air and water, but it was sufficient to his needs.

He formed the spell he wanted in his mind. Some mages
murmured words to help them twist their thoughts into the
pattern to accomplish a particular task. Some used talis-
mans; objects whose shape and texture helped them focus.
Falk disdained such things. He needed only his will to bend
his mind just . . . so . . .

With a sound like breaking twigs, the water around the
corpse froze solid for a foot in every direction. Mist
wrapped the charred remains. An instant later the mist had
vanished and the ice broke apart into chunks; but the dead
body continued to glisten, as though encased in frost.

Locked in magical stasis, it would deteriorate no further until released from the spell, or until the spell wore off naturally, which wouldn't be for some days.

That task done, Falk spun and waded out of the water. He shot a look at the bridge. A dozen figures were crossing at a run, silver breastplates and helmets flashing on ten of them, the eleventh, wearing gray, close behind them, and the twelfth wrapped in a green robe, bringing up the rear and falling farther behind with every step. Falk crouched by the Prince. "The First Healer and First Mage are coming, Your Highness."

"I told you, I'm not hurt," Karl said, though his face was pale and his teeth chattering. "I don't know *why* I'm not hurt . . . but I'm not."

"The First Healer will make sure of that," Falk said. He straightened, looked to see how far the three searchers he had sent along the shoreline had gotten, then turned to Karl's bodyguard. "Teran," he said, voice cold as the ice still bobbing around the corpse. "What happened?"

Teran, ramrod straight, looked past Falk rather than directly at him. "The assassin rose out of the water, Lord Falk," he said. "She fired a small crossbow at the Prince. But when the bolt touched him, both she and the ground surrounding the Prince were burned by a sizable blast of magical flame. The Prince was knocked to the ground, but seemed to be unhurt. He waded into the water to look at the corpse, threw up, then at my urging returned to the shore and sat down to await the arrival of help."

Teran had kept his voice neutral, reciting the bald facts without emotion. Falk knew why, of course. Teran hated and feared him, with good reason, since Falk had "recruited" him to spy on the Prince by the simple measure of threatening his mother and sister, who lived under his control in the Enclave.

He let Teran sweat for a moment, while he turned to face the line of bushes screening him from the bridge, impatient to see Tagaza, but the First Mage had yet to appear. After a moment, he glanced back at Teran. "Very well," he said. "Return to the Prince's side. I may have more questions later."

"My lord," said Teran, giving just enough of a nod to avoid being insubordinate. Rather than return immediately to the Prince, however, he trotted up the bank to where a chest and a backpack waited, retrieved the backpack, and then headed back down to the lake and the barely-covered Prince. A moment later he was pulling clothes out of the pack and handing them to Karl. Falk watched the Prince start as Teran touched his shoulder, look up, look at the pack, and then almost convulsively get to his feet. Shock, Falk judged. Well, that was certainly to be expected. But he was alive, and that was all Falk cared about. *And only for now*, he thought.

The additional guards, led by Captain Fedric, jogged into sight. Falk ordered Fedric to have his men join the other three in conducting a thorough search of the area. Hannik, the First Healer, had gone straight to the Prince. As the guards spread out, the First Mage finally arrived, puffing around the bushes. His rather shapeless green robe hid his alarming bulk, but his bald pate, tattooed with blue-and-green flowers, glistened with sweat. The First Healer, a short, thin man who, though balding, still had more hair than Tagaza, glanced up from the Prince as Tagaza leaned on his knees, gasping for air, and got to his feet, as though afraid his services would be needed to deal with Tagaza's apoplexy rather than whatever had happened to the Prince.

Six weeks, and you can drop dead at your leisure, Falk thought irritably. *But not before.*

The First Mage's face had gone from gray to flushed. The Healer seemed to take that as a good sign; he knelt by the Prince again.

Finally Tagaza gathered enough air to speak. "What ... what happened?" he puffed. "I was in the ... garden ... heard the bang, but didn't ..."

Falk jerked his head toward the lake and led Tagaza down through the grass. Tagaza gazed at the crisped body floating in the water within the glimmering sheen of stasis.

"She was lying in wait beneath the water," Falk said. "She emerged, fired a crossbow at the Prince . . . and then died, because whatever spell she intended to kill the Prince seems to have claimed her instead. Examine her and tell me what you find." He lowered his voice. "She was wearing an Unbound symbol," he murmured.

Tagaza shot a glance at him, eyebrows raised.

"I have removed it. We'll discuss it later." He looked again at the Prince, now clothed, standing, and shooing Hannik away with an irritated gesture. "The Prince will ask you questions. Be careful what you tell him."

Tagaza's face had gone pale now, as he gazed at the corpse; pale, with a touch of green. "I always am, my lord."

Falk strode to the Prince, his boots raising clouds of gray ash from the circle of burned grass. He looked first to Hannik. "First Healer?"

"He's essentially unharmed," Hannik said. He looked around at the burned circle. "Though, for the life of me, I can't figure out why."

"We're working to determine that," Falk said. "Thank you. You may return to your regular duties."

"I do not require your permission to do so, my lord," Hannik pointed out with a touch of acid in his voice. "I serve at the King's pleasure, not yours." He turned from Falk, bowed to the Prince, then turned and strode back to the bridge. *They'll soon enough be one and the same, old man*, Falk thought savagely as he watched him go.

Karl had opened his shirt for the Healer's examination; now he buttoned it up again, ran a hand through his shaggy blond hair, and glared at Falk. "Someone just tried to kill me, Lord Falk. Isn't it your job to prevent such things?"

Falk clamped down on his temper. *Soon*, he thought. *Soon.* Out loud, he said only, "My lord, such an attack is unprecedented. In fact, I would have said it was impossible. I am hoping the First Mage," he nodded toward Tagaza, who had waded into the water to look at the corpse, robes hitched up in one hand to reveal massive, hairy calves as big as tree trunks, "may shed light on how it was done. But at the moment, I can tell you nothing."

"Then let us consider the 'why.'" Karl's eyes never wavered from Falk's face. "Why would any Mageborn want to murder the Heir? It accomplishes nothing."

He's got the nub of it, Falk admitted sourly to himself. "It could be a personal, rather than a political, attack," he suggested out loud. "If someone hated you enough . . ."

". . . you would surely know it," Karl said. "As would I. I can think of no one who hates me at all, much less enough to go to such elaborate lengths to kill me. There are easier ways."

Falk let slide the notion that no one could possibly hate Karl enough to kill him, since he personally would have slain the Prince without a qualm if he didn't need him for a few more weeks, and admitted to himself that Karl had a point. A rock from the roof, poison in his cup, a thrown dagger, an ordinary crossbow bolt from hiding . . . the Prince moved and mingled freely within the Lesser Barrier, because in almost eight centuries, there had never been a plot against the Heir. As Karl himself said, killing the Heir would ordinarily accomplish nothing. And killing Karl in *particular*, Falk thought, would accomplish nothing . . . though only a few people knew that.

He frowned. That wasn't quite true, of course. Killing Karl would accomplish one thing; it would disrupt Falk's plans. And the Unbound symbol in his pocket lent that possibility more weight than he would ordinarily have given it.

He tucked that thought away to consider in more detail later. *First, gather information.* "Did Your Highness see anyone nearby before the assassin attacked?" he said.

"No one," Karl said.

"Your Highness . . . ?" Teran said. Karl glanced at him, then frowned.

"Oh, right. We did see a Commoner, outside the Barrier, a few minutes before the attack."

"A Commoner?" Falk turned and looked back toward

the Barrier. If anything, the storm out there had worsened. They appeared to be inside a glass dome immersed in dirty milk, the outside world entirely hidden in swirling gray and white. "In that weather?"

"He couldn't have had anything to do with the attack, anyway," Karl said. "The attacker used magic."

"But you can't be certain that the person you saw outside the Barrier was a Commoner, Your Highness," Falk pointed out.

Karl's eyes widened. "I never thought of that."

Of course you didn't, Falk thought scornfully.

The Prince's gaze narrowed again. "But even if he was Mageborn, he could have done nothing to trigger or abet the attack. Magic cannot pass through the Lesser Barrier."

"Not entirely true," said Tagaza, coming up behind the Prince.

Karl turned toward him. "Master?" he said.

"I'm not teaching you now, Your Highness," Tagaza said with a slight smile.

Karl laughed a little. "Sorry. Force of habit. First Mage, then. Are you saying magic *can* pass through the Lesser Barrier?"

"Not easily," Tagaza admitted. "But of course it is designed to allow *some* magic through. The smoke and ash from the MageFurnace, for instance, must be transported out to the Chimneys through the Barrier. And there are . . . other reasons."

" 'To allow the MageLords to strike at the Commoners should they prove rebellious,' " Karl said, as if he were quoting.

Tagaza smiled. "And I thought you were asleep during that lesson," he said.

"But that's all magic originating *inside* the Barrier. Surely it is designed to prevent any magical attack from *outside*."

"It is, Your Highness. But there are laws to magic. The Barrier cannot be even slightly permeable in one direction and remain completely impermeable in the other. So it is *theoretically* possible that someone could strike at you magically through the Barrier. Even, I suppose, that someone could find a way to bodily pass *through* the Barrier. But it would be very, very difficult to accomplish." He spread his hands. "I am First Mage, and I know *I* could not do it."

"Still, the man you saw in the snow could have been the mage who placed and armed the assassin, out there to observe the results of his efforts," Falk said. "Or, indeed, he may have been a Commoner ... which in some ways is an even more troubling prospect."

"Why would a Commoner want to kill me?" Karl protested. "I've represented the Crown in New Cabora for years. I want them to know that, even if the current King is ... uninvolved ... the next King will keep the Commons' interests in mind. I cut the ribbon to open the new clock tower of their city Hall just three months ago!"

"Ribbon cutting only goes so far," Falk said dryly. "You are still a symbol of what they call MageLord 'oppression.' There are some Commoners who might see killing you as a way of making a very loud, very public statement."

Karl frowned again. "Are you thinking of the Common Cause?"

"Not the public version, Your Highness, but as I have told you, there is a hidden, far more dangerous side." Falk glanced at the milk-white world outside. The Common Cause's public adherents insisted they were loyal to the MageLords and the King, but lobbied, as much as the Commoners *could* lobby, for greater control over their own affairs. Falk found them irritating, but left them alone as a kind of safety valve, a way to release the rebellious pressure constantly bubbling beneath the surface in the streets of the city.

But he knew well there was a shadowy side to the Common Cause, secret adherents who drew heart from the fact that once before, eight centuries gone, Commoners had risen up against the MageLords, had driven them out of the Old Kingdom to Evrenfels, terrified them so much they had built an impenetrable wall to protect themselves. Perhaps, those Common Causers suggested, it was time for history to repeat itself . . .

Fools, he thought. Commoners could not rise up against the MageLords without rebellious mages to fight at their side, and no such traitors existed.

Maybe they think a "Magebane" will arise, he thought, and snorted to himself. The mysterious master of antimagic that old legends claimed had helped the Commoners defeat the MageLords in the Old Kingdom had been conclusively proved decades ago to be a myth, probably designed to cover the asses of the incompetent MageLords who had allowed the rebellion to get so far out of hand.

What could they do, after all, against a superhuman who hurled their own magic back at them, destroying whole armies and cities? It wasn't *their* fault they'd lost the Kingdom. It wasn't *their* fault they'd fled to a howling wilderness on the far side of the world. It wasn't *their* fault they'd been so frightened of being hunted down, even here, that they had wrapped their new Kingdom inside an impenetrable, magical Great Barrier, a circular wall of protection six hundred miles in diameter.

It wasn't *their* fault they'd trapped their descendants in that self-made prison for some eight centuries and counting.

Oh, wait, he thought. *Yes, it is.*

"But I still don't understand what they could hope to accomplish," Karl said. "What message did they hope to send with my death?"

"The message, Your Highness," Falk said, trying to keep his annoyance at the boy's thickness out of his voice, "that even inside the Lesser Barrier we are not safe from them. The message that they are committed to the eventual overthrow of the MageLords . . . and might even have a hope of succeeding."

Karl shook his head. "That's stupid. The Royal guard

alone could drive off any attack with ease. We wouldn't even need to call on the army."

"I know that, Your Highness," Falk said, this time not entirely successful at hiding his irritation, "but they may not."

"So how was the attack carried out?" Karl glanced at Tagaza. "First Mage?"

"I cannot tell for certain through the stasis field, of course," Tagaza said, "but from the nature of the attack, I assume your attacker was, indeed, a Commoner. She still clutches a spellstone in one hand and a crossbow in the other. The spellstone probably allowed her to remain hidden in the water until you came within range; the crossbow is perfectly ordinary, but the quarrel it shot was no doubt also charged with magic." He glanced at Falk, who knew he was thinking about the Unbound symbol. "Perhaps she also had . . . something else . . . which stored a magical charge. When the bolt touched your skin, the magic was discharged."

"But not into me," Karl said. "How do you explain that?"

Tagaza spread his hands. "Poor enchanting skills," he said.

"All of this lends credence to the idea that Commoners are behind this attack," Falk said thoughtfully. "Not only was the attacker a Commoner, but they would have had to find a Mageborn to enchant the spellstone and quarrel . . . and any Mageborn reduced to working for Commoners is hardly likely to be one with any great ability."

Karl stared out at the Commons. "Someone would murder me just . . . to prove they can?"

"Essentially, Your Highness," said Falk. He looked around; the guards were returning, having searched the parkland from the bridge to where the water ran right up to the Barrier. "Captain Fedric, report!" he called.

Fedric saluted smartly. "We found nothing unusual, my lord."

Falk hadn't expected that they would. "Escort His Highness back to the Palace. Swords in your hands and spells ready in your minds. Then launch a thorough search of the grounds and the Palace. All papers checked and double-checked. Any Mageborn or Commoners who cannot properly account for their presence within the Lesser Barrier are to be detained for questioning. The Gate is to remain closed until further notice. Also, send a wagon, a coffin, and two men to collect the assassin's corpse."

"Yes, Lord Falk," snapped Fedric. He turned, barking orders. The guards started to form a protective cordon around Karl, but he pushed his way out from among them. As he confronted Falk, Falk noticed for the first time that the Prince's eyes were now level with his own. *When did that happen?* he wondered.

"I will expect more definitive answers from you very soon, Lord Falk," Karl said. "You may consider that a Royal Command."

Anger boiled up in Falk, but he let none of it show on his face. "Of course, Your Highness," he said. "Now, please, I must insist. Return to the Palace, and remain in your quarters until we have searched the entire grounds."

Karl took one more look at the corpse in the water, then turned and let his guards lead him back toward the bridge, leaving Falk with Tagaza. Once the guards had passed beyond the screen of bushes, Falk pulled the Unbound symbol from his pocket and held it out toward Tagaza. "She was wearing this."

Tagaza took it, and immediately said, "This was the storage device. Exhausted now, but I can feel a trace of power still clinging to it." He raised an eyebrow at Falk. "Is there a traitor among the Unbound?"

Falk took the emblem back and glared at it. "I can't believe that," he said. "Mother Northwind has examined every one of them. If any harbored thoughts of treachery, she would know."

Tagaza nodded. "Indeed she would." He looked back at the corpse. "You will have her examine the body?" he said. "That's why you put it in stasis?"

"Of course." Falk sighed. "That means a trip to my manor."

Tagaza shrugged. "You were going to have to go there soon anyway. Brenna . . ."

". . . must be brought to the Palace, yes, I know." He frowned. "Why would a Commoner be carrying an Unbound symbol?"

"To throw you off the scent," Tagaza said promptly. "To make you look to the Unbound instead of the Common Cause, or whoever is really behind the attack." He smiled. "Everyone knows of your bitter hatred of the Unbound. You have executed several of their leaders."

"Perhaps," Falk said. "I hope you are right. Because the other possibility is that someone knows that I am actually the Master of the Unbound, that the Unbound I have executed were ordinary criminals enchanted to lie about their membership in the Order, and that this assassin carried the Unbound symbol so that, after Karl was dead, I would know why he was murdered."

Tagaza frowned. "You have a devious mind, my lord."

Falk snorted. "That should hardly be a surprise to you, old friend."

"If you're right," Tagaza said, "then this attack was not really aimed at the Prince at all. It was aimed at you. At *us*."

"Someone who does not want the Barrier to fall," Falk said, "and knows how close we are to making that happen."

Tagaza shook his head. "An unsettling thought, my lord."

"Indeed." Falk glanced at the corpse once more, then up at the bridge. The Prince and his bodyguard were bright specks at its far end. "I'll leave for my manor tonight and take the corpse to Mother Northwind to examine. And when I return, I'll bring Brenna with me. I want all the pieces we need for our endgame close at hand. It may be we'll want to advance the date. I can easily give some excuse for why I want to inspect the Cauldron early this year."

"I concur," said Tagaza.

"Wait here with the body until the men come to collect it," Falk said. "I must get back to the Palace." He took one more look at the snow-wrapped world outside and let his anger boil up again. "When this storm clears, the Commoners will face one that is far worse!"

He reared back and hurled the Unbound symbol as far as he could out into the lake. The silver circle glittered as it spun end over end, then vanished beneath the waves with a tiny splash of foam.

Falk turned his back on Tagaza and strode toward the bridge.

———

Tagaza watched Falk stalk away, and sighed. He had left a large and particularly tasty glass of wine in the garden, not to mention a plate of his favorite cheese and some fresh-baked crusty bread, and now he was stuck on the far side of the lake from the Palace—howling wilderness, as far as he was concerned—waiting for guards to come and collect a crispy corpse.

He'd also been left quite alone (if you didn't count the aforementioned corpse), which he found a not-particularly pleasant state of affairs so soon after an assassination attempt. *Especially*, he thought uneasily, *one that Falk suspects may actually have been aimed at disrupting his plans*.

He supposed he should say "our" plans. After all, there would be no plans if he hadn't figured out, over years of research, how the First Twelve had created the Barriers, and—more importantly—how to bring both of them crashing down.

But although he and Falk both wanted the Barriers to fall, their reasons differed. Far more, in fact, than Falk knew.

Tagaza had seldom been as near to the Lesser Barrier as he was now. With a glance at the corpse, which he was reasonably confident was not going anywhere, he strolled north from the lake the hundred yards or so to the Barrier, and looked through its faint shimmer into the swirling storm beyond. *Such an amazing achievement*, he thought in admiration. Not as amazing as the Great Barrier, which absolutely *was* impermeable to magic, completely and totally . . . and, not coincidentally, to light as well. The Lesser Barrier was something you could see through. It was not the dome it appeared, but a giant sphere, half a mile in diameter, the Palace at its center, extending as far beneath the ground as it did into the sky above.

Even more remarkably, it somehow had been carefully tuned to allow air to pass through it, and the stream that fed the lake, without also allowing rain and wind and snow. A very fine piece of magic indeed, and Tagaza knew that the skills of the ancient MageLords that had accomplished it were long lost.

But the skill to bring it crashing down remains, he thought with pride. *It remains in me!*

And a good thing, too, because the ancient MageLords had badly miscalculated when they'd set an arbitrary expiration date for the two Barriers at a thousand years after their creation. *Did they not know?* Tagaza thought, reaching out a hand, not to touch the Barrier, but just to feel the power emanating from it.

Perhaps they didn't. The Old Kingdom, the histories agreed, had sprung up on an "inexhaustible" lode of magic. Tagaza did not believe such a thing existed, but if it were sufficiently large, the ancients might have, since they had never run up against its limit.

But *this* lode, the one on which the Palace had been built, the one to which they had transported themselves and all their more-or-less loyal followers eight centuries ago, was certainly *not* inexhaustible: not when the Barriers were drawing incredible amounts of magic from it day and night, and had been for centuries.

Tagaza had stumbled on that hard truth during his student days at the College of Mages. There were methods for measuring the amount of magic available in any particular location. The central lode in the Old Kingdom had been surrounded by many secondary lodes, avidly sought by magic miners. Cities sprouted where those lodes were found (making the miners who found them immensely wealthy).

But this lode, directly opposite the Old Kingdom on the sphere of the world, had no secondary lodes. It existed in solitary splendor, spread through the Kingdom only by a few veins, stretching out into the countryside like the spokes of a wheel. It was on the strongest of those veins that the First Twelve had established their demesnes.

With all the magic in Evrenfels so well mapped, the old magic-prospecting techniques had been long lost . . . until Tagaza, seeking an interesting focus for his graduate thesis, had decided to research them. Deep in the University archives he had found scrolls and ancient books detailing the methods the magic-miners had used. They weren't particularly difficult, and in short order he had created one of the enchanted magic-measuring devices he had read about in the histories. He had calibrated it carefully, and then decided to test it by measuring the strength of the central lode itself, which had been precisely measured and carefully recorded when the Twelve arrived.

He still remembered his bewilderment when his first reading had shown the lode considerably underpowered from what the ancients had measured. He'd checked again, recalibrated his measuring device, and checked *again*. A hundred times he'd checked, double-checked, rechecked. The reading never changed.

Unable to find any fault with his equipment, he had been forced to assume that either the founders of the kingdom had made an error, or that the lode was slowly being drained of magic.

His instructors had laughed at him. But Tagaza had continued to research and ask questions, and though no one else would believe him, he had come to the inescapable conclusion that the Kingdom of Evrenfels was running out of magic. And from further research, he had come to the equally inescapable conclusion that the cause was the Barriers. Magic did replenish itself, slowly, over time; no one knew how, exactly, but the effect had been measured. But it did *not* replenish itself as quickly as the Barriers were drawing it out of the lode.

Tagaza had graphed it. In no more than fifty years, probably less, the level of magic in the Kingdom would reach the point where all of it would be going to the Barriers. The Mageborn would find themselves without the use of magic for the first time in history. And when that happened . . .

Tagaza drew back his hand from the Barrier. *When that happens*, he thought, looking out into the snowstorm outside, *nothing will stand between us and the anger of the Commoners we have mistreated and exploited for so long.*

He shuddered and turned his back on the Barrier. Which was why the Barriers had to come down. With only the Mageborn's normal use of magic, the lode would be inexhaustible, or nearly. They could live without the Barriers . . .

. . . but only if they came to some better accommodation with the Commoners. Tagaza had argued over and over with Falk that the MageLords had to reform the way they governed, had to give the Commoners more rights . . . had, in fact, to adopt many of the policies the Common Cause—at least, the legal, public version of it—espoused.

If Mageborn and Commoners could live peaceably together, then the Lesser Barrier wouldn't be needed. As for the Great Barrier . . . well, if the histories were true, nothing waited outside the Barrier except wilderness and savages. Ordinary force of arms could secure the borders well enough.

And if the outside world *had* found this land in the time since the Old Kingdom fell, it was a world ruled by Commoners. *All the more reason to reach an accommodation with the Commoners within the Kingdom, before facing those without,* Tagaza thought.

He heard a rattling from the bridge, and looked up to see an open wagon, a coffin in the back, rolling across the cobblestones with two men on the seat. He walked slowly back toward the corpse in the water.

Knowing the Barriers had to fall, he'd researched that

little problem, too, and had figured out how to do it . . . but had also realized it was both fiendishly difficult and posed ethical problems, to say the least. It required the simultaneous murder of the King and the Heir.

At that point Tagaza might well have given up, if a certain tall, intense young man, a fellow student, had not come to his quarters one blustery winter night to ask him a few very pointed questions about his research into the construction of the Barriers.

The young man had been Falk, and though he hadn't said much that night, over time he had revealed that he belonged to the forbidden sect known as the Unbound, and that the Unbound shared Tagaza's desire to bring down the Barriers. Tagaza had been intrigued by Falk and the insights he offered into the Unbound. Tagaza thought their professed belief in some great "SkyMage" who guided and protected the MageLords as silly as the ancient legend of the Magebane, the "anti-mage" who supposedly had turned the MageLords' magic against them during the Rebellion that destroyed the Old Kingdom, but the fact that they had held on to that belief, and their belief that the Barriers had been a cowardly mistake, for eight hundred years, fascinated him.

The Unbound taught that the Mageborn were a chosen people, gifted with magic by the SkyMage so that they could have dominion over the entire world. Their roots lay in the religious beliefs of the Old Kingdom, but the impetus for their coming together into an actual organization had been the First Twelve's decision to hide the new Kingdom of Evrenfels behind the Great Barrier, and the King and Council behind the Lesser. The Unbound saw that not only as cowardly, but also as a direct affront to the will of the SkyMage.

Over the centuries Kings, Queens, and MageLords had persecuted the Unbound to a greater or lesser degree, but the cult had never faded away entirely, new recruits joining regularly, usually from the ranks of the young. *Not too surprising*, Tagaza thought. *The Unbound message boils down* to *"you're special, you're better than everyone else, and unlike them, you know The Truth."* *It might have been crafted specifically to appeal to young men.* He snorted. *Maybe it was.*

Then, a little less than a century ago, the Unbound's fortunes had taken an enormous turn for the better when, for the first time in their long secret history, a MageLord had joined their ranks: Lord Falk's grandfather, Lord Excar.

Tagaza knew the story well enough to know that Excar's conversion had had nothing to do with a sudden eruption of piety. It had been humiliation and fury that had driven him to the Unbound. *And that message of being special and destined to rule would have* really *appealed to him,* Tagaza thought.

That was because Excar had been the Heir Apparent, son of King Severad. Like Karl, he had grown up in the Palace. The dynasty had been unbroken for two and a half centuries at that point, so no one had doubted that, in time, the Keys would come to him. The First Mage didn't even test him when he turned eighteen, the youngest age at which the Keys' magic could be detected in their future recipient: there was no Confirmation Ceremony in those days.

The reason there was one *now* was because, when King Severad had died . . . the Keys had gone elsewhere. Five days after his death, five days of confusion and wondering in the Palace, a twenty-year-old Mageborn girl named Castilla had ridden up to the Gate of the Lesser Barrier, driven by an unbreakable compulsion to make the long journey from her father's horse ranch near Berriton. The First Mage had examined her and declared that she now held the Keys, and she had immediately been crowned Queen Castilla: the first ruler of Evrenfels to arise from the ranks of the ordinary Mageborn rather than from one of the families of the Twelve.

The statue of her on the horse she had arrived on now stood at the foot of the ceremonial gardens in front of the Palace, and her grandson, King Kravon, now sat on the throne (figuratively speaking, Tagaza thought, since he so rarely made an appearance in the Great Hall for court functions).

Excar, now Lord Excar, had not been there to see her arrival. He had fled the Palace for good, returning to the family manor far to the west, near the Great Barrier. Young, bitter, still a MageLord, still wealthy, still powerful, but not King, he had known the Keys would never return to his family.

Tagaza suspected Excar's real reason for joining the Unbound, offering his manor as a meeting place, providing money and resources, was to strike back at Castilla. In any event, he had quickly become the leader of the Unbound, as was his son after him, and his son after him: Lord Falk.

The Unbound had long faced a serious difficulty: to fulfill the SkyMage's will, as they saw it, they had to bring down the Barriers. But as far as anyone knew, there *was* no way to bring down the Barriers.

Until Tagaza came along.

Early on in their discussions Tagaza had told Falk his belief that magic was fading, and would disappear entirely unless the Barriers fell. Falk had scoffed at that. He believed magic came from the SkyMage and could no more fade and fail than the sun, and that the lode of magic beneath the Palace was simply a conduit for the SkyMage's power. He also vehemently disagreed with Tagaza's argument that the MageLords and Mageborn had to find a way to share more power with the Commoners, treat them more as equals. The Unbound saw the Commoners first as an underclass, there to serve the Mageborn, and second as a potential threat. After all, it had been Commoners who had risen up in rebellion against the MageLords in the Old Kingdom, with the help of traitorous mages, of course, since it was unthinkable they could have defeated the Mageborn on their own.

"Treat them well as long as they keep their place," Falk said. "Punish them without mercy if they don't."

Their differences were great, but their goal was the same. Both wanted the Barriers brought down.

And when Tagaza finally, one night over a bottle of wine ... or possibly two, he couldn't remember ... told Falk how it could be done, Falk had grown very silent, excused himself early, and disappeared for several weeks.

When he'd reappeared, he'd asked Tagaza to work for him upon graduation. Tagaza had agreed, of course—it would have been foolish to turn down such a request from the heir of a MageLord even if he didn't share Falk's goals—and a few years later, when Falk's father had died and Falk had ascended to the Twelve, Tagaza had (officially, though not in practice) left Falk's service to join the Magecorps, advancing rapidly. When the King named Falk Minister of Public Safety, some years later, he had also named Tagaza First Mage, in which position he had remained now for twenty-five years.

Twenty years ago they had finally been able to begin the process of bringing down the Barriers. Until the Heir turned eighteen, and the presence of the Keys' magic could be confirmed, they'd been unable to act. Having finally made that confirmation, they were within weeks of carrying out their long-laid plans ...

... and now, this.

Tagaza looked uneasily again at the corpse in the water. Could Falk's darkest suspicions be true? Could someone *know*, and was that someone working against them?

Mother Northwind may be able to find out, he thought, and shuddered. The old renegade Healer frightened him more than a little. He knew she had only to touch him to read his mind like an open book, and so he never let her touch him. But to think she might also be able to read the mind of a corpse ... that was frightening on a whole new level. *A man's secrets should be safe when he's in the grave*, he thought.

Although he had to admit that he fervently wished her luck in obtaining information from *this* corpse.

The wagon sent to retrieve the body had almost arrived.

About time, Tagaza thought. *My wine should still be waiting in the garden. I might not even be called on for the Prince's afternoon tutoring session. An assassination attempt is a pretty good excuse for skipping class.*

He smiled a little as he thought about how Karl had stood up to Lord Falk . . . and how much it must have galled Falk to show the respect due to a Prince to the youngster.

Karl would make a far better King than Kravon, Tagaza thought. Perhaps a very fine King indeed. *Too bad he's not really the Prince, or the Heir, at all.*

He sighed, and went to meet the approaching wagon.

CHAPTER 3

KARL WAS GLAD TO SEE THE DOOR of his quarters, and even more glad to usher Teran into them and firmly shut the other guards out. With the door closed and locked behind him, and suddenly feeling much older and more tired than any eighteen-year-old had any right to feel, he reached down and pulled off his boots, then went over to the fireplace, enjoying the feel of the thick white carpet on his bare feet.

Someone had obviously managed to warn his servants he was coming, because a fire blazed in the hearth. It wasn't really needed for warmth, since the MageFurnace provided all the hot air anyone could want, piped into every room in the Palace through floor vents, but there was something about a fire that made you feel warmer in a way mere heat could not.

Except he took one look into the hearth and turned away abruptly as a chance arrangement of embers reminded him of the blackened, staring face of his attacker.

Teran stood at attention just inside the door. "Take off your helmet," Karl told him. "I'm going to have a glass of asproga ... do you want any?"

"Not on duty, Your Highness," Teran said shortly. "Thank you."

Karl, on his way to the sideboard next to the window, shot him a sideways glance. "Since when? Was that some other guard I saw swigging ale down by the lake?"

Teran's face turned red beneath the helmet. "I would appreciate Your Highness not mentioning that to anyone," he said.

Karl, at the sideboard, paused in the act of pulling the top out of a crystal decanter filled with a bright yellow liquid. "Oh," he said in sudden understanding. "Falk. I saw him talking to you." He felt a sudden flush of anger. "If he blamed you . . ."

"He did not, Your Highness," Teran said. "But I do blame myself. I was on duty, and did not perform as my training dictates. I find myself embarrassed."

Karl made a rude noise, poured his liqueur, and picked up the little crystal glass. "There was nothing you could have done. Except possibly die if you'd been between me and that crossbow bolt."

"Your Highness," Teran said, "the best definition I know of my job is to be willing to die between you and a crossbow bolt."

"I'd rather you didn't." Karl reconsidered. "What I mean is, I'd be very grateful to you if you did, but I hope it doesn't come to that."

"It should have come to that today, Your Highness. If I had remained closer."

"Then you'd be dead, and I might be, too," Karl said forcefully. "Because I think that crossbow bolt would have killed you for sure." He hesitated, but then rushed on. Suddenly keeping it a secret didn't seem so important anymore, not if it had just saved his life. "Teran, I think I know why the assassin's attack failed."

Teran frowned. "Your Highness?"

"Do you remember that night when we were twelve, and we sneaked into the maids' bathing quarters?"

Teran's face flickered into a smile. "I am unlikely to forget, Your Highness."

"That door had *not* been left accidentally unlocked, Teran. I unlocked it."

Teran blinked. "A magical lock? But as Heir, you . . ."

". . . have no magic. Indeed."

"I don't understand."

"I don't either, exactly. But . . ." Karl explained about his strange ability. When he was finished, Teran looked . . . frightened. Which wasn't exactly the reaction Karl had expected.

"Your Highness," said Teran. "You know what that sounds like."

"What do you mean, what it sounds like? It sounds like what it is. I have this ability. It's probably because I'm the Heir, but . . ."

"Your Highness, that is not what I meant," Teran said. He took a deep breath. "That sounds like the Magebane."

"The Mage—" Karl gaped. "But that's . . . crazy. The Magebane is a myth. Tagaza says—"

"'Tagaza says,'" Teran mimicked. "Of course he does! But the common people . . . they are not as dismissive of the stories of the Magebane. Particularly the Commoners. After all, the Magebane, it is said, is the one who delivered them from the MageLords in the Old Kingdom."

Karl snorted. "I'm not the Magebane, Teran. I've got a minor ability. Like I said, it's probably related to the fact I'm the Heir—"

"Your Highness, forgive my bluntness, but you're being a fool."

For a moment Karl was *not* inclined to forgive his bluntness. He felt a rush of anger. But he tamped it down and said, "Why do you say that?"

"Because if someone among the Mageborn thought you might be the Magebane . . . or even thought you might be *taken* for the Magebane by the Commoners . . . that alone might be enough reason to kill you."

Karl gaped. He'd never thought of that. "But . . . no one knows."

"Your Highness, surely you have lived long enough now . . . as have I . . . to discover that many of the things you did as a child that you thought were secret were in fact well-known to the adults in your life."

"Um . . ." Karl couldn't deny *that*. "Lord Falk did not

mention the possibility," he said. "So I don't think *he* knows . . ."

"Perhaps not." Teran's voice grew guarded at the mention of Falk. "Though I would be . . . reluctant to make assumptions about what Falk does or does not know."

"I'm assuming you won't tell him," Karl said, lightly, as a joke, but Teran's face grew still and closed. "Teran?"

"No, Your Highness." For some reason, the words didn't seem to come easy. "No. I will not tell him."

"Well . . . good." *What was* that *all about?* Karl wondered as he took his first sip of the fiery yellow liqueur in his glass, then forgot about it as he considered Teran's suggestion that a Mageborn might want to kill him simply to prove to Commoners he wasn't the Magebane. That made . . . some kind of sense, he supposed. Except, of course, for the complete failure of the plan. If any Commoners really thought he was the Magebane, they must be completely convinced of it now that he'd walked away from a magical attack that had incinerated his attacker.

The other thing that worked against Teran's suggestion was the simple fact that the Mageborn most likely to want to eliminate someone who might stir up the Commoners was Falk, and if Falk had wanted to kill him, he could have done it any time in the last eighteen years.

But he didn't like Falk's suggestion that Commoners were behind the attack either. He had gone out of his way to reach out to the Commons, at Tagaza's urging; the First Mage had often told him he hoped there would someday be better relations between Commoners and Mageborn. He had attended any number of balls and festivals and grand openings in New Cabora, filling in for the King. He'd always gotten along well with the Commoners he met. After all, officially he didn't have any magic either.

Besides, there were surely greater acts of terror a determined Commoner could come up with, acts that would have far more impact, than the murder of the Heir, since the only thing killing him would accomplish would be to pass the Keys on to some other Heir outside of the current line of succession. Should Kravon's line die out with Karl, it wouldn't even be seen as a great loss, Kravon being . . . what he was.

He sighed. Too many questions, and no answers. "It's beyond me," he said. "I guess we'll just have to hope Falk figures it out."

"Falk is very resourceful, Your Highness," said Teran.

Taking another sip of asproga, Karl sat down in one of the two high-backed blue armchairs set in front of the fire on either side of a round marble-topped table. "I'm tired of thinking about my narrow escape from death," he said. "It was interesting for the first hour or two, but . . ." He grinned, and after a moment Teran grinned back.

"Aye, Your Highness, it is becoming tiresome," he said.

"Let's talk about something else. I've been meaning to ask you: I heard a rumor that Verdsmitt's Players are coming to the palace. True?"

Teran nodded, his grin widening. "Yes, Your Highness. I meant to inform you after your swim. I knew you'd be pleased. They're scheduled to perform in the Great Hall the day after tomorrow."

"It's been . . . what, three years?"

"Yes, Your Highness. A long time, for Verdsmitt. He used to premiere a new play every year, but he seems to have struggled with this one."

"What's it called?"

"*The Hidden Kingdom*."

"Historical?"

"No one seems to know," Teran said. "It's a mystery to everyone . . . well, except the actors, I presume."

"Intriguing," Karl said. Over the centuries, Court entertainment had solidified like kitchen grease left outside the Barrier in midwinter. The same songs, the same plays, the same stories, sung, acted, or read in the same way as ten years ago, and fifty, and a hundred. All had become part of Tradition, and though it was only Tradition, and not Law, in some ways it held more force than mere Law could ever muster. Within the greenhouse-like climate of the Court, the potential loss of face from flouting Tradition was far more feared than a mere fine or flogging. *Nothing has changed around here for decades*, Karl thought . . . but then the memory of the attack that morning struck him like a blow. *Until now*.

He shoved the thought away and took another sip of asproga. "I can't wait to see it, Teran." He leaned back in his chair and closed his eyes, savoring the warm glow of the liqueur in his belly.

"That makes two of us, Your Highness," Teran said.

Lord Falk descended a long flight of stairs into the basement of the Palace's east wing, halting at an iron-bound door. Frost had painted it in glittering white, the sure telltale of powerful magic at work. Falk pulled his black gloves from his belt, put them on, then placed both hands flat on the door. Closing his eyes, he reached out with his mind for the energy all around him, and the magic welling up from the lode deep beneath the Palace. He twisted his mind into the necessary shape, and willed the door to open. Even through his gloves he felt a sudden bitter chill, then the door swung wide, fog briefly enveloping him as the warmer air of the dungeon contacted its frosted exterior.

Two Royal guards awaited him, swords drawn, their blades frosted like the door had been. "Password," growled the one on the right.

"Periwinkle," Falk said gravely.

"Hyacinth," the one on the left proclaimed, and sheathed his sword, a small flurry of ice crystals sprinkling the flat square tiles of the floor. "Welcome, Lord Falk."

"Timos, Anders." Falk gave them both a smile, then shook his head. "I think I'll tell Brich to stay away from flowers next password cycle. I feel silly every time I come down here."

The guards laughed and stepped aside. Falk smiled at them, but the smile vanished the moment he passed them. As much as possible, he preferred to be liked by those he commanded, both to cement their loyalty and to ensure they carried out their duties as efficiently as possible. In truth, *he* had insisted on the silly signs and countersigns, just to give him something to joke with them about. Brich, his secretary, had agreed with an amused smile of his own. After twenty-five years in Falk's service, he knew how the Minister of Public Safety's mind worked.

He was also one of the few who knew what it worked *toward*.

Falk's offices in the basement of the Palace were actually in the topmost of the dungeon's three levels. Here, high, thin, horizontal windows located just above ground level still let in a modicum of natural light. A dozen relatively comfortable cells on this level were reserved for Mageborn who had fallen under suspicion of something-or-other but had to be well treated while those suspicions were investigated. All those cells were currently empty.

Not so the ones in the levels below, where no light penetrated, and less hope. As Falk walked to his office he reviewed his mental list of those held there. There were a couple of Commoners down there with links to the Common Cause; they'd be worth another round of questions. But he could think of no one likely to shed any light on the question of who had mounted the attack on the Prince.

Falk's dungeon was not primarily a place to incarcerate wrongdoers—far larger and more secure prisons on the outskirts of New Cabora and Berriton served that function, with separate facilities for Mageborn and Commoners. Rather, it was a place for gathering information.

Few people knew exactly *how* he gathered information, though, because no one who descended into those lower levels emerged with the ability to talk about it. Many never emerged at all, and those who did had had their memories carefully removed.

Falk considered that a merciful act.

Brich was hard at work in the outer office, seated at an enormous oak desk beneath a towering painting of an uncharacteristically regal King Kravon. *Artistic license*, Falk thought, as he usually did when he glanced at it.

Brich's fingers flew across the keyboard of one of the mechanical text-stampers recently invented by some clever Commoner and now being mass-produced in a smoke-belching factory up in New Cabora's northeast sector, where a lot of manufacturing enterprises had begun to cluster. The constant clacking that had replaced the much more soothing sound of a pen nib scratching across paper annoyed Falk whenever he was in the outer office, but at least it didn't penetrate his inner sanctum, and he had to admit that Brich's reports had gotten much easier to read since the machine was installed.

More and more such clever contraptions were emerging from the Commons, attempts by the Commoners to circumvent their lack of magic through mechanical artifice. Falk considered them harmless curiosities, for the most part, though he kept a close eye on anything that could be developed into a weapon, and had already confiscated an ingenious device for spraying liquid fire. The inventor had claimed, during questioning, it was only an "agricultural aid" for burning brush out of farmers' fields.

He didn't much like the idea of *that* ending up in the hands of the radical, secret half of the Common Cause. Not that it would matter much in a very short time, if all went according to plan, but precisely because things were approaching a critical juncture, he really didn't want any more disruption. The radical faction of the Common Cause wanted to overthrow the King, the Council, and the rest of the Twelve, and while Falk garnered a modicum of private amusement from the fact that was also what *he* intended to achieve, it wouldn't stop him from ruthlessly exterminating those traitorous Commoners . . .

. . . if he could ever find out who they were. So far, they had maintained a remarkable and frustrating anonymity. He knew that they called their leader "the Patron," but he had utterly failed to identify him or her, or any of his/her lieutenants.

It annoyed him, and puzzled him, since when questioned by his most skilled interrogators, very few people would fail to tell all they knew, sooner or later.

Well, no doubt that simply meant that he had not yet brought in the right people to question. He needed to dig deeper, and with a sharper shovel. And now, of course—he allowed himself a small, tight smile—the attempt to assassinate the Prince had given him the perfect opportunity to do so.

If it actually pointed him to the person behind the assassination attempt, that would be pure gravy. He didn't think it would, because of the Unbound symbol. It was stretching the limits of coincidence to think that the assassin would have worn that particular symbol purely by chance. It had been intended to taunt him. *Someone knows*, he thought. *And they're working against me.*

Still, being a man who lived by the motto "never let a crisis go to waste," Falk stopped by Brich's desk. "Brich," he said.

The secretary stopped text-stamping and blinked up at him with watery blue eyes. Brich had looked eighty years old for the last twenty years; Falk had no idea how old he really was. He pushed one of the few strands of gray hair that still spanned his brown-spotted scalp back from his forehead. "Yes, my lord?"

"Prepare orders for all of our operatives in the Commons. They are to arrest for questioning anyone they know or suspect has ties to the Common Cause."

Brich raised an eyebrow so high it almost disappeared behind the hair he had just pushed back. "There are many who profess sympathy with the Cause," he said. "That number of arrests will cause an uproar . . ."

"Let them roar," Falk snapped. "Issue the orders. And make certain that the word also goes out to all the Commons' newssheets that this is a direct response to the most heinous crime ever attempted in Evrenfels: the attempt to murder Prince Karl, Heir Apparent to the Throne and the Keys."

"You believe the Cause is behind it?" Brich unwound paper from the text-stamper's platen, picked up a fresh piece, and wound it in.

Falk snorted. "No. But this seems like the perfect excuse to ensure the Cause doesn't interfere with the Plan, however inadvertently."

Brich rested his fingers on the levers of the text-stamper. "Then who *do* you think is behind it?"

"I don't know," Falk admitted. "But I intend to find out." He said nothing to Brich about the Unbound symbol. Brich was Unbound, too . . . which, perhaps for the first time ever, put him within the realm of suspicion. "And when I do," Falk continued, showing his teeth in a predatory grin, "then the Rock of Justice awaits." He turned his voice brusque. "Now carry out my orders!"

Brich knew the limits of Falk's patience to within the breadth of a rather fine hair. "At once, my lord. Will there be anything else?"

"Yes," Falk said. "There is a . . . resource . . . at my own estate I need to consult. Order my magecarriage brought around to the west entrance, ready to leave at noon. I believe Robinton is the driver on call?"

"Yes, my lord."

"We'll need a second. We'll be driving straight through."

"Of course, my lord."

"Have the body of the attacker loaded aboard. Not in a coffin—that's too obvious—an ordinary packing crate. Magespeak Gannick and tell him I will be traveling overnight and will arrive at the manor by noon tomorrow."

"When may I expect your return, my lord?" Brich said. He sounded uncharacteristically tentative, as if reading something of Falk's mood. "You have four meetings scheduled for tomorrow alone, and the operatives will ask—"

When I'm good and ready, Falk almost snapped—a sign of how much the attack worried him, he realized even as he bit off the retort, not to mention another sign of how well Brich knew him. "The earliest I can be back is late the day after tomorrow, but it will more likely be the day after that," he said in a level voice instead. "Reschedule the meetings with my apologies. Prepare a daily précis for me of any reports or information that make their way to this office during my absence. I will magespeak with you each evening."

"Yes, my lord." Brich blinked at the paper in the text-stamper for a moment, then began pulling again at the padded levers, fingers flicking as though he were scratching a dog behind the ears.

Falk let the clacking sound drive him into his own office, where he spent the next hour dealing with the most pressing paperwork: arrest warrants, incarceration papers, orders for execution. Toward the end of that time Brich came in with a preliminary report from Captain Fedric on the search they'd conducted inside the Lesser Barrier for anyone who shouldn't be there. They'd found nothing. Everyone had the proper permissions, the proper papers, or the proper breeding. Falk frowned and went back to his work.

Half an hour later he had cleared his desk of the most pressing matters, and went into the outer office again. "Carriage?" he said to Brich.

"It's ready, my lord."

Falk nodded and headed toward the Palace's west entrance.

He could understand Brich's confusion as to why he would leave just after ordering a roundup of suspects, but he did not really anticipate receiving any useful information from the Commoners his operatives would arrest. They might be sympathizers of the Cause, but they wouldn't be its ringleaders. Some, in fact, would simply be innocent victims of whispering campaigns organized by their enemies.

The leaders, if they truly existed, would be far more deeply hidden. Most of them were no doubt thought of as fine, upstanding citizens. But the roundup would be a sharp reminder that Falk would not stand by indefinitely while sedition brewed in the Commons . . . and even though he considered it unlikely, there was always the possibility that someone might give him a name or a place, a tiny loose thread he could begin to pull at until he unraveled the whole web, revealing the mysterious Patron crouched like a fat spider at its center.

A better hope for beginning that unraveling process lay with Mother Northwind, but to see her, Falk had to go home.

His carriage hadn't yet pulled up as he stepped out under the pillared portico. The Magecorps had scheduled rain for that evening, and so a thick gray mist was beginning to obscure the magesun. Falk leaned against a pillar, idly slapping his black gloves against his knee with his right hand and holding the briefcase full of paperwork he had packed in his office with the other. He gazed across the broad lawn beyond the drive to the line of trees that marked the edge of the Mageborn Enclave; he could just see the chimneys of the house he maintained there for . . . special guests.

He would have been returning home soon in any case, he thought. Tagaza was quite right: with the execution of the Plan so close, it was time to bring Brenna to the Palace to stay.

He didn't think she would object—not that it made any difference, but it would be easier if she came willingly. She had turned eighteen half a year previously—at the same time as Prince Karl, of course—and he had often told her, setting the stage for the long-awaited culmination of his plans, that when she was of age he would bring her to New Cabora and find a position for her as a maid within the Palace or, if she preferred, in the Commons.

Falk's feelings for his ward were not at all fatherly, but neither were they lecherous. He saw Brenna more as . . . an investment. Or perhaps a gamble, though that word carried with it far more sense of uncertainty than he felt about the chances of the Plan's success. He did have some affection for her, doomed though she was—or perhaps because of that; he wasn't a monster, after all—and resolved to ensure she enjoyed herself during her final few weeks.

His magecarriage came rolling up the drive from the

outbuildings south of the Palace. Painted black, with no device to mark it as belonging to him, it trailed smoke as it
approached. At the tiller in front sat his usual driver, Robinton; beside him was a young man he didn't know.

Robinton pulled the brake lever to bring the magecarriage to a stop, then clambered down from the high seat.
"Sorry for the delay, my lord," he said. "I felt the coal bin
should be topped up for an overnight drive in this weather,
and then, of course, there was the crate to load." He pointed
to the carriage roof, where the large rectangular box
containing—though Robinton surely didn't know it—the
assassin's charred body, magically preserved, had been
strapped. "Heavy, that. Cold, too."

"Quite all right, Robinton," Falk said. "Better to delay
the start of the journey than to be stranded halfway. And
though the crate *is* awkward—and cold—it is also the reason for my journey." He glanced up at the young man, who,
like Robinton, wore Falk's gray livery. "And you are . . . ?"

"Shand, my lord," said the young man, looking very pale
and serious.

"I'm sure it was very short notice for you, Shand," said
Falk. "Thank you for agreeing to help Robinton." He
sighed. "Normally I would take two days for the journey,
but this trip is urgent. We'll be driving straight through, and
at top speed." Shand, he noted, was wearing a heavy fur
coat, with enormous fur mitts and a fur hat on the black
leather of the seat beside him. Falk glanced at Robinton; he
wore no extra layers at all. "Will you be warm enough?" he
said skeptically.

"Oh, yes, my lord, thank you for asking." Robinton
pulled off his broad-rimmed black hat and turned it over.
"Gift from the missus. Enchanted silver threads in the lining. I give 'em a kick before I set out, and they wrap me in
nice warm air for most of a day. Plenty of time to get us to
the valley. And just in case, I've got my old beaver-fur coat
in the trunk."

Falk laughed. "You have a wise missus, Robinton."

"Thank you, my lord. Though I'm not certain a truly

wise woman would have chosen to marry *me*." He opened the door. "My lord . . . ?"

Falk settled himself in the well-cushioned red-velvet interior, warmed by the heat of the coal burner that also provided energy to the enchanted gearbox that magically turned the magecarriage's wheels, settled his briefcase on his knees, and with a brief push of magic, unlocked it.

Before the carriage had rolled through the Gate at the end of the bridge, out of perpetual spring into the still-falling snow of late winter, he was deep into work once more, never once raising his head to look out the window.

Otherwise he might have glimpsed, here and there in the snow-choked streets of New Cabora, the bright blue uniforms of the Royal guards making the arrests he had ordered.

CHAPTER 4

ANTON DASHED THROUGH THE DESERTED STREETS of Elkbone, the mixture of slush, mud, and horse manure a recent thaw had created splattering his leather pants, even reaching as high as his sheepskin coat. The boardwalks on both sides of the street, fronting the few shops the cattle town could boast (half of which were saloons), were covered with ice, and he couldn't risk a fall ... not now, not today. The sky overhead had just turned to blue from pink as the sun rose above the horizon, and for the moment, at least, there was no wind: perfect flying weather.

Elkbone nestled in a low valley, sheltered from the cold winds that scoured the prairie above by the valley slopes and a few straggly trees ... if you could call them trees.

If you could even call Elkbone a town. Lord Mayor Ronal Ferkkisson liked to call it a city, but perhaps that level of delusional grandiosity was to be expected from someone who also insisted he was not just a mayor, but "Lord Mayor."

Elkbone wouldn't even have made a good-sized neighborhood in Hexton Down, Anton thought as he skidded around a corner, and Hexton Down was small compared to the truly great cities of the Union Republic, like Summerfell and Hawksight. Even the harbor town of Wavehaven, more than a thousand miles to the west and the largest settlement in the Wild Land, barely qualified as a city by Anton's standards.

Cities, for instance, usually had tall buildings, whereas in Elkbone the Temple Tower, rising ahead of him, was the only structure that exceeded two stories . . . except for what rose, albeit temporarily, just *beyond* the tower. Blue like the sky, shaped like a breadloaf, made of the finest silk, the envelope of Professor Carteri's airship tugged at its constraining netting as though longing to leap into the air . . . as it would, momentarily.

As it would have already if the Professor . . . *oh, all right, if I* . . . hadn't forgotten the telescope, thought Anton. The Professor was not the sort of master who beat his apprentice. But he was also not the sort to simply let an oversight like that slide, and Anton knew he'd be hearing about it all day.

The emptiness of the streets he had run along was due to the presence of the airship, of course. The town's entire population seemed to have come down to the Temple courtyard to see them off. As Anton dashed through the slush and finally onto good solid cobblestones, he couldn't even see the Professor, though he knew Carteri had to be standing by the wicker basket, impatiently awaiting his apprentice's return. All he could see were the backs of people's heads; but, of course, as he started to make his way through the crowd, those heads turned in his direction, and then, as though he'd parted the seas like the Prophet in the old Temple tale, the crowd opened up before him, giving him a straight run to the rope barrier surrounding the airship . . . and Professor Carteri. The Professor, standing with the Lord Mayor and a red-robed priest from the Temple, appeared completely calm, but he frowned just enough in Anton's direction as Anton reached the barrier to let him know that he definitely would hear more about this later.

Anton ducked under the rope barrier, accompanied by a barrage of flashes from the imagers of the newssheet reporters gathered along one side. Anton knew most of them, since they'd all made the long journey from Wavehaven together, their stagecoaches accompanying the wagon hauling the Professor's airship over the rutted trails. In fact, several of them he knew from as long ago as that day in Hexton Down when, after weeks of work helping his new master assemble and test the airship, he had stood at Professor Carteri's side as he announced his grand plan to fly his airship over the top of the mysterious Anomaly in the heart of the Wild Land. The skepticism and outright derision that had followed had not deterred him. More importantly, it had not deterred the Academy of Natural Philosophy, which was funding the expedition.

"Are you ready to go now, Professor?" one of the reporters shouted.

"Hey, Anton, sure you want to go through with this?" yelled another, to the laughter of his colleagues.

Anton ignored them. The Professor had made it clear that any comments concerning the expedition should come from him alone ... although Anton suspected the reporters had already garnered plenty of other comments from the people of Elkbone, who were relishing the excitement of having Professor Carteri and his amazing airship in their midst, but were convinced that once he flew over the Anomaly—if he even made it over—they'd never see him again.

He'll prove you all wrong, Anton thought as he handed the telescope to the Professor.

"Thank you, Anton," the Professor said gravely. "If you would be so good as to board and conduct the final preflight check, I'll just say a few words to the press."

Anton nodded, and went up the wooden steps behind the professor to the platform the town had built for the launch, apparently using the plans they normally followed for constructing gallows. The airship, already afloat in the air but tethered to the same stout posts that formed the corners of the rope barrier, dipped slightly as he stepped aboard. He immediately began following the checklist he'd long since memorized, scrutinizing ropes for wear, counting sandbags, inspecting the large tank of compressed rock gas and the burner above it (only flickering at the moment, putting out just enough heat to keep the airship bobbing on its tethers) and the tiny steam engine, with its own tank of rock gas, that powered the propeller at the gondola's stern. He tapped the glass of the instruments on their wooden panel, then swung the tiller, the blocks squeaking, and glanced up to make sure the giant rudder on the back of the envelope swung properly. All the while, he was listening with half an ear to the Professor's speech . . .

". . . since its discovery twenty years ago, the Anomaly has been the greatest scientific mystery of our age . . . until recently no way to investigate it, but with the advent of my airship . . . understand the dangers, but advancing human knowledge is worth any amount of risk . . . my thanks to the Academy for supporting this important expedition . . ." Anton had heard it all before.

He finished his checklist with a look in the stores cupboards in the bow and then went back to the gondola's door. The Professor knew to a tee how long the check took; he was just wrapping up. " . . . we do not know what we will find. But that is precisely why we must make the attempt. Thank you."

The Lord Mayor had made his speech *before* Anton had realized he'd been missing the telescope, and the Priest had already offered his blessing; knowing how the Professor felt about religion, Anton was almost surprised he'd accepted it—but then he thought of the reporters and understood.

The Professor's farewell said, he turned and climbed into the gondola with Anton. "About time we got away," he said under his breath, and Anton smiled sheepishly.

The Professor closed and latched the gondola's door. "I'll take port, you take starboard," he told Anton, and Anton crossed to the other side of the gondola to look down on the two beefy police constables in green uniforms standing ready at the posts on that side. "Untie!" the Professor shouted, and the constables undid the ropes from the posts, but kept a tight hold. The airship barely moved, the air in the envelope having cooled enough that it was on the verge of sinking. The Professor turned to the burner in the center of the gondola and opened a valve. Instantly the faint murmur of burning rock gas rose to a thunderous roar. Anton glanced up to see the enormous yellow flame shoot up into the envelope, then turn to blue, then turned his attention back to the two constables to make sure they didn't let go too early, the heat from the burner warming the back of his neck.

The crowd matched the roar of the gas with a roar of its own, mostly cheers, though there were a few jeers and catcalls in the mix as well. Until the Professor had shown up, most of the residents of Elkbone had never even *heard* of an airship, much less seen one, and more than a few of them didn't really believe it would fly.

Well, you're about to learn different, Anton thought.

He could tell from the increasingly strained expressions of the constables that the heat was building rapidly in the envelope. The ropes drew taut. One constable staggered forward a few feet, and the gondola lurched upward at that corner.

"Hold fast!" Anton shouted. He glanced over his shoulder. The Professor was still watching the burner, but now at last he turned back to the other side of the gondola. He raised his hand. Anton raised his.

"Let go!" shouted the Professor, and chopped his hand down, Anton mimicking him an instant later.

The constables released the ropes. The airship began to rise, the roar of the crowd so loud in Anton's ears it felt almost as if the airship were riding sound rather than hot air into the sky. But the noise dwindled rapidly as they gained altitude. Anton hurried to the starboard bow and began hauling in and coiling the rope there, the Professor doing the same in the port stern. By the time all four ropes were aboard, they were five hundred feet in the air and beginning to drift to the east. Anton took a look over the side of the gondola and saw Elkbone, strung out in its little valley;

then he looked up, across the rolling prairie, and saw their destination dead ahead.

From this distance, twenty miles or so out, the Anomaly looked like a fog bank: high, gray, crowned with clouds, impenetrable. They weren't nearly high enough to see over it, even if there was anything to see. What would they find on the other side? Anton wondered. Could they even *get* to the other side?

He glanced at the Professor, expecting him to order the engine started, but the Professor, looking over the side, said nothing for a moment. "There's little wind, but it's taking us in the right direction," he said at last. "We'll drift, lad. Our fuel supply is limited and we'll want it for the return trip."

Drift? Anton took a look over the side. They were moving, but very, very slowly. He could still see the crowd in the Elkbone Temple Square, waving. He took another look at the Anomaly. Four hours at this rate, he thought gloomily, sighed, and went to the bow to keep a lookout.

The morning passed slowly. The wind rose with the sun, but not very much. Elkbone dwindled out of sight behind them at last, hidden in its valley. The Anomaly grew closer. Periodically the Professor lit the burner, so that they continued to rise, until they were five thousand feet above the snow-covered prairie below. Anton, looking down, saw a huge herd of bison, oblivious to their silent presence, grazing peacefully.

But after three hours, the Professor, who had been examining the Anomaly ahead with the telescope Anton had belatedly delivered to the airship, abruptly straightened and closed the telescope with a snap. "I believe it's time to make steam, Anton."

"Aye, aye, Professor!" Anton said. At last!

He hurried to the stern, and took the tiller, flipping the loop of rope that had been holding it centered off of the end. The Professor turned his attention to the steam engine. The boiler was hot, but like the envelope, needed more heat before it would do them any good. He cranked open valves, checked gauges, double-checked the boiler's safety valve, then waited stoically for the pressure to rise.

"Pressure's up," he said after a few minutes. "Engage the gearshaft."

Anton pushed a lever by his left hand. "Gearshaft engaged."

"Quarter steam," the Professor said.

"Quarter steam it is." Anton pushed a second lever forward half as far as it would go. The little steam engine gave a gasp and began to puff . . . and behind Anton, the propeller began to spin, slowly at first, but rapidly picking up speed. As it did so, he felt air moving against his face for the first time. He pushed at the tiller, and the nose of the airship responded . . . sluggishly, but it responded. It would respond faster at a higher airspeed, but of course the Professor still wanted to preserve as much rock gas as possible.

"Our heading will be due east," the Professor said. "I'll take the tiller once we are closer to the Anomaly, but for now, carry on. Keep us at five thousand feet."

"Due east at five thousand it is," acknowledge Anton. He didn't move the tiller; they'd been drifting due east the whole time. The altimeter showed them dipping below five thousand; he reached out for the burner control and gave the envelope a brief kick of flame.

"I believe we will make it half steam," said the Professor.

"Half steam, aye," Anton said. He pushed the throttle ahead another quarter. The puffing of the engine increased in tempo, the rhythmic whirring of the propeller grew louder, and the light breeze blowing past Anton's ears became a stiff one, and a cold one, at that. He reached up and undid the snaps holding the earflaps of his helmet, so they dropped over his ears, and then pulled his goggles down over his eyes.

Meanwhile the Professor had opened a compartment in the bow and pulled out a fine-grain imager, a huge black box with a lens on the front that he attached to a mount. He began taking pictures of the Anomaly as it drew nearer and nearer. Not that its appearance changed; it remained a towering bank of fog. It looked like they could sail right through it, but, of course, Anton knew better. Deep within that fog was the true Anomaly, an impenetrable black wall of nothingness, so cold that the unlucky discoverer of the Anomaly (a now-elderly gentlemen whom Anton had met in person during a trip with the Professor from Hexton Down to Summerfell to argue for more funding from the Academy) had lost not only his fingers but his whole hand and a large portion of his arm after reaching out and touching it.

Calculations based on the apparent curve of the Anomaly indicated it formed a circle some 1,800 miles in circumference, roughly six hundred in diameter, encompassing an area of more than 280,000 square miles (assuming it really was a circle; no one had yet penetrated far enough into the Wild Land from its mountainous eastern shore to encounter the Anomaly from that direction). Its height was uncertain, due to the fog and clouds associated with it, but was generally estimated to be between 13,000 and 18,000 feet.

Closer and closer drew the wall of fog. Periodically Anton lit the burner to keep them at five thousand feet. Mostly he watched the back of the Professor's head, waiting for the next order, and finally it came. "Slow to one quarter," he said. "I think it is time to ascend."

"Yes, Professor," Anton said. He pulled back on the throttle. The Professor checked the gauge on the rock gas tank, frowning slightly, then shrugged and opened the main valve. The flame roared, and the airship began to rise through the cold prairie air.

Five thousand . . . six thousand . . . seven . . . eight . . . up and up they went, and still they could not see over the Anomaly. At nine thousand feet their rate of ascent slowed, and the Professor, frowning again at the rock gas tank, said, "I believe we will release ballast, Anton. If you would open the tank? One-quarter turn, I think; we don't want to ascend too quickly, and we'll want to save some ballast if we can."

"Yes, Professor." Anton bent down and turned a knob

protruding through the floor of the gondola at his feet. The entire base of the gondola was a water tank—their water supply, should they need it. However, considering the entire prairie around them was covered with snow and ice, it seemed unlikely they would. The water also made ballast, and now, as Anton turned the valve, that ballast began to flow out of the bottom of the tank. The airship lurched, then rose much faster than before.

Ten thousand feet. Eleven thousand. Twelve, and they were slowing again. The water tank was empty, they were almost to the wall of fog marking the Anomaly, and still it rose above them, an impossible cliff of white, swirling vapor. Was it his imagination, or could he feel the chill from it even through his warm leather flying gear?

The Professor peered up into the fog. "I think we need another two to three thousand feet," he said, his voice grim but determined. "Release ten sandbags, please, Anton."

"Ten sandbags, aye," said Anton. The sandbags festooned the outside of the gondola; one hundred in all, in five ranks of ten bags each, port and starboard. The cords holding them were rigged with quick release buckles at his end. He let the tiller go for a moment, took hold of the top buckles on each side, and pulled hard.

The ropes dropped from the side of the gondola, the sandbags slipping off them to plummet toward the prairie below . . . and the airship resumed climbing. Anton seized the tiller. "Head to port!" yelled the Professor above the constant roar of the burner. "Parallel until we get enough altitude!"

Anton pushed the tiller to port, but he knew they couldn't really fly parallel to the Anomaly, not with the prevailing westerly pushing them toward it. Of course the Professor knew that, too. *If he really thinks we're going to hit, he'll want to turn right into the wind and try to fight our way away from the wall*, Anton thought tensely. *I'll have to be ready to—*

"Ten more sandbags," called the Professor, cutting his thought short.

"Aye, aye!" Ten more plunged away.

And still the wall of fog rose above them, so close now that they were within the outer reaches of it, the moisture beginning to freeze onto the rigging and metal, forming ice that would weigh them down, slow their ascent. Anton, squinting up, could see no end to the fog. Yet from a distance he'd been able to see the top. They must be close....

The Professor was glaring up through the fog as though he took the Anomaly's ridiculous height as a personal insult. "Release all ballast, Anton."

Anton swallowed. Without any ballast, they'd have no way to gain altitude rapidly the *next* time they needed to. A gust of wind swung them farther into the mist, making the Professor go suddenly ghostly in the bow. *On the other hand*, Anton thought, reaching for the quick-release buckles, *we're liable to smack hard right into that thing any minute, and what that kind of sudden freezing will do to the airship* ...

... well, he really didn't want to find out, not at this altitude.

He pulled all the remaining quick-release buckles. Just as the last snapped open, an enormous updraft seized them.

It felt like a giant had grabbed them and hurled them, spinning, into the sky. The airship shot up, so fast and suddenly that both Anton and the Professor were flung to the floor of the gondola. Anton struggled up again and grabbed the tiller, but they had no headway, the propeller churning uselessly behind them. He couldn't stop the spin. The world whirled through his vision, wall of fog, sunlit prairie, wall of fog, sunlit prairie. Anton felt his gorge rising. He was going to be sick ...

The spinning, mercifully, stopped, but hard on its heels came the unmistakable sound of tearing silk. Anton twisted his head around.

The complex network of pulleys and ropes that gave the tiller control over the rudder had come apart in the violence of the spin. The rudder had swung too far, puncturing the envelope. And now, as he watched, the hole grew.

The airship lurched. A powerful westerly wind had them now. All around were the tops of clouds, but there was something odd about them, almost as though they were in a river, rushing toward a waterfall . . .

"Downdraft!" screamed the Professor, who had been clinging to the bow of the gondola. As pale and green as Anton felt, he lurched to his feet and flung himself on the burner, twisting the valve wide open. Flame roared, filling the envelope . . . but the edges of the rip near the stern fluttered, and Anton knew the heat roaring into the envelope was spurting out of it nearly as fast.

And then they swept over the edge of the cloud waterfall, and Anton's stomach leaped up as they dropped like a stone toward the snow-covered ground far beyond. Groaning, Anton clung to the edge of the gondola, stared down at the strange new lands beyond the Anomaly that were rushing up toward them with alarming speed, and threw up into them.

The Professor shoved him out of the way. He grabbed the tiller, wriggled it uselessly, then seized the throttle and shoved it to full ahead. The steam engine sputtered and shook, and the propeller spun into an invisible blur. Anton turned around. "It won't last five minutes at full throttle," he gasped.

"We've got to get out of this downdraft," the Professor said grimly. "It will smash us to kindling if we can't." He peered up at the envelope. "We should be able to maintain some lift if we can only get into still air . . . not enough to stay airborne, but maybe enough to make some sort of landing . . ." He scrambled aft. "I'll take the tiller. Lighten the ship. Everything you can find. Throw it overboard. Start with the stores."

Anton swiped his leather-clad arm across his mouth, hauled himself to his feet, staggered forward, and began emptying the ship of everything they had so laboriously loaded the day before, while all the while the ground below grew closer.

It's not going to work, he thought. *It's not.*

Since the day he'd fled his abusive father, he'd fully expected to die young. But now that the prospect was imminent, he found he didn't relish it.

You're not dead yet, he snarled at himself. Grabbing a trunk of scientific instruments, he heaved them up and over the side, the wind roaring in his ears. He glanced toward the stern to see the Professor's face, pale and set, staring bleakly at him. And behind the Professor, the vast bank of fog that marked the Anomaly grew higher and higher.

It looks just the same from this side, Anton thought. *So why did we bother?*

And then he turned to look for something else to toss over the side.

———

Brenna tugged aside the heavy green drapes that covered her window to peer down into the snow-filled courtyard outside. Nothing moved down there, or on the steep white hillsides beyond the outer wall of Lord Falk's estate: not so much as a bird or a hare, much less a human. "When was the last time we had a visitor?" she asked the mageservant sweeping in the corner, where crumbs from Brenna's just-departed lunch had somehow flung themselves. "The Moon Ball? That was more than two months ago!"

The mageservant didn't say a word. Brenna would have been terrified if it had, since it was essentially a marionette, animated by magic and programmed to perform the same rote tasks day after day. Its round wooden face, on which the magical symbol that enchanted it glowed faintly blue, remained half-turned away. For a moment Brenna considered smashing something on the floor—one of the delicate pieces of glass fruit decorating her mantelpiece, perhaps— just to get its attention and watch it scurry to clean up the mess, but as usual, the impulse passed before she acted on it. *Just as well,* she thought. She would eventually run out of things to smash, and still nothing would have changed, except her room would be even drearier than it already was.

The door opened and another mageservant entered,

carrying a fresh load of wood that it stacked, with inhuman precision, beside the fireplace. "I'm going for a walk," Brenna told it. It kept stacking wood. "Why, yes, I know it's cold outside. Thank you *ever* so much for your concern. I promise you I shall dress warmly."

The mageservant placed two logs from its newly made pile onto the fire, adjusted the remainder so they looked as neat as before, then went out. Brenna went to the closet, grabbed her warmest coat—ankle-length, hooded, and made of wolverine fur—checked to make sure her red woolen scarf and rabbit-fur mitts were still in the pockets, and followed the mageservant, whose passing had left a faint chill in the air by the door.

The hallway outside her ran left and right, turning at either end to form the two wings of the manor house that wrapped the central Great Hall in their embrace. There were broad, curving staircases at either end as well, leading down to the main floor.

Doors opened only off the side of the corridor where her room was located. The other side of the hall was punctuated by tall, vertical slits, about two hands' breadth in width, filled with delicate wooden latticework. As Brenna pulled on her coat, she glanced idly down through one of those slits into the Great Hall, expecting to see it empty and dark.

Instead, it blazed with light. Servants, both human and mage, wove around it in a complicated dance, cleaning floor tiles, polishing tabletops, buffing brass candlesticks, never duplicating one another's efforts or getting in one another's way.

All that bustle could mean only one thing: Lord Falk was coming home.

Which made it even more urgent that Brenna go outside *now*. Once Lord Falk arrived, she would be expected to be close at hand. It also meant she couldn't, as she had planned, simply cross the Hall to the antechamber on the other side and go out from there through the big double doors of the main entrance. If Gannick, the head of the household, saw her, he might not—almost certainly *would* not—allow her out at all, on the theory that Falk might wish to see her the moment he arrived. Even if she weren't stopped, Falk would not be pleased to hear, as he certainly would, that she had chosen to leave the estate knowing his arrival was imminent.

Better to plead ignorance than beg forgiveness, she thought.

Fortunately, there was more than one way out of the estate, and she knew them all.

So rather than go to the end of the corridor and down into the Great Hall, Brenna went only halfway along it and through a door that opened into a servants' staircase, very narrow to make it easier for servants to lean against the wall and support themselves while carrying laden trays.

Once in the basement, she followed the corridor of whitewashed brick that ran beneath the lavish rooms that visitors saw. Brenna knew all these behind-the-scenes corridors like she knew her own face in the mirror, having roamed them since she was a child. At regular intervals she passed steps leading up to between-room hallways that allowed the servants to access rooms unobtrusively to change bed linen or feed the heating stoves, without troubling Lord Falk or his guests.

At one point she passed another staircase going down. It led to the only part of the manor she rarely visited: the sub-subbasement, deep beneath the manor, where Falk's Magefire roared, a brilliant tower of blue and yellow flame, fed by a constant flow of rock gas from a reservoir untold fathoms beneath the ground. That reservoir of gas was one of two reasons Falk Manor had been built where it was: the other, of course, was the even more important fact that beneath the manor ran one of the veins of magical power that spread out from the lode beneath the Palace like the tentacles of one of the monsters that supposedly swam the oceans of the world ... oceans Brenna had read about in Falk's extensive library but never expected to see, cut off as they all were from the outside world by the Great Barrier.

In the Palace, Brenna knew from her annual visits there, the MageFurnace both provided energy for magic *and* heated the hundreds of rooms and dozens of corridors. The Magefire in Falk's basement could surely have done the same for his much smaller manor, but Falk preferred to heat his home with coal, reserving the Magefire's energy for other uses—such as charging and programming the mageservants.

Once, as the corridor she followed testified, the manor had boasted a full staff of actual living humans, but unlike his ancestors, Lord Falk seemed to prefer to have as few people about the place as possible. Besides Gannick, there were only a half-dozen servants in the entire manor, and they mostly kept to themselves, usually speaking to Brenna only when their duties demanded it. Like all MageLords, Falk had his own Mageborn men-at-arms to keep order within his demesne; a score of them dwelt in the compound just outside the estate's front gate. They, too, were taciturn in her presence—but then, they rarely *were* in her presence. In the ordinary course of affairs, the only living humans Brenna saw were Gannick and her tutor, Peska, a middle-aged woman with a pinched face, a nasal voice, and no more warmth of personality than . . . well, than one of the mageservants.

Brenna knew all the servants by name, of course, but no matter how informal she was with them, they were always deferential to her. It had to be by Falk's orders: she knew, and they had to know, too, that she was no more Mageborn than they were. As a child, she'd simply accepted things as they were, but when she'd gotten old enough to start to ask questions, she'd wondered why she didn't have parents like the children in Overbridge, the nearby village.

Falk had sat her down in his study one night and told her that her parents had been Commoners in his employ who, during a journey north on his business, had been killed by the Minik savages. Falk, in their honor, had raised her from infancy. But sometimes, she thought, he seemed to forget she had done a considerable amount of growing since then, until now, past eighteen, it was surely time he took her to the Palace to stay. He had promised to help her find a position within the Palace, or, failing that, within the city of New Cabora.

A position in the Palace would mean serving either Falk, one of his fellow MageLords, or, she supposed, the King (and someday his Heir, Prince Karl). Falk seemed to take it for granted that was the option she would most desire. But in her heart, Brenna thought she would prefer the other. New Cabora amazed her every time she visited it. She saw magic every day, but the things in the Commoner city ... gaslights, water that poured from pipes without magic, fireworks that painted the sky with light ... amazed and delighted her because they were all created by Commoners. Commoners like her.

She'd met the Heir a few times. He seemed a pleasant enough boy, certainly a *handsome* enough boy, tall, well-built (not that Brenna entertained any fancies on that score; the thought of the Heir of the Kingdom taking a romantic interest in a Commoner was ludicrous), so if she *did* end up serving in his household, it might not be the worst of fates. Still ...

The corridor ended in another narrow staircase leading up to a metal door. She pushed it open, its hinges squealing, to reveal the coal shed, a wooden lean-to against the back of the manor house lit only by dirty glass skylights in the high, sloping ceiling. At the beginning of the winter, the coal had stood in piles higher than her head, wagonloads having arrived weekly during the summer to ensure the manor would stay warm even when winter storms made further deliveries impossible. Now, with spring putatively just around the corner, the piles were poor, depleted wraiths of their former selves, and the loose coal scattered across the floor made walking treacherous.

On the wall to Brenna's left hung a dozen red coal buckets. She walked past them, then picked her way through the scattered coal to the exit, a double door that she could open from the inside but that would lock behind her when she pushed it shut. That didn't worry her: she would return through the front door, so that she could express the proper surprise and remorse for her tardiness when she discovered that Lord Falk had either returned or was about to.

Out she went into the snowy rear courtyard, with its own locked gate to the outside world and other doors leading into the manor, one into the kitchen storeroom, one into the dry goods storeroom, and a third into a central hallway that ran to the back of the Great Hall. Over the course of the winter the swirling wind had pushed the snow into deep drifts, some as high as Brenna's head, all around the walls, but had left the worn cobblestones in the center exposed, though covered with ice. Sometime since she had looked out through the window of her room the snow had stopped falling. Heavy gray clouds continued to scud overhead like boats on one of the Seven Fish, the long, narrow lakes strung like a fisherman's catch on a line along the bottom of the Grand Valley that sheltered the estate, but patches of blue sky showed between the clouds. *Not a blizzard, then*, Brenna thought. *Just a line of flurries.*

Which meant she didn't have to confine herself to moping around the manor grounds. She could safely go down to the lakeshore, or up the hill. It didn't really matter. Just being out of the house for a while always made her feel better, freer . . .

The hill, she decided. She felt the need for an expansive view.

A small, heavy door opened through the wall next to the big padlocked freight gate. The door was bolted but not locked. The manor's walls were more for show than anything else, since no one but another MageLord would dare to steal from a MageLord, and walls offered no protection against *that* sort of attack. Not that Brenna could imagine anyone, Commoner, Mageborn *or* another of the Twelve, daring to attack Lord Falk.

She unbolted the door and pushed it open, grunting a little as she forced it through the drifted snow on the other side. She slipped out and glanced up and down the blank expanse of the manor's back wall. Except for the gate and door from which she had just emerged, there were no other openings in the wall on this side of the manor—which made it that much easier for her to escape unseen.

Around the front, the manor boasted ornamental shrubs, shrouded in canvas this time of year; statuary that, being mostly of the heroically nude variety, currently looked both silly and uncomfortable; and, most impressively, a magical, multicolored fire fountain that played one of a selection of tinkly musical tunes whenever someone passed by. Utterly impractical and an enormous waste of magical energy, it had been installed by one of Falk's more ostentatious predecessors as a way of proclaiming that here dwelt a MageLord. Brenna had long wondered why Falk had not had it pulled out.

This side of the manor actually seemed to fit Falk's personality better: a few distinctly nonornamental shrubs, a few winding graveled paths (all currently buried under snow, of course). Brenna grinned a little. *All right, maybe that weird limestone sculpture of a giant frog doesn't exactly say "Lord Falk,"* she thought. But the rest of it: plain, direct, utilitarian. That was Falk to a tee.

Beyond the manor's outer fence of black iron, perhaps fifty yards away, a forest of aspen, birch, and pine began, but it spread only halfway up the tall, round-shouldered hill that backed the manor before petering out into shrubs and then into undisturbed snow, the smooth white surface marred only by the occasional rocky outcropping.

Brenna trudged toward the fence, the snow, calf-deep everywhere and over her knees in spots, pulling at her legs. The newest layer, fluffy as eiderdown, covered the hard crust left behind by the recent thaw. Below that were layers of old snow, strata marking every storm of the long winter.

The wind, though it whipped long, ghostly tendrils of snow around her feet, lacked the bitter bite of midwinter: cold, certainly, but not the knifelike unbearable cold of winter's depths, the life-stealing cold that could freeze exposed flesh in less than a minute. When *that* kind of cold settled over the land, no one went out any more than could be helped, and then only for short periods of time.

This, though . . . this she could bear all day, warmly dressed as she was. The relative warmth was the first whisper of spring, still weeks away, but drawing closer every day. It couldn't come soon enough for Brenna, who loved watching the frozen landscape shake off its mantle of ice and come to new, green life . . . and she particularly loved the spring equinox, when the manor was full of life for one glorious evening as the leading citizens of the villages came to celebrate Springfest, one of only four occasions—the others being the Sun Ball on the summer solstice, the Moon Ball on the winter solstice, and the Harvestfest in fall— when the manor was filled with people. There would be music, dancing, dramatic readings, lectures, maybe even a play. She'd heard that Davydd Verdsmitt was about to premiere a new work at the Palace. What she wouldn't give to see his players on the stage of the Great Hall! *And no doubt Lord Falk could order it, if he so chose*, she thought, but she couldn't imagine asking him.

Springfest also offered something else in short supply in the manor of Lord Falk: young men.

At the Moon Ball, the son of the Reeve of Poplar Butte had asked her to dance. Just turned nineteen, he'd been a bit awkward, a bit shy, and definitely not much of a dancer . . .

. . . but he had also had a nice smile and the most beautiful brown eyes she had ever seen, and she really thought she'd like to dance with him again.

Although, to be completely honest, she would be glad to dance with *anyone*. Except possibly the baker's son, who was fighting a two-front war against acne and overweight, and losing both.

Brenna reached the fence and clambered over it easily, then plunged in among the trees. The snow wasn't as deep here, since some of it had been intercepted by the overhanging branches throughout the winter, although occasional deep drifts and deadwood, betraying its presence only by the slightest of bumps in the snow, made the footing precarious. But Brenna plunged ahead, knowing she was doing something she really shouldn't, knowing it could even be dangerous—if she turned an ankle, it might be hours before anyone found her—but getting perverse pleasure out of that very fact.

The going got even harder as the land sloped up. The new snow was moist enough to compact under her feet as she climbed, turning icy. She had to hold onto bushes and branches to keep from sliding backward, but eventually she emerged from the forest onto the bare hillside. Up here the winter winds had driven most of the snow into drifts. By carefully picking her way, she could follow a path where dry grass still showed through the thin white blanket that covered it, providing some traction. Though the wind continued to snap slithering snakes of snow at her, she was working hard enough now that she felt too warm in her fur, and she unbuttoned it a little to let in some fresh air.

She had a specific destination in mind, an outcropping of rock to which she often climbed in the summer. It was a good deal easier to get to then, she thought, panting; but there it was now ahead of her, and a few minutes later she reached its broad, tablelike top and turned to survey the landscape.

Below her sprawled Falk Manor, the large main building with its white walls and red roof and multiple smoke-spewing chimneys surrounded by an untidy cluster of smaller structures. From the manor's front gates, a road ran past the compound of the men-at-arms, white wooden barracks behind a stockade of peeled logs, through snow-covered fields down to the edge of the lazily meandering river, still frozen solid. To her left and right along the Grand Valley, the Seven Fish showed as broader, flat expanses of alternating dark gray ice and white snow.

The road ran alongside the river, eventually disappearing to her left around the shoulder of another hill. As she looked that way, Brenna saw a black dot roll into sight, trailing smoke, and recognized it at once as Lord Falk's magical carriage. Once he had returned to the Palace after the Moon Ball, Brenna ordinarily didn't see her guardian again until spring; since he had the option of living in the perpetual warmth of the Palace grounds, she could hardly blame him. But there he came. *I wonder what's happened?*

And then she forgot all about Lord Falk and everything else as an enormous glowing blue *something*, roaring like a dragon, burst over the crest of the hill behind her.

CHAPTER 5

FIVE HUNDRED FEET ABOVE THE GROUND, the downdraft became a powerful westerly wind, hurling the airship out over the snow-covered prairie, the straining propeller adding to its eastward momentum. Freezing wind roared through the gondola. The envelope fluttered and twisted. Anton, staring over the side, saw the ground both streaming past and growing larger at an alarming rate. He looked forward. And ahead . . .

. . . hills. Not very big hills, but big enough. Anton watched the clump of trees on the hill in front of them grow rapidly nearer. It would be a very near thing, but he thought they might just . . .

Another loud tearing sound. The hole in the envelope grew larger. The airship lurched downward and twisted, and the tip of a towering pine, the tallest tree on the hilltop, tore through the side of the gondola like a blunt knife. The impact threw Anton forward; only a frantic grab at the rigging saved him from being tossed out.

In the stern, the tip of the pine slammed into the Professor's left leg. Anton heard the bone break, a sickening sound, then the wind flowing over the hill tossed the airship skyward again, ripping the tree free of the gondola.

The Professor dropped to the bottom of the gondola, eyes wide with shock. Anton scrambled toward him. The burner continued to roar, but Anton knew it couldn't last much longer. At the Professor's side, he peered out through the splintered hole in the wickerwork. Forest, a river . . . a road? A house? "Professor, there are people down there!"

The Professor's eyes, which had closed, fluttered open. "Inhabitants? Inside the Anomaly?" He tried to roll over and look, but groaned with pain and flopped back. A sheen of sweat covered his white face.

"Maybe they can help us!"

The Professor closed his eyes. "If the gas won't lift us and the ballast is gone, lad, no one can help us but God." He coughed and smiled weakly. "Too bad I don't believe in Him."

The torch flared hugely and went out. The Professor's eyes fluttered open, and he looked up at the envelope's torn blue silk. "It appears He doesn't believe in me, either," he said softly.

With the roaring of the burner gone, the only sounds Anton could hear were the creaking of ropes and the rush of wind in the treetops below . . . and not very far below, at that. "Hold on, Professor," he said desperately. "I think we're almost down." He guided the Professor's hands to one of the rope-loop handholds in the gondola wall and seized one himself. He closed his eyes. "Any second now . . ."

Ten seconds passed. Twenty. And then . . .

They struck.

Crunching, tearing, ripping sounds; tumbling, no up or down; a flash of green, then white; violent blows to his body; a horrible stabbing pain in his leg . . . it all happened in an instant.

For a timeless period, nothing . . . and then Anton abruptly opened his eyes to find himself hanging head-down, tangled in ropes, six feet above the snowy ground. The gondola hung upside down above him. The burner had ripped out of it and lay steaming in the snow. Folds of blue silk hung like a stage curtain all around.

Something dropped past his nose. Where it struck the ground, the snow turned red. As he watched, another red drop fell, then another. It took him a long, dazed moment to realize the drops were blood . . . his blood.

He felt suddenly dizzy and sick and swallowed hard, fighting not to vomit yet again. "Professor?" he called weakly, but heard no answer.

Instead he heard footsteps, crunching through the snow, coming nearer at a run. And then a girl appeared beneath him. She wore an enormous fur coat, its hood thrown back to reveal tumbling curls of dark brown hair. Her eyes, just as dark, peered up at him from a pale, heart-shaped face. She said something to him. It sounded like a question, but he couldn't quite understand the words . . .

"I need . . . help . . ." he said, and then promptly threw up all over her. The retching seemed to tear something loose inside him, and agonizing pain bludgeoned him once more into darkness.

———

Brenna gaped at the . . . thing . . . that had appeared from nowhere in the ragged gray sky. It was a huge bag of blue cloth, shaped like a loaf of bread, with a round opening at the bottom. A kind of giant wicker basket, badly broken, hung from it on ropes, and as it swept away from her, she glimpsed a white face inside that basket. A tall chimney rose from something like a heating stove in the center of the basket, but instead of belching smoke, it shot a roaring tongue of blue flame, like the manor's Magefire, into the interior of the blue loaf-shape, lighting it up like a lantern but somehow not setting it on fire. At the back something like an overgrown version of a child's whirligig spun lazily.

She took all of that in in an instant as the thing shot past. She heard shouts from inside the basket—there had to be a second passenger she couldn't see—and then, suddenly, the fire turned orange and went out. For a few seconds the thing flew down the slope in eerie silence, lower and lower . . .

. . . and then it crashed into the forest at the bottom of the hill.

The big blue loaf-shape, which she now realized was

made of cloth, collapsed in on itself. The basket upended. The Magefire-like burner ripped free with a tremendous noise and smashed into the ground, releasing a huge cloud of steam that obscured everything even before the blue cloth settled over the scene like a shroud. Yet even as the thin fabric drifted into place, Brenna was scrambling down the slope as fast as she could. There had been people in that basket. They must be hurt . . . or worse.

But even with that horrible thought in her head, another part of her jumped up and down like a little girl at her first Moon Ball. *They were flying!* she thought. *Like birds . . . well, like dandelion seeds, anyway. But still, they were flying!*

No one that she had ever heard of—not Lord Falk, not First Mage Tagaza, not even the First Twelve—had ever been able to use magic to fly. *I'd give half my life to fly like that*, she thought. *Fly right out of Falk Manor. Fly right over the Great Barrier, even . . .*

Over the Barrier . . .

Could it be . . . ?

The possibility, if it were a possibility, both thrilled and horrified her. If people from outside the Barrier could fly over it, then Brenna's whole world—the whole kingdom of Evrenfels!—was about to change forever.

All this time she had been hurrying down the slope, slipping and half-falling more than once, catching herself with her hands, sliding a few feet, then running once again. Ahead she could see the blue tentlike canopy the loaf-shape had made as it deflated and settled over the treetops. A confused heap of metal, ropes, and crates lay beneath it. She pushed through the undergrowth and cautiously stepped under the hanging fabric. She looked up to see a young man, her own age or slightly younger, tangled in a mass of ropes like a fish in a net. Blood dripped from him, flowing steadily from a hole in his leg. It wasn't spurting, though—she knew enough to know *that* would have quickly meant his death. *Punctured the muscle but no major blood vessels*, she though clinically, pushing the horror of the blood and the wound into the back of her mind by concentrating on what her tutor, Peska, had taught her of anatomy. *He might have a permanent limp.*

His eyes were open. He was looking at her, though he seemed to be having some trouble focusing.

She opened her mouth, not sure what to say to him. She didn't even know if he spoke her language. Maybe that was why what actually came out was quite possibly the most inane thing she had ever said to another human being. "Are you all right?"

He didn't seem to understand her. He said something, his voice a hoarse croak—and then he groaned, his eyes rolled back, his mouth opened, and bloody vomit poured down on her head.

She ducked at the last instant to keep it out of her face, but she felt the hot stickiness foul her hair and dribble down the back of her neck. Screaming, she threw herself backward and promptly tripped over something in the snow.

When she saw what it was, she spun away and threw up her own breakfast.

The glazed, open eyes of the body on the ground watched her dispassionately, the viscera and pooled blood that had spilled from the enormous gash in its belly still steaming in the cold air.

After several minutes of cleansing her mouth and hair with snow, she regained her composure enough to go back under the blue canopy and look up at the surviving passenger of the . . . flying device.

He remained unconscious, and still dripped blood, not only from his leg, now, but also from his mouth and nose. *I've got to get him down from there*, she thought, but she knew she couldn't do it alone.

Fortunately or unfortunately—she had a feeling she wouldn't know for some time—she didn't have to. While she still dithered, Lord Falk and a half-dozen men-at-arms came crashing through the wood, swords drawn.

Her guardian skidded to a halt, his lean, sharp-angled face so startled he looked almost comical—well, as comical as the supremely *non*comical Falk ever could. "Come away from there!"

"Lord Falk, there's someone hurt!" She pointed up at the dangling youth. "Look!"

Lord Falk looked, then turned to the men-at-arms and began snapping commands. In short order they had cut the boy down, laid him on a travois made of spruce boughs, bound up his wounds, and begun dragging him toward the manor. Brenna doubted that was the best way to treat someone who might have internal injuries, but on the other hand, what choice did they have? One of the men-at-arms had already been dispatched to fetch Healer Eddigar. With luck, the Healer would reach the manor at almost the same moment as the boy.

Falk turned his attention to the dead man. Brenna forced herself to look at the corpse. At least someone had had the decency to close his staring eyes and drape a cloak across his ruined torso, and with that dreadful wound hidden, the man might almost have been asleep . . . if not for the red slush that surrounded his body. Falk knelt beside the corpse, fingering the strangely cut suit of leather it wore. A blood-spattered white scarf of some incredibly fine material was wrapped around the dead man's neck, and he wore a close-fitting leather helmet. Round glass lenses, framed in copper, had been shoved up on his forehead. One of the lenses had shattered in the impact.

Two men-at-arms remained at hand; Falk stood and ordered them to build a second travois and transport the body to the manor for closer examination. "Put him in the coal shed," he said. "He'll keep well enough in there. No need to waste energy on a stasis spell."

Brenna had to swallow hard to keep her gorge down again. As the axes of the men-at-arms rang among the trees, Falk gazed up at the wrecked flying device. "Astonishing," he said. He spotted something in the snow, and leaned down to pick it up; when he straightened, he held a leather, glass-goggled helmet like the one the dead man had worn. *The boy's*, Brenna thought.

And then Lord Falk turned his ice-gray eyes toward her, and she quailed.

Lord Falk might be the closest thing she had to a father, but that wasn't very close at all. He never called himself that; he simply said he was her "guardian." He was not at all cruel to her. In fact, he was quite generous, frequently bringing her presents from the city, and of course once a year he even took her there. He had introduced her to the other MageLords, even the King and the Heir; sent her shopping (with an armed escort, of course) in New Cabora. But she never sensed any personal warmth from him. He seemed to regard caring for her as a duty, a not particularly onerous duty but not a particularly pleasant one, either. And, of course, most of the time, he simply wasn't there at all, and she was left to her own devices.

When she had been very small, she had been tended to by a woman from the village, affectionate enough in her own way, but always taciturn and withdrawn. She had died "of an influenza," in Falk's words, when Brenna was eight.

Her current tutor, Peska, spoke to her only about her schooling, but at least she wasn't entirely uninformed about events in the rest of the kingdom, even during the long months Falk left her alone.

The manor had a mageletter, a large sheet of enchanted parchment that filled each day with brief stories about the latest happenings at the Palace. Brenna devoured every word of it, even though it focused almost entirely on court gossip, with events involving Commoners mentioned only when they, in some way, impacted life inside the Lesser Barrier.

The Commoners of New Cabora kept *themselves* informed through a nonmagical thing called a newssheet, printed daily on cheap paper by the use of a clever mechanical device, and distributed on street corners by a network of children who kept a portion of the price of each newssheet sold for themselves. That was what Brenna *really* longed to read each day, but unless Falk chose to send copies to his manor she had no way to obtain one, and Falk did not so choose. And so Brenna had to be content with reading about who had worn what to the latest ball, speculation as to which highborn young lady would wed Prince Karl, and the excruciatingly boring details of the latest shuffling of the undersecretaries of the Council.

Commoner though she was herself, she rarely got to visit the local villages. Twice a year she accompanied Falk to Overbridge, enjoined to sit in strict silence while he heard whatever grievances had accumulated in the months since his last visit.

Falk would dispense justice—and, Brenna had to admit, did so thoughtfully and fairly—then bring her back to the manor. He said the trips were part of her education into the political system of the Kingdom, but sometimes she wondered if they were really meant as a simple but forceful reminder that Lord Falk held absolute sway over this corner of the Kingdom.

And over her. Rescuing the boy and having the corpse hauled away had distracted him for a few minutes, but now he frowned at her. "Brenna. Why are you out here by yourself?"

"I often take a walk in the woods near the manor, Lord Falk," she said. "I did not know you were coming home today, or I would have been there to greet you." *Almost true. . . .* "I was up on the hill, enjoying the view, when that . . . whatever-it-is . . . suddenly appeared."

"From the other side of the hill?" Falk gazed west, up the slope to the rock formation she had climbed to earlier. "From the direction of the Barrier? You're certain?"

"It almost knocked me off the rock," Brenna said.

Falk squinted up at the crest of the hill, and Brenna knew what he was thinking, because she had thought it herself. On a clear day, when you climbed to the top of that hill, you could actually *see* the Great Barrier, a wall of fog, ten miles away across the bare prairie. To left and right the Barrier dwindled away in the distance. How tall is it? Brenna suddenly wondered. A mile? Two? She'd never heard.

She had never been to the Barrier herself, of course, but

she had been told what it was like to come too close. Despite drawing its energy from the great lava-filled Cauldron almost three hundred miles north, it greedily sucked heat from the air as well, creating a chill that deepened to bitter cold within twenty-five feet of it and became unbearable to the point of agony within ten. The cold created the ever-present fog that both hid it from view and revealed its location. You could walk into that fog, until the cold drove you back. If you were dressed warmly enough, you might even get right up to the Barrier itself—but you would still see nothing but fog until the moment your outstretched hand touched it and the excruciating pain of having that hand instantly frozen drove you back.

After which, of course, the resulting amputation would keep you too occupied with your own misery to think much more about the incredible feat of magic the Barrier represented.

The Lesser Barrier was more like a nearly invisible glass wall in the air, or so Brenna had been told. Cold enough to freeze bare skin, but if you touched it with a gloved hand, all you felt was a sensation like running your hand over a sheet of ice. But the Great Barrier was, literally, untouchable. And, of course, impenetrable.

But the Lesser Barrier was a dome, whereas the Great Barrier was only a very tall wall . . . which meant a flying device could, conceivably, pass safely over it.

A flying device like this one.

Falk turned back to Brenna. "You're filthy," he said. "And you stink of vomit."

"I'm not used to seeing—" she shot an involuntary glance at the body, just being rolled onto the new travois by the men-at-arms, "—such things."

"Nor should you be," Lord Falk said. "But I do not believe you contrived to vomit on your own head. That must have come from above. So, the boy was awake when you came upon the wreckage?"

"Yes," Brenna said. Falk hadn't gotten where he was by being either dimwitted or unobservant.

"Did he speak?"

"Barely. I asked him how he was. He said something I couldn't understand. Then he threw up on me. And then he passed out."

Falk's cold gray gaze was, as always, unnerving. Not for the first time, Brenna wondered if her guardian used a little magic at such times to ensure she spoke the truth. Not being Mageborn herself, she couldn't know. *What if he can read my mind?*

But, no, Peska had told her that was impossible, at least for a mage like Falk. A powerful Healer, a master of soft magic, could possibly do it . . . but soft magic required touch.

She hoped Peska had been telling the truth, and hadn't simply been ordered to tell her that mind-reading was impossible so that Falk could then read her mind without her being aware of it . . .

She shook her head. Did all Commoners feel this paranoid around MageLords? She suspected they did, but it wasn't something she could ask anyone. Not even the Reeve's son at the Moon Ball.

"Get back to the manor. Get cleaned up," Falk said abruptly. "I'll talk to you later."

Brenna knew a command when she heard one, and this one she was only too happy to obey.

She desperately wanted a bath.

Falk watched Brenna trudge away through the snow. The girl—the young woman, he corrected himself—was bright and observant, and as he had expected, beginning to chafe under the restraints he had put on her life.

Well, no matter. He could certainly manage whatever willfulness she might muster in these final few weeks. No doubt the excitement of returning to the Palace with him would temper much of her rebelliousness. In any event, she was important not for what she did or didn't do, but simply for who she *was*.

He put Brenna out of his mind and instead turned his

attention to the thing hanging in the tree over his head. Reaching up, he took hold of a fold of soft blue fabric. He held it between thumb and forefinger for a moment, concentrating fiercely. But no matter how deeply into its intricate structure he mentally delved, he could find no trace of magic about it.

He released it. It was a thing of artifice, then, its provenance Commoner, not Mageborn. What made that astonishing was that its creators had accomplished without magic something that the Mageborn could not with it.

To keep a man aloft was beyond the abilities of even the greatest mages, because the energy required could not be drawn from the surrounding air. Nor could it be accomplished with a coal burner like that in his carriage, because the added weight ate up most of the additional energy provided, leaving the mage no better off; worse, if he had somehow managed to get himself aloft before the energy ran out.

Of course, the fact that this device had crashed was proof enough that nonmagical solutions posed their own hazards. But what it represented . . .

Falk walked out from under the shadow of the flying device and looked once more up the hill. The disappearance of this flying device would probably mean that it would be a long time before anyone else from beyond the Barrier would risk the attempt, but where one had come, another would surely follow.

The one weak point in the Unbound's great plan to bring down the Barriers and move out into the world to rule as the SkyMage intended had always been, as Falk had long recognized, the fact they had no way of knowing what lay outside the Great Barrier. Eight hundred years ago it had been wilderness, inhabited only by the primitive Minik tribes, a thousand miles inland in a continent even the sailors of that day had never seen. But as the flying device testified, things had changed.

As I anticipated, he thought with satisfaction. Since King Kravon had appointed him Minister of Public Safety twenty-five years ago, he had been expanding and strengthening the army, for most of Evrenfels' history only a tiny force used to put down the occasional minor Commoner uprising. His excuse, on those rare occasions he was questioned by other members of the King's Council (though never by King Kravon, who didn't care about such things and was probably not even aware of them), was the need to protect the northern villages from what he called "the increasing threat" from the Minik, scattered tribes of fur-clad savages who lurked among the lakes, rocks, and trees of the far north.

The Minik were the only surviving descendants of the aboriginal inhabitants of the wilderness into which the remnants of the Old Kingdom had been magically transported. Their ancestors had attacked shortly after the arrival of the MageLords and their followers in a burst of magical energy so great it had blackened and blasted an area some ten miles in diameter, larger than New Cabora now occupied. The southern tribes had been quickly routed, those savages who survived fleeing into the rocky, swampy forests of the north. Hunting them down in that difficult and essentially useless terrain was clearly a waste of resources, and so they had been allowed to remain there since. Mostly they kept to themselves, and even traded furs to some of the northern Commons villages for food, tools, or knives, but occasionally a group of hotheaded young warriors raided a village or farm. Falk had been very careful, though he certainly had his men attempt to track down and punish those responsible, not to put an end to those raids entirely, because if they stopped, why would he still need to grow the army?

Twenty-five years had been more than enough time to install those personally loyal to him as commanders; many, in fact, were members of the Unbound. The army now numbered about five thousand men, armed with both normal weapons and some of the magical weapons of old, resurrected by Tagaza from ancient scrolls.

Even five thousand men were too few to be everywhere

at once around a Barrier more than 1,800 miles in circumference. So the army had been split into four divisions, each responsible for the regular patrol of the segment of the Barrier in their quadrant. As far as the soldiers knew, those patrols were simply training exercises, although occasionally they did lead to clashes with the Minik. When Falk had control of the Barrier and was ready to bring it down, those patrols would become crucial to planning the best way to move out of the Kingdom into the outside world.

Even if the Kingdom proved to be surrounded by Commoner communities when the Barrier came down, Falk had been confident his troops, trained not only in the use of sword and bow, but in the battlefield use of magic, would have no trouble overwhelming any opposition, which after all would be taken completely by surprise, since they surely would not expect a Barrier that had stood for centuries to simply vanish into thin air.

But if he had *accurate* information about what lay outside the Barrier before he brought it down . . . he smiled. The boy was a gift: a gift from the SkyMage himself.

Falk judged the boy badly wounded, but not mortally so, given the ministrations of a talented Healer such as Eddigar . . . who should already be examining him, down in the manor.

Falk turned on his heel and left the wreckage behind. He had already ordered his men-at-arms to free it from the trees and drag it down to the courtyard for further examination. He had no fear of anyone else attempting to salvage anything from it: the local villagers well knew that stealing from Lord Falk would have unpleasant consequences.

He needed to talk to Eddigar, to find out how soon he could question the boy.

And now, more than ever, he needed to talk to Mother Northwind.

———

While Brenna stripped off her filthy coat and clothes in her bedroom, two mageservants hauled in a bronze bathtub, placed it in front of the fireplace, filled it with steaming water and scented oils, then whisked her clothes away for cleaning as she lowered herself into it.

When she had been younger, Brenna had felt shy about disrobing around the mageservants; now she didn't give them a second thought as she settled with a sigh of pleasure into the warm embrace of the water. She plunged her head under, then scrubbed her dark curly hair furiously with soft lilac-scented soap from a bowl the mageservants had placed at the side of the tub.

Half an hour later—clean, dry, warm, and *much* better-smelling—she donned a forest-green gown of soft velvet, buckled a belt of gold chain around her hips, brushed her hair until it shone, tied into it a bit of gold ribbon that set her hair off nicely and matched the belt, then examined herself in the full-length mirror on the bedroom side of the bathroom door. She wondered if perhaps she wasn't just a *little* overdressed to do what she intended to do next, which was to try to see the injured youth.

He's probably not even conscious, she told herself.

But she didn't change her clothes.

Instead, she went into the corridor, and this time followed it past the staircase that curved down into the Great Hall and turned into the West Wing, where the guest quarters were located.

Two men-at-arms stood in front of one of the half-dozen closed doors on the right side of the hall. She strode up to them and stopped. "I'd like to greet our guest," she said.

"Sorry, miss," said the bigger of the two, a red-bearded giant she'd met before . . . Buff? Biff? Skiff? . . . something like that. "Lord Falk's orders. No one is allowed in."

"He didn't mean *me*," Brenna snapped, though she suspected that was a lie. "I've already seen the boy. I found him, remember?"

The big man's expression didn't change. *Kuff, that's his name.* "That's as may be, Miss Brenna. Lord Falk did not tell us of any exceptions."

The other guardsman, whom she didn't know at all, kept

his eyes focused on the opposite wall, as though he had never seen anything more fascinating.

"And what will you do if I simply push past your silly pikes?" Brenna said. "Skewer me?"

"No, ma'am. But we *will* restrain you and take you to Lord Falk."

Bluff called, Brenna could do nothing but try to save face. "No need," she said coolly. "I'll talk to him myself and see what he has to say about your impertinence."

"Perhaps that would be best, ma'am," Kuff said.

All her cards played and trumped, Brenna turned and not-quite-stomped (not wanting to appear childish, though it certainly would have felt good) back down the hall to her own room . . .

. . . where she promptly slipped out through the hidden entrance near the stove into the servants' corridors. She went down the same narrow stairs she had taken when she'd gone out through the coal shed earlier, but this time went past the entrance to the shed, into the servants' quarters themselves, plain rooms on the bottom floor of the West Wing, strung out along a corridor that ended in the kitchen but was punctuated by a series of staircases leading up.

Just as in her part of the manor, each of those stairways led to a corridor running between two guest rooms, providing hidden access for servicing stoves, changing linens, delivering food, retrieving dirty dishes, and all the other servantly functions. There were rooms for two-score servants, but they were mostly empty, the few living servants all clustering near the kitchens.

Brenna could hear noise from that direction as she entered the servants' wing, but there was no one in the hallway, lit sparingly by a magelight every ten feet or so. The stairway she wanted was the second one. She slipped up it without being seen. It doubled back on itself on a tiny landing halfway up, then delivered her into the corridor between the room where the boy lay and an empty room on the other side.

As Brenna reached the top of the stairs, she heard

voices. At the same instant the pine planks of the floor creaked beneath her feet. She froze. But, after all, the old house was full of creaks and groans, and the owners of the voices took no apparent notice.

Brenna couldn't make out any words, but recognized the bass growl of Lord Falk. Very slowly, she crept over to the door to the boy's room, and put her ear against it.

"... wake?" That was Lord Falk.

"I have put a sleep on him to keep him unconscious until morning," said a voice she now recognized as that of Healer Eddigar, whom she'd met many times through the usual sicknesses and mishaps of childhood, the last time just a few months ago when she'd cracked a rib after a slip in the tub. She'd been black and blue for days, but he'd knitted the bone and taken away most of the pain in short order.

"When he wakes," Eddigar continued, "he will be very weak and very hungry. However, I have stopped the internal bleeding and sped the healing of the wound in his leg. I have also cleaned that wound and his various scrapes and cuts. There should be no infection. I expect him to make a full recovery."

"As long as he is able to answer questions," said Falk.

"He will be *able* to answer them," Eddigar said. "Whether he *will* answer them is of course beyond my control."

Footsteps receded, and when Falk spoke again, his voice was more muffled. *He must have gone to the door*, Brenna thought. "When will he awake?"

"I cannot be more precise than I have been, my lord," Eddigar said. His voice, too, was more distant. "Sometime in the morning, but whether early or late, I cannot say. It depends not only on my magic but on his body's powers of recuperation ... and level of fatigue."

"Hmm. Well, I'll leave the guards. It wouldn't do for him to wake and wander off, would it?"

"Those decisions are yours, my lord."

Brenna heard the two men go out and the door close

behind them. Falk's voice rumbled indistinctly for a moment; presumably he was speaking to the guards. Then, silence.

Brenna waited a moment for her racing heart to slow a little, then opened the servants' door and entered the room.

The curtains on the floor-to-ceiling windows, twins of those in her own room, were drawn tight, so that the only light in the room came from the lamp—an oil lamp, not a magelight—barely aglow on the table beside the bed. At first all Brenna could see of the bed's occupant was an indistinct lump, but as her eyes adjusted she recognized that the young man she had last seen hanging upside down and bleeding from a tree outside the manor grounds now lay on his back beneath a thick red comforter, his head on a feather pillow and his bare shoulders exposed. Brenna stepped farther into the room and closed the concealed door behind her.

She took one step, and a floorboard creaked. The boy stirred, his head turning slightly. His breathing had become faster and louder. Brenna froze, watching, but after a moment the boy's breathing settled, and he was once again as quiet and motionless as when she had first seen him.

He's in a magic-induced sleep, she reminded herself. *He's not going to wake up because of a creaky floor.*

But there were also guards outside the door, and so she took the remaining few steps toward the bed as carefully as though she were walking on eggshells instead of pine.

Finally she stood beside the bed and could look down on the sleeping youth's face. He appeared younger than she'd first thought, now that his face was cleaned of grime and blood, but whether he was younger or older than she, she could not tell; she was not a good judge of the ages of young men, having met so few of them.

Remembering the blood dripping from the wound on his leg, and curious to see how Eddigar had dealt with the wound, she moved around to the other side of the bed and lifted the comforter to take a look.

Beneath the blanket, he was naked.

Brenna blinked, stared, realized she was staring, and dropped the comforter in confusion. Even though she was alone, she felt her face flush. *I didn't mean—I never thought—*

Her thoughts stammered to a stop inside her head, and a cooler, sardonic voice said, *And if you had known, you would have looked on purpose, wouldn't you?*

She couldn't answer that question. But then, she hadn't really seen what condition his leg was in. And she wasn't hurting anything by taking another look. He was asleep, he'd never know—

Her hand was on the comforter again when, horrified by her own thoughts, she decided she'd seen enough. (*More than enough*, that sardonic inner voice commented.) There was no point risking discovery when the boy wasn't even able to talk to—

And then his head tossed right and left, his eyes opened—and he looked straight at her.

CHAPTER 6

FOR A LONG MOMENT, Anton couldn't make sense of what he was seeing. Where was Professor Carteri? Who was this curly-haired, brown-eyed girl looking at him with a strange expression?

He blinked, swallowed with a throat that felt like sandpaper, and finally found his voice. "What happened?" he croaked, in a credible imitation of a bullfrog. "Where am I? Where's the Professor?"

There was something wrong with his tongue ... and his ears. It felt like heavy snow was falling inside his head, piling up, muffling everything, trying to bury him once more in darkness. Had he been drugged? But it didn't feel the same as the one time he *had* been drugged, when he'd broken his arm as a child, before his family fell apart, and had been sedated while the doctor set it. This felt ...

He didn't know how it felt. He'd never felt anything like it before, like someone from outside himself pushing a smothering pillow down on his consciousness.

The girl appeared horrified that he had spoken. She turned in a hurry and headed toward a narrow door ajar in the dark-paneled wall, next to a gilded stove, the glow of burning coal showing through the metal grill in its round belly.

"Don't go...." he said, as urgently as he could through the strange lethargy gripping him. "Tell me ..."

She paused, her back to him, then turned and stepped

back toward him again. She pointed at herself. "Brenna," she said.

He managed to pull one arm—it felt like lead—free of the covers and laid his hand palm-down on his bare chest. "Anton. Do you ... can you understand me?" He spoke very slowly and clearly, as though talking to a deaf old woman.

The girl put her head to one side, studying his face. "Oondehrrrshtant you? Awlmoost.... yoor wahrrrds ur shtrrranjuh."

"My ... words are strange?" *But not incomprehensible!* he thought with a surge of excitement. *They don't speak another language; it's just a dialect—an accent.*

The Professor was right. There are people inside the Anomaly ... not monsters or ghosts as the superstitious would have it. People, people like us ... but people from the past ...

The Professor! Anton felt ashamed for not thinking of his friend and mentor sooner. "Where is the Professor?" he said. "The man I was with," he added, when the girl gave him a puzzled look.

She frowned, as though trying to work out his words. "The man ..." Already he was becoming accustomed to her accent. "I am sorry. He is dead. He died when your ... flying thing ... crashed into the trees. Was he ... your father?"

"He's ... dead?" Anton couldn't believe it, couldn't accept it. The Professor ... dead? *He can't be. He can't be! He was all I had ... Without him, I'd be all alone, back on the streets of Hexton Down ...*

But sympathy filled the girl's face, and he couldn't doubt her. She had been there moments after the crash. She must have seen the Professor's body herself ... and arranged for his rescue.

A friend, then?

Too soon to tell. He didn't know if he *had* any friends here. A stranger from outside the Anomaly? If they had truly been isolated in here for centuries, the appearance of someone like him would hit them like a grapeshot grenade thrown into a crowded room. And if their politics were anything like those of the Union Republic, everyone who learned of his existence would try to use him for their own purposes, or at least prevent their enemies from using him for theirs.

And without the Professor . . . he would have to deal with that, all of it, on his own.

The darkness pushed down harder. His eyelids drooped. He saw the girl reach out a hand toward him, but this time he didn't fight the lethargy. Instead, he was glad to let it take him, burying him in blank forgetfulness.

Brenna gazed at the sleeping youth, pitying him—she had seen from the look on his face how much the man he had called "The Professor" had meant to him. But she was also astonished that he had awakened at all. Healer Eddigar knew his business, and he had said the spell would keep the stranger unconscious until at least morning. Here, practically on top of the Magefire of Falk Manor, there was no chance his spell had been too weak.

So how had this strange youth from beyond the Barrier managed to overcome it, even for a little while?

Brenna knew she was pushing her luck, staying so long in the boy's . . . Anton's . . . room. She went to the servants' door, but even as she reached for it to swing it wider, the main door opened. She jerked her head around to see Lord Falk looking at her.

She froze.

Falk's eyebrows rose. "I see you found a way through my security arrangements," he said dryly. "Perhaps we should have a talk about that."

He stepped to one side and motioned for her to come out. Mute, heart pounding, she crossed the room and stepped out into the hallway. The guards turned as she emerged. Kuff's face paled. "Lord Falk, I swear, we didn't let her pass! I turned her away myself not twenty minutes ago—"

"At ease," Falk said. "She came through the servants' corridors. Which I had not bothered to guard because I was more concerned about the boy escaping than anyone trying to sneak in to see him, and he would have been unlikely to find them. So the fault is mine, as much as yours." He gave Brenna a stern look. "But not," he added, "as much as yours."

"Lord Falk—"

"I said we would talk about it, and we will. But not here. Come with me."

He led her down the corridor in the direction of her room, but rather than taking her around the corner, stopped at another of the guest rooms. He opened the door and motioned her through.

The room looked much like the one in which Anton lay, except that the furniture was shrouded and the air icy, the stove in the corner unlit. Falk gazed into empty space for a moment, eyes narrowed, and an untethered magelight appeared, a glowing ball of bright blue light floating in the air over his head. Falk returned his attention to her. "I should have remembered the servants' corridors, of course," he said. He reached out and pulled the covers from two chairs and a table near the door, the floating magelight following him wherever he went. He motioned for Brenna to sit down, and she did so, though without relaxing, keeping her back straight and her hands folded primly in her lap. "I wandered them often enough as a boy," Falk went on, sitting down across the table from her, "so I can hardly be surprised that you know them well. But I really did not expect anyone from within the household to defy my wishes and try to see the boy. . . .especially you."

"You didn't tell me I couldn't see him, Lord Falk," Brenna pointed out, while wondering a little at her own temerity. "And it is my home, too."

Falk cocked an eyebrow at her again, but said nothing.

He studied her in silence for a long time. She became increasingly uncomfortable under that gaze, but held still, waiting to hear her punishment.

Lord Falk surprised her. "Perhaps it is as well," he said. "The youth, after all, is wounded and alone. He will need a friend and companion when he awakes. He will find me cold, and possibly even sinister . . . and he will thus be less likely to tell me what I need to know, whereas to you, he may speak freely."

Brenna felt shock, then anger. "You want me to be your spy?"

Lord Falk made an impatient gesture with his right hand, as though flicking water from his fingertips. "I mean him no harm, Brenna. But we cannot be certain he does not mean harm to *us* . . . or, if not him personally, those who sent him." He leaned forward. "He comes from beyond the Barrier. If two men can cross the Barrier, then an army can. And if those who have found their way to the Barrier from the outside world share the traits of their ancestors . . ."

Brenna's tutor had taught her well. She knew exactly what Falk was referring to. "But the Mage Wars were eight centuries ago," she said. "Ancient history, inside or outside. The MageLords are probably little more than legends out there . . . if they remember them at all. Why would they attack?"

"*We* remember the Mage Wars," Falk said. "Why shouldn't they? And even if they do not, think of what they will find here: a lush, civilized kingdom, carved out of the northern wilderness, rich in natural resources, developed cropland, fresh water . . . if whatever powers are out there are like every other power in history, they will see us as fruit ripe for the picking, especially if they know nothing of magic and believe themselves to have the edge in military might."

Peska had told Brenna of the atrocities committed against the MageLords and their followers during the Mage Wars. The rebel Commoners had slaughtered men, women, and children. They would have eradicated the Mageborn entirely if the Twelve hadn't found the Evrenfels magic lode and used all the magic and energy of the Old Kingdom to transport themselves and their followers halfway around the world. Rebounding from their near-eradication, they had carved civilization out of wilderness here—and Brenna, Commoner though she was, did not want to see all that destroyed any more than Falk did.

She took a deep breath. "I'll learn what I can," she said. "But I would have anyway. I'm not your spy."

Lord Falk nodded solemnly. "I understand. And of course I will question the boy myself. But if you learn anything you think I should know . . . please tell me." He held out his palm, and the magelight descended to rest in his open hand. He blew gently on it; it drifted away from the puff of air. "One secret above all I hope he will share with either you or me: how that flying conveyance works."

Brenna blinked. "Magic, surely. It carried a mageflame. I heard it roaring—"

Lord Falk shook his head. "There is no magic about it at all. I tested it myself. It is a plain, unenchanted object, like a broom or a table. It works by artifice, not magic." He flicked a finger, and the magelight dropped like a rock to the floor. He raised his hand, the light rose slowly again. "So what held it up?"

Dinner that night was a quiet affair. Lord Falk and Brenna ate alone in one of the more intimate dining rooms off of the Great Hall. Falk had never been one to encourage idle chatter, and he considered any queries about his official business impertinent. Nevertheless, emboldened by their earlier conversation, Brenna ventured to break the silence as they waited for dessert. "Why did you come home at this time, Lord Falk?" she asked cautiously, then decided to venture a small joke. "Is it true what the villagers say, that you know everything that happens here before it happens?"

To Brenna's surprise, a corner of Falk's mouth actually

quirked upward. "Well, I certainly wish that were true, but . . . no. No, I came because of an alarming incident at the Palace. You've met the Heir . . ."

"Prince Karl," Brenna said. "Has something happened to him?"

"Almost. Someone tried to kill him yesterday morning . . . *inside* the Lesser Barrier."

Brenna blinked. She had been taught the Lesser Barrier protected the King and his Heir as effectively as the Great Barrier protected the entire Kingdom.

As securely as that? she thought uneasily, remembering Anton, guarded and asleep upstairs. *Are both Barriers failing?*

The thought felt like heresy.

"But I don't understand," she said. "Why should that bring you here?"

"There is someone here I think might be able to help me figure out who was behind the attack," Falk said.

Brenna frowned, thinking. "Mother Northwind?"

Falk raised both eyebrows this time. "Well done. Yes, she is the one I came to see. May I ask why you named her?"

Perversely pleased to have surprised her notoriously unflappable guardian, Brenna shrugged. "Who else could it be? Aside from me, I doubt anyone else here besides Mother Northwind has ever been more than twenty miles from Overbridge."

"Well-reasoned," Lord Falk said. "Yes, it is she I came to talk to."

"But what information could *she* have?" Brenna asked, curious.

Falk shook his head with a small smile. "That, I'm afraid, I cannot tell you."

Dessert arrived, a trifle of whipped cream and fresh blueberries that had been magically preserved through the winter. While she ate, Brenna thought about Mother Northwind.

The old woman—Brenna had no idea *how* old—had lived in her cottage, nestled against the valley wall not far from the manor, for as long as Brenna could remember, but certainly she had not *always* lived there. No one knew, or at least no one had ever told Brenna, precisely where she came from, or everything she had done in her long life.

One thing Brenna knew; though she lived among the Commoners, she was Mageborn. More than that, a Healer, who assisted Eddigar, focusing her efforts mainly on the women of Lord Falk's demesne, easing the pains of childbirth and occasionally exerting extra effort to attempt to save the life of a mother or child—attempts which were, more often than not, successful.

Falk had been eating in silence. Now he put down his spoon and picked up his wineglass. As he drank from it, he gazed at her with cool thoughtfulness. "You are now eighteen years old," he said as he put down the glass. "A grown woman. And that, too, has brought me here."

Brenna froze, spoon halfway to her mouth, wondering what was about to come. *If he tells me he's arranged a marriage . . .*

"When I return to the Palace, I want you to come with me . . . to stay."

Brenna's heart skipped a beat. "To stay? Not just for a visit?"

"To stay," Falk confirmed. "It's time." He smiled. "Spring is scant weeks away. Wouldn't you enjoy celebrating Springfest in New Cabora?"

Brenna felt her face spreading into an enormous smile. "There is nothing I would love better, Lord Falk!" she said fervently.

"Excellent." Falk took another swallow of his wine. "Then it is settled." He pushed away from the table. "And now, if you will excuse me . . ."

In her bed that night, Brenna found it hard to sleep, her brain whirling, wondering what it would be like to move to the city permanently. New people, new friends . . . she smiled in the darkness . . . a lover, a husband . . . ?

But then, for some reason, her thoughts leaped back to the youth, Anton, not just her brief exchange with him in the bedroom, but what had come just before that, when she had lifted the covers . . .

She blushed in the darkness, and set herself to determinedly counting nice, fat, woolly (definitely *not* shorn and naked) sheep.

She was up to two hundred and forty-seven before she finally drifted off to sleep.

CHAPTER 7

LORD FALK, ALONE AND ON FOOT, walked out through the manor's front gate.

He strode past the stockade of the men-at-arms without slowing. He needed no escort. He had no fear of the darkness or anyone who dwelt in the valley. Not all of the Commoners loved him, but that hardly mattered. Certainly they all feared him, and none would dare test his magical defenses by attempting to harm him in any way . . . a wise choice.

Mother Northwind lived alone, in a hut not too near the village but not too far from it either, up one of the wooded draws that wound into the high, steep slopes of the Grand Valley. He was not the first to walk that way since the snowfall, nor had he expected to be, but he did take a moment to study the footprints to assure himself that those who had gone ahead of him with their heavy load had returned the same way.

He smelled the smoke of Mother Northwind's fire before he saw her cabin, almost invisible in a copse of poplar and ash at the very back of a long, narrow draw. In warmer weather a stream ran down into the draw from the hillside above, but now it existed only as a series of icicles hanging from the rounded rocks that defined its bed above the cottage.

The cottage itself was nondescript, a simple structure of logs caulked with clay, roofed with slate. It might have been there forever, but Lord Falk knew it had been built new, magically, literally overnight just eighteen years before: knew, because he had had it built, when Mother Northwind had entered his service (if that was quite the right phrase for it) and set him on the path that would shortly lead to the destruction of the Barrier . . .

. . . if the attempt to assassinate Prince Karl did not upset everything.

Well. That was why he was here. He strode forward, boots crunching through the crusted snow.

As he came nearer to the cottage, he heard singing. The tune was a well-worn old folk tune, but the words described the improbable adventures of one Axnay the Well-Hung. *She's home, then*, Falk thought wryly, as he stepped up onto the low porch and knocked three times.

The tune cut off in mid-verse, "leaving poor Axnay embarrassingly unsatisfied. "Enter, then," said a woman's voice, and Lord Falk pulled the door open and stepped into the warm yellow glow of the cabin's interior.

Mother Northwind sat in a rocking chair by the cheerily crackling fire, a sky-blue shawl drawn around her shoulders and a bright red scarf covering most of her gray curls. She looked pretty much exactly how someone raised on children's stories and the skits of traveling players would expect someone named Mother Northwind to look. Lord Falk, however, knew that her image as a harmless old hedge-mage living in a storybook cottage in the wood was very carefully crafted. It endeared her to the Commoners of his demesne, who saw her as "their" Healer far more than they did Eddigar (especially the women), while keeping her accessible to Falk when he had need of her more . . . exotic services.

Mother Northwind was, in fact, the most powerful practitioner of soft magic in the Kingdom, a Healer without equal. But that was not why Falk valued her. For Healing, he had Eddigar. Much of Healing was actually a form of hard magic, anyway: the knitting of a broken bone was no different in principle from the welding together of rock to make a wall. What set Healers apart was the ability to soothe troubled minds, relieve pain, erase nightmares. The other difference between the two branches of magic was that while hard magic required an outside source of energy (heat from the air, from the Palace's MageFurnace, from the Magefire in the manor's basement), the energy for soft magic came from the body of the mage him- or herself. Falk recalled how exhausted Eddigar had been after dealing with a series of serious injuries following the collapse of a granary under construction in Overbridge. Only one man had died, thanks to the Healer, but Falk had feared Eddigar would be the second.

But Eddigar was to Mother Northwind in his abilities as a Mageborn child who had just learned to illuminate a magelight was to Lord Falk. And it was from Mother Northwind that Falk had learned the other way in which a powerful soft mage could obtain the energy for her work—not from herself, but from the person she touched.

Mother Northwind could heal with a touch, and so she did. But Mother Northwind could also kill with a touch, willing a man's heart to stop. She could alleviate pain, but she could also, without leaving a visible mark, cause pain so great that a man's throat might be ripped to bloody shreds by his screaming.

More, Mother Northwind could get inside a man's mind without his knowing she had violated it, and recover nuggets of information he would much rather have kept hidden: nuggets suitable for blackmail, nuggets providing evidence of treason or graft, nuggets that might betray his dearest friends to their blackest enemies.

Supposedly such magic required touch, and for that reason Falk never allowed Mother Northwind close enough to touch him. Of course, "supposedly" was not the same as assuredly. But Mother Northwind also knew that if Falk ever suspected she had been inside his mind, he would blow her into shreds of bloody meat with a flick of his hand.

In such mutual fear and respect, they had become something almost like friends.

Well, perhaps not friends, Falk amended. *Coconspirators*.

Twenty-five years ago, shortly after he had become Minister of Public Safety, and he and Tagaza had begun to despair of arranging the complex circumstances for bringing down the Barriers, Mother Northwind had come to him one night at the manor, presenting herself as a Commoner from Overbridge with a grievance. He had had her ushered in, and in the privacy of his office, she had revealed that she knew exactly what he wanted to do (though she had never explained *how* she knew), and just how impossible it seemed. And then she had offered a solution. "The King," she said, "needs an Heir. The necessary act has appeared to be beyond his capabilities, but I have it on good authority . . . a Healer within the Palace . . . that that is about to change.

"There will be an Heir, Lord Falk. Nine months from, oh, this time next week. And he—or she—can be yours."

"Why?" he had asked her. "Why would you help me in this?"

"Why do you care?" she had said. "Suffice it to say I want the Barrier down as much as you do. And you *cannot* accomplish that task without my help."

Falk had not pressed more deeply; he dared not, with the solution to his problem delivered so neatly to his doorstep.

Nine months later, as Mother Northwind had promised, King Kravon's wife had given birth. The baby had lived; she had died. The Royal Midwife, apparently distraught at having failed her Queen, committed suicide that same night. And a week after that, while the Mageborn were still both mourning the death of the Queen and celebrating the birth of Prince Karl, Heir Apparent to the throne of Evrenfels, Mother Northwind had brought to Falk, waiting in his manor, a squalling female bundle which he had given over into the care of a woman from the village. "Call the child Brenna," Mother Northwind had told him. "And now let us discuss the cottage you are going to build for me . . ."

Now Falk stood inside the door of that same cottage, looking at Mother Northwind in her chair by the fire. The flames struck sharp red sparks from her eyes, bright and hard as a crow's. "Lord Falk," she said. "So nice to see you again. Did you have a pleasant trip from the Palace last night?"

"There's nothing pleasant about spending most of twenty-four hours in a magecarriage," Falk said. "But all that matters is that I am here . . . although I trust I am not the *first* visitor from the Palace you have had today."

Mother Northwind laughed, a hearty, fruity laugh, not at all like the thin cackle she normally affected, which better suited her carefully crafted appearance. "Indeed you are not," she said. "Your men dropped off my other . . . guest . . . a couple of hours ago. She wasn't nearly as lively as you, though. Dead on her feet, you might say. Charry, but not cheery."

Lord Falk sighed. Mother Northwind had an . . . iconoclastic . . . sense of humor. "But did she have anything to say?"

Mother Northwind's smile widened. "She did, indeed! You did well to get her into stasis so quickly. I was able to retrieve more than I expected when you first sent word."

Falk leaned forward. "And?"

Mother Northwind tsked. "So eager," she said. "Rushing to fulfillment is no way to please a woman."

"*And?*" Falk repeated, putting an edge into his voice.

Mother Northwind spread her hands. "And," she said, "she went to her death firmly convinced that she was carrying out the wishes of . . . the Master of the Unbound."

"*I* am the Master of the Unbound!" Falk snarled.

Mother Northwind's eyes widened. "Really? And you are the Minister of Public Safety. It's a scandal!"

"*I* did not give an order to attempt to assassinate the Prince. What purpose would it serve? Especially *now*?"

Mother Northwind shrugged. "You hardly have to convince *me*. But I haven't finished telling you what I learned."

"Go on."

"She believed she was carrying out the wishes of the Master of the Unbound . . . in alliance with the Common Cause."

That was so unexpected Falk was struck speechless for a moment. "The Unbound in alliance with Commoner rabble-rousers?" he said at last. "Who could believe that?"

"Our would-be assassin, apparently. A Commoner herself, and a—call her a foot soldier—of the Common Cause, she was acting on orders from the Cause . . . but had been told that the magic that made her attack possible had come from the Unbound. What she thought of that, I cannot tell. There are limits to what may be retrieved from the dead." She smiled sweetly. "But perhaps, Lord Falk, you are not as fully in control of the Unbound as you think."

Falk's eyes narrowed. "You have personally vetted every member of the Unbound, have you not?"

"Every member you identified to me," Mother Northwind said. "But there could be others you do not know of. A secret cult within a secret cult."

Falk considered that, then shook his head. "Unlikely. Something would have come to my attention, through any of a hundred different channels."

"And yet . . . *someone* provided this Commoner with the means to assassinate the Prince," Mother Northwind pointed out. "Someone who wanted the Unbound blamed for it."

"Someone who wanted to hide their own tracks," Falk said. "Someone with their own reasons to want the Prince eliminated."

Mother Northwind held out her hands to the fire. An enormous tabby cat that had been snoozing on the hearth stood up, stretched, and walked over to her. She rubbed its head, and even from across the room Falk could hear the animal's purring. "And who would that be, exactly?"

"I don't know," Falk admitted. "You say the assassin was a "foot soldier" of the Common Cause, but I do not understand why the Cause would want to kill the Prince any more than the Unbound. Even Commoners would know that would accomplish nothing, that the Keys would simply be passed on to someone else. And Karl . . . at Tagaza's urging . . . has spent a lot of time representing the Crown in the Commons. They *know* him. Why risk bringing to power a King who might be less sympathetic to Commoners?" He scratched his chin thoughtfully. "The only reason I can think of is the one I told Karl: that the Cause might have wanted to kill him simply as an act of terror, to show they can strike inside the Barrier. But my dungeons are already filling with those arrested in response, and they must have known that would be the response. So what did they hope to accomplish?"

"It's a quandary," Mother Northwind said. "I wish you luck in figuring it out." She patted her lap, and the cat leaped up, turned itself around, and settled down happily, kneading her leg with its claws as she continued to pet it.

Falk tapped his fingers on the table. "I suppose it could be a . . . bargaining tactic," he said slowly. "Perhaps they believe if they cause the MageLords enough pain, we will negotiate more self-rule for them." He shook his head. "They talk about the 'will of the people,' as if you could choose a leader just by letting everyone have a say in the process . . . as if it that would not inevitably lead to chaos and anarchy, with so many conflicting interests in play."

"Not nearly as neat and tidy as now," Mother Northwind said, and he shot a glance at her, uncertain whether she was being sarcastic. She gazed back blandly. After a moment, he went on.

"They're mad, but still . . . that *could* be their motivation. But why did they involve magic in their attack? And how? What mage would work with them? And why tell their assassin the Unbound were supposedly in alliance with them? Why not carry out the attempt through nonmagical means, and then claim *full* responsibility? As I said, Karl is often in the Commons. They could have killed him at any time."

"All good questions, Lord Falk."

Falk grunted. "Well, then, here's another. *Why did the*

attack fail? The corpse in your cellar isn't Karl's. The magic intended to kill him killed his would-be assassin instead."

"Very mysterious," Mother Northwind said. "But I do not understand the workings of hard magic as well as I do soft." She scratched the cat behind the ears. "It is all beyond me." The cat had suddenly had enough; it got up, stretched, and jumped onto the floor. "Oh, I almost forgot. I did . . . acquire . . . one other piece of information. A name, prominent in the girl's mind."

Falk sat very still. "And you 'almost forgot' to mention it?" he said, his voice dangerously soft.

Mother Northwind smiled, brushing cat hair from her apron. "I'm mentioning it now, aren't I? Besides, it's hardly a name one should be surprised to find in the mind of someone living in New Cabora."

"Someone well-known?"

"Extremely." Mother Northwind met his eyes. "The playwright, Davydd Verdsmitt."

Falk felt a kind of . . . pleasure . . . at hearing that name. He had long suspected Verdsmitt of being involved with the radical side of the Cause. "Why would she be thinking of Verdsmitt at the moment of the attack?"

"Another good question, Lord Falk."

Falk snorted. "You give me more questions than answers, Mother Northwind."

"I am a simple country healer and midwife," Mother Northwind said. "What answers could I possibly offer someone as highly placed and powerful as you?"

Falk let that pass. "Well, as always, I thank you for the information you have provided. I will send my men to remove your . . . guest . . . in the morning."

"Always happy to serve," Mother Northwind said. She smiled again. "And now, I suspect, you intend to ask my help in the matter of your unexpected visitor from beyond the Barrier."

I shouldn't be surprised she knows about that, Falk thought. *But I wish I knew* how *she knew.* "Yes," he said. "I cannot simply rely on what he might freely tell me—"

"Or Brenna?"

"Or Brenna," Falk said, again startled by Mother Northwind's knowledge, though he let nothing of it show on his face. "I need to know . . . everything he knows."

"My humble abilities are entirely at your command," Mother Northwind said. "But as you know, Lord Falk, 'everything' is a very great deal indeed. I can strip his mind of all knowledge, but you know what that would do to him."

Indeed, Lord Falk knew. Among those publically executed as members of the Unbound, to demonstrate his hatred of the cult, were the drooling, blank-eyed results of that kind of questioning.

"We need not go that far," Falk said. "Not to start with, at least. The boy may have other uses. But whatever you can find out without harming him, I must know. In particular, how that flying device of his operates."

Mother Northwind nodded. "I would be interested to know that myself. Very well, Lord Falk. When would you like me to call on you?"

"Let's say . . . an hour after sunrise. In my study in the manor."

"I am not an early riser, Lord Falk, but for you . . . I suppose I can make an exception."

Falk stood. "Thank you," he said. "Until the morrow, then. Good night, Mother Northwind."

"Good night, Lord Falk."

Falk let himself out and, deep in thought, walked back toward the manor. So the assassin had had Davydd Verdsmitt front and center in her mind . . . and shortly the playwright himself would be inside the Barrier, presenting his new play at the Palace. Falk needed to be there. He would have to leave on the morrow . . . after Mother Northwind had extracted whatever information she could from the boy from Outside, and he had decided what to do with him . . . and with his flying machine.

A great deal would depend on whether the machine could be made to fly again. If so, then until others could be trained in its operation—and more of the machines could be constructed—he would need the boy as a pilot. Even if the machine could not be fixed, the boy would continue to be useful as a source of information and even, possibly, a hostage once the Barrier was down.

More useful if he's loyal to me, Falk thought. *Tomorrow I'll speak to Mother Northwind about taking care of that, too.*

He turned his thoughts back to the matter of the Common Cause. Tomorrow he would magespeak Brich and find out what, if anything, his interrogators had learned from those he had ordered arrested. He needed to know the exact nature of the plot he was certain was afoot, and whether it posed any real danger to the Plan. And if he could not find out from those arrested thus far, he could certainly get the truth from Verdsmitt.

Could Verdsmitt even be the elusive "Patron"?

Maybe. At the very least he would likely be the most highly placed member of the Cause Falk had yet had the chance—or reason—to question . . . and whatever Verdsmitt knew, he *would* tell. Falk was very good at extracting information, even without Mother Northwind's unique talents.

He felt a surge of anger at the unknown conspirators who had chosen *this* moment to attack the Prince. For more than thirty years he had been preparing, ever since he had first met Tagaza at the College of Mages and learned that the Barriers could, indeed, be lowered, though it involved an extremely complex spell . . . and, of course, the simultaneous murders of the Ruler and Heir.

Tagaza claimed he had spent many sleepless nights when he had first discovered that fact, had claimed he had worked weeks longer looking for some other way, with no success. Despite his insistence that he felt the Barriers must fall (though Falk didn't believe his claim that magic would fail if they did not; the SkyMage would not permit such a thing), he had told Falk over and over how much he regretted the awful necessity of that double murder. It was almost as tiresome a constant in his conversation as his harping on the topic of Commoners, and how the Mage-born had to treat them more fairly if the Kingdom were to survive.

Falk had felt no regret or horror at learning that the only way for him to obtain the power to lower the Barriers required two deaths. For him, there had been only a feeling of exaltation; the thing could be done. It would be difficult, but *it could be done*.

How difficult had become clearer as Tagaza had further studied the spell. The energy required was so enormous that the spell could only be performed on the very edge of the Cauldron, the vast open lake of lava that provided the energy for the Barriers. One of the two, either King or Heir, would have to be slain on its blackened shore.

Nor could it be done while the Heir was still a child, since the Keys would not transfer to an Heir who was not yet an adult, and intercepting the transfer of the Keys, in effect grabbing them away from the Heir at the very moment they attempted to leap from dying Ruler to future Ruler, was the whole point of the spell.

The logistics were almost as complicated as the spell itself. Killing the Ruler and Heir at once within the Lesser Barrier would have been a simple matter—especially when the one who wanted them dead was the Minister of Public Safety, whose duty was supposedly to protect them, and who commanded the Royal guard—but getting either to the Cauldron had seemed an insurmountable task, exacerbated by the simple fact that King Kravon, at the time Falk ascended to the King's Council, had not yet produced any heir at all.

And then Mother Northwind had come forward and offered her invaluable help.

Falk reached the edge of the trees and began walking along the much better marked road that led to his manor. Almost two decades had passed. Brenna and Karl had both turned eighteen six months ago. No one had ever expressed doubt that Karl was both the true son of King Kravon and the Heir to the Keys. Why should they? After all, the First Mage himself had Confirmed Karl as Heir.

But, in truth, *Brenna* was Heir to the Keys and Karl the orphaned Commoner.

He sighed, thinking of Brenna. He *was* rather fond of the girl, despite having done his best to keep his distance from her over the years. He'd been amused by her determination to sneak in and see the boy, impressed by her willingness to do so against his wishes, and impressed again by how quickly she had realized Mother Northwind must be the one he had come see, even though she had no inkling of Mother Northwind's true powers. He thought she would probably have made quite a good Queen—certainly a better Queen than her father Kravon had made a King— but, nevertheless, when the moment came, he would kill her without a qualm. It was a shame, but there was no help for it.

So she sacrifices her life for the greater glory of the Kingdom and to fulfill the will of the SkyMage, he thought. *I have already sacrificed mine.* He had forgone marriage, children, the many pleasures prestige and power provided for other MageLords, focusing always on the Plan, which would culminate with him becoming King: the first King of Evrenfels with the ability to lower the Barriers at will.

It was all so close, now. He had a man in place ready to kill the King. He had long made it his practice in early spring to travel to the Lake of Fire with the First Mage on an "inspection trip"—no one would remark when he did so again. This time he would take Brenna; the ward he'd have recently brought to the Palace to live permanently, to "further her education." No one would remark on that, either.

Once there, using a magelink with his operatives in the Palace, he would order the King murdered—and at the moment of that death, Falk, with Tagaza's help, drawing on the vast energy of the Cauldron, would strip the Keys—and her life—from Brenna, transferring the Keys to himself, and transforming those Keys to give him power over the Barriers.

With the army and Royal guard already loyal to him and his plans twenty-years matured, and now with the information he hoped to get from the boy from Outside about what awaited them on the other side of the Great Barrier, he would prepare for the moment when the Mageborn would *all* be Unbound, free from their self-imposed prison, and ready to take their place once again as rulers in the world Outside, as the SkyMage willed.

And he, at last, would erase the family shame—the failure of their dynasty, two generations before, when Kravon's grandmother had received the Keys instead of Falk's grandfather. He would be King, as he always should have been.

The vision was as clear and sharp and rainbow-hued in his mind as a crystal goblet lit by the sun, and had been for years, but the attempt on the Prince's life had cast a shadow across it.

He stopped on a footbridge that crossed a tiny creek, its summertime burbling stilled by months of deep winter cold, and gazed down at the ice-covered rocks. If the Prince were to die, leaving the current King apparently Heirless, there would be demands for Tagaza to conduct a magical search for the new Heir. The First Mage before Tagaza had developed the spell, and its existence was unfortunately well known to the King's Council and the rest of the Twelve. There would be no way to refuse. But such a search, if carried out fairly, would, without fail, point to Brenna, exposing all Falk's machinations.

If it were carried out fairly. The search would of course be led by Tagaza, who would certainly not expose Falk's—

Falk's eyes narrowed. *Or would he?*

Whoever had arranged the attack on the Prince, if it had indeed been intended to disrupt the Plan, had to be someone with intimate knowledge of that Plan.

Someone like Tagaza.

Tagaza, Falk well knew, did not share the Unbound's belief. He had always been open about his reasons for wanting the Barriers to fall, with his preposterous claim that they were eating up the Kingdom's magic. Falk was prepared to overlook that as long as Tagaza continued to work toward their shared goal, and so far, he had.

But Tagaza also had a soft spot in his heart for the Commoners. In fact, some of the things he'd said to Falk over the years about improving the lot of Commoners could have come straight from the Common Cause's manifesto. Falk had never believed Tagaza would actually act on those beliefs . . . but what if he had? What if *Tagaza* had arranged the assassination attempt, hoping to bring about the search that *he* would lead—and which he could then use to reveal Brenna as Heir, expose Falk, and halt the Plan?

It made some kind of sense, if Tagaza had finally realized that his theory of magic failing if the Barriers remained in place was the nonsense Falk had always believed it to be. If he no longer believed the Barriers had to come down, then he might very well want to prevent Falk from becoming King, knowing that King Falk would certainly never negotiate the reforms with the Commoners Tagaza supported.

He must know I would kill him for it, Falk thought. *Whether I became King or not.*

Unless he thinks he could be protected somehow by . . . the Cause?

Falk turned around and looked out over the snow-covered fields to the few flickering lights of the nearest village. Smoke rose into the starlit sky in tall, unbroken streams from a hundred chimneys.

To craft the magic that could hide an assassin in a bubble of ice on the bottom of a lake, and another that could blast the Prince to oblivion, and enchant objects so that even a Commoner could use that magic . . . it was the work of a master mage.

Maybe even the First Mage.

Then why did the spell fail? Falk thought, frowning—and thinking—furiously. *Because it was being used by a Commoner?*

Or . . . had Tagaza always *meant* the assassination to fail? He was fond of Karl . . . too fond, Falk had often thought. By staging the attempt on Karl's life, and planting the Unbound symbol on the assassin, he might have been aiming to sabotage Falk's Plan, deflect suspicion from himself, and save Brenna's and the King's life, all at once.

Which would also mean he had sacrificed a Commoner, but Falk didn't believe even Tagaza would flinch at that when the stakes were so high. He might want them treated better, but he was still Mageborn, and they were just Commoners, their lack of magic bearing unimpeachable witness to their inferiority. Falk treated his own Commoners well, judging their disputes, ensuring the villages had clean water, access to Healers, farm equipment, etc. But he treated his animals well, too, and he still wouldn't hesitate to butcher one if he needed the meat.

Fury was starting to burn in Falk's chest like a tiny, redhot coal. He sucked in a lungful of freezing air, as if that would cool it, then let it out in an explosion of white steam. He and Tagaza had been friends and coconspirators, but lately the friendship had faded. And as for the latter . . .

Tagaza had crafted the spell that would transfer the Keys from Brenna at the moment of her and the King's deaths, and transform them to give power over the Barriers. Falk could hold it perfectly in his mind, but could not use it and receive the Keys at the same time. The plan had always been for Tagaza to perform the spell. But Falk had taken the precaution of teaching it to another mage, as well, someone who could step in if something happened to Tagaza.

Which meant Tagaza was no longer necessary to the Plan, and had not been for some time.

Falk turned and walked the last few feet to the gates of his manor. *A pity*, he thought. *But we must all live or die with the consequences of our choices. If Tagaza has betrayed me . . . then his choice is made.*

Mother Northwind listened to the sound of Falk's footsteps crunching away through the snow, then, chuckling, hauled herself to her feet.

So easy to manipulate, she thought. *So unable to see the truth.*

She shuffled into the kitchen, her knees stiff after sitting so long in her chair, and stoked the fire, then placed another log on the coals. A wheel of cloth-wrapped hard cheese lay on the lovingly polished table of golden oak, next to half a loaf of crusty bread. She took a knife from the counter and sliced two pieces of the bread, then hung them on a toasting fork, pulled the table's sole accompanying chair close to the fire, sat down with a grunt, and held the slices over the flames.

It was true enough, as Falk believed, that she and he shared a goal: both wanted the Barrier to fall. What Falk had never known, never guessed, she suspected, for he could not imagine a Mageborn would even think of it, was that she wanted the Barrier to fall, not for the greater glory of the MageLords, but to destroy them utterly.

Staring into the fire, she saw, as she always did, another fire from long ago: the flames of a burning Minik village, as men, women, and children she had come to help were slaughtered by a MageLord and his men, and she stood helpless on the hillside.

Lord Starkind had been one of the Twelve, but not of the King's Council. He had come north with his entourage on a hunting trip, but their prey had not been deer, moose, or bear.

He had come to hunt the Minik.

He had set up camp on the outskirts of Stony Creek, the Commoner village where Mother Northwind lived (though that had not been her name then). He had ordered the Commoners to act as forest guides for him and his drunken companions. The locals were on good terms with the Minik and did everything they could to prevent Starkind from finding them, but he soon caught on to what they were up to—and in retaliation executed the village mayor, splitting him in two from head to crotch with a blue-white blade of ice conjured from thin air. Terrified, the guides took him to the Minik village the next day.

When Starkind and his men, blood-spattered and smelling of smoke, grinning, drunk, and laughing, rode back into Stony Creek, the villagers begged him to let them flee south with him and his men. But Lord Starkind jeered at them and rode away, forbidding them to follow. They waited until he was out of sight, then began their own desperate journey south, abandoning everything but what they could carry, the men, women, and children struggling along the forest trails on foot.

By sunset that first day of their journey, none were left alive . . . except Mother Northwind, spared by the vengeful kin of the slaughtered Minik for the Healing help she had always provided them. Taken prisoner, she served the next ten years as Healer to the Black Bear Clan, and as his last action before he died, the old chief set her free. She had set out south at once.

Lord Starkind, grown too fat to ride to any kind of hunt in the ten years since the massacre, shortly thereafter went violently insane, servants rushing into his room when they heard him screaming in the middle of the night, watching in horror as he plucked out his own eyes, chewed, and swallowed them. He had eaten all the fingers off his left hand, his own cock, and was halfway through his second testicle when he finally expired.

Every one of the Mageborn who had accompanied him on his hunting trip north soon met similarly unpleasant fates.

And meanwhile, a new Healer, Mother Northwind, settled down to a quiet life in New Cabora, where she was very welcome, since so few Healers were willing to devote themselves to the care of Commoners . . . and regularly visited the city's library, repository of the documents the Commoners had thought most important down through the centuries. Ostensibly she was researching the ailments of Commoners; in truth, she sought to learn everything she could about the Magebane, the antimagical force that had supposedly helped the Commoners defeat the MageLords of the Old Kingdom.

The toast was done. She pulled it out of the fire, cut a slice of cheese, laid it on top of one of the bread pieces, and munched contentedly. Mother Northwind's hatred of the Mageborn had only intensified during her years in New Cabora. She had seen too many lives torn apart by the casual cruelty of the MageLords: too many abused children, pregnant teenagers, Palace servants crippled by multiple beatings, released prisoners bearing the marks of torture, though with no memory of how it had happened or what they had said to their interrogators in their distress. Even with her extraordinary skills, she could do nothing to help some of those who came to her; ease the pain of their bodies, perhaps, but not their scarred minds.

Oh, she understood perfectly *why* the subjects of the ancient MageLords had risen up. And she knew that the Magebane, by counteracting magic, had given them the victory. But where had the Magebane come from?

Though she found hints in the Commoners' official library, she finally discovered the answers she sought in what she thought of as the *unofficial* library: books, scrolls, letters, songs, and legends, passed down within families, and above all, kept hidden from the Mageborn (for early in the Kingdom's history all talk of the Magebane had been ruthlessly suppressed). From one crumbling scroll an old woman showed her, Mother Northwind learned that the Magebane had been the bastard offspring of a MageLord and a Commoner. From a book hidden beneath a floorboard in a grateful father's kitchen, she learned that the Magebane had not been born, but made. Like a crow collecting shiny things, she pecked and scratched and hid away the fragmented and sometimes contradictory bits of information she uncovered, until at last she thought she could detect the shape of the truth.

The Magebane had been the creation of a great Healer named Vell, who had forced the conception of that bastard child, then molded the fetus within the womb, melding its Mageborn and Commoner halves, creating a very special whole: a man who, though he could not *use* magic, could counteract it—and not *just* counteract it, but *turn it back on its source*.

Vell had raised the child as his own, while secretly fomenting rebellion among the Commoners and a few renegade Mageborn. When the time at last came for open revolution, he had placed that child, then a young man, at the head of an army of Commoners, and when the MageLords contemptuously called down magical fire on the Commoners' heads, it was they who died instead, blasted apart by their own magic.

Without magic, the Mageborn had been hopelessly outnumbered. With the myth of their invincibility so thoroughly shattered, Mageborn began to die even in places where the Magebane had never been seen. They were poisoned, arrow-shot from hiding, burned alive in their homes while they slept. From every corner of the island Kingdom, panicked Mageborn had fled to the capital of Stromencor. There the twelve surviving MageLords of the Great Council had drawn on all their knowledge and resources to find, on the far side of the world, another lode of magic to rival that of the Old Kingdom. They would use the connection between that lode and their own to magically transport themselves to what was now Evrenfels, along with the surviving Mageborn and the Commoners who were supposedly loyal to them, but were in fact, Mother Northwind believed, simply trapped.

As they had been trapped ever since, inside the Great Barrier the First Twelve had crafted to protect their fledgling kingdom from the Commoners and their cursed Magebane, who they feared would pursue them even here.

Mother Northwind knew her abilities well. What Vell had done, she could do. To understand *how* he had crafted the Magebane, though, she had needed access to the libraries of the Colleges of Mages and Healers, and the archives of the Palace, and so she had changed her appearance and her name and offered her services to First Healer Jimson, predecessor to Hannik, as "Healer Makala." Jimson had tested her and, astounded by her abilities, welcomed her. For the next few years, while she tended to the complaints of the mages she secretly detested, she had also delved into ancient magical lore. She had learned a great deal that had made her own magic even stronger . . . and eventually, she had learned enough to be confident she could do what Vell had done.

She, too, could make a Magebane.

Mother Northwind brushed crumbs off her apron, decided not to eat the second piece of toast, and instead heaved herself to her feet, picked up the lantern from the kitchen table, and went to the door that opened onto the stairs into the basement. Holding onto the wall with one hand, the lantern in the other, she descended into the dim depths. The crate in which the body of the dead assassin had arrived leaned against one wall. The corpse itself lay on a wooden trestle table in the middle of the dirt floor. The lantern's flickering yellow light played over the blackened, skull-grinning face, the bulging white eyes, cooked in their sockets. Falk had removed the stasis field on his arrival, and a faint odor of cooked meat, with a hint of beginning corruption, hung around the body.

The grisly sight didn't faze Mother Northwind, who had seen much worse, some of it at her own hands. She set the lantern on the edge of the table, went to the head of the casket, then reached out and laid both hands on the corpse's forehead. Exerting just a little of her will, she reached into the rapidly decaying brain and purged it of the fragments of memories still lingering in its tangled, crumbling pathways. She did not believe Lord Falk would have another Healer check her work, or that there would be enough left of the brain for it to matter if he did, but there was no point in taking chances; not when there was, in fact, not a hint in the dead girl's mind that she'd even heard of the Unbound, much less thought she was following orders from it. She was Common Cause, through and through. Nor, of course, had she had a thought about Verdsmitt, whom she knew only as a playwright.

There. Mother Northwind took a deep breath as a wave of fatigue flowed over her. Once she would hardly have felt such a minor outlay of energy, but she could not deny that she was getting old.

Well, she thought, *at least I'll last long enough to see the MageLords brought low*. She wiped her hands on her apron, picked up the lantern, and climbed back out of the cellar.

She regretted the death of the assassin—Jenna, she thought; the least she could do was remember the girl's name—but there had been no other way. For two reasons, Karl *had* to face an attack, a potentially fatal attack involving magic. First, it was the only way she could be certain she had succeeded in creating a Magebane. If he survived the attack then, without question, the half-breed boy whose existence she had shepherded from coerced conception to birth was indeed what she hoped.

But there was a second, even more important reason. The Magebane *had* to face a lethal magical attack in order to become the Magebane. Only when faced with mortal peril would his power fully awaken.

She suspected Karl had had flashes of power as a child: spells going awry in his presence, enchanted objects failing to work, that sort of thing. But such things could and would be written off as coincidence, especially in an era when no one believed the first Magebane had ever existed.

Neither the Mageborn father nor the Commoner mother had ever understood why they were so consumed by lust one day in a horse barn near Berriton. Nor had they had much time to wonder at it. She had arranged for the father's "accidental" death shortly thereafter, and watched over the mother during her pregnancy and eased her into the netherworld during the birth.

She had molded the child in the womb in the manner Vell had first perfected all those centuries ago. But to activate his power, the Magebane *had* to be attacked. And so she had arranged for just such an attack, through the other thing she had so carefully nurtured through the decades: the Common Cause. If the attack had succeeded, and the supposed Prince had been slain, it would have been proof of her failure, but at least it would have still been a heavy blow against the MageLords.

But the attack *had* failed; the magic directed against Prince Karl had rebounded on Jenna. Which meant she had succeeded: Prince Karl was a Magebane. And that meant Mother Northwind's own great Plan was, like Falk's, moving rapidly toward fruition.

Mother Northwind set about tidying the kitchen, though there was little enough to tidy. She'd learned of Falk's Plan during those years she worked in the Palace, every healing laying-on-of-hands on every Mageborn allowing her a glimpse of the contents of his or her mind. Falk himself had come to her for ministrations in those days, though she had had a different name and a different face and she was certain he had never made the connection between mousy Healer Makala and herself. And that was when she realized how her Plan could be realized, under the ironic and unintended cover of his.

The Magebane, her research and her own knowledge had convinced her, could do far more than just counter the magic hurled at him: *he could destroy magic entirely.*

To do so, he had to be present when the Keys were transferred from Ruler to Heir. That magic, the greatest ever worked, drew from every living mage, each providing one of the threads from which the fabric of the Great Barrier was woven.

If the Magebane were there when the Keys transferred, touching the Heir at that moment, the Keys would not only fail to transfer, they would shatter. The Barrier would fall— and the magic it contained would rebound through every living Mageborn.

She didn't think it would kill them. Not all of them. But Mother Northwind was convinced that not one of them would be able to use magic thereafter . . .

... except, possibly, those who practiced soft magic. Healers, who drew energy from within themselves rather than without, might—she hoped, though she could not be certain—retain their powers to help and heal the mind, if not the body. But the hard mages, those who used their powers to manipulate and destroy, would find themselves reduced to mere Commoners. And the true Commoners, led by the Common Cause, outnumbered them.

The Kingdom would fall. A new country, free of the tyranny of magic, would take its place.

Falk also wanted the Barrier to fall, Mother Northwind had learned as she eased the pain of his sprained wrist one day in the Palace. And he knew how it could be done without the Magebane, but his scheme needed an Heir to sacrifice, and the King showed no interest in producing one.

Mother Northwind also needed the Heir, not to sacrifice, but to bring into contact with the Magebane at the crucial moment. So up to a point, her agenda was compatible with Falk's; and, of course, she'd never told him about the part that *wasn't*.

From there, everything had advanced like clockwork. Trusted by the Palace, she had managed, *through one of my greatest feats of magic*, she thought sardonically, to temporarily turn King Kravon into enough of a man to father a child on the Queen. Shedding her guise as Makala, she had gone in her own person to Falk to offer him the Heir to raise.

Back in the Palace, she had disposed of both Queen and Royal Midwife, switched the infants, left Prince Karl, her hoped-for Magebane, in the Palace ... and then Makala had disappeared forever and Mother Northwind had arrived at Falk's manor with Brenna. He had built this cottage for her. And since then ... she had waited.

Foul deeds, she freely admitted, to slay innocents ... but deeds, she firmly believed, justified by the great end toward which she worked.

Now, that great end was very near. Falk also had to wait until Tagaza could confirm Brenna was the Heir, which he had done secretly during her last visit to the Palace. Now he was through waiting. He had set the spring equinox, when he would normally travel north to inspect the Cauldron with Tagaza, as the date he would attempt to seize the Kingship and control of the Barrier. That had forced her hand: she dared wait no longer to discover if Karl were a Magebane, and so, in her guise as the Patron of the Common Cause, she had sent Jenna to test the Prince.

She took a last look around the kitchen and, satisfied, picked up the lantern and moved through the sitting room toward her bedroom. A dark shape flashed through the flickering light, right across her feet, and she gasped, then laughed. "Mousebreath, you did give me a fright."

The cat meowed and vanished into the shadows, no doubt to slip out into the night through the swinging cat-sized door she had made for him, to terrorize field mice in their tunnels beneath the snow.

Falk would take Brenna back to the Palace. He would arrest Davydd Verdsmitt—even if her dropping his name hadn't been enough to arrange that, Verdsmitt's play would certainly do the trick. With Verdsmitt, the Heir, and the Magebane all in place, only one more piece in her great game needed to be positioned: herself.

It was time for Makala to return to the Palace.

Mother Northwind blew out her lantern, undressed in the darkness, pulled a warm flannel nightgown over her head, and lay down on her bed. It was a pity, because she really liked the cottage Falk had built for her, but it couldn't be helped.

Mother Northwind was not one to lie awake worrying about things, but she did spend a few extra moments that night thinking about the unexpected appearance of the boy from outside the Kingdom. Did he change anything?

She couldn't see how. He was only one boy, and it was hardly a surprise that there were people on the other side of the Great Barrier, after all these years. Soon enough, the Barrier would fall and the people of Evrenfels would once more be part of that world. It didn't much matter to her what that world was like, as long as it didn't include MageLords or Mageborn . . . and she intended to make certain of *that*.

In any event, in the morning she'd know as much as the boy about that outside world. If any adjustments to her plan were necessary, she could decide on them then.

She closed her eyes, and within two minutes was fast asleep.

As the winter night wore away, she stirred only once, when Mousebreath returned from his nighttime perambulations, jumped onto the bed, and curled up against her, purring loudly.

CHAPTER 8

WHEN ANTON WOKE AGAIN, in the bright light of a wintry morning, the young woman—Brenna—he had seen in the night was there, this time accompanied by a thin, neat man wearing a dark-blue tunic and trousers. Something indefinable about him made Anton think, "Doctor."

Brenna confirmed his guess, nodding to the man. "Thank you, Healer Eddigar. You may leave us." Although her accent was as thick as ever, the fog in his head seemed to have lifted, and he found it easier to follow than when he had first heard it.

Healer Eddigar nodded. "The guards are right outside if you need anything," he said, his accent as thick as Brenna's. He gave Anton a cool, dispassionate look. "His leg should heal normally now. He may rise with a crutch when he is ready."

I'm right here! Anton thought. *Probably thinks I can't understand him.*

Well, then. "Thank you, Healer," he said.

Eddigar started, but did not reply. He just gave Anton a hard look, then nodded to Brenna and swept out through the inner door. A moment later Anton heard the outer door open and close.

"Good morning," Brenna said to him then. "Do you remember meeting me last night?"

"Of course I do," he said. "You introduced yourself then. Brenna, right? And then you said—" And suddenly, so fast and hard that, like a punch to the stomach, it drove a sob from his throat, he remembered what else she had said. "The Professor—"

Brenna pressed her lips together and her eyes turned bright. "I'm afraid it's true." She reached out and covered his hand, lying on the coverlet, with her own. "I'm so sorry. He was dead when I saw him. There was nothing anyone could do. But you are lucky to be alive yourself."

He knew that. A crash into the trees was every airshipman's nightmare. Only an in-flight fire was more terrifying. But he didn't feel lucky. He felt . . . lost. *What do I do now? Professor? What am I supposed to do now?*

No answer came floating through the ether from beyond the grave. The Professor had believed in no gods, no soul, no hope for life beyond that enjoyed in this world in the physical body. Anton shared, or thought he shared, that same hard-nosed, practical belief . . . or lack of belief. But now he wished the Professor had been wrong, and that, as the god-followers claimed, words of comfort from the newly dead could truly be heard if only he prayed hard enough.

Brenna cleared her throat and said gently, "Your name is Anton?"

He blinked away the tears that had fogged his vision and said, "Yes."

"That's all? Just Anton?"

He felt his face flush, but she couldn't be expected to know that in Hexton Down his single name was a mark of shame, that with no known father he could not take a family name until he was twenty-one years of age.

But then, he wasn't in Hexton Down anymore, was he? And though he was still three years from his age of majority, he knew already what name he would take. "Anton . . . Carteri." *That's for you, Professor,* he thought. *I always meant to take your name when I came of age. I just did it a little too early . . .*

. . . and a little too late. His eyes stung with fresh tears.

"Well, Anton Carteri. You are in the manor of Lord

Falk, Minister of Public Safety for His Royal Majesty Kravon, King of Evrenfels, Holder of the Keys to the Lesser and Great Barriers."

Anton blinked. None of those names or titles meant anything to him. "Congratulations," he said. "You managed all that with one breath."

She grinned, her nose crinkling and her eyes twinkling and her apparent age suddenly dropping several years. "I practice a lot," she said. "Well, Anton Carteri. Would you like to join me for breakfast? As you heard, Healer Eddigar said," she managed a credible impersonation of the Healer's rather pompous tone, "you may get up if you use a crutch."

As soon as she mentioned breakfast, Anton realized he was starving. "Would I!" He started to fling back the covers, realized something, and hesitated. "Um, Brenna? I'll, uh, need some clothes . . . ?"

Her grin widened just a bit; there was something mischievous about it. "Of course, Anton. Lord Falk . . . my guardian . . . summoned a tailor from the village. He's waiting outside with a selection of clothing. I'll send him in."

"Thank you," Anton said.

"Don't mention it," Brenna said. "You are our guest here. Whatever you need, you have only to ask." She turned and went out through the door, closing it behind her; a moment later it opened again to reveal an elderly gentleman in a plain black tunic and leggings, arms laden with clothes.

The man offered him underwear, then turned his back while Anton swung his legs out from under the covers. He glanced down at the injured one. It bore an angry red scar, and certainly it was sore . . . very sore, he realized when he tried to put weight on it . . . but how had the wound closed so rapidly? Without a single stitch?

Puzzled, he pulled on the underwear, then let the elderly gentleman measure him.

Half an hour later, dressed in plain black trousers and an open-necked, rather puffy-sleeved white shirt (the tailor having promised to provide him with a wider selection of clothes within a day or two), and also washed, shaved, and combed, Anton found himself sitting down to breakfast in a flower-bedecked breakfast nook filled with rainbows from the sun streaming through the chiseled edges of the many tiny panes of glass above and all around.

Brenna, who had stood as he hobbled in with the help of the crutch he had found leaning against the foot of his bed, sat opposite him, took her napkin, and delicately spread it on her lap, the linen, white as the snow outside, in brilliant contrast to the thick red velvet of her dress.

Anton wondered if he'd hit his head harder than he'd thought when he crashed. That was *not* the sort of the thing he usually noticed.

But then the food arrived, and he forgot everything else. In fact, he was so focused on the fresh bread, butter, honey, scrambled eggs, bacon, and sausage piled on his plate, that it took him a moment to realize the servant who had put it before him had only three fingers, made of jointed, polished wood. He started, his first bite of sausage halfway to his mouth, and looked up.

The servant had no face, either: just a round wooden head emblazoned with a symbol in paint that glowed faintly blue. A chill air flowed off of it, as though it were made of ice.

He gaped at it, sausage momentarily forgotten. "What—?"

"Hmm?" Brenna had calmly taken a bite of bread and honey. She followed his gaze. "Oh, the mageservant. We have quite a few; more of those than the human kind, actually. Lord Falk likes them. Now, please try the eggs, they're from our prize-winning—"

"It doesn't have a face!"

"Of course not. What would it do with one?" Brenna cocked her head to one side. "You've never seen a mageservant before?"

"No." Now that he was over the shock, Anton was fascinated. He put down his fork. "So how is it done? Is it like a . . . a marionette? Does it have a motor inside? Or

clockwork? How on Earth can you give it instructions to
do something as complicated as serving? Perforated tape,
or—?"

"Motor? Perforated tape?" Brenna frowned. "I don't
know what those words mean. No, it has nothing inside.
Though I suppose you *could* think of it as a marionette,
except of course it's moved by magic, not strings. Its duties
are written into the spell that motivates it, and can be
changed as need. The spell is renewed once a week or so."

Anton stared at her. "Magic? You . . . the people here . . .
you believe in magic?"

From the expression on her face, you'd have thought
he'd suddenly sprouted horns and a tail. "Do we 'believe in
magic?' What an odd question. It's like asking, 'Do you believe in the sun?' There's not much choice, is there? I mean,
it just *is*."

Anton felt like a shipwrecked sailor floundering in a
tossing sea. "But . . . magic . . . it doesn't exist. Not where I
come from. There are legends from long ago, and some
people enjoy reading magical-adventure novels or going to
the wonder plays, but those are just stories. You're saying
that here magic is real?" The mageservant stood by, impassive. Anton suddenly got up and limped around the man-
nequin, looking for strings or pulleys. "It's not a trick?" He
reached out a finger toward the glowing blue symbol on the
mageservant's "face."

"Don't—" Brenna said sharply, but not before Anton's
finger contacted the blue-glowing paint. He jerked it back
at once.

"Ow!" For a moment he thought the symbol had been
hot, and he'd burned himself; but when he examined his
fingertip he saw a dead-white patch and realized it had actually been intensely cold; he'd frozen the skin.

"—touch it," Brenna finished. She sighed. "Most children learn not to touch symbols when they're toddlers."

"I can see why." He shook his hand ruefully. "You can
actually use magic!"

"Not me personally," she said softly. "I am a Commoner,

not Mageborn. But Lord Falk, whose house this is . . . and whom you'll meet shortly . . . is a very powerful mage. And this house is built on one of the veins of the Evrenfels magic lode, and above a great source of energy, an eternally burning rock gas flame deep in the cellars. Falk has more mageservants than any other MageLord in the Kingdom, I've been told. More than the Palace, in fact, where they prefer to use Commoners."

The mageservant, which had stood as still as furniture while Anton examined it, suddenly came to life, making Anton jump back. It turned on its spindly wooden legs and clattered on oversized wooden feet to the sideboard, where it filled a glass with red-purple juice from a moisture-dewed crystal decanter. It brought the glass back and held it out to Anton. As he took it gingerly from the three-fingered hand and stared again at the convoluted glowing symbol on the blank wooden head, he thought, *Magic is real.*

He could almost see the Professor's scowl. "No, it is *not*," he would have said. "There is a rational explanation. We just have to find it."

Just as he had been convinced that the Anomaly must also have some natural explanation, Anton thought. *But then, if magic works . . . and it obviously does . . . than I suppose it* is *natural. By definition: anything that exists is natural.* He smiled a little sadly. Though it had been his thought, that had sounded very much like Professor Carteri.

The Professor would have been the first to admit that natural philosophers did not yet know all the secrets of the workings of the universe. Confronted with the undeniable, he would have made room within his beliefs for magic . . . and then he would have set about learning everything he could about it.

Grief, momentarily forgotten, crashed in again. Professor Carteri was dead. Anton was alone, utterly alone, in a place far stranger than either of them had ever dreamed of finding inside the Anomaly. Anton stepped away from the bizarrely animated wooden figure and sat down hard in his chair. Head down, he blinked furiously to clear the embarrassing evidence of weakness from his vision, then raised his eyes to see Brenna looking at him compassionately . . . and curiously . . . from across the table. She smiled, and a bit of the strangeness receded. At least he seemed to be a guest, not a prisoner, in this strange new world . . . and to have found a most pleasant guide to its mysterious ways.

And at least they weren't going to starve him. The delectable smells wafting from his plate drove away his fears and doubts, at least for the moment, and he gave himself over to filling the deep, empty pit his stomach had become while he slept.

When the need to eat had become a little less urgent, Anton began to ask questions. The answers he received sounded like they came straight from one of those cheap magical-adventure novels he'd mentioned to Brenna. He would have dismissed it all as ludicrous fantasy if not for the unmistakable, solid fact of the mageservant, quickly and efficiently clearing away the dishes while Brenna talked.

What she told him boiled down to one astonishing fact. Within the mysterious Anomaly he and the Professor had come to this remote part of the world to investigate lay a hidden Kingdom where magic worked—a Kingdom, in fact, ruled by magicians: the MageLords.

Anton had never been very good at history back in Sutton Sterling's Preparatory School, even before he'd run away and taken to the streets of Hexton Down. He'd focused most of his intellectual powers on the considerable challenges of evading the unwelcome attentions of the older boys, and sneaking off the school grounds to run wild through the streets. But he'd learned a few things during his apprenticeship with the Professor over the past three years, and he'd always been a voracious, if indiscriminate, reader. "MageLords" was a word he had come across before; it was the name given to the tyrannical rulers of an ancient empire that had once held sway over the great island now known as Krellend and a large portion of the west coast of the First Continent, including what was now the city of Hexton Down but had then been a tiny fishing village.

The MageLords had been driven from the mainland to Krellend, pursued by an army, retreating at last to their capital city of Stromencor. Presumably there had been a siege, and perhaps even a final battle. Stromencor might have fallen, or the MageLords might have rallied to push back the attackers. No one knew, because the city, the MageLords, and the surrounding armies of Commoners were all destroyed by an enormous natural disaster of some kind, a vast explosion—presumably volcanic—that had reduced the city to rubble, flattened forests and fields with a scorching wind, and burned every living thing caught within it to charred bones and drifting ashes. To this day, nothing grew on Krellend, where the very soil had been turned to glass and cinders.

On the mainland, the alliance against the MageLords had been short-lived. Petty kings had arisen and fought, towns were built, laid waste, rebuilt, abandoned. Gradually larger kingdoms had coalesced; and finally, some two hundred years ago now, the Union Republic had been forged from a dozen of those squabbling kingdoms. After a couple of civil wars, a new era of peace had unleashed a golden age of science, philosophy, art, and history.

From the very beginning of their study of the MageLord Empire, historians had been divided over exactly who or what the MageLords had been, and what the old records meant by "magic." Since, self-evidently, magic was not real, the MageLords could not really have been the powerful wizards of the old stories. The prevailing opinion was that the MageLords had somehow leaped past their neighbors in technological know-how, their greater ability being interpreted as magic by those they conquered. The successful rebellion had supposedly been led by someone calling himself "The Magebane" (obviously a *nom de guerre*), who apparently stole the MageLords' own "magical" technology and outfitted his own armies with it, allowing them to use their superior numbers to overrun the kingdom. The final cataclysm had simply been a coincidence, an astronomically (or perhaps geologically) unlikely coincidence, but a coincidence nonetheless.

But if Brenna spoke truth, the MageLords had been exactly what their name implied: lords of magic, with inborn abilities to manipulate matter and energy simply by force of will. They had used that power to create and then rule an empire. Cruelly, according to the history Anton had been taught; benevolently, according to Brenna. She claimed those long-gone MageLords had used their magic to help the nonmagical "Commoners" they ruled live happier and healthier lives. According to her, the uprising had not been against oppressive government, but based on religion. A new cult had sprung up that saw magic as a tool of the King of Demons, and had used the latent resentment of the MageLords among the various conquered peoples to eventually ignite the revolution that forced the MageLords to flee for their lives.

Anton had never heard of such a religion, but said nothing.

The conflagration that had destroyed Krellend, Brenna said, must have been the backlash of the enormous energy the MageLords had expended in transporting themselves and their loyal followers instantly to the other side of the world . . . here! . . . where they had founded the Kingdom of Evrenfels, and hidden themselves safely behind the Great Barrier.

That Barrier, Brenna said, would stand for at least another two centuries, then the MageLords would emerge peacefully into the larger world once more, a world hopefully purged of the superstition that had driven them into hiding, and once more bend their magical abilities to the betterment of all humanity.

"At least, that's what I was taught," Brenna said as she finished. Anton looked at her sharply—was that doubt in her voice?—but her expression was smooth and with her accent, he couldn't be sure. He reached for another scone, wondering if Brenna shared his feeling that they were both skating on thin ice, circling the open water of the fact that he was descended from those who had driven the Mageborn into exile, and that his presence here meant the Mageborn were no longer safely isolated from their former enemies; and the fact that Brenna, though not herself Mageborn, was the ward of one of the most powerful MageLords in the kingdom.

And then someone came into the breakfast nook from the hallway outside, and Anton suspected the ice had just given way.

Tall, thin, with a sharp-edged face and hair the color of frosted steel, the new arrival wore a gray tunic and trousers, boots so highly polished they might have been covered with glass, and a similarly polished belt into which a pair of black leather gloves were neatly tucked. Around his neck he wore a plain disk of gold on a fine-linked chain.

A cool draft seemed to follow him in from the hall, as though winter had accompanied him into the room. Brenna, seeing him, got to her feet at once. Anton didn't know why, exactly, but he copied her a heartbeat later, though his leg twinged beneath him.

"Anton," Brenna said, "Allow me to present my guardian, Lord Falk."

Anton wondered if he should bow, but settled for raising his hand. "Hi," he said, sounding incredibly lame, even to himself.

"Welcome to my home," said Lord Falk. "And to the Kingdom of Evrenfels."

"Um . . . thank you."

"Did you enjoy your breakfast?"

Anton glanced at the all-but-empty table. "Very much," he said truthfully.

"How is your leg?"

"Still a little sore, but I didn't expect to be able to walk for a week, so I can't really complain."

"I've asked for another Healer to examine you. Not that Eddigar is not very good, but Mother Northwind has exceptional skills. Possibly she can relieve the pain you are still feeling."

Anton glanced at Brenna, who wore a puzzled frown.

Falk indicated the door. "She's waiting in my study, if you'd care to accompany me?"

"Uh . . . sure," Anton said. He didn't exactly feel he had a choice. He took his crutch from where it leaned against the breakfast table and limped out in the wake of the tall gray figure. Brenna started to follow, but Lord Falk stopped. "I don't think you need to accompany us, Brenna," he said. "Mother Northwind may want privacy for her examination."

Brenna stopped. "I'll talk to you again later," she called after Anton, who gave her a quick wave with his free hand.

To Anton's relief, Falk's study was on the same floor as the breakfast nook, just inside and to the left of the big front doors. He'd managed to descend the stairs with his crutch, but he wasn't looking forward to the return trip.

Dark wood panels covered those few parts of the study's walls not hidden by locked, glass-fronted bookcases lined with tomes Anton would dearly have loved to get a good look at. He had not donned shoes that morning, and his stockinged feet sank into thick, dark-red carpet. That color repeated high above on the ceiling, showing between criss-crossing beams of dark wood, in the upholstery of the chair behind the desk . . . and in the armchair in the far corner, right beside one of the two tall, narrow windows, where a figure, half-hidden in shadow, awaited them.

Falk sat behind the gnarled desk. It appeared to have been carved out of a massive tree stump, the polished top revealing several centuries of rings. The only things on that desk were a stack of fresh white paper, a fountain pen, and a bottle of ink. Anton was relieved to see that not *everything* in this strange place was done by magic.

Falk gestured to the two armchairs, identical to the one in the corner by the window, facing him across the desk. "Please, be seated," he said.

"Thank you . . . Lord Falk." It felt odd and archaic to be

calling someone "Lord," but when in Evrenfels . . . With a glance at that shadowy figure in the corner, which had yet to speak or even move, he seated himself carefully, leaning the crutch against the arm of the chair.

"Allow me to present Mother Northwind," Lord Falk said, nodding to the seated figure. For the first time it moved, raising its arms and pulling back the hood that had shrouded its face, then leaning forward to reveal . . .

. . . the kindly face of an old woman who could have been Anton's grandmother.

Not that he knew who his grandmother was.

The reality was so much less ominous than the foreboding born of light and shadow that Anton almost laughed out loud.

"Good morning, young man," said Mother Northwind. "Welcome to Evrenfels."

"Thank you . . . um, Mother?" *That* felt even odder in his mouth than "Lord," and he wondered if it was the correct greeting, but it seemed to be. Mother Northwind did not correct him.

The old woman got to her feet, joints audibly creaking. "Now, then, young man," she said. "If you'll just take off all your clothes . . ."

Anton gaped, not knowing what to say, and Mother Northwind laughed a long, cackling laugh which for some reason earned a raised eyebrow from Lord Falk. "Well, it was worth a try," she said. "Just joking, youngster. You can stay dressed."

"Um . . . thank you," Anton said. "I'm afraid I would get chilly, otherwise." He hadn't been around old people very much . . . well, not at all, really . . . and was a little shocked at her sense of humor, but he found himself liking Mother Northwind—even more so when she laughed again.

"All I need to do is touch you for a few minutes," said Mother Northwind.

"Touch me *where*?" Anton said dryly.

Mother Northwind chuckled. "Your hands will do, young man . . . for now."

"All right."

Mother Northwind sat down in the other chair in front of the desk, then leaned toward Anton, holding out her hands, palms up. Anton placed his hands in hers, and her fingers, dry and bony, closed around them.

"Close your eyes," Mother Northwind said. Anton did so. "Now . . ."

Something . . . happened. The sensations were sudden, disorienting. A feeling of pressure, then of dizziness; a rushing sound, a smell of burning; a sense of cold, then heat, then tingling; images, snatches of conversation; a moment's heart-stopping pain, gone almost before he registered it . . .

Anton found himself slumped in his chair, bathed in sweat. He blinked and shakily straightened. "What—"

Mother Northwind stood over him, a strange expression on her face. "You're perfectly healthy, young man," she said. "Healer Eddigar has done his work well." She glanced at Lord Falk.

"Thank you, Mother Northwind," Lord Falk said. "If you'll see Gannick, I'm sure he can find you some breakfast. I'll talk with you a little later on."

Mother Northwind nodded and went out without another word.

What just happened? Anton thought. He remembered the strange feeling he'd had when he'd awakened in the night to find Brenna in his room, that feeling of something outside himself pushing down at his consciousness. This had been similar, only far more intense—something from outside that had somehow found itself into his inner being. *Magic!* he thought. He was beginning to hate the stuff. No wonder his ancestors had revolted.

"I'm pleased Mother Northwind has found you healthy, Anton," Lord Falk said. "I apologize if there was any discomfort."

Anton still felt a little shaky, but the feeling was fading quickly. "I'm all right," he said. "I'm just . . . unused to the way you do things here."

"Ah, yes. Magic. Well." Lord Falk leaned forward and

rested his elbows on the edge of his desk. In anyone else it might have seemed casual, almost friendly; in Falk it was more intimidating than anything else. "We are equally unused to the way you do things outside the Kingdom, it seems. You flew into our Kingdom in a . . . machine. Something we have never seen before. So . . . I need reassurance from you. I need you to reassure me that you are not a scout for a planned aerial invasion of our Kingdom."

Anton blinked. He hadn't expected *that*. "I'm not, sir," he said. "Uh, Lord Falk. In fact, most of the people back in Elkbone—the village the Professor and I launched from— thought we were crazy. They certainly weren't preparing to follow us. They thought we were committing suicide."

And in the Professor's case, they were right, he thought, another stab to his heart.

Falk sat back again. "Village," he said. "Then there are not great numbers of people outside our Barrier?"

Anton shook his head. "Elkbone is the largest town I know of on the other side of the Barrier, and it's only got three or four hundred people, cattle ranchers and coal miners, mostly—they ship cattle and coal down the Swift River by barge to the bigger towns to the west. There's a saying that once you're in sight of the Anomaly, you know you've reached the end of the world."

"Anomaly?"

"The wall. The . . ." What had Brenna called it? "The Barrier."

"I see. And these bigger towns to the west? How big are they, and how far away?"

The conversation—interrogation, really, Anton soon realized—continued in that vein. Anton answered as truthfully as he could, seeing no reason to lie and suspecting he wouldn't get away with it anyway. Falk reminded him of the police sergeant he had known back in Hexton Down, a man who had the uncanny ability to see through any subterfuge . . . and a man who had the power to lock Anton away for a long time, if he chose, though he never had. Maybe it was because Anton had never lied to him, though he'd sometimes not told him everything he knew when he wanted to protect his friends.

Lord Falk, Anton had quickly realized, held his life in his hands. Minister of Public Safety, Brenna had called him. Men with titles like that not only enforced the law, they *were* the law. If Falk decided that Anton should disappear, that he and the Professor should never have arrived in Evrenfels at all, then that would be exactly what happened.

So he answered all the questions that were put to him, though just as with the police sergeant, he didn't tell everything he knew.

When asked about the weapons available to his country's military, for instance, he left out a few things, like steam-powered repeater guns and cannon that could hurl a shell five miles, though he was more than willing to talk about the other recent technological advances, from the pneumatic tube systems that provided rapid communication within cities to the smoking, bellowing motivators that ran, as many as a dozen wheeled carriages packed with people in tow, over the increasingly common railpaths stretching across the Union Republic.

"And who are your enemies?" Falk asked. "You have a military, so you must have enemies."

"The Concatenation," Anton said. "A dictatorial regime that would spread like a cancer across the world if we did not oppose it."

Falk cocked his head. "Indeed? And does this . . . Concatenation? . . . know of the Anomaly?"

"Everyone knows about the Anomaly," Anton said. "But the nearest Concatenation settlement in the Wild Land is hundreds of miles east of here, on the other coast, and the Concatenation capital two thousand miles farther yet, across the ocean. Nor, as far as we know, have they yet developed airships. You won't be seeing any of them any time soon."

Falk smiled. "Ah, yes, your airship. I find it fascinating. Are there a lot of these airships in your world?"

"Not a lot," Anton said. "There are a lot more balloons—

just big bags filled with hot air or gas that float up in the sky as military observation platforms, allowing a bird's-eye view of the battlefield. But Professor Carteri and a few others realized that you could make a balloon navigable if you changed its shape, added a rudder, and found a means of propelling it . . . turned it into a 'ship of the air.' They're proving invaluable in mapping the world's unknown regions. Stegra Eisfeldt down in South Molska used one smaller than ours to discover the ancient ruins of—"

"But how does it work?" Falk interrupted. "There is no magic in your world, you say. And yet you can fly."

"It's not magic, it's just physics," Anton said.

"I do not know that word. But go on."

"Well, you know that hot air rises . . ." Anton did the best he could, though he realized he was a little shaky on the details himself as he tried to explain the principles behind the airship. Nevertheless, Lord Falk listened in silence, then nodded.

"Interesting," he said. "And very clever. I'm surprised our own Commoners have not yet hit upon some such scheme." He leaned forward again. "Can you rebuild this airship of yours?"

"I haven't taken a good look at it," Anton said. "So I don't know for certain. The burner fell, and I don't know what happened to the engine and propeller. If either are too badly damaged . . ."

"Never mind the damage," Falk said. "Damage can be repaired . . . provided you have the required knowledge. Do you?"

"I know how all the pieces fit together. But—"

"Excellent." Lord Falk suddenly pushed his chair back and stood up. Anton hurriedly got to his feet—and shot a startled look down at his leg.

It had quit hurting. His head, on the other hand . . . there was a feeling of . . . well, if it wasn't inside his skull, he would have said bruising: a faint ache, getting stronger.

"Let's get you started on repairing it, then," Falk continued.

Anton looked up at him. "Now? But—"

"I am a busy man, Anton," Lord Falk said. "I need to return to the Palace almost at once. I would like to see this airship of yours fly before I do so, so I can take a full report to the King and Council."

"But, Lord Falk, it will take days, maybe weeks, to—"

"I doubt that very much," Falk said. "Come with me, tell me what needs to be done, and we will do it."

Anton could only shake his aching head as he followed Falk across the vast marble-floored Great Hall. Brenna, who had obviously been waiting for them to emerge, ran across the hall to join him. "Your guardian is . . . intimidating," he murmured under his breath.

"What happened?" she asked. "Where's your crutch?"

"Mother Northwind fixed my leg," he said. "But she also . . ." He let his voice trail off, unsure how to explain what had just happened. "I don't know. Something very odd."

Brenna's brow furrowed. "Like what?"

"I don't know." The pain in his head was increasing. "All I know is, my leg doesn't hurt any more . . . but my head sure does."

They passed through a set of double doors on the far side of the Great Hall that led into a broad corridor with doors on either side that ended in what was apparently the manor's back entrance. Falk stopped at the last door on the left. "Gannick," he said. "You've looked after Mother Northwind?"

"Having breakfast in the kitchen, Lord Falk," came the reply in clipped tones.

"Excellent. Please call all the mageservants into the courtyard where we stored the wreckage of the flying machine."

"Yes, Lord Falk."

Lord Falk headed toward the end of the hall. Anton glanced through the door he'd just vacated, and saw a small, bald man wearing the same gray as Falk—some kind of livery, Anton thought—with his hands palm down on a simple wooden desk, eyes closed. A beam of light finding its way through the room's curtained windows lit steam rising from the desk's surface.

Magic, Anton thought again, and shuddered.

On the wall of the corridor next to the back wall hung several fur-lined coats; on the floor were several pairs of fur-lined leather boots. Anton found a coat and pulled it on; Brenna helped him tug on a pair of boots, and again he marveled at the complete recovery of his leg. He followed Falk and Brenna through the back door into the icy cold of an enclosed, cobblestoned courtyard, snow piled man-high around its walls. In the cleared space in the middle lay Professor Carteri's airship: gondola on its side, ropes tangled all around it, envelope a shapeless blue mass. The rudder and steering mechanism lay in a heap against a snow pile, and the burner rested on its side next to them. Falk gestured at the wreckage. "Well?" he said. "Can it be fixed?"

Anton momentarily forgot his headache as he hurried across the courtyard to the most important item, the burner, the one thing he did not believe could be fixed anywhere nearer than Wavehaven. He ran his hands over it. Though blackened and dented, it was intact, as was the rock gas tank. He turned his attention to the rest of the airship. The engine and its separate rock gas tank had miraculously remained in place inside the gondola, and the propeller appeared to be undamaged. He turned to the envelope. Of course it had the one large tear that had brought them down, and he thought there must be others, but nothing that couldn't be fixed.

Some ropes had snapped and would need replacing. The rudder and steering mechanism seemed, like the burner, beat up but not seriously damaged. The gondola was badly damaged, of course, from the encounter with the tree that had broken the Professor's leg, but that could be fixed as well.

He felt a surge of relief. The airship could be made airworthy again . . .

. . . and then the relief faded. Yes, given skilled workers

and enough time. But where would he find such helpers here?

The door opened. Anton glanced up, and a chill ran down his spine as a small army of mageservants emerged into the courtyard: clicking wooden limbs, faces blank but for the blue-glowing insignia, every movement unnaturally fast, every stillness unnaturally still. He counted two dozen in all as they lined up against the wall of the manor and froze in place, obviously awaiting further direction.

"Tell me what you need done," Lord Falk said, "and they will do it."

"I don't know if I can explain well enough," Anton said.

"Try," said Lord Falk.

He didn't seem to have much choice. With Brenna watching silently, he began pointing out to Lord Falk how the pieces of the airship went together, where ropes needed replacing, silk restitching, wicker patching. Lord Falk listened intently, asking questions now and then. "Very well," he said. He walked over to the mageservants and stood in front of each of them in turn for about thirty seconds, a look of intense concentration on his face. When he had finished with the last one, he crossed back to where Anton and Brenna stood, faced the line of mageservants once more, and made a quick flicking gesture with his right hand.

As one, the mageservants came to life. As one, they moved away from the wall and advanced on the airship. And as Anton watched, openmouthed, they began the repairs he had detailed to Falk. Methodically, mechanically, never getting in one another's way, they undid ropes, carried away the gondola, righted the burner, began rolling up the envelope . . .

"The repairs should be done by tomorrow morning," Falk said. "If the mageservants discover something they cannot fix, or that their instructions are unclear, they will report to Gannick, who will fetch you to issue clarifications. There's no need to watch. Let's go back inside where it's warm."

Anton nodded and hurried after Falk, falling in beside

Brenna again as they reached the back door. She shot a glance at him, but he said nothing to her, lost in amazement at what he had just witnessed.

What would an army of mageservants be like? he thought, and for the first time, wondered if, rather than the Hidden Kingdom fearing an airborne invasion from his world, his world should be fearing the sudden reappearance of the MageLords they had thought lost in the mists of history.

CHAPTER 9

BRENNA, AS SHE WALKED WITH ANTON down the long back hall of the manor, led by Lord Falk, felt shaken and disturbed, like the still water of a pond a horse had just splashed through, leaving behind chaotic ripples and swirling mud.

She wasn't sure exactly what Mother Northwind had done to Anton, but she was sure it hadn't been anything as simple as a healing, even though he no longer limped. From his description, it sounded like . . .

But that's forbidden! Lord Falk is Minister of Public Safety. He's supposed to uphold the law. If a Healer used her power to steal memories and thoughts from someone, he'd arrest her. He'd . . .

Except, clearly, he had not.

Was that why Mother Northwind was sequestered on Lord Falk's demesne? So he could use her for "unofficial" interrogations?

She felt furious at Falk, furious at herself for not realizing it sooner, and furious at the old hag, off somewhere having breakfast.

But she didn't tell Anton what she suspected Mother Northwind had done. How could she? She was the ward of Lord Falk, Minister of Public Safety of the Kingdom of Evrenfels, the direct representative here of King Kravon himself. If the Minister of Public Safety believed that knowing what Anton knew was important enough to resort to that kind of mind-rape, who was she to argue with him?

She was his ward. Anton wasn't the only one over whom he had the power of life and death.

So she walked with Anton in silence, trailing Falk.

But it wasn't only what Falk had done to Anton that troubled her. It was also what Anton had told her.

The . . . technology, to use Anton's word . . . of the Outsiders (as Brenna had begun to think of them) seemed capable of doing *without* magic almost everything the MageLords did *with* magic; indeed, as the airship in which Anton had arrived demonstrated, technology could already do things that magic could not. *A civilization of Commoners, no MageLords to rule over them . . .* even thinking such a thing seemed subversive.

But she wanted to know more about that amazing world, and she wanted to hear it from Anton, not predigested and preselected by Falk. She glanced at him. Surely he would now rush off to talk to Mother Northwind . . . ?

He didn't disappoint. "I will leave you in the care of Brenna," Falk said as they reemerged into the Great Hall. "We'll talk again later."

"Of course, Lord Falk," Anton said.

Falk nodded to Brenna, then strode toward the doors into the kitchen.

Brenna smiled at Anton. "Shall we find somewhere to sit down? I'd like to talk to you some more about—"

Her voice trailed off. Anton's face was quite pale. "My head," he said. "I'm sorry, I think . . . I think I'd better just go back to my room and lie down."

"Of course," Brenna said. "I'll walk with you." She took him back up the stairs, with him showing no sign of a limp, said good-bye to him at the door to his room, then stood in the hallway, feeling almost as pale and shaky as Anton had looked.

The more she thought about what she thought Mother Northwind had done, the more it frightened and infuriated her. *But maybe I'm wrong,* she thought. *I don't know everything about Healing. Maybe what she did was entirely harmless. Maybe she was trying to help him in some way.*

Maybe. Or maybe not.

She had to know. And so she headed off to do something she had never in her life dared to do before: confront her powerful guardian.

She knew he was in the kitchen with Mother Northwind. The shortest route was down the servants' stairs. As she reached the bottom, though, she froze, because some quirk of the corridors allowed her to hear, as clearly as though she was sitting with them, the conversation between her guardian and the witch.

"... boy told you the truth," Mother Northwind was saying. "But not the whole truth. He held back information about the weapons of their military, for instance: things called repeater guns, powered by steam ... I confess I don't understand how such a thing works, but they seem to hurl pieces of metal with great force and rapidity, hundreds per minute. Very nasty."

"Magic can deal with anything this Commoner technology can create, if it comes to that, though it *will* be good to be prepared," Falk said dismissively. "Never mind their weapons. What about their *intentions*? Is Anton telling the truth about him and this dead Professor of his being lone adventurers? Is there truly nothing on the other side of the Barrier but a few tiny communities?"

Mother Northwind snorted. "He was telling the truth. From the images in his mind, his Professor was considered by most at best a crank, at worse a lunatic. And he believes that if he does not return to tell the outside world what happened to them, no one will make the attempt again for years, convinced the Barrier destroyed them. For all their talk of 'technology' and 'natural laws,' many of the Outsiders seem to regard the Barrier—the Anomaly, they call it— with superstitious awe. Anton does not seem to be religious, but there are those who see the Anomaly as the work of ... they call it God, but I suppose you would call it the Sky-

Mage . . . and believe that any attempt to circumvent it is sacrilegious."

"Excellent," Falk said. "We will emerge to find scattered and terrified Commoners who will quickly submit to our rule. Better yet, we'll be able to seize whatever technology they have so that we can study it and learn how to counter it with magic." A pause, then Falk spoke again in a lower voice, but one freighted with more than a hint of threat. "And did you learn anything *else* you should be sharing with me?"

"I can tell you all about the day he lost his virginity to an inn maid twice his age, if that sort of thing interests you," Mother Northwind said. "It certainly interested *me*." She gave a lusty cackle, and Brenna felt a little sick . . . and, disturbingly, a little jealous. "Seems she 'accidentally' walked in on him while he was—"

"No, thank you," Falk said, coldly. "Very well. There is no threat from these Outsiders. And we have this airship to put to our own uses, once it is repaired. *If* the boy can be convinced to provide details of its operation." A pause. "And that, I think, tells me what is to be done with him. He is only useful for as long as he cooperates. I think we will call him down for a second 'consultation' with you. You will see to it that afterward he will be unquestioningly loyal . . . *personally* loyal . . . to me."

What? Brenna sagged against the wall, her knees suddenly weak. Forcing someone to loyalty, twisting their mind against their will? That was worse, far worse, than rummaging through his memories and thoughts. The latter was punishable by imprisonment, but twisting someone in the way Falk was suggesting was punishable by death. Falk was Minister of Public Safety. How could he . . . ?

She hoped Mother Northwind would respond with equal disgust, equal outrage; but instead, all the old hag said was, "Very well. But I cannot do it today, not so soon after rummaging through his mind. I'm not as young as I was, and that is a major undertaking. And too much manipulation in short order could cause ... damage. He will be of little use to you if he's reduced to nothing more than a flesh-and-blood mageservant, unable to even wipe himself without orders."

"Hmmm." Another silence. "Well, there's no hurry, I suppose. I have to return to the Palace at once; Verdsmitt's play is tomorrow night, and I have preparations to make. I had intended to take Brenna with me, but that was before I knew about Verdsmitt. I'll take care of that matter, then return for her and the boy ... no more than three or four days, I expect. Can you have the boy ready by then?"

"Of course, Lord Falk," Mother Northwind said. "I am, as always, your most obedient servant." The words dripped with oily sincerity, fatally undercut by the fruity cackle that followed.

"No doubt." Brenna heard the doors from the kitchen into the Great Hall swing open and closed. Suddenly afraid that Mother Northwind might have some magical way of detecting her presence ... though if she did, it was surely already too late ... she scurried back up the servants' stairs to the second floor, and her own room.

She sat by the tall, frosted window, staring blankly out at the gray sky. She didn't know what the "Plan" Falk had referred to was, but it sounded ... unthinkably ... as though Falk expected the Great Barrier to fall, and the Mageborn to emerge into the Outside world—Anton's world—and launch a war of conquest to take back what they lost eight centuries before.

She seemed to have some part in that Plan, though she couldn't imagine what it was. And now Anton ...

They were going to twist his mind, remake him, force him to be loyal to Lord Falk. He wouldn't be the same person after that. He wouldn't be a real person at all, but a puppet for Falk to use as he saw fit, probably to fly the airship for him and help him attack his own people.

Brenna shivered. The Barrier was meant to stand for a thousand years. Two centuries more, at least. The only people she knew of who spoke of destroying the Barrier were the Unbound, the cult that Falk himself had persecuted unmercifully for years, notching up numerous executions.

Brenna's hands were showing an alarming tendency to shake. She gripped the arms of her chair, not wanting to believe what logic told her must be true, but unable to explain it away.

Lord Falk wasn't battling the Unbound, *he was one of the Unbound* . . . and Mother Northwind with him; and Falk, to serve the purposes of the Unbound, had just casually ordered the destruction of Anton's mind.

She had to *do* something, had to warn Anton, save him somehow . . . tell someone who *mattered* what she had heard . . .

And then the germ of an idea sprouted.

Her hands quit shaking.

She couldn't tell "someone who mattered" because there was no one who mattered more than Falk in the entire Kingdom, barring the King and the Heir, whom she could no more contact without going through Falk than she could fly.

But that was the thing. Maybe she *could* fly.

Neither she nor Anton could escape the manor on foot, not in the winter, with men-at-arms at the gate who would be after them on horseback the moment they were found missing. But with the airship, even now being repaired by Falk's own mageservants . . .

Falk was providing them with the perfect opportunity, returning to New Cabora that very day to "take care" of the matter of Verdsmitt—though what possible concern Falk could have with the famous playwright she couldn't imagine. If she could convince Anton of the danger he faced, and if he could fix the airship, launch it and fly it by himself without his Professor before Falk returned, and before Mother Northwind was ready to render him incapable of doing anything at all without Falk's approval . . .

All big ifs. But Brenna saw no other hope.

Her guardian had revealed himself as a monster, and whatever his Plan, she would not be a part of it.

Once he left, she had her own plan to put into action.

Mother Northwind sat in the kitchen of Lord Falk's manor and sipped the last of her meadowsweet tea, reflecting on the jumble of images and memories she had gleaned from the boy's mind. As she had told Falk, and as was to be expected in a young man, his fumbling and extremely limited sexual experiences had been close to the top of his thoughts; unlike what she had told Falk, and the image she liked to portray, they didn't really interest her. She had little interest in men or boys of any sort for any reason at this time in her life. But she did have an interest in cultivating a certain image with the Minister of Public Safety.

She had told Falk the truth about what he would face Outside when the Barrier fell. Why not? He was confident magic could overcome anything the Commoners might throw at him. He didn't have a clue that, if her plans came to fulfillment, it would be those Commoners with their technology who would certainly hold the upper hand in any engagement. She pictured the repeater gun she had seen in Anton's mind spraying its hail of lead through the mounted ranks of defenseless Mageborn, or the devastating shells hurled by "cannons" raining down on the Palace, and smiled at the thought.

What had interested her more had been what she had seen in Anton's mind of the social order Outside. No Mageborn, no Commoners, all equal, all given a say in the governing of their land ... though there were other lands, including something called the "Concatenation" that Anton thought of with a sense of worry and foreboding, where that extraordinary freedom did not exist.

Still, his own "Union Republic" sounded very much like the fulfilled dream of the Common Cause.

Verdsmitt would be fascinated and heartened to hear it. So was Mother Northwind; not so much for the specific details of how it was done, but simply because it was done at all, without MageLords, and without hard magic. Let the Outsiders sort themselves as they would, so long as they finished the task of the first Magebane and threw the MageLords and their hard magic onto the ash heap of ancient history where both belonged.

Soft magic, she hoped, would survive, offering healing and succor . . .

. . . and a little manipulation of minds as required? her inner voice commented, a little disapprovingly.

As required, Mother Northwind thought firmly. *For the good of all. Not to rule, but to shape; not to dominate, but to help.*

Of course, she felt badly about what she had done and would have to do next to the boy, just as she had felt badly about Jenna, just as she had felt badly about Karl's mother (though not his Mageborn father), eased into death at the very moment of birthing new life, and felt badly about the Queen, who had suffered a similar fate on the night Brenna was born, and felt badly about the midwife present at that birth, who had also met a sudden and untimely end.

She knew full well she had done things most would call evil. If Falk's SkyMage or the God of the Outsiders actually watched over all that went on in the world, perhaps someday she would be called to account for them. But she would argue before any god or man, if it came to that, that out of her "evil" actions would come nothing but good: an end to the tyranny of the MageLords, an end to the Great Barrier, a return to the mainstream of history for the tens of thousands of prisoners locked up in Evrenfels more than eight centuries ago.

She shook her head. She regretted nothing she had done, or planned to do.

She sipped the last of her tea, put the cup down on the table, tugged her cloak closer, and went out. The next step of her plan was in Falk's hands, though he didn't know it. When he "dealt with" Verdsmitt, arresting him at the Palace, he would be doing exactly what he was supposed to.

Mother Northwind smiled as she stepped out of the front door of the manor into the cold embrace of the still wintry air. She had only been inside Falk's head that once, when, as Healer Makala in the Palace, she had learned of his Plan. She had never manipulated *his* thoughts as he wanted her to manipulate Anton's. And yet off he would go this very day to do *exactly* what she wanted and needed him to do.

Mother Northwind found that very satisfying indeed.

CHAPTER 10

PRINCE KARL SPENT THE AFTERNOON before Davydd Verdsmitt's much-anticipated premiere in a boring meeting of the King's Council—although using "boring" to describe a meeting of the King's Council was redundant.

Still, this one was even more boring than most, due in part to the absence of Lord Falk, who had not yet returned from his manor, though he had passed word to the Council through his secretary, Brich, that he "anticipated with delight the prospect of being in the audience" that evening.

Karl had had some hope that the meeting might be livelier than most due to the attempt on his life just three days before, and had looked forward to Falk's report on his investigation into it, but with Falk absent, the matter was simply deferred and he was left slumped in the magnificently carved, richly upholstered, and hideously uncomfortable throne that was his reserved seat at the table, feeling his buttocks going numb and wishing that, just once, King Kravon would attend his own King's Council meeting in his own Royal Person.

But that, alas, was about as likely as a bald eagle erupting from his blood-starved butt and warbling a popular pub tune.

When he had seated himself, he had given the usual fiction about the King being indisposed, when he knew very well, as did every member of the Council, that the King was at that moment sleeping off a hangover in his massive bedchamber high in the central tower of the palace, probably in the embrace of some beardless youth who might, if pressed, give the lie to the King's reputation for being omnipotent . . . or potent at all.

Prince Karl tasted the bitterness of his own thoughts and felt ashamed. *He's my father*, he thought.

Sometimes that unpleasant realization frightened him. When he became King, would he take after the old man?

We're nothing alike, he told himself vehemently. *We don't look alike, we don't think alike, we don't act alike.*

Which he supposed meant he took after his mother . . . but there was no way to know for certain, since she had died when he was born.

In the past, he had given tours of the Great Hall to groups of Commoner children from New Cabora, a task he enjoyed, because it represented a break from monotony, and at least some connection with the majority of the Kingdom that did not breathe the rarified, stultified air of the Palace. (He had been scheduled to give such a tour that very morning, but with Falk currently suspecting Commoners of having attempted to kill him, all such visits had been canceled.) He always envied the children, staring wide-eyed at everything he showed them, awed that the Heir to the King was personally conducting their tour. They might be Commoners, forced to live a life of drudgery without the comforts provided by magic, but they each had parents who loved them and cared what happened to them, and in that respect they were richer than he had ever been or ever could be.

Instead of a parent, he had been taught by a series of tutors, including Tagaza. Tagaza was closer to a father to him than his own: or perhaps Tagaza was more like his mother, and Falk his father, ready to correct and discipline as required. Although now that he was past eighteen, Falk's authority no longer seemed as absolute as he had once thought it. He was the Heir, after all, and would be King.

I will be King, he reminded himself again that morning. But for now, he was just the Heir Apparent, and so, even though he had the grandest chair in the Council chamber and represented the Crown, he wasn't permitted to speak. He was expected simply to listen and learn—though mostly what he learned was that it was a miracle the Kingdom operated at all, and had not long since devolved into squabbling satrapies.

The Council did not meet in the vast and echoing Great Hall, though the heavy oak doors Karl now faced opened into it. Instead, it met in this much smaller chamber, as close to utilitarian as any room in the Palace could be. Karl had long since exhausted every possible bit of interest to be gleaned from the examination of the meager furnishings: plain marble walls, plain marble floor, long wooden table, plain wooden chairs (except his, unfortunately). Instead, he studied the five Councillors. Of course, he'd examined them in minute detail multiple times as well, but this time, as he studied the Councillors, he found himself wondering if any of those who sat with him at the oval table could have been behind the assassination attempt.

Lord Athol, Prime Adviser to King Kravon, sat at the opposite end of the table from Karl, chairing the meeting as always. Enormously tall and enormously fat, he took up the space allotted to any two normal people, and it sometimes seemed to Karl that his bristling gray-streaked black beard took up the space of a third.

The fact the Kingdom managed so well without any significant input from its King was a tribute to Athol's effectiveness. But Karl had never warmed to the man, who seemed to regard him as a child who couldn't be trusted with anything important. Still, that very disdain argued against him having any reason to attempt to kill the Prince.

Lady Estra, the King's Purse, sat to Athol's right. She was a little on the small side, which made her look positively elfin next to Athol, though there was nothing elfin about her habitually sour expression, as pinched as though she had just bitten into an unripe crabapple. Perhaps it was being in charge of the Kingdom's finances that gave her that expression; the previous King's Purse, an elderly man who had died when Karl was a small boy, had had a similar look about him and used to terrify Karl whenever they crossed paths.

To Estra's right, Karl's immediate left, sat Lady Vin. Tall and thin, she had a natural expression that also tended toward the dour—though not as dour as Estra's—but one she made up for with a ready, radiant smile that took twenty years off her age and made it impossible for Karl not to smile back.

As Goodskeeper, Lady Vin was responsible for agriculture and internal trade. She awarded the government contracts on which many merchants depended—and for which they were prepared to bribe government officials. Throughout the Kingdom's history the Goodskeeper's office had been more or less corrupt, depending on who was running it. At the moment, it tended toward the "more" side of that balance, but nobody seemed to mind because Lady Vin, despite rolling in presumably ill-gotten wealth, was so personally likable and generous.

Across from Lady Vin, to Karl's right, sat Tagaza. As First Mage, he was responsible for the magical lifeblood of the Kingdom, including maintenance of the Barriers (not that any had ever been required), long-distance communication via magelink (for those Mageborn who could not manage the necessary spell themselves), and, most importantly, the MageFurnace, source of energy for the Lesser Barrier and other magic of the Palace. (He also had responsibility for the Cauldron, the vast lake of molten rock that powered the Great Barrier, but since giant lava lakes tended to look after themselves rather well, in practice that just meant maintaining the road to it and accompanying Falk on the annual trip north to inspect it.)

There was one other member of the Council, but he did not sit at the table with the others. In a corner of the room the Commoner sat at his own small table, papers strewn across it.

He had a name, of course, but it was never spoken. He was just "The Commoner," the liaison between the Council of MageLords and the Commons. Chosen by lottery every four years, he had given up his personal identity for the duration. It was he who passed on the decisions of the MageLords to the Commons, and he who brought petitions from the Commons to the MageLords.

The Commons had its own Council, a group of twelve men and women chosen, again by magic-guided lottery, from an approved slate of candidates drawn up by the Prime Adviser's office. The Commons Council had limited powers but was permitted to deal with matters of land ownership, roads and sewer systems, and the like. Anything outside its purview it sent to the MageLords via the Commoner.

Although the Commoner attended all Council meetings, he was magically prevented from saying anything about what he heard in the Council Chamber outside its walls. Within the chamber, he could only speak at specific times, or when asked a question. He was not permitted to take part in any discussion, or to express an opinion, without being invited, and he was seldom invited.

Karl had given him a sympathetic smile when he first sat down on his throne. He rather thought he knew how the Commoner felt. The Commoner had very slightly bowed his head, but made no other response.

At the end of his term, the Commoner would be greatly rewarded. If he failed to serve out his term, he would receive nothing. It gave him great incentive to behave himself precisely as the MageLords expected him to behave.

As well, at the end of his term, the Commoner's memory of the meetings he had attended would be magically removed. As a discussion of which of two Commoner firms should have the snow-clearing contract for a bridge over the North Evrenfels River in Berriton dragged on, Karl rather wished *he* had that option.

The meeting was well into its fourth hour, and Karl feared he would never walk again, when Lord Athol finally said, "I therefore declare us adjourned. We will reconvene in three days, at which time Lord Falk will tell us of the preliminary results of his investigation into the attempt on Prince Karl's life." He smiled. "In the meantime, I expect I will see many of you tonight at Davydd Verdsmitt's play." There was a murmur of assent, then the Councillors began to get to their feet. Athol hurried to catch up to the King's Purse. "Lady Estra, a word . . ."

Lord Athol and Lady Estra exited together, talking in low voices. Tagaza nodded to Karl as he gathered up his notes and trailed along. The Commoner remained where he was, reading over papers, as did Lady Vin, who was still studying the final report the Council had received. Karl stood and stretched, and Lady Vin raised her head. "Will you be at Verdsmitt's play, Your Highness?"

"The first new play by Verdsmitt in three years, Lady Vin? You'd have to tie me up to keep me away." *Or assassinate me*, he thought, and grinned a little sourly, wondering if Falk had considered *that* unlikely motive for the attack. He glanced up as Teran, relegated to the hallway outside during the Council meeting, came in to see what was taking him so long. "You *will* sit behind me, won't you?" he said to his bodyguard, who stood a head taller than he did. "If you sit in front of me I won't be able to see a thing."

A grin flicked over Teran's face. "I could slouch. But no, I won't be sitting in front of you."

"Nor in front of *me*, I trust," Lady Vin said lightly. She stood and gathered her papers, then hesitated. "I . . . was alarmed when I heard of the attack on you, Your Highness," she said, her voice warmed by concern, though whether real or feigned, Karl couldn't tell. "It would be a tragedy if the Kingdom were to lose you."

"Well, *I* certainly agree with you," Karl said, keeping his own voice light. "But Falk has taken every precautionary measure. I'm reasonably confident that no attacks on my august person will disrupt tonight's performance . . . or if they do, I promise to step outside and die quietly in the hall so as not to disturb the rest of the audience."

Lady Vin laughed. "Your solicitude is appreciated, Your

Highness. Fare well until this evening." She swept out, leaving Karl alone with Teran and the Commoner.

Karl strode over to him, and he scrambled to his feet and bowed respectfully. "Please, sit down," Karl said. The Commoner bowed again, and resumed his place behind the table. Karl glanced down at the papers there. "What are you reading?"

"More about the bridge contract, Your Highness," said the Commoner. "I have some . . . concerns."

Karl cocked his head. "You don't think the Council made the right decision?"

The Commoner lowered his head. "As you know, Your Highness, it is not my place to say."

"It is if the Prince asks you for your opinion," Karl said softly. "And I'm asking."

The Commoner's head came up again, slowly. "Then, Your Highness . . . no, I do not think the Council made the right decision."

Karl sighed. "As it happens, neither do I. The contractor was chosen because Lady Vin conducts non-government business with him. He gives her a very good price on that work, and in exchange she arranges for him to snare overpriced government contracts."

The Commoner's face went blank. "If you say so, Your Highness."

"I'm not trying to trap you," Karl said tiredly. "It's obvious, and everyone knows it. But nobody cares."

The Commoner raised his left eyebrow. "But you do, Your Highness?" he said softly.

"Yes," Karl said. "I do. But I'm still only the Heir. When I'm King . . ." He spread his hands. "I don't know what I can do then, either, to tell the truth. But I hope to do better than our current King. And I hope to craft a Council that does better as well."

The Commoner's right eyebrow went up as well. "I would . . . welcome that, Your Highness."

"Well . . . I'll let you get back to work," said Karl, and headed for the big oak doors, Teran close behind.

In the Great Hall, Teran said, "That was an interesting conversation."

Karl glanced over his shoulder. "You don't think I should talk to the Commoner that way?"

Teran smiled. "Hardly. I think that's *exactly* the way you should talk to him. But not many Mageborn would, and no MageLords. It's particularly interesting considering Falk seems to think the Commoners were behind the attack on you."

Karl shrugged. "All the more reason to try to make the point with any Commoner who will listen that I hope to be a different kind of King than they're used to, isn't it? Not that the MageLords will make it easy." He reached back and rubbed his rear end with both hands; it was tingling now that blood flow had been restored to it. "Damn, I hate that chair."

Teran laughed. "Not very Prince-like, Your Highness."

"Even Princes get sore butts, Teran."

As they strode through the corridors leading to Karl's quarters, they passed the Royal Theater, a grandly named but rather small auditorium that held no more than a hundred audience members. The doors stood open, and Karl, glancing in, saw workmen on the stage, hammering away at set pieces lying facedown on the black-painted wood. He felt a thrill of anticipation. A new Verdsmitt play! He could hardly wait.

Falk had never shown any interest in plays of any kind, by Verdsmitt or anyone else, as far as Karl knew. He wondered why the Minister of Public Safety was making a special effort to be back for the performance.

He snorted to himself as they moved on down the hall, the sound of hammering following them. Of course, with a moment's thought, he *knew* why. Verdsmitt was widely whispered to be sympathetic to the Common Cause, though how much of that was truth and how much merely a smear campaign by his less-known (and less-talented) rivals Karl did not know. Nevertheless, if *Karl* had heard those rumors, surely Lord Falk had, as well.

So why hasn't he canceled the performance? Karl wondered. If he hadn't, he had good reason for it. Falk did not simply overlook things.

"It should be an interesting evening," Teran said, voicing what Karl had been thinking, and while such a thought could sometimes fill him with excitement, on this day, it filled him with foreboding.

———

Three hours later, following a light supper of hot barley soup and cold fresh walleye (there would be a surfeit of food at the reception following the play), Karl entered the Royal Theater, dressed in his finest white tunic and scarlet trousers. A featherweight gold cape floated from epaulets on each shoulder, and a golden circlet, with an enormous ruby centered in the middle of his forehead, proclaimed his rank. Glittering black calf-high boots and a ceremonial sword completed his faux-military ensemble.

He felt like a fool, really, but it was his duty as representative of the Crown to dress the part and impress upon the Verdsmitt Players the honor a Royal Performance represented.

Of course, for *real* honor, the play should have been attended by the King, but once again, the King was "indisposed."

Karl had vague memories from when he was a small child of his father laughing uproariously at performances in this very theater. When had all that changed? He hadn't seen his father in the flesh for . . . what? Two months? In fact, the only reason he could be certain the old man was still alive was that the Keys had not come to him, an event which Tagaza had assured him he would not overlook.

"When the King or Queen dies," the First Mage had told him, "the Heir to the Keys immediately feels faint and may even black out. There is reportedly a feeling of disconnection, as if the mind and body have been separated. Next, consciousness enlarges. Previous Heirs have reported that for a brief but overpowering moment they felt connected to every Mageborn in the Kingdom, a feeling followed by an equally overpowering sense of loss as the sensation passes and mind and body reunite. All of this frequently is followed by a splitting headache and nausea."

"Charming," Karl had responded. "The effect of becoming King appears to closely mimic the effect of eating bad mussels."

Tagaza had diplomatically ignored that comment. "Next comes the Call, an irresistible urge to journey to the Great Hall, no matter how far away the Heir may be. In your case, of course, you will most likely be in the Palace, but even should you be, oh, driving a dog sledge across the northern wastes—"

"That seems unlikely."

"—you will instantly turn your steps toward the Palace, and will not be able to rest until you sit upon the Throne. The compulsion will be lifted. And you, my prince, will be the new King. After which, of course, comes the coronation, but that is a mere formality."

Karl sighed and settled himself in his high-backed, nicely padded (unlike that cursed Council Chamber chair) theater seat. None of that had happened; therefore, the King still lived.

But still he felt a pang as he glanced at the empty seat to his left, always reserved for the King, but never filled.

When had his father withdrawn so completely? And why?

He heard the rustle of brocaded gowns and courtly robes as those MageLords present in the Palace and some of their favored Mageborn followers took their seats behind him, as had Teran.

The house lights, magelights all, dimmed, leaving only the curtain warmers, flushing the rich red curtain with a dim glow. A lone figure, silhouetted against that glow, stepped in front of the curtain from stage right and made his way to the center. An instant later a spotlight, a particularly powerful magelight magically focused to a tight round circle of light, lit his face. The crowd murmured as they, like

Karl, recognized Davydd Verdsmitt, the most famous playwright, Commoner *or* Mageborn, in the Kingdom's history.

"My Lords and Ladies," Verdsmitt said. He was an actor as well as a playwright, and his voice carried easily to every corner of the theater. "Welcome to the first performance of my new play." His face, boyish and smooth-skinned though he was halfway through his fourth decade, crinkled into a grin. "And possibly the last, if it doesn't go well!"

The audience laughed, Karl included.

"I will tell you nothing about it up front, so that its action and themes may be a surprise," he said. "But I did want to appear before you to personally welcome His Highness Prince Karl, Heir Apparent to the Keys of Evrenfels. Your Highness, I am particularly pleased you can be with us tonight in light of the recent attempt on your life."

Around him, the audience had stilled into frozen discomfort at Verdsmitt's effrontery. If Verdsmitt noticed, he gave no indication. "We have a saying in the theater that the show must go on, Your Highness. Your presence here tonight, so soon after the attack, is proof to me that you are, indeed, a true patron of the dramatic arts, which, as an old actor and rapidly aging playwright, gladdens my heart.

"But enough prattle. Your Highness, My Lords and Ladies, Verdsmitt's Masters of the Stage present the premiere performance of *The Unlocking: A Romance of the Far Future.*"

With that, the curtain swept up, and Verdsmitt stepped back onto the stage and into the revealed scene—a representation of the Great Hall.

But not the Great Hall as Karl had seen it just hours earlier. This Great Hall lay in ruins, and ancient ruins, at that. In the foreground broken stone and shattered bricks half-buried one of the great beams from the roof. The painted background showed a crumbled wall, through which could be seen trees and weeds growing wild in the Palace grounds. The sight shocked Karl, like a stinging slap to the cheek. A horrified murmur ran through the crowd.

As the play progressed, those murmurs grew in volume and displeasure.

In Verdsmitt's play, the unthinkable had happened: the Barriers had fallen. That alone was close to heresy, but what was worse was the reason he gave for it. It was not because the thousand years had passed. Rather, in his world, magic had simply . . . failed. Vanished.

No, not just vanished, been *driven* from the world, never to return, by the appearance of . . . a Magebane.

Had the entire play consisted of nude actors engaged in an onstage orgy with farm animals, Verdsmitt could scarcely have offended his audience more. (Indeed, Karl suspected the former would have been wildly, if secretly, popular among the MageLords.)

Worse, the mythical Magebane, in Verdsmitt's play, was a MageLord himself, and not just any MageLord, but the last King of Evrenfels—the last, because he chose to destroy the Keys, magic, and himself in order to usher in a new era in which there would no longer be any distinction between Commoners and MageLords, who, in the play's "happy ending," decided to build a new land together where there was no magic and no king, the people instead choosing their own rulers from among their own numbers.

The play ended, after only one act, with Verdsmitt's character, the ex-Prime Adviser of the last King of Evrenfels, joining with a young Commoner to lift the beam that had fallen from the roof of the Great Hall and begin, both literally and symbolically, to rebuild the land.

Verdsmitt must have decided to limit the play to one act because he assumed no second act would be allowed to proceed, Karl thought. And indeed, as the curtain fell, the audience grumbled and muttered. No one applauded.

Karl knew he should be as horrified as the other MageLords; more so, in fact, as Heir. And yet a part of him found the play's concept exciting rather than revolting. For him, after all, more than for anyone else, the Kingdom of Evrenfels, its Barriers, and the Keys that would one day come to him were a prison sentence, locking him into a future he did not want but could not escape. To imagine that those bars could be dissolved . . .

Of course it was a fantasy . . . but like many fantasies, it held a powerful appeal. And wasn't theater about fantasy, about challenging what *was* with the possibilities and even the impossibilities of other ways, other worlds?

And with that thought Karl, seized with sudden fury and disgust at the brocade-bound, robed and stuffed Palace-dwellers all around him, leaped to his feet and began to clap.

Teran stood first, as duty required, but everyone else followed a heartbeat later. You did not stay seated when the Prince stood. Nor did you refuse to applaud, and so applause there was, just enough to be almost polite, as the eight actors, five men and three women, took their bows. To Karl, they appeared pale and frightened . . .

. . . all but Verdsmitt. He bowed as though receiving the greatest accolades of his career, then joined hands with the rest of the cast and bowed again.

And at that moment, the first Royal guards burst onto the stage.

They rushed on from the wings, down from the back of the theater, from behind the set. Someone screamed, whether on stage or in the audience, Karl couldn't tell, but it was over in a moment. The actors, hands bound, were dragged away. Lord Falk himself took charge of Verdsmitt, who accompanied the Minister of Public Safety into the wings with his head held high and even a hint of a smile on his face.

Karl watched it all in stunned silence, then was furious at himself for saying nothing. He was the Prince! He could have stopped the arrests—

But even as he thought that, he knew that he could do nothing of the kind. Falk would not answer to him. His orders, he would surely say, came from the King, and the King would certainly never gainsay him.

And then, to his shock, Teran seized his arms and pulled him toward the exit, almost as though he were under arrest himself. "What are you doing?" Karl shouted at him, pulling back.

"Please, Your Highness," Teran said, a note of near panic in his throat. "Lord Falk ordered me to get you out of here when the arrest happened."

That shocked Karl even more, and he let himself be pulled out into the hallway and toward his quarters, even as the rest of the audience spilled out behind him. But once they were in his sitting room, he rounded on Teran. "You *knew* about this arrest?" He remembered Teran's comment that it should be an "interesting evening," and his anger burned higher. "You knew, and you didn't tell me?"

"Your Highness," said Teran, looking pale. "I had my orders. From Falk."

"I am your Prince," Karl snarled. "And your friend!"

"Yes, Your Highness," Teran said softly. "But Lord Falk is my supreme commander. If I failed to obey his orders . . ." His voice trailed off. "I cannot disobey his orders, Your Highness."

"You can if I tell you to!"

"But you didn't tell me to, Your Highness. You did not order me to tell you of Falk's plans to arrest Verdsmitt."

"How could I order you to tell me about something I didn't know about?" Karl shouted.

Teran flinched, but stood firm. "Even so, Your Highness. And so I had to obey the orders I was given, by Lord Falk."

In disgust, Karl spun away from him, strode to the sideboard, and poured a glass of asproga. "And what are your orders now?" he said, then downed the fiery yellow liqueur in a single gulp.

"Lord Falk requests that you await him here, Your Highness," Teran said.

"Then perhaps *you* had better wait for him outside, so you can confirm you carried out your instructions," Karl said coldly.

"Yes, Your Highness," said Teran. He went out into the hallway, and closed the door.

Karl, upset with himself, furious at what he had just witnessed and at Teran's part in it, stripped off his ridiculous finery, donning in its place plain black trousers and a white shirt. Barefoot, he padded to the window and gazed out over the Palace grounds. The night was moonless, but globular magelights on metal poles cast circles of cold illumination every few yards along the paths that wound through the formal gardens. Their illumination revealed nothing out of the ordinary.

He squinted. Unless . . .

Karl had an enchanted device known as a "magniseer" beside his window. Tagaza had provided it to him so that he could study the stars. Somehow it canceled out the faint shimmer of the Lesser Barrier, allowing him a clear view. But now he seized the chill metal tube and pointed it downward, toward the Palace grounds.

There. Near the bronze equestrian statue of Queen Castilla, down at the far end of the gardens. Karl pushed at the focus lever, and turned the knob that made it as light sensitive as possible. The action of the magic within drew energy from the air around the device, frosting the controls. Karl blew on his fingers to warm them, then took a closer look through the magniseer. Even with the adjustments, he could not make out any features of the two figures lurking in the shadow of the statue. Still, they were obviously hiding—waiting for a signal, perhaps.

A signal that Davydd had been taken prisoner? And then what?

Karl watched them for the next few minutes, but they did nothing but lurk. He straightened up to relieve his back just as he heard the door opening in the other room.

Instantly he pointed the magniseer up to the ceiling, and was at the bedroom door before Lord Falk finished closing the main door. "Lord Falk," Prince Karl said in his haughtiest I-am-royal-and-you-are-not voice, "I demand to know what is going on!"

"Of course, Your Highness," Lord Falk said. "That is precisely why I have come."

"*On your orders*, Teran came perilously close to

dragging me to my chambers, Lord Falk. I am still Prince, am I not?"

Lord Falk spread his hands, though his face remained expressionless. Karl suspected Queen Castilla's statue could show more emotion than Falk when he didn't want to reveal anything. "I trust Your Highness will forgive him," Falk said. "He was following my orders. I feared there might be some unrest following the arrest of Davydd Verdsmitt and his troupe. As it turned out, those fears were unfounded, Verdsmitt's play having scandalized even his most ardent supporters in the Palace."

"Are you mad, Lord Falk?" Karl said. "Davydd Verdsmitt is the leading playwright of the kingdom and much beloved by the Commons. You may have arrested him without any 'unrest' in the theater, but when word of this reaches the Commons—"

"Unrest among Commoners is of little concern," Falk said. "While magic lives, the Commons pose no threat to the rule of the MageLords. And despite the fond wishes of radical Common Causers like Verdsmitt, magic is not going to fail."

Karl's eyes narrowed. "If you aren't worried about the Common Cause, why have you arrested him?"

"Not because he is a threat to the Kingdom, Your Highness," Lord Falk said. "Because he is a threat to *you.* It was he who ordered and organized the attack on your person."

"*What?*"

"My source is unimpeachable," Falk said. "Verdsmitt ordered the attack."

"Three days before coming to the Palace to perform?" Karl did not try to keep the skepticism out of his voice.

Falk shrugged. "Hubris. He either believed we would never find out, or else he believed he is untouchable because of his fame. In either case, more fool he."

"But *why* would Verdsmitt want to kill me?"

"My working assumption is, as I told you earlier, as a simple act of terror. But I'm sure his exact motivation will become clearer after a thorough interrogation. Which I had best be about. If Your Highness will excuse me . . . ?"

Karl waved a hand. "Of course. Please keep me informed." Falk bowed and took his leave. Teran looked in momentarily, then stepped back into the hall, closing and locking the door behind him.

Karl went back to the magniseer.

The mysterious figures still waited in the dark. But even as he watched them, they moved.

He didn't know what he had expected them to do. Approach the Palace, perhaps, maybe attempt to free Verdsmitt, armed with enchanted weapons provided by the same renegade mage who had provided the one that had mysteriously failed to kill him. But instead they went the other way, to the shore of the lake; and then, as he watched, they got into a boat and rowed out onto the water.

Their course, he saw immediately, would take them to the wildest part of the far shore, a tangled jungle of cattails and rocks and brush that the Palace gardeners had left in its natural state.

There was nothing there. Nothing to interest Mageborn *or* Commoners. Unless . . .

How had Karl's attacker come through the Lesser Barrier? Falk had suggested that perhaps she had been smuggled in as a Commoner worker, a servant for some MageLord. But Falk had provided no more information. That proved nothing, since Falk had little inclination to share information with Karl at the best of times. Still . . . what if the attacker had *not* been smuggled in? What if she had . . . somehow . . . come straight through the Barrier?

What if the mysterious renegade MageLord who had enchanted the crossbow was more powerful and connected than they had yet guessed . . . powerful enough that he could open the Barrier at will?

It wasn't impossible. After all, the Gate, the only existing opening in the Lesser Barrier, had been crafted by a powerful ancient mage. Why couldn't some modern mage have likewise figured out the secret?

Karl knew he should tell Teran about the two lurkers in the night, have him call out the guard. He knew what he was about to do was foolish beyond belief. But anger still burned in him at the cavalier way Falk treated and belittled him. If he could discover how the assassin had gotten inside the Barrier, it would give him an edge in his dealings with the Minister of Public Safety for years to come. And though he was not King yet, Karl already knew he needed every advantage he could get over the fractious and powerful MageLords and Mageborn that made up the government, from the Council on down to the regional governors and town mayors.

Besides Teran right outside his door, there would be other guards farther down the hallway, more guards at all the Palace entrances, guards everywhere . . .

. . . except right outside his window.

Karl had long ago discovered that it was a simple matter to climb down from his third-story window to the ground below. The cut stones that emphasized the massive solidity of the Palace also made excellent foot- and handholds. When he had been much younger, he'd frequently slipped down the side of the Palace and roamed the lakeshore and gardens in the dark, sometimes swimming in the moonlight, sometimes just lying on the grass and staring up at the stars through the shimmer of the Lesser Barrier. He'd never been caught, either, and so no one had ever thought to put a guard below his window.

The descent was easiest barefoot, and the night, as always, was warm. Karl went to his closet for a pair of boots— not the silly dress boots he'd been wearing in the theater, but his favorite pair of comfortable, ordinary boots— opened the casement, dropped the boots out the window, and then turned and lowered himself out of it as well, his toes finding the remembered cracks with ease. He descended quickly and quietly, although he had one bad moment when his right foot slipped—the cracks between the stones didn't seem nearly as deep to him now as they had when he was ten. Still, he recovered without falling, and a few moments later stood, a little breathless, on the be-dewed grass, damp and cool beneath his feet. He grabbed his boots and immediately slipped into the darkness of the line of trees that, framing the ornamental gardens, stretched down to the lakeshore.

Hidden in the shadows, he tugged on his boots while he peered across the lake. He could see nothing of the boat the two strangers had taken, out there on the dark water, but it had certainly been one they had somehow brought with them, for the four boats usually moored at the pier at the foot of the garden for the use of pleasure-seeking Palace dwellers bobbed right where they always were. Karl climbed into one, undid mooring ropes fore and aft, then unshipped the oars and pulled away from the shore.

It was cooler on the water and there was a little dampness on the seat. But he put the slight discomfort out of his mind. Rowing would soon warm him up, he thought, and so it did; by the time he had traveled a hundred yards, he was sweating.

With his back to the bow, he had a good view of the re-ceding Palace, lit, like a jewel set in black velvet, by giant magelights. He watched for signs of alarm at his absence, or an attempt to rescue Verdsmitt, or anything at all out of the ordinary, but saw nothing. The Palace appeared serene, calm, and utterly unconcerned about possible threats.

The reflected Palace lights sparkled off the water all around him, his wake a glittering broken V-shape within it. When he glanced over his shoulder, he saw the shore as a nearing band of black. Some distance beyond, he could see the sparse yellow lights of New Cabora on the other side of the Barrier, slightly distorted by its shimmer, but between the Barrier and those lights was more parkland, a kind of snowy moat symbolizing the impassable divide between the Commons and the Mageborn.

He was suddenly horribly aware that he must be as vis-ible as a wart on an actor's nose, cutting through the reflec-tions on the water, but there was nothing he could do about it except hope that the Commoners he pursued were look-ing ahead, and not behind.

A few moments later he stole another look over his shoulder, saw that he had almost reached the shore, backwatered with his left oar to spin the boat around, and then shipped his oars and used just one to scull over the stern until the bow grounded, with a wet squelching sound, on the lakeshore.

He clambered over the bow and promptly sank knee-deep into thick, gooey mud. He struggled forward, lost one boot and then the other, fell forward and plunged elbow-deep into the black muck. Crawling, he finally reached firmer, weed-grown ground beyond. Giving up his boots as a lost cause, he forced his way barefoot through a thick hedge of bushes that grabbed at his clothes like grasping fingers, trying with every step to be silent and horribly aware just how miserably he was failing.

Once he was through the hedge, thankfully, the going became easier. He could see almost nothing, though, the lights of the Palace cut off by the hedge, the lights of New Cabora more emphasizing the darkness ahead than alleviating it.

He stopped and listened. Was that a murmur of voices? He stretched out prostrate on the grass, lowering the horizon, raised his head slightly—and perhaps another fifty paces ahead saw the silhouettes of men against the city glow. They seemed to be working on something, heads close together. Light flared, so bright it hurt Karl's dark-accustomed eyes, and must have hurt the mysterious men's eyes as well, since he heard a sharp curse. The darkness that followed seemed even deeper and more impenetrable than before, but then there came another flare of light, softer, and a different color, too, a dim blue that Karl associated with magic . . . except that around its edges it flared red. As he watched, it swelled, expanding like the glowing rim of flame spreading out through a piece of paper set alight by a candle.

And suddenly he realized what he was seeing: a hole, an opening in the Lesser Barrier, burned through it by something the two men carried.

The moment the hole was big enough, the two men slipped through. They turned, and pointed the whatever-it-was at the Barrier. The hole began to shrink, like a puddle draining from the middle. Without waiting to see it closed, the men turned away and began crossing the snow-covered parkland toward the city.

Suddenly realizing that he knew nothing about them, that he had no proof to show Falk of their existence, much less their ability to slip through the Barrier, Karl scrambled to his feet and dashed toward the Barrier, determined to make it through that impossible breach before it closed.

He might have made it, if the Barrier had closed at a steady rate. But when it was just big enough that he thought he could still fit through it, it suddenly collapsed, the red rim racing in toward the center of the blue glow like the last dregs of water slipping down a drain.

It was too late for Karl to stop his headlong rush. Knowing he was about to crash into the Barrier, hard and cold as a wall of ice, he turned himself at the last second so that his shoulder would take the brunt of the blow, steeled himself for the impact . . .

. . . and went sprawling into the snow on the other side of the Lesser Barrier, passing through it as though it was so much thin air.

The sudden cold took his breath away. He yelped, heard a surprised shout ahead of him, and then the two men he had followed across the lake were on him, one slapping a hand over his mouth and twisting his arm behind his back, the other holding a dagger to his throat.

A light flashed in his eyes: not a magelight, but something yellower, a lick of flame attached to a short piece of wood. It only lasted a moment, then was blown out.

"It's the Prince!" hissed the man who had lit the flame. The dagger point pricked his skin, and he held perfectly still.

"That's impossible," said the one holding Karl. "How did he get through the Barrier?"

"It must not have closed . . ."

Karl felt, rather than saw, the first man shake his head. "No. You know how it closes with a rush at the end. He couldn't have made it through."

"But he did."

"Yeah." A pause. "So now what do we do with him?"

"Not our call. Gag him, bind him, bring him with us. The Patron will decide."

"Then let's be quick," said the first man. "We've been here too long already, and this damned snow makes it too light. One of Falk's bloody patrols could be by at any second."

"Right." Karl, already shivering, was rolled over and his face pushed down into the snow. He felt his hands seized, jerked behind him, and bound together with rope or cord of some kind; then he heard a ripping sound as his own shirt was torn apart, exposing even more of his skin to the chill air, but providing a strip of cloth that a moment later was pulled over his mouth and tied tightly behind his head.

His legs were left free. His captors hauled him to his feet and forced him to walk, his bare feet sinking into the snow with every step, already moving beyond cold to a kind of agonizing numbness.

After a few more steps, though, he had no words at all, and few thoughts. There was only one unbearable step after another, shivering so hard his teeth would surely have smashed themselves to flinders if not for the gag keeping them apart, as he was driven like a Commoner criminal away from the Palace and into the streets of New Cabora.

CHAPTER 11

FALK'S PRELIMINARY INTERROGATION of Davydd Verdsmitt was unsatisfactory. The playwright didn't seem to know what kind of trouble he was in, and simply sat there, a slight smile on his face, not responding to any of Falk's questions. "Your celebrity status in the Commons will not protect you against charges of sedition," Falk warned him at last.

"I do not expect it to," Verdsmitt said. "But it does protect me against you doing what you would really like to do, which is torture me into confessing . . . something. Probably being behind the assassination attempt on Prince Karl."

"Does it?" Falk growled.

"Not indefinitely," Verdsmitt said. "I'm not naïve enough to suppose that. But even you, Lord Falk, must hesitate before flouting the law so publicly as to torture a political prisoner—a very popular prisoner, if I do say so myself— who was arrested in full view of so many witnesses. I have many fans among the Mageborn—even among your fellow MageLords—as well as among the Commoners." Verdsmitt shrugged. "If I had been writing the scene, I would have had the seditious playwright arrested in secret after the play had ended, and spirited away somewhere while a fictitious story of his being suddenly taken ill was spread about. No one would have believed it, but it would have provided cover. But you . . ." He shook his head. "Who writes your material, Lord Falk?"

And the trouble was, Falk thought as he ordered Verd-smitt returned to his cell, that Verdsmitt was absolutely right. He had been so eager to seize the troublesome play-wright, to finally find a chink in the too-smooth armor of the Common Cause, that he had thought the public arrest would actually serve his ends ... when in fact, as Verdsmitt had just pointed out, quite the opposite was true. The play had been provocative, certainly; yet he knew well enough there were those within the Twelve, and even within the Council, who would argue he had overreacted, seeing an opportunity to perhaps bring him down a notch.

Nor could he very well present his evidence that Verd-smitt had been involved in the assassination attempt against the Prince, when that evidence consisted of the word of Mother Northwind, and had been taken from the brain of a corpse.

Well. Verdsmitt himself would soon give him all the evidence he needed, he was certain. He would bring Mother Northwind to the Palace. He could not openly or legally use her special abilities to interrogate prisoners, but once she had the contents of Verdsmitt's mind, she could surely point Falk to those who could be ... convinced ... to provide more conventional evidence against the playwright.

I'll bring her back here when I bring Brenna, he thought. *In the meantime, Verdsmitt can rot in that cell.*

He went to his own bed after that, confident that the recent upheavals still posed no threat to the Plan. He had a couple of other matters to deal with that could not wait, but in two days he would return to his manor, collect Brenna, collect Mother Northwind, collect the newly compliant An-ton, see this mysterious airship in action ... if it worked ... and then return to New Cabora, where his Plan would un-fold as he had always anticipated it would, with smooth, devastating efficiency.

In six weeks, two months at the outside, he would be King. And once his power over the Kingdom had been se-cured by his hidden allies and Unbound followers, he would lower the Barrier and the MageLords would emerge from their Hidden Kingdom and take back their world.

All was well; soon, all would be even better.

Lord Falk settled into his bed and fell instantly and dreamlessly asleep, as close to carefree as he had ever been.

But that same night in Lord Falk's manor house, Anton's sleep was interrupted, once again, by Brenna at the foot of his bed.

He had been horribly ill for the rest of the day after his meeting with Mother Northwind, and the day after that, his head in agony, nausea gripping him. Shortly after returning to his room he'd thrown up every bit of the wonderful breakfast he'd had with Brenna. Healer Eddigar, summoned by Gannick, examined him, frowning, and declared he had obviously suffered a head injury in the crash that he had somehow missed on his first examination. He put Anton back into a magical sleep and watched him closely through the first night, then insisted he stay in his room resting for all of the next day, allowing him to sit and look out the window but not to go down the stairs. Brenna had visited him, looking pale and worried, which touched him, but Eddigar limited the time she spent with him.

By the end of that day he was feeling much better, and ate something approaching a full meal for supper. Despite having rested all day, he found himself exhausted again shortly afterward and went to bed early, falling asleep at once . . . only to be awoken by Brenna.

Not that he knew it was Brenna at first. All he knew was that he had been dragged out of deep, dreamless sleep by . . . something. At first all he could see was a flickering candle flame. It took another moment or two for his fogged brain to recognize the face of the girl holding the candle.

Brenna wore a long white dressing gown, cinched at the waist. "Anton," she said in little more than a whisper, and he realized it must have been her speaking his name that had wakened him in the first place.

He raised himself on his elbows. "What . . . what is it?" he said.

"I need to talk to you."

"In the middle of the night?" No light showed through the window. "What time is it?"

"Three hours past midnight."

Anton dropped his head back on his pillow. "It couldn't wait until morning?"

"No. And keep your voice down." Brenna came and sat on the edge of the bed. He was suddenly acutely aware of her nearness, and of the fact he was nude beneath the blankets. "The guards are still outside."

"All right, all right." He stayed lying down, looking up at her as she turned her upper body toward him to look down at his face. "What is it?"

"You're in terrible danger," Brenna said. "You have to escape the manor within the next couple of days, before Lord Falk returns." She held his gaze steady, her eyes wide black pools in the dim light. "And I have to come with you."

"Danger?" Anton was certain that Lord Falk wouldn't hesitate to harm him if he thought it would help the MageLord kingdom. But . . . "But I answered Lord Falk's questions truthfully. Why would he harm me?"

"He already has," Brenna said. "Mother Northwind—"

"The Healer?"

"She's more than a Healer," Brenna said. "She's a powerful mage in her own right—soft magic, different than what Lord Falk uses. And she . . . raped you."

Anton blinked. "Um . . . I think I would have noticed."

"Not that kind of rape," Brenna said impatiently. "Mind-rape. She went inside your mind and stole your thoughts, stole them so she could give them to Falk. Things you didn't think to tell Falk, or things he didn't think to ask about, things that she had no business knowing, things no one should know about another person . . . she took them all. That's why you've been sick. It's the aftereffect."

"I—" I don't believe it, he intended to say, but remembering how he had felt when Mother Northwind had touched him, and the strange way that horrible headache had come on afterward, he let the protest die unspoken. "How do you know?" he said instead.

"I heard them talking about it," Brenna said. She looked down at her feet, cheeks flushed. "Maybe this will prove it to you. She mentioned a certain maid at an inn, twice your age, she said, who . . ." She left the sentence unfinished, and it was Anton's turn to blush . . . but hard on the heels of embarrassment—bad enough Mother Northwind had learned about that very-brief-but-messy encounter, but for Brenna to know, too!—came an emotion Anton had once known intimately when he lived on the streets of Hexton Down but had had little use for since the Professor took him under his wing: rage. Pure, unadulterated anger.

He sat up, the blankets falling to his waist. Brenna glanced at him, then averted her eyes again at once, but he hardly noticed. "I'll kill her," he said, and in that moment, he would have done it gladly, with a knife, with a gun, with his bare hands. . . .

"No," Brenna said. She still wouldn't look at him. "You couldn't. She's protected." She took a deep breath. "But that's not all. Falk wants her to do . . . something else to you. Something worse."

"Something worse than stealing my memories?" Anton snarled.

"Yes." And now Brenna *did* look at him. "Falk wants her to twist your mind. To make you loyal to him, and him alone. To make you his puppet."

Anton felt sick. "That can be done?"

"It can," Brenna said. "It is the worst kind of violation, even worse than what that old witch has already done to you. The punishment is death . . . or would be, if Lord Falk weren't the one tasked with enforcing the law forbidding such things!

"The worst of it is that after it is done, you would *remember* it being done and remember everything you knew and thought *before* it was done—but none of that would make any difference. You would be, now and forever, Falk's creature, and would obey him to the death in all things."

"But why?" Anton cried, forgetting to keep his voice down. Brenna shot a frightened look at the door, and he dropped it to an agonized whisper. "Why would he do that to me? What possible use could I be to him?"

"He wants you to fly that airship for him," Brenna said. "And he thinks you might be useful later . . ." She shook her head. "It's hard for me to believe this part, either, but I think Lord Falk is of the Unbound. They're a . . . a cult that wants to destroy the Great Barrier. It's impossible, of course, but I think he thinks he can do it. He wants the MageLords to rule your world as they do this one, as they did centuries ago."

Anton would have said that was a fool's hope, knowing what he did of the modern might of steamships and airships, of repeater guns and explosive shells . . . but he had seen too much already here in Evrenfels of what these MageLords could do, and knew he must have seen very little of what they were truly capable of. And on this whole continent, there were just a few troops and maybe a couple of cannon in Wavehaven, weeks away. The true military might was on the far side of the world, where the Union Republic squabbled with the Concatenation in a hundred ways, battling by surrogate in small, splintered countries or staring each other down along long, heavily fortified borders. If the Anomaly fell and the MageLords emerged, it could be weeks before word of it even got back to the Union Republic's government, and quite a bit longer before any major military campaign could be launched. Who knew what deviltry the MageLords would have in place by then?

"But I don't understand," Anton said. "The Anomaly has stood for centuries. How can he bring it down?"

"I don't know," Brenna snapped. "It's not like methods of destroying it were part of my education." She paused. "I'm sorry," she said more softly. "But time is short. You have to escape the manor . . . and you have to take me with you."

Anton sat cross-legged on the bed, carefully arranging the blankets to preserve his modesty, though it sounded like he had already been stripped naked by Mother Northwind. "I'll agree *I* need to escape," he said. "But why do *you*?"

"I'm part of this Plan of Lord Falk's, too," Brenna said. "I don't know how . . . but I don't want anything to do with it. I can't imagine I'm a crucial part, but maybe if I'm not here when he needs me, it will jam a tree branch into his spokes."

"But this is your home. He's your guardian." *Yes, he is*, an inner voice whispered. *How do you know this isn't all some trick of Falk's?*

He mentally thrust the doubts away. He had to trust *someone* in this bizarre kingdom where wooden puppets walked and worked and a little old woman could rape your mind with a touch of her hand. Brenna was the only candidate.

"He's my guardian, and I'm his ward. But he's not my father, and I'm not his daughter," Brenna said, her voice rising a little with emotion. "I'm his prisoner, and he's a monster." She held up the candle so that he could see her face more clearly as she met his eyes squarely. "So be a good fairy-story hero and rescue me."

"But how?" Anton said. "How do we—"

There was a noise outside the door; very slight, but enough to tell them both that one of the guards had shifted position. Anton could almost picture it, the guard turning, putting his ear to the door . . .

"Airship," Brenna whispered. "Fixed. Only hope." And then she fled for the servants' door in the corner, closing it silently behind her just as the door into Anton's room opened.

By that time, of course, he was fast asleep again, though tossing and turning and even mumbling out loud. After a moment he stopped and lay still. A moment after that he heard the bedroom door close.

He sat up and waited to see if Brenna would come back. When she didn't, he lay back down again. Putting his hands under his head, he stared up into the darkness.

The airship fixed! All well and good . . . but could he really fly it without the Professor? Could he even get it off the ground? How would they fill it with hot air? Where could they get rock gas for the burner and engine?

And even if they did get it airborne, as his own painful and tragic arrival here had proved, flying the airship wasn't the problem: landing it was.

But Brenna was right. It was their only hope.

He just wished it was a brighter one.

———

Though Karl had been into New Cabora many times, as representative of the Crown, he had never been in this part of it, far away from City Hall and the other grand public buildings that were his usual venues for official appearances. At any other time he would have been fascinated by the narrow streets, the four- or five-story buildings leaning over them, the coal-oil streetlamps casting yellow circles of illumination on snow-covered cobblestones, but otherwise doing little to alleviate the gloom, the darkened shops with half-glimpsed goods, mysterious and alien to Karl, displayed in their windows. . . .

But this was not any other time. Barefoot and lightly dressed, all Karl could think of was pain and cold. His feet had become blocks of ice he could no longer feel, though once when he looked down he saw blood on them and knew he must have cut them on the sharp stones of the streets. His ears felt like knives were slicing at them. Even his lungs hurt. *I'll be dead before we get where we're going*, he thought, but he wasn't. They didn't really penetrate very far into the city streets before he was pulled down a narrow passageway between two grim, unlit brick hulks. One of his captors rapped a rapid-fire knock in a complicated sequence on a rusty metal door. The door opened silently. Beyond was pitch-blackness, and Karl hung back for an instant as he was propelled into it . . .

. . . but only for an instant, because inside it was warm.

He reveled in that warmth for a moment, though he still couldn't feel his feet. The door closed behind them, shutting off the pale gray rectangle that proved however dark it might have seemed out there, it was far darker in here.

The space had the feeling of somewhere small. No one spoke, but they moved a short way down what felt like a narrow hall and rounded a corner. Another knock, different from the first, and another door opened. Beyond this one, there was not only warmth, but light.

It seemed blinding, though it was really, Karl realized a moment later, only the glow of a small fire burning inside a tiny hearth, combined with the gleam of a single oil lantern sitting on the mantelpiece. Together, they illuminated a small room furnished with a table, four chairs, and nothing else—unless you counted the burly, grim-faced Commoner facing them with a drawn sword, who had just stepped back from opening the door. His eyes, brown beneath bushy black brows, widened as he saw Karl. "Creator! What the rutting hell are you doing with *him*?"

"Nice to see you, too, Shiff," one of Karl's captors said. Karl took his first good look at him. He was smaller and slimmer than Karl, which made him about half the size of Shiff, but he radiated a sense of suppressed strength and energy, like a coiled spring. "And as for him," he indicated Karl, "he *followed* us."

Karl's other captor grunted. Nondescript in every way— smaller than Karl, thicker than his companion, graying hair, features that had a kind of blobby, unfinished look to them—he was someone no one would have taken a second look at in any crowd, and couldn't have remembered five minutes later even if they had. *Useful for a revolutionary*, Karl thought. Because he was certain that was what he had fallen in with: radical members of the Common Cause, the ones who wanted to overthrow the rule of the MageLords and let Commoners rule themselves.

The ones, and his throat and gut tightened at the thought, *who may have tried to kill me once already*.

"Followed us through the Barrier," the nondescript man said, his voice as unremarkable as the rest of him, a kind of generic baritone. "*After* it closed."

There was a fourth man in the room, behind Karl, the one who had opened the outer door. Now he slipped around in front, and from the looks the others gave him, Karl guessed he was the leader here. He was about Karl's height, but at least twice his age, with a face as angular and chiseled as an unfinished sculpture, and eyes, in this dim light, as black as coal.

"Prince Karl," the fourth man said thoughtfully. "Most unexpected."

"I say we kill him," growled Shiff. "We already tried once. Jenna died—"

Karl felt cold, and this time it had nothing to do with the weather.

The leader shook his head. "No," he said. "The Patron was quite clear. No more attempts on the Prince's life. His survival changes things, somehow. I don't know how. But the Patron wants him alive." He studied Karl. "Although the Patron, so far as I know, did not expect him to just place himself in our hands like this."

The feeling had at last begun to return to Karl's feet, a burning and tingling progressing rapidly toward pain. His ears and cheeks felt on fire. He could feel the cuts on his soles now, too. He tried to shift his weight from one foot to the other, but that only intensified the pain in the one he stepped down on, and he gasped involuntarily.

The leader glanced down. "Barefoot?" he said. "In this weather?" He glanced at Shiff. "Fetch the Healer."

"I say we let his feet fall off," Shiff snarled.

"And I said 'Fetch the Healer,'" the leader said softly. Shiff tensed for a moment, then grunted, sheathed his sword, and went out.

"Sit down," the leader said to Karl, who gratefully complied, collapsing onto one of the rough wooden chairs with a groan. He clenched his fists against the pain in his feet.

The leader remained standing. "Denson, guard the outside door. Jopps, find us something to eat and drink."

Denson, the wiry one, nodded and slipped out. The nondescript Jopps went through the only other door in the room, on the far side, leaving it open to reveal a slightly larger room with four beds ranged along the walls. Beyond that, through an archway, Karl saw a fire burning. Jopps went through the archway and turned left, disappearing from view.

"How did you get through the Barrier?" the leader said softly.

"What's your name?" Karl countered.

A moment's stillness. "Call me Vinthor."

"Not your real name?"

A small smile. "It is not the name I was born with. Nor were the other names you have heard given my associates by their parents." The smile vanished. "Now answer the question."

"I don't know," Karl said. "I tried to get through the opening your men made, but I was too late. Yet somehow I went through anyway." *And how* did *your men make that opening?* he wanted to ask. They were Commoners, so they must have used an enchanted device of some kind, but he would have sworn, and he thought Tagaza would have backed him up, that no mage now living could create such a device.

"Can the Heir move through the Lesser Barrier at will?" Vinthor said.

Karl shook his head. "I have never heard of it." But in the back of his mind came the thought that perhaps, just perhaps, slipping through the Lesser Barrier was all one with his strange ability to cancel out minor spells and make enchanted objects stop working. But he wasn't about to say anything about *that* to Vinthor.

"'For even the wisest, the wide world holds endless

mysteries and wonder,'" Vinthor said, and it took Karl a second to figure out why that sounded familiar. It was a quotation from *The Eagle Falls*, one of Verdsmitt's earliest but still most popular plays.

Was Verdsmitt this mysterious Patron, then? But Falk had arrested him. Surely the Patron would not have allowed himself to be captured by the Minister of Public Safety!

Unless there was some reason he *needed* to be inside the Palace . . .

"Could your father have died this very evening, making you King without your knowing it?" Vinthor continued. He asked the question softly, but there was some hidden depth to it that Karl couldn't fathom. "Perhaps the King has the power to pass through the Barrier."

"I've never heard that, either," said Karl. "And when my father dies, I *will* know it."

"Hmmm." Vinthor glanced at the fire for a moment, thinking. Karl closed his eyes and pounded his fists silently on his legs, willing the agony in his feet to retreat. It didn't work.

Jopps bustled in with a plate piled with slices of bread, cheese, and meat of some kind, though Karl couldn't quite decide what it was aside from gray and slightly slimy. Jopps went out again, returning in a moment gripping four mugs by their handles with one hand and an open wine bottle with the other. He slopped wine into the mugs, put the empty bottle aside, and went to the door, opening it to hand one of the mugs to Denson in the darkness beyond; then he closed the door again, picked up his own mug, and plopped down on the chair closest to the fire, between Vinthor and Karl. Placing a piece of cheese and a piece of meat between two slices of the bread, he ate noisily, apparently oblivious to both his leader and the Prince.

Vinthor gave him an irritated look, then nodded to Karl. "Eat, if you're hungry."

The expected after-show reception having failed to materialize, Karl *was* hungry, but the pain in his feet made it impossible to eat. "No, thanks," he said, voice strained. "But I will take that wine." He grabbed the goblet and took a large mouthful, prepared for something pretty vile, but pleasantly surprised to find it quite good. Not that he cared—it was the alcohol he wanted, hoping it might dull his increasing agony.

"The Healer will be here shortly," Vinthor said. "Perhaps then." He nodded toward the back room. "Perhaps you would be more comfortable lying down while you wait. And as I find I have lost my appetite," he gave a significant look to the oblivious Jopps, who was chewing with his mouth open, "I will see if I can contact the Patron. And then, Prince Karl, Heir Apparent to the Keys and the Kingdom of Evrenfels, we will see what is to be done with you."

He got up and disappeared back into the kitchen. Jopps kept eating, but his eyes followed Karl as he got to his feet, drained the rest of his wine in one long draft, and then limped, gasping with each step, into the next room. There he lay down, gaining some slight measure of relief when he lifted his feet from the floor. Throwing his arm over his eyes, he waited for the Healer . . . and his fate.

Lord Falk's feeling of contentment did not survive breakfast. He was just spreading butter on a second piece of toast in the private dining area of his suite, enjoying the play of the sunshine on the lake outside, when he heard voices in the outer room and knew someone had come to call on him. He ignored them, and went on buttering his toast. There was always some new demand on his time, but toast only stayed hot for a minute.

He was halfway through the slice when Brich appeared. Falk swallowed, set the remaining portion of toast down on his plate (recently denuded of a healthy helping of ham and eggs), and said, "From your expression, Brich, you have something to tell me you suspect I will not enjoy hearing."

"You're quite correct, my lord," Brich said grimly. "My

lord—" and the fact he used the honorific twice in such quick succession was more testimony, if any were needed, to just *how* grim he felt, "Prince Karl is missing."

Falk sat very still for a long moment, then said just two words, though each carried enough savagery to make even Brich pale a little. "When? How?"

"Sometime in the night, my lord," Brich said. "His absence was discovered when his manservant went in this morning with breakfast. His bed had not been slept in. As to the how . . ." Brich licked his lips. "His window was open, my lord. It appears he simply climbed down the wall of the palace to the ground."

"And Teran, his bodyguard? The other guards I left posted outside in the hallway?" Falk said softly. "They heard nothing?"

"No, my lord, but the thickness of the . . ." Brich's voice trailed off, as though he thought perhaps it wasn't wise to make excuses, even if they weren't for himself.

"I shouldn't be surprised," Falk said, almost to himself. "He grew up in the Palace. As Brenna has recently reminded me, children have a way of finding secret ways of getting to places they aren't supposed to be." He took a deep breath. "Well, no doubt he is hiding somewhere on the grounds, enjoying the frantic search for his Royal Presence. The Heir may look a grown man on the outside, Brich, but he is still enough of a boy to enjoy such childish pranks." He got to his feet. "Let us indulge him. Turn out the guard. Search everywhere. He must be inside the Lesser Barrier, after all." He paused. "And send Teran to me," he added softly.

"He's already waiting in a cell," Brich said.

Falk nodded once, and went to find him.

Teran sat on the cell's bed, hands folded in his lap, head down. He looked up as Falk came in, then jumped to his feet. "Lord Falk, I—"

"Teran," said Falk coldly. "How is it that the man to whom I have entrusted not only the Prince's safety but also the task of keeping me informed as to his whereabouts and actions has once again failed at both duties?"

"My lord," Teran said again. "He ordered me from his room. He was angry that I had not told him about the impending arrest of Verdsmitt."

"It's as well you did not," Falk said. "What did he tell you?"

"Nothing, my lord," Teran said. "As I said, he was angry. He pointed out that he was both the Prince and my friend. I told him that you were my supreme commander and I had to follow your orders unless he had specifically countermanded them ... which he had not."

"And he said nothing that indicated he intended to sneak out of the palace, Teran?" Falk said.

"No, my lord," Teran said. "The last I saw of him he was pouring a drink. He seemed ready to settle in for the evening."

"And you heard nothing?"

"Nothing, my lord."

Falk gave Teran a hard look. "It seems to me," he said softly, "that you have now failed your duty twice."

Teran paled. "My lord—"

"The terms of your service," Falk said, "have always been that you *serve* me well, and your mother and sister *remain* well. If you do not serve me well ..." He let his voice fall to a silky whisper. "Would you say you have served me well in these past few days, Teran?"

"My lord, I beg of you—"

"Your begging does not interest me." Falk stood up. "Fail me again, and your mother and sister will find their lives suddenly very difficult. As will you ... though in your case, it will be both difficult and short." He jerked his head toward the door. "Join the search for the Prince. But I may wish to speak to you again later."

Teran nodded and fled, and Falk dismissed him from his mind.

The day wore on. The searches turned up nothing. At

noon, Falk, to general though muted outrage, ordered the Royal guard to search all personal quarters. By three o'clock, there could be little doubt: Prince Karl was no longer inside the Lesser Barrier.

Two boats had been found on the far side of the lake, one of the Palace pleasure boats and an ordinary rowboat no one could remember seeing before—but that meant little, since there were numerous boats tied up here and there around the lake, and if anybody was missing one, he was unlikely to claim it when it might implicate him in the disappearance of the Prince. Both boats were unmoored, and it could have simply been the breeze that pushed them so close together along that weedy bank ... but the breeze had not churned the mud, flattened the weeds, and pushed through the thicker growth above the shore to the very edge of the Lesser Barrier.

It had snowed heavily again during the night, obliterating any tracks there might have been on the other side of the Barrier, but the signs seemed unequivocal. Prince Karl had passed through the Lesser Barrier, perhaps following someone else.

Which was utterly and completely impossible.

Or so Tagaza has always said, Falk thought. His calm response to the original news of Karl's disappearance had long since vanished in rage burning hot enough to scour the streets of New Cabora with fire, had he unleashed it magically. But he could not turn that rage on the Commoners ... not yet, at any rate. When he was King ...

... except he might never be King if Karl had stupidly allowed the Common Cause to finish the job of assassination it had botched so spectacularly just days before. If Tagaza were not to be trusted, the magical search for the next Heir that the MageLords would insist upon would point straight to Brenna, and that would raise questions even Falk could not dance around. *I'd have to kill her*, he thought. *Quietly and quickly*. The Heirship would pass to someone else. Tagaza's search would point to someone else. No one would ever know she was Heir, and Karl was not ...

. . . and twenty years of careful planning would collapse into chaos. Who knew if he could come out the other side of that chaos with even his life, much less the Kingship?

And if he did not become King, then the Hidden Kingdom would remain hidden for another two hundred years: forever, from his point of view.

All of which drove him to Tagaza's office, two carefully selected guards in tow.

Time to answer a few questions, old friend.

CHAPTER 12

TAGAZA HADN'T SPOKEN TO FALK since the Minister for Public Safety had returned from his manor, though he'd been expecting to be summoned at any time.

He'd been even more shocked by the subject matter of Davydd Verdsmitt's play than most. Magic running out, the Barrier crashing down . . . it was *exactly* what would happen if the Barriers were not brought down and were instead allowed to exhaust the magic lode. It was to prevent that happening that he had joined forces with Falk. But how had Verdsmitt, a Commoner, come up with the idea?

And then he'd been shocked all over again when Falk and the guards so suddenly arrested Verdsmitt. *What's Falk playing at?* he wondered as he stood in the theater, watching the playwright taken away, the actors arrested, the Prince hurried out by Teran. *He can't* really *believe Verdsmitt had anything to do with the attack on the Prince, can he?*

But of course he could. And if he did, then Tagaza could only assume that the reason was something he had been told by their mutual acquaintance and coconspirator: Mother Northwind.

After the arrest, he returned to his quarters and waited, certain Falk would come to explain his actions. But he didn't. Tagaza went to bed, had his usual breakfast of egg-on-toast in front of his open window, enjoying the breeze blowing in from across the lake, then went out and through the bustling corridors of the Palace to his office, located in the same wing as Falk's but on the top floor rather than in the basement. He passed through the rather ordinary oak door into the outer office, decorated in dark blue panels separated by marble pilasters. His secretary, Sintha—perhaps not as efficient as Falk's Brich, but being half Brich's age, female, slim, and with long black hair she liked to wear loose, considerably easier on the eyes—sat behind the marble-topped oak desk. She got to her feet as he entered.

"First Mage," she said breathlessly. "Have you heard the news?"

Tagaza's heart sank. In his experience, nothing good ever followed that particular phrase. "About Verdsmitt's arrest? Of course, I was there—"

"No, First Mage." Sintha shook her head. "Apparently, sometime in the night, Prince Karl disappeared from his locked room."

That bit of information did more than just make Tagaza's heart sink; it damn near stopped it cold. "What?"

"None of the guards heard a thing," Sintha said. "But when the servants went in to dress him and bring him his breakfast . . . he wasn't there. His bed hadn't even been slept in."

Tagaza thought for an instant he might be sick. Cold sweat broke out all over his body. Without the Prince, the plan he and Falk and Mother Northwind had been working toward for two decades was about to unravel . . . and it might unravel him along with it.

Brenna, he thought. *She'll have to go. They'll call on me to search out the new Heir . . . it can't be her.* He was sure Falk would want him to lie about who the next Heir was, if he had to do that spell; but the magic wouldn't let him lie. He'd have no choice but to reveal the true Heir. *Falk will have to dispose of her . . .*

That thought made him feel even sicker. He had met Brenna every year since she was ten, which had been the first time Falk had brought her to the Palace. She had been a brown-haired, brown-eyed, grave, curious, and very intelligent child, whom he had led by the hand around the Palace, showing her all its wonders, once even carried her to bed when she'd fallen asleep after a concert.

And you always knew she was doomed, a cold voice deep inside him pointed out.

But that was different. It was one thing to sacrifice her for the greater good, to ensure the Barriers could come down and the drain on the magic lode be reduced before magic failed entirely. Regrettable, but absolutely necessary. But to eliminate her just so Falk and he could avoid discovery . . .

It was monstrous.

He saw Sintha's concerned look, and smiled at her weakly. "I hope he's found unharmed," he said. "I've grown very fond of the boy."

"I hope so, too," Sintha said. "He's been very pleasant to me."

"Lord Falk has not requested my help in the search?" he said.

Sintha shook her head. "No, First Mage."

Tagaza nodded. "Very well. I'll be in my office." He hurried through the inner oak door. His office was white: white carpet, white walls, white ceiling, white desk, all trimmed with gold. Just as in his quarters in the east wing, the windows were thrown open, letting in air and light. He went over to the window and peered out across the lake. He could see guards even then combing the lakeshore, guards in boats, guards on the bridge.

He gazed down at the ornamental gardens, down toward the boathouse, and even from that distance recognized the slim gray figure of Falk, talking to someone. *He'll want to see me now*, Tagaza thought. He turned away from the window, went to the desk, and sat down; then, after a moment, got up again and went to the sideboard beneath the giant portrait of King Kravon, looking far more regal than he'd ever looked in real life, opened a decanter of asproga, and poured himself a glass of the fiery anise-flavored liqueur, which he'd introduced the Prince to some years ago. His hand shook slightly as he took it back to his desk. For a moment he just sat there, staring across its white marble top at the two empty chairs on the other side; then, with a sigh, he folded his mind into a simple spell he'd crafted many years before and said into empty air, "Sintha, I might as well get started on those inspectors' reports. Please bring them in."

"Yes, First Mage." He heard her voice clearly in his mind as she responded to the magical call. A few minutes later she entered with a stack of papers. "Here you are."

"Any more news on the Prince?" he asked, as casually as he could, reaching for the top sheet.

"No, First Mage."

"Let me know if you hear anything."

"I will."

He gave her a dismissive smile, and she curtsied a little, then went back into the outer office, closing the door behind her. Tagaza started reading the paper on the desk. *Magelight Inspection Report, Royal Palace, Royal Quarters. Greetings, First Mage Tagaza. As noted in my last report, we continue to suffer mysterious failures of the enchanted light-stones near the Prince's quarters. It could be due to some natural interfering material in the stonework. I propose . . .*

Tagaza read on, making notes. He found it hard to concentrate at first, but gradually the rhythm of the never-ending paperwork reasserted itself and he became engrossed in the work. The day passed swiftly. He ate lunch at his desk, Sintha bringing in a plate of cold meat, cheese, and bread, and a bottle of Old Evrenfels Amber, Commoner-brewed but the best beer in the Kingdom for all that. By midafternoon, he had reached the bottom of the pile; but as he reached for the last report, the door to his office crashed open. In strode Falk . . . and two grim-faced guards. Beyond them, in the outer office, he could see Sintha, craning her neck to see what was happening.

Tagaza froze for an instant, hand on the last report; then he forced himself to pick it up as though completely unconcerned by the First Minister's unannounced arrival. "Lord Falk," he said. He laid the report on the desk in front of him, then picked up his pen, enchanted so that it magically transported ink from a reservoir in his desk as needed and thus never ran out. It was wrapped in an insulating leather sheath so it didn't freeze his fingers as he used it. "Have you found the Prince yet? Is there anything I can do to assist?"

Falk glared at him, mouth a thin line. "First Mage Tagaza," he said, voice colder than the wind outside the Barrier, "In the name of His Majesty King Kravon, I arrest you for the crime of High Treason."

Tagaza's fingers were warm on the pen, but the rest of him froze at those words. He couldn't seem to process what the Minister of Public Safety had just said.

Falk turned to the guards. "Take him," he said.

The guards stepped forward, eyes cold and bright beneath the silver shine of their helms. Tagaza put down the pen and got to his feet. Shock had given way to fear . . . and anger. "You have no authority—"

"I am Minister of Public Safety," Falk snapped. "My duty is to protect the King and Heir. Someone tried to kill the Heir. Now he's missing. And I have reason to believe you are involved."

Tagaza's eyes widened. "What? What did Mother—"

Suddenly, he couldn't speak at all. He tried, once, twice, but his throat seemed numb and his lips and tongue wouldn't move. He recognized the spell; he had taught it to Falk. He stopped struggling against it and glared at Falk. Falk ignored him, turning to the guards. "Take him," he said, and swept out.

Tagaza heard the sharp click of enchanted manacles locking onto his wrists, and felt their anti-magic field wrapping around him, heavy and cold as a wet woolen blanket. He had no choice but to go with the guards.

This will all be straightened out, he told himself. He even managed a reassuring smile to Sintha as the guards led him past her desk, though he was feeling far from reassured himself. *Falk has made a mistake. That's all. He needs me, and after a little reflection, he'll realize it.*

But he still couldn't suppress a thrill of fear as the guards took him down the stairs toward Falk's dungeon, into which so many men, Mageborn and Commoner alike, had disappeared forever.

———

Let him stew for a few hours, Falk thought as he stalked away from Tagaza's office, *and then we will find out how he did it.*

That he *had* done it, Falk no longer had much doubt. Who else but Tagaza, who with Falk had delved more deeply into the secrets of both Lesser and Greater Barriers than anyone else alive, could have the knowledge or skill to open a hole in the Lesser Barrier and spirit the Prince out through it?

He went through the magical door into his offices with none of his usual banter with the guards, though the sign and countersign ("Snapdragon." "Honeysuckle.") were no less silly, and strode up to Brich's deck. Brich took one look at him and jumped to his feet. "Yes, my lord?"

"We have been too quick to forgive the Commoners," Falk said, every word clipped and weighted. "Prince Karl is somewhere in New Cabora. See to it that we find him ... by any means necessary. I don't care if you have to tear the city apart stone by stone." He paused as a thought struck him, then smiled, or at least showed his teeth. "In fact, I think that is *exactly* how we should begin. Starting with their precious City Hall. Let us remind them of the power MageLords can call on if need be."

Brich paled, but he did not argue. "It will be done, Lord Falk."

"Yes," Falk snarled. "It will."

———

Mother Northwind received word of Prince Karl's disappearance some time earlier than Lord Falk; in the middle of the night, in fact, when a glowing ball appeared in the air above her bed and made a squawking sound rather like a chicken having its neck wrung—Mother Northwind's own choice, since it was such a horrible noise it could hardly fail to wake her up.

Nor did it this time. She closed her eyes again momentarily and used magic to sweep the sleep from her brain, then, as alert as if she had had a good night's sleep and a morning dip in a cold pool, said, "I am here. Who speaks?"

A magelink *could* carry an image, but she had chosen to make this one transmit only sound. Not only that, but the voice the person at the other end heard coming from it would not be the quavering tones of an elderly woman, but the sonorous voice of a middle-aged, powerful man. It was a sorry reality that men and women alike were more likely to respond to a man's orders than those of a woman . . .

. . . something else Mother Northwind hoped would change in the New World that would follow the destruction of the Great Barrier. Some of what she had seen in Anton's mind had hinted that, though far from perfect, things were somewhat more equal for men and women Outside—but for now she had to deal with the world as it was, not as she hoped to make it. And so she talked to those within the Common Cause whose help she needed with the voice of a man . . . and the title of "Patron."

She smiled a little, thinking of how long Falk had sought that elusive individual, when in fact the Patron lived in a cottage he had had built within his very own demesne.

"Cell Leader Vinthor, Patron," the voice said. His cell had been tasked with placing certain objects in the Palace grounds in preparation for the final act of her plan to destroy the Barrier. She tensed. Had something gone wrong?

"Yes, Vinthor," she said. "Was there a problem with your mission?" Already she was thinking ahead. If those devices had not been placed, she would have to activate a backup plan. A riskier one, but if necessary—

"No, Patron. The devices were placed successfully."

"I am glad to hear it," Mother Northwind said with relief. "Then why do you contact me?"

"There were complications after the completion of the mission," Vinthor said. A long pause followed. Mother Northwind declined to fill it. "Patron," Vinthor said at last, "we seem to have inadvertently taken a prisoner."

Mother Northwind frowned. "What kind of prisoner?"

Another pause. "Patron, it is the Heir. Prince Karl."

Mother Northwind had been holding up her end of the conversation while remaining comfortably prone beneath her down comforter. Now, though, she shot upright. "The *Prince*? How? *Why?*"

"As I said, Patron, it was inadvertent."

"Forgive me if I find it difficult to imagine how one inadvertently captures a prince, Cell Leader Vinthor," Mother Northwind said, her tone biting.

"I know it is hard to believe, Patron," Vinthor said. "But inadvertent it was, nonetheless. Prince Karl seems to have spotted our men in the garden—how, I do not know—and somehow sneaked out of his quarters and followed them across the lake. He saw them leave through the Lesser Barrier. He followed."

"Through the opening they had made?" Mother Northwind said, though she suspected she knew the answer.

"No," Vinthor said. "He tried, he said, but it closed too quickly. He just . . . passed through the Barrier. As though it weren't there."

Magebane, Mother Northwind thought. As if there were still any doubt after the assassination attempt . . .

She waited a moment before speaking, thinking. The Prince's disappearance would certainly put a kink in Falk's Plan, though it might or might not be a fatal one, depending on how cleverly he managed it. But as for her *own* Plan . . .

It made no difference, she decided. In fact, if anything, things would be easier to manage with the Prince in her hands.

I'd have ordered him kidnapped myself if I'd thought we could get away with it, she thought wryly.

"Very well," she said at last. "An interesting development. Vinthor, you must get the Prince out of the city tonight, before he is missed from the Palace. Lord Falk will tear New Cabora apart to find him. Use the safe house in Mouse Valley. You must get him there before daybreak. Can you do that?"

"Yes, Patron," Vinthor said.

"Good. Also, warn all of your contacts, and have them warn *theirs*, that Falk is about to launch a crackdown on the Commons unlike anything we have seen thus far. We may be advancing the timetable."

"Yes, Patron."

"Thank you for contacting me, Vinthor. And congratulations on the successful completion of your mission. Death to the MageLords—liberty for the Commons!"

"Death to the MageLords—liberty for the Commons!" Vinthor echoed, and the magelink vanished with a soft pop.

Endgame, Mother Northwind thought. *Though perhaps not playing out quite as I foresaw. Still, I can make it work.* She lay down once more. So Prince Karl had passed through the Lesser Barrier as though it weren't there. Could he do the same with the Greater?

She suspected he could. *Magebane*, she thought with great satisfaction. *The only weapon with which one can strike at the tyranny of the MageLords . . .*

. . . and a weapon that now is firmly in my grasp.

CHAPTER 13

IN THE MORNING, it was as though the strange midnight visit with Brenna had never happened.

Anton sat in the same breakfast nook as he had two days before, eating the same breakfast, albeit with slightly less desperation. In fact, he found he was hardly hungry at all this morning, and picked at the food.

For her part, Brenna chatted blandly about the weather, and the upcoming Springfest, and would Anton like to visit the village of Overbridge, and what kind of music did they play in the Outside world, and . . .

Anton understood why she was doing it, with one of the few human servants standing by, but it still almost drove him mad to talk about such inconsequential things after what Brenna had told him in the night.

But after what seemed an eternity, though it was really only about an hour, Brenna dabbed her lips with her handkerchief—Anton gave his own a quick wipe, as well—and got to her feet. "Well," she said. "Let's see how those mageservants have gotten on with your airship, shall we? I'm sure Lord Falk will want a progress report magelinked to him."

Magelinks, Anton had guessed, must serve the same purpose inside the Anomaly as electromissives did outside. "Yes, let's," he said with false brightness to match Brenna's own, which earned him a slightly annoyed but also amused warning look in return.

Despite Falk's assurances, Anton had not really believed the mageservants could repair all the damage to the airship in ... what, a day and three quarters? But when he and Brenna, after nodding to Gannick, bent in concentration over that eerie desk of his, emerged into the back courtyard, he gasped.

There was the airship—the Professor's airship—looking exactly as it had when the Professor had first showed it to him, just before terrifying him by informing him that someday soon he would be flying in it.

"I don't believe it," Anton said. He circled the gondola, examined the connections between it and the burner and the engine, noted the fresh sandbags hung on the outside of the wicker basket like heavy brown fruit, checked the rigging, the rudder, and the propeller. "It's ... perfect."

"Then it will fly?" said Brenna, still brightly, but with an undercurrent of the urgency she had expressed in the middle of the night.

"No," Anton said. "Not until we can fill the envelope." He pointed to the long, flat blue worm of cloth lying on the ground beside the gondola.

"And that's what the burner does?" Brenna gestured at the copper stovelike device in the middle of the gondola.

"Yes," Anton said. "But it needs fuel."

"Fuel?"

"Rock gas," Anton said. "Compressed rock gas. We were out when we crashed. Without it ..." He shook his head. "Without it, the airship won't fly."

"But it's *got* to," Brenna said, the false cheeriness replaced by naked desperation. "We can't be here when Lord Falk returns. Either of us."

"I can't just snap my fingers and make it fly," Anton said. "It's not ..." He bit off the last word.

"Magic?"

"You know what I mean."

"Yes." She stared at the airship. "So what you really need," she said slowly, "is hot air."

"To fill the airship, yes," Anton said. "But we also have

to have a source of hot air on board. Otherwise, we go up, but we come down very fast ... about seven hundred feet a minute. You can slow that some by throwing out ballast. If you can lift with a lot of ballast, you can stay aloft longer, because you have more ballast to toss away as you lose altitude."

"And this 'ballast' ... that's the sandbags?"

"Yes," Anton said. He studied the gondola, hung with new sandbags the mageservants had somehow made. They didn't look like the sandbags they'd left Elkbone with, but they were bags, and they were filled with sand, so they'd do. "Twice as many, if we can get them. There's a water tank in the base of the gondola, too, but I don't think we should fill that; in this weather, it would freeze and it would be impossible to empty it ... but, Brenna, this is *all* impossible. If we don't have the burner, we can't fill the airship, or stay aloft long enough to get very far away. We'll have to risk escaping on foot."

"Suicide," Brenna said. "Even if the men-at-arms don't get us, the cold will." She glanced over her shoulder; a man-at-arms, no doubt sent by Gannick, had emerged and was watching them. "I've been remiss in my duties as host," she said, brightly and loudly. "I have yet to complete your tour of the house."

"But—"

"I'm sure you'll find it 'uplifting,'" Brenna said. Anton got the hint, though he couldn't imagine what she could show him that would solve their problem ...

... until, after touring him past some rather pedestrian statues on the front lawn and the covered hulk of what he was told was a magical musical fountain, Brenna took him through a door in the kitchen into the servants' corridors, and from there through another door and down a long flight of stone stairs.

As they started their descent, Anton heard a distant roar. It grew in volume until, as they emerged into a vaulted underground chamber, it sounded like an enormous waterfall. But Anton couldn't see anything except for a strange blue glow, like and yet very unlike the glow of the ubiquitous magelights. Brenna didn't try to talk above the noise, just led him through the first strangely warm chamber into an adjoining one that was more than just warm: it was stifling.

Anton gaped at the source of both the heat and the noise: a massive torch, a shrieking, howling blue flame, balanced over a fissure in the rock and splaying tentacles of fire across the ceiling above. "The energy source for all the magic in Lord Falk's demesne," Brenna shouted. "The manor was built here because of this natural outpouring of rock gas. It was set alight more than seven hundred years ago and has never faltered."

"The biggest burner of them all," Anton shouted. If he took even half a dozen steps forward, he was sure its heat would singe the hair from his arms and eyebrows. "But how do we get hot air from down here into the airship?"

Brenna pointed up. Anton blinked, trying to see through the heat-shimmer and licking flames. There were dark openings in the rock above, which made sense; they would have been asphyxiated long before they descended to this level, and the fire would burn itself out in moments, if there were no outlets for the byproducts of its combustion.

"Where do they come up?" he shouted.

"Various places," she shouted back. "One of which is not far from the airship . . . a chimney on the back of the manor, that heats the servants' quarters."

"A chimney?" Anton shook his head. "No good. How do we get the air down from a chimney to the airship?"

"We don't," Brenna shouted. "We take it from the bottom of the chimney. We knock a hole in it—"

"How?" Anton demanded.

Brenna spread her hands. "My guardian is not the only one who can command mageservants," she said.

"There's still the problem of replenishing the hot air while we're in the air," Anton said. "Otherwise it'll be a short trip and a hard landing."

"I've got an idea for that, too," Brenna said. She told him what she had in mind, and for the first time, Anton felt a flickering of hope. If they could fill the airship, get away before the men-at-arms realized what was happening, and keep it aloft for a reasonable amount of time . . .

. . . and land it without killing themselves, he thought uneasily . . .

The winds would blow them east, deeper into the Kingdom. With no fuel for the engine, he couldn't take the airship back over the Anomaly. Still, they'd be somewhere else, somewhere far away from Falk and his mind-destroying witch.

"We'll need a hosepipe," he said, thinking.

"We can get one," Brenna said.

They made their way up to the courtyard. The man-at-arms hadn't followed them down into the cellar, from which there was only the one exit, but he was waiting for them when they emerged. He planted himself on the back steps, looking bored, and paid them little heed as they walked over to the chimney. Even on this side it was hot enough to melt the snow from the cobblestones, so that a ragged semicircle of pavement gleamed wetly despite the icy chill, which had deepened since Anton's arrival.

Anton glanced at the man-at-arms. "Won't *he* try to stop us?" he said in a low voice.

"Why should he?" Brenna murmured back. "He knows we're supposed to be getting the airship ready to fly. He doesn't have a clue how it works, so anything we do . . ."

" . . . is all right with him," Anton finished. "Nice." He touched the chimney's bricks, then snatched back his hand. "Lots of heat," he said. "Now if only we can get it into the envelope."

"We can," Brenna said. Although many of the mageservants had gone back to their regular tasks of household maintenance, a half-dozen stood idle in case more work was required. "I can't just *will* them to act the way Lord Falk does," she said. "No one else in the household can. We have to use this." She pulled something from her pocket, a short, narrow cylinder of wood with a glass ball on one end that glowed blue.

Anton couldn't help laughing. "A magic wand?"

Brenna gave him a curious look. "I suppose you could call it that—it's magic, and it's a sort of wand. But I don't know why you find that so funny."

Anton only shook his head, thinking of street "magicians" he had seen gulling a living from tourists with their misdirection and sleight of hand. They *all* used magic wands. He'd even heard one once claim that *his* magic wand was an ancient artifact of the legendary MageLords. But their wands were usually much longer, much more impressive, than this little stubby . . .

He grinned suddenly. *Well*, he thought, *they do say that size isn't everything*.

Brenna was looking at him curiously, and he flushed, glad *she* couldn't read his thoughts. "So . . . how does it work?"

"It's been enchanted to take verbal orders and . . . translate them, I guess is the word . . . to magical orders for the mageservants. It's how Gannick orders them about." Holding the "wand" in her gloved right hand she went over to one of the mageservants and touched the blue symbol on its polished wooden head. "These orders are for all mageservants within this courtyard," she said clearly. The five other mageservants suddenly twitched and stood up straighter. She lifted the wand from the glowing symbol and looked at Anton. "Tell me what they need to do, and I'll repeat it to them," she said. "Be as clear as you can. They're . . . very literal."

Anton remembered a childhood fable, "The MageLord's Apprentice," in which the hapless helper of a MageLord learned enough magic to set the MageLord's magical minions to scrubbing the stonework, but not enough to stop them from scrubbing it to dust, so that the MageLord had returned to find his castle in rubble and his apprentice buried within it.

He also remembered that at the end of the story the MageLord turned on his heel and walked away, leaving his apprentice to suffocate beneath the weight of his own folly.

He shuddered. "I'll be precise," he said, and he did the best he could.

Brenna placed the wand back on the symbol on the mageservant's face, and repeated the instruction almost word for word—almost, because she took it on herself to rephrase some of his clumsier sentences. He thought of "The MageLord's Apprentice" again, and couldn't blame her.

"Carry out my orders," she said at last, and lifted the wand.

The man-at-arms watched with interest as two of the mageservants, having disappeared momentarily in the direction of the tool shed in one corner of the courtyard, returned with hammers and chisels. He actually descended the steps to watch as they attacked the chimney bricks with inhuman strength and precision. "Should they be doing that?" he said.

"Yes," Brenna said shortly. "They should." He gave her a skeptical look. "Lord Falk wants this flying device operational," she said. "I don't think he'll begrudge a few bricks from a chimney to achieve that."

"Miss, I personally think you and the young man here are *both* a few bricks short of a chimney if you think you can get this pile of rubbish to fly without magic," the man-at-arms said with equanimity, and returned to his post.

Despite having been on the receiving end of that bit of wit, Anton still grinned appreciatively.

While two of the mageservants were dismantling a section of the chimney, the others disappeared inside. In a few minutes, two of them emerged with more of the odd-looking sandbags, which Anton had finally realized were flour sacks. "Where are they getting the sand?" he asked Brenna as he watched the magical marionettes hang the bags on the ropes on both sides of the basket.

"Groundskeeper shed, out front in the gardens," Brenna said.

The other two came out with something quite different: a small stove, with a tall, narrow chimney. Anton watched them bring it over to the gondola and place it inside, and as they next headed to the coal shed, he climbed into the basket and manhandled the stove into place next to the useless burner, pointing the chimney up into the envelope. The small stove normally resided inside the extra magecarriage Falk kept at the manor, and came with bellows to fire it up when more heat was needed quickly. Brenna had suggested, and Anton hoped, that perhaps, if they pumped the bellows, they could produce enough heat to slow their descent, though he knew it could never put out enough to keep them aloft indefinitely. *At least it will be extra ballast we can throw overboard in an emergency*, he thought.

The mageservants returned with a bag of coal each. While he lit and stoked the little stove, the two working on the chimney abruptly opened a small hole, scorching air roaring out, creating a plume of white fog that billowed skyward. Anton jumped over the side of the gondola and ran over to where Brenna stood by the chimney.

Two of the mageservants that had been carrying sandbags now emerged from the house with a huge coil of canvas hosepipe, also liberated from the gardener's shed, Anton figured. The two that had brought him the stove and coal went into the tool shed, coming out after a moment with a piece of heavy wood and an assortment of tools.

Anton's instructions—at least as modified by Brenna—seemed to have been clear. Within moments the mageservants had cut a round hole in the wood exactly the right size to take the hose, bound the hole in place with a set of brackets that might have once held torches (the mageservants bending the heavy iron with alarming ease to clamp the hose in place), and spread a thick putty normally used for sealing windows all along the back edge of the board. They placed the wood over the roaring hole in the chimney and pushed it hard against the brick. When they stepped away, Anton went over and felt along the edge of the board. He couldn't feel as much as a breath of hot air escaping.

Instead, that hot air roared out of the end of the hose, creating a narrower, more focused plume of white as it met the cold air.

"It's going to take a long time to fill," Anton warned. "And at some point, our clever guard over there is going to get suspicious."

"Let him," Brenna said. She took the wand and went over to the nearest mageservant. What she told it, Anton couldn't hear, though he did hear the beginning admonition that "these orders are for all mageservants within this courtyard." The mageservants didn't do anything different after she finished, but she came back to Anton looking satisfied.

"If we're lucky, that'll do it," she said.

Anton didn't ask any questions. Unbelievably, the time had come. He was glad Brenna had insisted they both dress as warmly as they possibly could before coming outside that day. There could be no going back for clothes or supplies . . . or water, he thought. *Well, without the burner it would probably freeze solid anyway.*

Anton took the hose from the mageservants and thrust it inside the envelope of the airship.

It filled with agonizing slowness. For a long time he thought it wasn't filling at all, or that the air from that giant gas flame in the cellar wasn't hot enough . . . but then the tip of the envelope twitched, and slowly, oh-so-slowly, began to swell.

The expansion seemed to pick up speed as it went along. The man-at-arms watched, obviously fascinated, but didn't interfere.

Once the airship had begun filling, the mageservants had moved to other positions, as Anton had instructed Brenna to order them. Each had taken the end of a rope from the gondola and tied it around something: a bit of stonework, the railing of the steps, the handle of the gate. Inside the gondola, Anton had rigged the ropes with the same quick-release buckles used to drop the sandbags, spare ones he'd taken from the stores cabinet under the pilot's bench at the stern, the only cabinet he hadn't emptied in his frantic search for stuff to throw over the side during the descent from the top of the Anomaly, because the Professor's feet had been in the way.

It wasn't until the airship rose off the cobblestones and slowly, as though it hardly meant it, began to swell toward the sky, that the man-at-arms came down the steps toward them. "That's amazing," he said. He leaned over and said in a voice just for Anton, "and a little obscene, if you take my meaning."

Anton grinned, but said nothing. He'd often had the same thought watching the long tube of silk inflate.

The envelope lifted completely free of the ground, and Anton had to scramble to make sure the hose remained pointed up into its interior. Leaving the guard behind, he climbed into the gondola. "Help me out here," he said to Brenna, who climbed, much more gracefully, in beside him. "Getting close," he said under his breath.

The man-at-arms continued to watch the airship grow with interest, rather than alarm. "Amazing," he said again. "And here I thought all this talk of flying was a load of horse apples." His eyes traced the ropes tied here and there. "Well, those make sense now," he said. "Making sure you two don't float away . . ." And then his eyes narrowed. "Hey," he said. "You've proved you can fix this thing. I think you should stop now."

"Got to be sure the envelope holds air," Anton said cheerfully. "Can't do that without full inflation."

The man-at-arms looked up at the airship now towering above them. The gondola creaked and shifted a little. "It's inflated now," he said, his voice suddenly hard. "Out of there, both of you."

"But the test isn't complete—" Anton said.

The guard, it was clear, was having none of that. He drew his short sword. "Out of it!"

"Carry out my orders!" Brenna shouted to the mageservants.

One of the magical puppets stood no more than ten feet away. It suddenly sprang to life, closing the distance between it and the man-at-arms with impossible speed. One three-fingered wooden hand closed around the short sword, yanked it from the man's hand, and threw it up and away so hard it sailed clear over the tool shed and disappeared beyond the courtyard wall. The other hand gripped the man's arm. He cried out. The mageservant turned and walked toward the stairs, dragging the burly guard across the cobblestones as though he weighed no more than a sack of potatoes . . . a small sack, at that. The man-at-arms writhed, but to no avail, and he abruptly quit moving after his head impacted the bottom step . . . and then the next one . . . and then the next one . . .

Anton hoped to the God he didn't believe in they hadn't just killed the man. He glanced at Brenna, who looked white and a little sick, but she pressed her lips together. "How much longer?" she demanded.

Anton studied the envelope for a moment, then leaned forward to look at the ground. "We'll lift in a couple of minutes," he said, straightening, shouting to be heard above the roar of the hot air pouring out of the hose. "But we need to keep filling as long as possible. We need to drive all the cold air out the bottom so we get the maximum amount of lift."

Brenna looked back at the mageservant as it opened the back door and tossed the guard's limp body through it. Then it closed the door firmly and stood in front of it.

"What did you order them to do?" Anton shouted to Brenna.

"To let no one into the courtyard but us," Brenna said.

"Can't Gannick countermand your orders?"

"Only one at a time," Brenna said. "And he has to touch them with the control wand to do it."

Anton could hear shouting now from inside the house. The door opened and Gannick took a step outside, wand in hand, but the mageservant reached for him and he backed up so quickly he fell hard on his rear end, then scrambled backward out of sight, his feet, kicking desperately for purchase, the last of him to disappear.

For a few more precious moments, no one attempted to enter the courtyard, but Anton could imagine what was happening on the other side. Gannick would be calling the men-at-arms. They'd be seizing weapons, rushing through the house. And the mageservants—

The mageservants couldn't stop them for long.

The back door flew open and the mageservant that stood there vanished in a blast of blue fire. The other mageservants raced for the door.

If they can use magic to destroy the mageservants, they can use it on us, Anton thought. "Time to go! Grab the buckles!"

He'd told Brenna what they would have to do. She seized the two buckles closest to her, he seized the others.

Another mageservant blew apart in a blast of blue flame.

"On a count of three," Anton shouted. "One . . . two . . . three!"

Brenna released her buckles. Anton released his. Majestically, steadily, but oh-so-slowly, the airship began to rise.

Two more mageservants became kindling.

"Too slow!" Anton yelled. "We've got to get out of here. They'll use magic—" He turned, grabbed another buckle on the inside of the gondola, hesitated only a moment—then, as the last of the mageservants shattered, opened the buckle; and, in quick succession, all of the other buckles as well.

The ropes on which the sandbags hung fell away, every sandbag plunged to the icy cobblestones, and the airship, like a tethered hawk suddenly set free, shot into the sky.

CHAPTER 14

THE HEALER, WHEN HE CAME, took a look at Karl's feet, ears, and cheeks, then checked his fingers for good measure, grunted, and said, "Going to have a blister on that one ear, nothing serious. Face is okay. Feet, I've got to do something with. Stay still."

Karl did the best he could, though the pain in his feet seemed to intensify rather than ease as the Healer placed his hands on Karl's ankles and closed his eyes in rapt concentration. But then, abruptly, the feeling changed. The pain diminished, replaced by what felt like a furious swarm of angry bees. That, too, dropped off rapidly, and when the Healer finally took a deep breath, released Karl's ankles, and sat down rather heavily on the bed across the room from him, the pain had settled to nothing more than a slight, throbbing ache.

"Thank you," Karl said fervently. Vinthor, who had stood by silently watching the whole procedure, now turned to the Healer.

"Can he walk?"

"Yes," The Healer said faintly. "Probably better than I can for the next minute or two."

"Jopps! Bring some food and a glass of wine for the Healer."

"My thanks," the Healer said.

"As for you, Your Highness," Vinthor said, "it's lucky for

you that you can walk, because whether you can or not, we're heading out."

"Tonight?" Karl quailed at the thought of facing the cold again. "Why?"

"You're the Prince. You're now officially missing. Once Falk twigs, he'll search inside the Barrier . . . and he'll find the boats and the tracks you made. He'll know you somehow came through the Barrier. Which means he'll be searching New Cabora for you next—and the kind of search he's likely to launch is all-too-likely to find you.

"So we're leaving. Tonight." He crouched down and pulled a worn pair of black boots from under his bed. "You're about my size. See if you can wear these." He reached under the bed again and pulled out a pair of not particularly clean-looking woolen socks. "Put these on first."

Gingerly, expecting more pain, Karl pulled on the scratchy socks, then slid his feet inside the scuffed-up footwear. The boots proved to be a big-toe's-length too long, but were far better than nothing.

Vinthor also produced an equally scruffy-looking brown leather coat lined with sheepskin, a knitted woolen cap, and a pair of gloves with holes in the palm. Once he'd put them on over his own clothes, Vinthor examined him critically. "You'll do," he said. "You don't look like the Prince."

"No, he looks like a cutthroat," the Healer put in unexpectedly. "He could get arrested on general principles."

"He looks like far too many Commoners look," Vinthor growled, and the Healer, who was, after all, Mageborn, though obviously a sympathizer to the Cause, wisely held his tongue.

The Healer left shortly thereafter. Vinthor waited another half hour past that, then doused the fires, blew out the lanterns, and led the way into the frosty alley, locking the door behind him. "Horses," he whispered, and that seemed to be enough for Jopps and Denson to know their destination. They moved through the deserted streets of the midwinter night, so dark and still and frigid it was hard to believe the sun would ever warm them again. They kept mostly to back alleys, slinking from shadow to shadow, Vinthor leading the way. Once he stopped at the corner of a dilapidated house and held up a fist. Instantly Jopps' big hand clamped itself over Karl's mouth and Denson seized his arms. He started to struggle, thought better of it, and relaxed. A frozen minute crept by, then another . . . and finally Vinthor lowered his fist. "Patrol," he mouthed, barely audible. "Gone past. This way."

After what seemed an eternity but logically must have been less than an hour—New Cabora simply wasn't that big—they reached the outskirts of the town, where a very unprepossessing inn stood guard at the intersection of two roads that, judging by the lack of either ruts or hoofprints in the snow, and the weeds sticking up through that snow, were seldom used by anyone. The slate roof sagged, but not as much as the porch; the wood had obviously not felt the touch of a paintbrush since before Karl was born, and even the light of the welcome lamp the law required inns to display had a sickly quality, glowing wan and yellow behind the paper used to replace several panes of the front window.

The inn sign hung askew above it. In the urine-colored light, he could just make out the faded image of a fat man holding his apron-covered belly and laughing uproariously. "The Jolly Host," Karl read.

They didn't go into the inn, though. They went around it, into the fenced yard at the back. Here, trampled snow and an unmistakable smell announced the presence of horses, and a third road, which had been much more heavily trafficked, led away through a copse of trees and between two low hills. *The inn's just cover*, Karl realized. *So the Common Causers can come and go unobtrusively.*

Like now. As he watched the horses, all of whom seemed grumpy at being woken (he really couldn't blame them), being saddled and bridled, he thought he should point something out to Vinthor.

"I can't ride," he said.

"What?" Vinthor turned to look at him in disbelief.

"Never had any reason to learn," Karl said. "You can walk around the Lesser Barrier in an hour, and when I've gone into the Commons it's always been in a magecarriage."

Vinthor sighed. "Then you'll have to ride double with Denson . . . he's the smallest. All you'll have to do is hold on. Can you do that?"

Karl nodded.

Riding, he soon discovered, was almost as painful as frostbite . . . though it involved different parts of his body. He jolted and bounced on the saddle, unable to find the rhythm of the horse's stride . . . if it had one . . . as they moved at a trot away from the lights of New Cabora along a road that by the looks of it no one else had traveled all winter. Then they began to gallop, and that seemed better at first . . . better until the cold started to find its way into his coat and boots, resharpening the dull ache left in his feet by the Healer's touch. But there was nothing he could do but hold on to the solid, wiry form of the little man behind whom he rode, and press his face to the back of his coat to keep off the wind.

Karl had no way of knowing how long they rode, alternating galloping, cantering, and walking. But at some point he noticed that he could see more of the other horses riding alongside; and then that he could distinguish the horizon; and then ever-so-slowly after that, dawn broke, the sun poking a semicircle of orange fire above the black rim of the prairie.

Before it had completely cleared the horizon, though, it was hidden again, as they abruptly came to a little valley and followed the road down into its depths.

A house nestled there among willows lining a frozen line of ice that in warmer times would be a stream. Karl realized he must be almost asleep in the saddle, because he first saw the house off in the distance, then blinked and suddenly discovered they were riding into its yard. And then Vinthor and Jopps were helping him down from the horse in the yellow glow of a lantern shining through the windows. He could barely walk, but the light that streamed out of the open door promised shelter and warmth, and that was enough of an incentive for him to force his aching muscles to propel him forward.

He'd expected to find another hard-faced man, some soldier for the Common Cause, inside the cozy farmhouse kitchen; but instead, it was a woman who greeted him, a woman as welcoming and comforting as her house. She said her name, but he didn't hear it, barely noticed as she helped him take off his boots and coat and hat and gloves. He climbed the stairs like an old man, turned to the bed she pointed him to, and two minutes later was blissfully asleep.

———

As the sun set on the day after Verdsmitt's arrest and Prince Karl's disappearance, Lord Falk stood in the central square of New Cabora, on the broad stone base of the larger-than-life bronze statue of some Commoner whose name Falk neither recognized nor cared about. He had sent his guards into the streets an hour ago, rousting people from their homes and the businesses they were just locking up, ordering them to assemble. They stood in silent throngs all around him now, their breath creating clouds of steam that the last orange rays of the sun, finding their way between buildings, slashed through in ever-shifting lines of fire.

Falk gathered his will, drew energy from the air, and tossed skyward a glowing ball that hung over the square. As he spoke, the ball, first cousin to a magelink, amplified his voice, throwing it out across the crowd in a booming, inescapable wave of sound.

"Commoners of New Cabora," Lord Falk thundered. "Last night, an unspeakable criminal act was committed. His Royal Highness Prince Karl, Heir Apparent to the Throne and the Keys of the Kingdom of Evrenfels, was kidnapped."

A murmur ran through the crowd. Falk was not foolish enough to believe it was an entirely disapproving one.

"This follows, of course, the attempt on the Prince's life three days ago. We have strong evidence that the terrorists behind both of these outrages were members of the criminal organization styling itself the Common Cause."

Another murmur, this time of denial; a few muttered "No!", even someone calling "That's the scuttle calling the hearth black!" Falk's eyes narrowed, but he didn't turn to look for the culprit, who would soon see where such petty defiance led.

"We therefore require anyone with knowledge of the Prince's whereabouts, or the method by which he was taken, or the identities and whereabouts of the leaders of the Common Cause, in particular the one known as the Patron, to make themselves and their information known to us."

He glared around at the crowd. The Royal guard hemmed those gathered with a line of blue and silver, insuring there would be no trouble. As reinforcements, Falk had even called in soldiers from the army barracks, their white winter uniforms harder to see among the snowdrifts around the square, stationed to prevent access to or from the surrounding streets.

The guards had shaped the crowd as Falk had commanded, so that to his right there was a large open space between the wall of the watchful guards and the red-brick-and-limestone City Hall with its recently added clock tower, officially opened by Prince Karl just three months ago. That tower, Falk had been told by Brich, boasted the latest Commoner cleverness, mechanical automatons in the shape of men and women and children and animals that emerged with clanging cymbals, jingling tambourines and ringing bells, to mark the passage of time. The Commoners, Brich said, had an inordinate fondness for the clock and City Hall itself, which had just reached the ripe old age of 150 years.

"Lest anyone thinks we are not serious about obtaining

this information," Lord Falk said quietly, "let this prove otherwise."

He had enchanted the object he pulled from his cloak himself, working for an hour to pour into it the necessary amount of energy from the roaring coal-fed fires of the Palace's MageFurnace. It was a simple wooden ball, such as a child might play with, but even through the heavily insulated glove he wore he could feel its deadly cold. It smoked, the very air that touched it condensing like water on its surface, then falling away in a puff of white.

"For every day that the Commoners of New Cabora fail to tell the MageLords what we wish to know about the disappearance of Prince Karl and the leaders of the Common Cause, this will be the fate of a building."

And with an effort of will, he hurled the smoking ball out of his hand, above the wide-eyed faces of the Commoners, over the helmeted heads of the guards and, with a tinkling crash, through one of City Hall's multi-paned windows.

Lord Falk waited just the right amount of time . . . and then exerted the very little bit more will required to activate the magic packed so densely into the ball.

Blue-white light, brighter than the sun, flashed through the windows of City Hall. The windows themselves simply . . . vanished, the wooden frames and glass alike instantly vaporized.

In the aftermath of the flash, the sunlight seemed faded. Gloom gripped the square. And then City Hall . . . collapsed.

The roof went first, falling into the suddenly hollow interior as the beams that had held it crumbled into ash. The walls followed. The tower stood for one moment all by itself, and then collapsed straight down, rock grinding to dust that billowed across the Square. The massive mechanism of the clock hit the stones with a great ringing crash that shook the pedestal on which Falk stood.

Falk heard soft sobs from the crowd of Commoners, then coughs as the dust clouds swept over them. "Every day, another building falls," he said, his voice thundering from the globe overhead. "Every day . . . until someone tells me what I want to know."

He raised a hand and flicked the glowing ball out of existence, then nodded to Captain Fedric. The guards pushed the Commoners out of the way, holding them back as Falk strode between them, back toward the Palace. He would not have been surprised to hear them cursing him, even surging forward to try to get their hands on him, but in fact they stood all but silent, as though numbed by the power he had just demonstrated.

We have been too lenient too long, Falk thought. *This Kingdom belongs to the Mageborn. It's time the Commoners remembered that.*

After what he had just done, he did not think they would forget again anytime soon. He allowed himself a small smile at that thought; a smile that vanished as he crossed the bridge that led from New Cabora into the Palace grounds and saw Brich waiting for him, face pale in the blue magelight glowing above the guardhouse at the bridge's far end.

Falk, seeing him, suspected that just when he thought his very bad day was almost over, it was instead about to get much worse.

"Lord Falk," Brich said as Falk and his bodyguards reached him. "I have . . . disturbing news."

"Why am I not surprised? One moment." Falk turned to Captain Fedric. "Dismiss your men with my thanks."

"Yes, my lord."

As Fedric turned to talk to his men, Falk nodded toward the Palace. "Let's walk." Once out of earshot of the guards, he continued. "Now, Brich. What news?"

"Brenna has fled the manor," Brich said.

Falk prided himself on maintaining a steely composure in the face of almost any provocation, but that simple sentence stopped him in his tracks. "*What?*"

"In the company of Anton, the boy from Outside," Brich continued steadily. "In his flying device."

Falk literally did not know what to say. The disappearance of the Prince was a disruption in the Plan. But the disappearance of Brenna was . . . catastrophic. Without her in his control, ready to be slain at the crucial moment, there *was* no Plan.

"Details," he grated out at last, and resumed walking, much more quickly, toward the Palace.

But of details, it seemed, there was a shortage. Gannick had been aware that the boy was trying to fix the airship, and had thought nothing of it, since that was the task he and the mageservants had been set, though he had made sure that a man-at-arms kept an eye on both Brenna and the boy. But then the back door had suddenly opened and that man-at-arms had been tossed, bleeding and senseless, into the hallway by a mageservant, which had then slammed the door shut.

Gannick had seized his control wand and tried to run out into the courtyard, but a mageservant, obviously under a command to let no one into the yard, attacked him so quickly he couldn't use the wand on it. As he scrambled for safety, he glimpsed Brenna and Anton in the gondola of the airship, which was straining at its ropes. He'd called out the other men-at-arms. The mageservants had been quickly dealt with . . . six destroyed, and despite everything else Falk winced at the thought of how much each of those cleverly made and fiendishly expensive magical marionettes cost . . . but they had given Anton just the amount of time he needed. The airship had shot skyward, "Quick as an arrow," Gannick said, rising so far and fast that it was only a tiny blue dot in the sky in seconds. They had watched it start to drift to the northeast. The men-at-arms had mounted and ridden after it, but the heavy brush and snow in that direction had slowed them to a crawl, and soon they had turned back, defeated.

"Are you certain there is no magic in that device, my lord?" Brich said. "Gannick said they opened the back of a chimney and drew on the heat of the Mage Fire."

Falk snorted. "He needed the hot air, Brich. That's all."

Brich frowned, clearly not understanding, but said nothing.

That suited Falk, who was thinking furiously, picturing a map of the Kingdom. Northeast would take the airship to the Great Lake, this time of year an enormous sheet of windswept ice rather than an inland sea. And northeast of that, if they somehow made it clear across, lay only wilderness, home to the Minik, the native people driven from the South by the arrival of the MageLords eight centuries ago.

What those primitive savages would make of a giant airship dropping into their midst, Falk couldn't imagine.

The trouble was he had no idea how far the airship could go. It had not traveled far in miles from the town Anton had described on the other side of the Barrier before coming down in Falk's backyard, but Falk suspected a lot of that had had to do with the unusual conditions that prevailed above the Barrier. If he understood the airship's principle well enough, it would gradually descend as the air in its envelope cooled. If the burner still worked, they could use it to stay aloft longer, but its reservoir of rock gas was empty and they certainly hadn't been able to fill *that* in Falk's manor. They could throw out ballast for a time to stay aloft, but eventually ...

If he only knew how far it had risen, how fast the winds were blowing, and the rate of descent, he could easily calculate their approximate landing point. But he knew none of those things.

During the last few moments of mutual silence, he and Brich had entered the Palace and were now descending to Falk's office. He waited until they were through the checkpoint and Brich had taken his accustomed place at his desk before giving his orders.

"Call out the army," he said. "Start ..." Again he pictured the map. "They're to start at Moose Leap and move northeast, questioning everyone they can find, adjusting their search as necessary based on whatever sightings of the airship are reported. When they find the airship, they're to secure it and have it transported back here."

"Here, my lord?" said Brich, who had been taking notes using pen and paper, as though he suspected the Commoner-made text-stamper was not something Falk would appreciate at that moment. He was right.

"Yes, here." Falk rubbed his forehead. "I may have use for it. Brenna, when they find her, is also to be brought here. The boy . . ." *Kill him*, he wanted to say, but all the reasons for not killing him remained valid. "Likewise."

"It will be done, my lord."

"And then, Brich, magespeak the manor. Tell Gannick to tell my men-at-arms they are to gently—gently, mind you, but firmly—insist to Mother Northwind that she, too, must come to the Palace. I need her talents."

"Yes, my lord." Brich's pen quit moving across the paper. "Anything else?"

"Yes. Verdsmitt. Has he said anything to his interrogators?"

"Only," Brich said dryly, "that he was sorry they did not appreciate his play and the next time he comes to the Palace, he promises to bring a musical comedy."

Falk smiled tightly. "Davydd Verdsmitt," he said, "believes he is untouchable because harming him will inflame the Commons. After what I have done this evening, Brich, perhaps he will understand that inflammation of the Commons no longer concerns me."

"Shall we make more . . . intense inquiries?" Brich said.

Again, Falk was tempted to say yes, to let loose the torturers. But though torture had its place, he did not place much faith in the information he received from it. Men in agony would say anything to ease that agony, and sometimes they even convinced themselves they were telling the truth, their own memories warped by the pain . . . in which case, even drawing out those memories would be useless.

He did not want Verdsmitt's mind warped. He wanted it crystal clear when Mother Northwind reached inside it.

"No," Falk said. "Stop all inquiries. Let him sit in silence and contemplate his misdeeds ... until Mother Northwind is here."

Brich nodded. He didn't know all of what Mother Northwind was capable of, but he knew enough.

"And Tagaza?" Falk said.

"The First Mage says he will speak only to you, and points out that he serves at the pleasure of the King, not you, Lord Falk," Brich said. "He says you have arrested him illegally and are abusing your authority. The Council has, of course, learned of his arrest and is demanding you account for it at the morning meeting."

"And so I will," Falk said. "After I've had a little chat with my old friend. Issue my orders, Brich."

"Right away, my lord."

Falk took a moment to divest himself of his winter coat and boots in his office, pulling on his indoor boots and making sure every thread was in place on his gray tunic and trousers before heading down the hall to Tagaza's cell ... just across the hall from Verdsmitt's, he noted with grim amusement. No doubt they would have had a lot to say to each other if not for the fact the cells were magically soundproofed to prevent any such communication ... magically, so that the soundproofing could be easily removed if Falk judged it worthwhile to have the sounds from one cell heard by other prisoners.

There was a lot of magic at work in that dungeon. It made it cold enough in the hallway that Falk could see his breath. Some of it held Tagaza's door closed. He reached out and adjusted the spell with his mind, then pushed the door open and stepped inside, closing and locking the door again with a quick magical flick.

The cell, eight feet wide by ten feet long, held a bed, Tagaza, a chamber pot, and nothing else. It had no window, the only light coming from a magelight in the ceiling. Reset once a day, it gradually faded as the day went along until it plunged the cell into pitch-blackness around midnight. Already it had dimmed far enough that the room seemed twilit. Falk gave it a quick boost, flooding the cell with harsh blue light.

"Falk!" Tagaza, tight-lipped, lumbered to his feet. "I have done nothing to deserve this. Have you gone mad? We're only weeks from—"

"Mad?" Falk said coldly. "On the contrary, I believe I am seeing much more clearly than I have for some time."

"I've been working with you for twenty years to bring down the Barriers," Tagaza said. "At the solstice that work will be done. How on earth can you believe I would sabotage two decades' labor this close to its culmination?"

"People change, Tagaza," Falk said. "I have noted for a long time your distaste for the sacrifices we must make to bring down the Barriers. You have grown inordinately fond of both Brenna and our *faux* Prince. And though you have always claimed you share the *goals* of the Unbound, you have *never* shared our reasons. You've claimed to believe that magic is running out, and will fail entirely if we don't bring down the Barriers. My guess is that you have realized you were wrong about that—as I've always said—and so you've decided to sabotage the destruction of the Barriers to save the lives of Brenna and the King. But did you really think I would not put two and two together when I discovered Commoners had found a way to pass through the Lesser Barrier and kidnap the Prince? Only a master magician, steeped in the lore of the Barriers, could accomplish such a thing. Only you, My Lord First Mage."

Tagaza's jaw and fists had clenched, as though he wanted to physically attack Falk. *I'd like to see him try*, Falk thought contemptuously as he glared at the First Mage's broad face. "That's . . . ludicrous," Tagaza said at last, voice tight with anger. "You have no evidence any of that is true. And I do not doubt my belief, Falk. The magic lode beneath this Palace cannot sustain both the Barriers and still meet the needs of the Mageborn forever. In a few more years, if the Barriers stand—"

"No evidence?" Falk snarled. "How many times have

you told me the Lesser Barrier is impenetrable? And yet it *has* been penetrated." Falk stepped closer to the First Mage, who squared his shoulders and glared back. "And there is more. You have long argued for giving the Commoners more say in governing this kingdom. I have heard from more than one source that you have even expressed a wish that there were some way Commoners could use magic, too. And now, it seems, Commoners can. Somehow they have gained access to enchanted weapons, and a key to the Lesser Barrier. Some mysterious, powerful mage has been providing the Common Cause with magical help. That is clearly sedition. It is clearly a threat to Public Safety. And therefore, clearly, the Minister of Public Safety has the authority and duty to arrest that mage. *You.*"

"Falk, listen to yourself," Tagaza said. "Why would I help the Common Cause assassinate the Prince? You just said I had grown too fond of him!"

"But they *didn't* assassinate him, did they? They spectacularly *failed* to assassinate him. You claimed it was incompetence on the part of the mage who crafted the weapons. But no one could be *that* incompetent. I believe rather than a sign of incompetence, it is a sign of *great* competence, by a master mage who knew exactly what he was doing, whose goal was not to kill the Prince but to disrupt plans *involving* the Prince . . . my plans. My *Plan.*

"And then the 'kidnapping.' The Prince left his room on his own, took a boat, rowed it across the lake, and exited the Lesser Barrier in the company of unknown Commoners. Almost as if it weren't a kidnapping at all. Almost as if the Prince had been told to flee . . . by someone who knew what was about to happen." Falk took another step closer, staring down at Tagaza with cold fury. "Confess, Tagaza. Confess willingly, or when Mother Northwind gets here, you will confess *unwillingly.*"

Tagaza held himself very still, eyes searching Falk's face. And then, to Falk's surprise . . . and fury . . . he had the gall to smile. "Bring her," he said softly. "Bring your pet mind-reader, Falk. I welcome her to look inside my mind. In fact," his voice grew stronger, "I *demand* it. *I have nothing to hide!*"

"Nothing?" Falk said. "You will have *no* control over what she gleans from your mind, Tagaza. Do not think that, because you are First Mage, you can stand against her. I have seen her work. You may be a master of hard magic, but she is the master of soft. You will not be able to keep *anything* hidden from her, Tagaza. *Anything.* Even if you are innocent of my specific accusations, is there *nothing* you are guilty of? Is there *nothing* hidden away in your head that you do not want known by me?"

And still the First Mage didn't quail. He met Falk's gaze and said, firmly and clearly, "Nothing."

Falk's eyes narrowed. He hadn't expected that; hadn't expected Tagaza to remain so constant in denial when faced with the threat of Mother Northwind rummaging through his memories. For the first time he doubted his suspicion. *Well,* he thought, *if this is more than simple bravado, there's an easy way for him to prove it.*

"If that is true," he said, "and if you still support the Plan . . . there is a way for you to demonstrate that."

Tagaza turned his head a little to one side and his eyes narrowed. "What?"

"Find Brenna."

Tagaza's eyes shot wide. "Find her? But—"

"She has fled the manor. Use the spell that finds the Heir. Tell me where she is."

Tagaza looked thoughtful. "Even if I do . . . you still won't have Karl."

"I can manage without him if I must," Falk said. "This close to the end, he's almost superfluous. Of course I must continue my aggressive search for him—to remind the Commoners of their proper place, if nothing else—but I am willing to consider the possibility you are telling the truth about not being involved in his disappearance—*if* you find Brenna for me."

"I'll be sentencing her to death," Tagaza said.

"You sentenced her to death when you crafted the spell to bring down the Barriers," Falk said harshly.

Tagaza nodded slowly. He stared at the floor for a moment, as if thinking, then raised his head again, met Falk's gaze, and said, "I will find her. Whatever you may think, Falk, I have never betrayed you. The Barriers must fall. Our reasons for wanting that have always differed. But we still share that goal." His eyes narrowed. "I had thought perhaps we shared a friendship as well," he said softly. "I see I was wrong."

"I don't need friends," Falk said, steel in his voice. "All I need are results." He went to the door, unlocked it, went out, then turned to face Tagaza through it. "I will send for you when I'm ready. Find Brenna, and you will be a free man again ... and I will keep Mother Northwind out of your mind."

"I eagerly await your summons, Lord Falk," Tagaza said, and his voice was as cold as the air in the hallway.

Falk closed the cell door, locked it, and strode away.

———

In the cell across from Tagaza's, the man called Davydd Verdsmitt sat quietly. He was not supposed to be able to hear anything from inside his magically soundproofed cell, certainly not supposed to be able to hear a conversation carried on inside another magically soundproofed cell ... but Davydd Verdsmitt had a great many capabilities he was not supposed to have, and he heard every word.

When Falk had left, he opened his eyes and frowned. His entire purpose in getting arrested had been to position himself inside the Palace, ready to strike when the moment came. But that moment would not come until Brenna was also in the Palace. He had expected Falk to bring her within a day or two. If she were missing ...

Verdsmitt believed deeply in what he had been sent into the Palace to do, both for noble reasons—he truly did want to see the MageLords overthrown, the Barrier cast down, and the Commoners free at last to choose their own destiny—and for far more personal ones. But he would not throw his life away. If Mother Northwind's plan failed, the Common Cause would still need his peculiar skills.

He would wait, he decided, but not indefinitely. He had always had in the back of his mind a secondary plan, one that would not accomplish the great goal of destroying the MageLord's rule, but one that would certainly create havoc enough. If Brenna could not be found, he could still strike hard at the MageLords—one MageLord in particular—and live to carry on the struggle in some other way.

He lay down on his bed again and closed his eyes. Anyone looking in would have thought he was asleep. In reality, he was writing the first act of a new play, though he had to admit the odds were stacked against it ever being performed.

It didn't matter. Davydd Verdsmitt was not his real name, and very little else that everyone thought they knew about him was real, either, but one thing was absolutely true: Verdsmitt was a writer, and a damn good one.

And a good writer never lightly passed over *any* opportunity to work for a long period of time without interruption.

By the time the guards came to Mother Northwind's door, she was ready for them.

She had known, of course, almost as soon as it happened, that Brenna had fled the manor with the boy from Outside. Why she had chosen to run, Mother Northwind didn't know. She had never been inside Brenna's mind, something which suddenly seemed an incredible oversight: why hadn't she insisted, why hadn't Falk insisted, that she make the changes in the girl's mind that would have rendered her absolutely compliant to Falk's wishes?

Because she always seemed compliant without that, Mother Northwind told herself angrily. *Because she was only a little girl. Because I'm a senile old fool and Falk is an idiot. Because . . .*

She took a deep, calming breath.

And also, she reminded herself, because there seemed a risk, however slight, that such manipulation might sever the link between Brenna and the Keys, rendering her an ordinary girl, and not the Heir at all.

She reached inside her own mind to cleanse it of the useless anger aimed at herself, while holding onto the core of cold fury that she had lovingly maintained like a prize rosebush, one with very long thorns, since the long-ago day she watched the MageLords massacre the Minik men, women, and children she had grown to love.

Little girls like Brenna, she thought. And that was another reason she'd never tried to manipulate Brenna's mind. Even though she knew Brenna's life was forfeit to the need to destroy the Barriers, she'd wanted her to at least have her childhood to enjoy, unlike the little Minik girls the Mageborn raped and slaughtered.

The scullery maid who had run all the way from Falk's manor to tell her of Brenna's escape had quailed before her fury that morning, when for a moment it had slipped through the kindly mask Mother Northwind perpetually wore. But she had hidden it at once, and reassured the poor girl that she had done the right thing. Then she had asked after the maid's invalid father, whose heart Mother Northwind had kept going far longer than it would have without her ministrations, and her pregnant sister, and had soon had the girl calmed down and smiling.

Now that she had also calmed herself—though she had no desire to smile—she wondered why Brenna had fled. Had she somehow figured out what was planned for her?

She snorted. *Hardly. She's eighteen years old and a handsome young man just literally dropped into her lap . . . right where she wants him, I'd wager.*

And who could blame her for that? But whether she had meant to disrupt Mother Northwind's plan—or Falk's—or not, that was what she had done, in as thorough and potentially disastrous fashion as she could have managed short of committing suicide.

She has *to be found*, Mother Northwind thought with an unfamiliar hint of desperation. *Verdsmitt is in the Palace. The Magebane is safely tucked away. I need only get Brenna and the Magebane together. Verdsmitt will strike. The Keys will pass to Brenna ... but the Magebane will intercept and destroy them. And since the Barrier is bound up intimately with magic in this kingdom, its power drawn from every hard mage, not only will the Barrier fall, it will drag hard magic down with it.*

They'll all be Commoners then. And we'll see how they like it, when the Commoners are running the show.

But none of that could happen without Brenna. So once again, it seemed, her needs and Falk's ran in tandem, however different the outcomes they desired. Karl's disappearance would be a nuisance for Falk, and he would have to act forcefully against the Commoners—*not that he's at all loath to do so, and I can't wait until he faces his erstwhile victims without the protection of magic.* But Brenna ... for his Plan, as for hers, Brenna was *essential.*

He has to find her, she thought. *And only one man knows how to do that, how to locate the Heir.*

Tagaza.

He'll turn to Tagaza for help. Tagaza will locate Brenna. Falk will bring Brenna back to the Palace. I have to be there to spirit her away to where the Magebane waits.

She had anticipated Falk returning to the manor in a day or two, and then traveling back to the Palace with him, Brenna, and Anton, once she had molded the boy from Outside as Falk had asked (or not *precisely* as he had asked; she had had her own thoughts about the best way to twist the boy's mind, turning him into her weapon instead of Falk's tool, but that was all moot now). Falk would not be coming now, of course, but she was confident he would still want her in the Palace ... to interrogate Verdsmitt for him, if nothing else. *He'll send men for me,* she thought. *Well, it never hurts to be thought omniscient.*

Which was why, when four men-at-arms came quick-marching behind their sergeant up the gully to her door, perhaps two hours after dark, they found her sitting on her front step, a flowered carpet bag containing a few clothes and other essentials on her lap. She reached for her cane and got to her feet as the sergeant called the men-at-arms to a rather startled halt.

"Took you long enough," she said cheerfully. "Well, come on, Sergeant. I've grown tired of the cold and the dark. I think it's time I paid a visit to the Palace, don't you? Always spring inside the Lesser Barrier, they do say." And she set off down the gully at such a pace, despite her cane, that the men-at-arms had to resume quick-marching in order to give her a proper escort.

CHAPTER 15

BRENNA HAD NEVER IMAGINED ANYTHING like the sensation that hurtling skyward in the airship produced. It felt as if she had left her insides behind on the ground, and at the same time was being pushed downward by some strange force. *Magic!* she thought, but, no, there was no magic in that entire incredible device: no magic in the enormous blue silk envelope above them, no magic in the rush of cold air as they soared above Falk's manor. Within seconds she found herself gasping for breath, both from the cold, which had become even more intense, and because she just couldn't seem to get enough air into her lungs . . .

"Air . . . thins . . . with altitude," Anton said, panting as though he had run a race. "Good thing we . . . didn't go much higher or . . . might have passed out." He was peering over the side. "We've found . . . a fast wind . . . making fifty miles an hour, I think."

Thin air? Brenna had never imagined such a thing. Surely air was air, and stretched all the way to the stars. But then, Brenna had never imagined being in the sky before, either, except in dreams of flying. And as for the speed . . . the fastest magecarriage—Falk's—could do twenty miles an hour (though few of the roads allowed that for more than a few minutes), and she found that terrifyingly fast. And yet, up here, she didn't feel like they were moving at all.

With a great effort she heaved herself up and peered

over the side of the gondola. What she saw made her gasp anew, not from lack of air, but from the sheer shock of seeing her world in a whole new way.

The manor was little more than a dot far below and far behind, almost lost in the glare off of the vast snow-covered plain that slipped steadily beneath them and stretched away as far as she could see . . . or almost as far: to the west, her view ended in the Great Barrier. It looked even more immense from up here than it did from the ground, a vast wall of fog disappearing into the distance to north and south . . . but not above.

In fact, she realized with an almost superstitious thrill, she was *above* the top edge of the Great Barrier. Which meant the distant land she could see over there, identical as far as she could tell to the land stretching out to the east, flat and snow-covered, with only occasional copses of trees, was *outside* the Barrier, out in the world she had never even wondered about until Anton had arrived so precipitously in her life.

Anton was looking that way, too. "If only . . . . the wind were from the east," he said despairingly, between heaving gasps of air. "Or we had fuel . . . we could . . . fly out." He looked away from the Barrier, and deeper into Evrenfels. "But we're . . . bound northeast. We might make . . . a hundred and fifty or two hundred miles . . . if the stove works . . . what's . . . out there?"

Brenna still couldn't tear her eyes from the Barrier and the immense sweep of land beyond it. *A whole world free from the likes of Falk and Mother Northwind*, she thought. *A world where no one even believes in magic, much less uses it to terrorize and destroy . . .*

She wished for a moment with all her heart that she *could* fly out of Evrenfels with Anton, leave Falk and his ilk to rot inside the Great Barrier. But they were at the mercy of the wind, and, blowing from the southwest, it was bearing them steadily northeast.

Already they were not quite as high, either, she realized.

She could see less of that land beyond the Barrier. Slowly but surely, it was vanishing.

She glanced at Anton. "A scattering of villages," she said. "And then the Great Lake."

"A lake?" Anton was peering ahead. "How big?"

"Enormous. Like an inland sea."

"We could be over the lake when we run out of altitude," he said, a note of worry in his voice.

Brenna thought what that would mean, descending onto the frozen lake, miles of ice between them and any possibility of shelter or help, and the air suddenly felt even colder.

But there was absolutely nothing they could do about it. They had literally cast their fate to the winds when they launched the airship, and now they could do nothing but wait and see how their cast played out.

Within a few minutes, they were breathing more easily. "We'll be on the ground in less than half an hour if this doesn't work," Anton said, indicating the magecarriage stove. "Guess we'd better find out." He knelt in the bottom of the gondola, gripped the bellows attached to the side of the stove's round belly, and began to pump.

Smoke belched from the chimney and poured up into the gondola. The stove began to roar. Anton, sweat starting on his face even in the cold, kept working the bellows. After a few minutes, the stove began to glow a dull red. Brenna could feel the heat radiating from it where she stood, and only hoped enough was going into the envelope to make a difference.

After five minutes, Anton released the bellows, his breath coming in great clouds of vapor as he let himself fall backward. "Hard . . . work . . ." he gasped. He got up, groaning, went into the stern, and checked the instruments there. "It worked!" he said after a moment. "We're descending much more slowly." He flexed his hands, then stretched his arms out, wincing. "It may kill me, but it works."

An hour went by . . . then two. Every few minutes, Anton worked the bellows. He quit talking altogether, just adding coal to the stove, pumping for as long as he could, sweat running from his increasingly red face, then letting go with a gasp, checking the altitude, and resting silently until it was time to pump once more.

Brenna offered to help, but discovered she simply couldn't work the bellows fast enough. "I'm sorry," she said, gasping, as she let go and got back to her feet.

"Just . . . keep a look out," Anton said, settling himself with a groan before the bellows once more.

Brenna nodded, and retreated to the gondola's rail.

She found the view even more fascinating as the ground grew closer, as it did despite all of Anton's working of the bellows and the roaring of the little stove. They passed over a village, miniature dark roofs and little wisps of chimney smoke slipping silently beneath them. Brenna wondered if anyone down there would look up and see them. She hoped not: Falk would certainly be on their trail and looking for eyewitnesses.

She said as much to Anton, as he rested between battles with the bellows. "But you must have known that from the beginning," he said. "What was your plan for when we landed?"

Brenna said nothing. In fact, she had *had* no plan: just the absolute certainty that they had to flee before Mother Northwind touched Anton again, before Falk returned to take them all to the Palace to further his mysterious Plan to destroy the Barrier, the Plan in which Brenna, unimaginably, somehow had a central role.

"I guess I was hoping we could find a friendly farmer to put us up," she said. "Then . . . I don't know. Flee north, I suppose. Few MageLords venture up there, and the Commoners who do appreciate that. They'd be unlikely to give us away."

"We have no supplies," Anton said. "Nothing but the clothes on our back. No food. No water."

"But at least your mind is still your own!" Brenna snapped. "Anton, I did the best I could. I couldn't get any supplies without making Gannick suspicious. We had to go when we did, as quickly as we did, or we weren't going to escape at all."

Anton said nothing. Then he sighed. "I know," he said. "It's rather ungracious for the rescuee to wish for a better-organized rescue, isn't it?" He shook his head. "None of this is what I expected when the Professor and I set out," he said. "But then, I guess none of us gets a choice in what life throws at us."

"No." Brenna thought of her own circumscribed life as Falk's ward. "No, we don't."

The airship drifted and dropped. Though Brenna couldn't feel it in the gondola, she knew a stiff breeze was scouring the prairie below, sending snow-snakes whipping over the ground, and she welcomed it, its force sending them farther from Falk every passing minute.

When they crossed the western edge of the Great Lake about three thousand feet remained between themselves and the ice, Anton reported. "Maybe we'll make it across yet," he said, settling himself at the bellows one more time. But this time he had hardly pumped a dozen times before the noise of the bellows changed, and he suddenly found his hands moving without resistance. He stopped, leaned over. "Damn," he said. "The bellows have busted. That's that, then."

"Won't the heat keep filling the envelope without the bellows?" Brenna said, looking up at the distended blue silk.

"Some," said Anton. "But not enough. And we've got to throw it overboard, anyway."

"What? Why?"

"It's full of hot coals, Brenna. When we hit, we're going to tip. And then . . ."

Brenna pictured what that could mean, and jumped to her feet.

The mageservants had carried the stove to the airship on a palette with four crisscrossed wooden staves forming handles. Together, she and Anton lifted it, still hot, teetered to the edge of the gondola, and tipped it over the side.

The airship lurched skyward as the weight left it. Brenna, looking down and behind, saw the stove crash to the ice, disappearing in a cloud of steam as it spilled its burning coals. A moment later Anton heaved what was left of the coal over the side, as well.

Anton went forward, Brenna trailing him, and together they gazed out over the ice. Snow blowing and drifting across it obscured the view ahead. They could see nothing but white haze: no sign of the far shore. "At least ice makes for a smooth landing," Anton said, as if to himself.

Brenna remembered the scene she had found when the airship had crashed in the trees outside the manor, Anton hanging from the rigging, dripping blood, the Professor dead in the snow, and swallowed.

They dropped lower and lower, flying in eerie silence broken only by the faint creak of rope against wicker as the gondola swayed. The snow-swept ice beneath them seemed to move faster and faster as they crept ever closer to it. The shadow of the airship, stretched out in front of them as the sun set behind them, grew bigger and longer every second.

"Any minute now," Anton said. He abruptly grabbed a rope, turned, sat down in the gondola, and pulled Brenna down beside him.

"What's the rope?" she said.

"Vent cord," Anton replied tersely, which did nothing to enlighten her.

Brenna had thought it frightening enough being able to see the lake surface rising beneath them. She found it absolutely terrifying to *not* be able to see it, to not know for certain when—

They hit the ice.

The first blow tossed her across the gondola on top of Anton, who pushed her away and gave the rope he held a furious tug. She heard a ripping sound above her.

They must have bounced; they came down again, not as hard. The envelope was deflating above them, and looking up, she saw the big square holes in the top of the envelope and realized that the rope Anton had pulled had opened them, letting the last of the warm air stream out. But the wind had its teeth into them now, dragging them across the ice like a dead rat in the mouth of a cat. The gondola tipped on its side, and only Anton's grip kept them both from tumbling out. She seized his arm with one hand and one of the loops of rope set as handholds inside the gondola with the other. She could hear the ice scraping beneath them, could turn her head and see the dark gray surface rushing by not a foot away. She could see nothing of what lay ahead of them, the envelope, now only a third its former size, still blocking the view. It shrank further, and then, abruptly, collapsed completely. The gondola slid forward into a welter of ropes and blue silk, spun slightly to the right, and then stopped.

Brenna found herself lying on top of Anton. She pushed herself off him, rolled over, and sat up. "Are you all right?" she asked.

He nodded, his face white. She realized suddenly that this second crash in an airship must have been even more frightening for him than for her. "I'm . . . fine," he said. "And I think the airship is undamaged, too." He gave her a crooked smile. "The Professor used to say any landing you could walk away from is a good one." The smile faded. "Neither one of us walked away from the last one. So this is definitely an improvement."

"Let's see where we are." Brenna scrambled out of the gondola, and stood up. She found herself facing southwest, staring along the long gray track the gondola had made as it had scraped snow from the ice.

Then she looked the other way.

They'd been closer to land than she'd thought. Just at the limit of visibility rose a line of spruce, shadows in the blowing snow.

And then a piece of shadow detached itself from that line. It rushed toward them, taking shape as it drew nearer, until she recognized it a sled drawn by a team of dogs.

"Company," Anton said from behind her. "Friendly?"

Brenna moved closer to him. "We'll know soon enough."
Silent, they stood and waited for the dogsled to arrive.

Karl woke to find himself lying, fully clothed, in a strange bed. He felt a moment of panic, trying to remember where he was . . . then the events of the previous night came rushing back and he sat up.

He had a terrible taste in his mouth, an urgent need to relieve his bladder, and a strong desire for fresh clothes: those he wore had a definite horsiness to them.

In the Palace, he had an enchanted chamber pot that instantly whisked all wastes away in a flash of blue light. The cracked porcelain pot he found under the bed . . . didn't. But it served the purpose. He closed it and put it at the foot of the bed, not knowing what else to do with it.

Then he went to the door and tried to open it. Rather to his surprise, it swung wide.

He'd had only a confused impression of the house the night before. He remembered climbing the stairs, and there they were, leading down; but he hadn't noticed that this upper hallway went on a lot farther than he would have thought from the way the house looked from outside. There was no one around, and though hunger was now clamoring for a place at his mental table, he told it firmly to wait and went exploring instead.

He quickly figured out how the trick was accomplished. The farmhouse wasn't just nestled against the hillside, as he had noted when they'd ridden up, it was *attached* to the hillside, the corridor extending not just under the slate roof that showed outside, but through an open door that (Karl confirmed) looked like a wall when it was closed. *A secret door, a secret hallway,* he thought. *I could be in one of Verdsmitt's mystery plays.*

He walked into the underground portion of the hall. There wouldn't be much point of a secret hallway if there weren't also a secret exit out of it, and sure enough, at the end of the hall another door opened into a narrow staircase he presumed climbed up to the top of the hill . . . though he could only presume it because, in the chamber at the bottom of those stairs, Jopps and Denson sat playing cards by the light of a lantern, a handful of small coins spread on the table between them. They glanced up.

"Um," said Karl. "Just exploring."

"Not this way, you're not," said Denson. He tossed a card on the table; Jopps swore and threw down his own cards. Denson scooped up the coins.

"That's ten gelts you've won off me," Jopps complained. "I'm beginning to think you're cheating."

"If I were cheating," Denson said, "I'd have won a hundred by now."

"What time is it?" Karl asked.

"Couldn't tell you," Jopps said cheerfully. "But getting on toward sunset, I'd say. You've slept the day away."

Sunset! By now Falk would know Karl was missing. He'd probably even discovered that he'd gone through the Barrier . . . into the Common part of New Cabora.

Which means he'll take it out on the Commons, Karl thought uneasily. *That's why they wanted me out of the city. But what will he do?*

"Where's Vinthor?" he said.

"Downstairs sipping wine with our host, I shouldn't wonder," Denson growled. "While we're stuck up here with each other."

"Shut up and deal," Jopps said. "At least we're inside. Them that are outside are envying us right about now."

Denson shrugged. "There is that." He shuffled the cards and started dealing.

Karl went back down the hidden corridor, into the "real" corridor, and down the stairs. Vinthor, it turned out, was *not* sipping wine with the matronly woman who had greeted Karl last night. In fact, he was nowhere to be seen. The woman was there, though, knitting by the fire; when she saw him she immediately put the needles and yarn aside. "And there you are, you poor frozen duckling," she said. "I won't ask if you slept well, since here it is getting dark again already and you just getting out of bed." She reached out to tweak his rumpled clothes, tsking. "And you slept in your clothes. I should have undressed you while I was about it, poor lamb."

Karl didn't know how to respond to *that*. "I am grateful, Madame . . . ?"

"Oh, don't bother with the Madame, sweetie-pie." The woman smiled. "Goodwife is good enough for me. Goodwife Beth."

Karl blinked, not sure she was serious. Goodwife Beth was the name of a character from *The Farmer's Mother*, a Verdsmitt one-act that was very popular with amateur actors because of its broadly comic characters. And now that he thought about it, Goodwife Beth in the play also called people "duckling" and "lamb" and "sweetie-pie." Even the most inappropriate people, like powerful MageLords.

He laughed, suddenly. He couldn't help it. *And Princes,* he thought.

Goodwife Beth—obviously that was no more her real name than Vinthor's was Vinthor—smiled. "Does my heart good to hear you laugh, and you so pale and frozen when you came in last night. Well, it looks like no permanent harm was done, honeybuns. Are you hungry?"

"Starved," Karl said. "But . . . I'd prefer some clean clothes, first. If there are any."

Goodwife Beth looked him over with a critical eye. "I dare say I've got something your size. Come along."

She led him into a main-floor bedroom whose most impressive feature was an enormous four-poster bed. She ignored the beat-up old wardrobe in the corner, instead moving aside a rug and pulling open a trapdoor beneath it. She disappeared down a ladder, and emerged a moment later with a handful of clothes. *Stores for the Common Cause's agents,* he thought. *I wonder what else is down there?*

Goodwife Beth showed no inclination to give him a

tour. She closed the door firmly behind her, then unrolled the rug over it again. She spread the clothes out on the bed; she'd brought up three shirts, two pairs of pants, even clean underwear—at least, he hoped it was clean. She held up the first shirt, tossed it aside, then held up the second and nodded. "There you are, moppet. Try that one on for size."

She waited expectantly. Feeling a little awkward, Karl pulled his own sweat-stained shirt over his head. "My, what a well-built young man you are, chickadee," Goodwife Beth said.

Karl felt himself blushing from forehead to navel, and quickly started pulling the shirt over his head. It was only half on when Vinthor stormed into the room. "That bloody bastard Falk has—" He stopped on seeing Karl, but only for an instant. "You'd better be worth it, you stupid, useless whelp!" Karl jerked the shirt down over his head and stepped back, bumping into the wardrobe, as Vinthor advanced on him. "Do you know what your rutting Minister of Public Safety has done?" He jabbed a finger at Karl. "Leveled New Cabora City Hall. And says he'll destroy another building every day until someone tells him where you are. New Cabora City Hall has stood for almost two centuries. You've only been around for two decades. We should have killed you like poor Jenna tried to do. But, no, I went and asked the Patron!" He suddenly snarled and drew back his fist, and Karl threw his arms over his face . . . but the blow never landed.

"As you were required to do," said Goodwife Beth, and she no longer sounded at *all* like the comic character from Verdsmitt's play. Vinthor froze, fist cocked, as the tone registered. Then he dropped his hand and turned. Karl lowered his own arms and straightened, looking past him. Goodwife Beth seemed somehow to have gotten both taller and a lot . . . harder.

"Goodwife . . ."

"The Patron needs this young man alive more than the Patron does you," Goodwife Beth said. "Which means you are to defend him to the death, if it comes to that. Do you have a problem with those orders?"

Vinthor's face had gone somehow solid, as though it were carved out of marble. "No, ma'am."

"I'm glad to hear it. And so will the Patron be, when next we speak." And then, suddenly, the iron vanished, hidden away behind the smiling face of the simple farm woman who had welcomed Karl to her house the night before. "Now, then," she said to Karl, "you just go ahead and try on those trousers and underwear. And don't worry, mooncalf. I'm not going to stay and watch." With a warm chuckle, Goodwife Beth bustled out of the room.

Vinthor gave Karl another hard look, but didn't speak. Instead, he followed Goodwife Beth out.

Karl pulled off his trousers and drawers, and quickly pulled on the clean ones he'd been provided. They fit perfectly. Goodwife Beth, he'd wager, had sized up more than one young man in her life. Whatever she was, or had been, she was definitely *not* just a simple farm woman.

And a good thing, too, or he might be lying on the floor spitting out teeth . . . or worse.

Falk destroyed City Hall? Karl thought. That seemed extreme even for him. Especially since he had to know Karl had left his room of his own free will and certainly wasn't "kidnapped," whatever he was telling the Commoners. *There's something else going on. He's worried about something . . . something big. Something I don't know anything about.*

He gazed around the simple room, so different from his grand quarters back in the Palace. *And something I am unlikely to find out anything about.*

He remembered thinking the Lesser Barrier was just one big prison, and longing to escape it. Now it seemed he had simply fled one prison for another, much smaller one.

But things were moving, out there in the big world. Falk was at the center of it, along with Davydd Verdsmitt . . . Tagaza . . .

. . . and this mysterious Patron.

It was like being buffeted from all directions by gusts of

wind, seemingly unconnected . . . but all harbingers of a much greater storm to come.

Stuck in Goodwife Beth's not-at-all-what-it-appeared farmhouse, it seemed all he could do was wait for the storm to break.

Well, he thought, *at least there's no reason to face it hungry*; and off he went to find something to eat.

CHAPTER 16

TAGAZA SPENT AN ALMOST-SLEEPLESS NIGHT
in his cell after Falk left him. He'd known Falk was ruthless
and utterly determined that his Plan succeed; he just had
never really expected to be on the receiving end of that
ruthlessness.

More than a quarter of a century we've known each other,
he thought. *I discovered how to bring down the Barrier. I
brought him that information. I've helped him every step of
the way. And yet on the flimsiest of circumstantial evidence,
he was ready to believe I would throw all that away.*

It was his own fault, he thought as he lay on the narrow
cot, staring up into the dark. He had been honest with Falk
when they were just starting out, and honest since. He'd
made it clear his reasons for wanting the Barriers removed
were not the same as the Unbound's. He'd thought that
didn't matter, as long as they both shared that ultimate
goal. But that was why Falk had been so quick to mistrust
him. *Falk doesn't believe magic will fail if the Barriers remain,* he thought bitterly. *I explained everything I've found,
but there is no room within the belief system of the Unbound
for magic that is a limited resource, like . . . like coal, or lum-
ber. They think they will always have magic, whenever they
need it, as much as they need. They think they can count on
using it to conquer the lands Outside the Great Barrier.*

But they're wrong. And now Tagaza was glad he had not
been *entirely* honest with Falk. For there was one thing his

research had uncovered that he had never shared with Falk, for fear *Falk* would be the one to decide the Barriers should remain in place: the First Twelve, while searching for the lode on which the Kingdom was centered, had found no other lodes of similar power anywhere else in the world.

Tagaza had a theory about that, too. The Unbound believed that the SkyMage had created the Mageborn to rule over the obviously inferior Commoners, that their ability to use magic was a sign that they were favored by the Creator.

But Tagaza did not believe in the SkyMage, or any other supernatural being. Tagaza believed that the Mageborn had appeared simply because their ancestors were the first people to settle the land above the great lode of magic at the heart of the Old Kingdom. Over time, the magic power surrounding them had changed them, altered them, generation by generation, until they could draw on its power and use it to change the world around them.

His theory was bolstered by the fact, otherwise inexplicable, that at rare . . . very rare . . . intervals, a child born to Commoner parents was found to have magical ability: to be, in fact, a brand-new Mageborn. This had historically been a matter for great rejoicing, both on the part of the Mageborn and the Commoner parents, whose child was then assured of being lifted out of servitude: although the rejoicing was tempered by the fact that the child was then promptly taken from its parents and raised by Mageborn surrogates. (Some Commoner parents had tried to hide their children's ability when it manifested, usually about the same time they started to talk; such deception was, of course, punishable by death.)

In any event, as far as the First Twelve had been able to determine there were no other lodes of magic anywhere in the world except for the site of the Old Kingdom . . . and the one deep beneath the Earth below Tagaza right now.

Why that should be so, no one knew. Tagaza leaned toward the theory that magic had arrived from outside the world, that it belonged to some other world, some alternate world invisible to this one but somehow close at hand, and had somehow leaked between the barrier hiding the one from the other: but that was just idle speculation, since there was absolutely no evidence one way or the other.

In any event, the scarcity of magic outside the two known lodes of it meant, Tagaza suspected—but had never dared suggest to Falk—that if the Unbound escaped the Great Barrier and set out on a war of conquest against the supposedly defenseless Commoners of the Outside, their conquest would be short-lived indeed, for they would soon find themselves outside the regions in which magic could be easily drawn upon.

What Tagaza had argued with Falk was that the best course for the Mageborn to follow was not to use their magic for conquest when the Barriers fell, but only to defend themselves. Best of all would be for them to seek cooperation with the Commoners. Surely both cultures had a lot to offer each other.

As Falk had just thrown in his face as evidence of his perfidy, Tagaza had long advocated a gentler approach to the Commons, pointing out that the Commoners greatly outnumbered and were outbreeding the Mageborn, and that reforms aimed at placating the Commoners were therefore only prudent.

Falk had rejected those arguments, too. And if he had now destroyed City Hall, and was threatening even more retribution for Karl's disappearance . . . then the opportunity for greater cooperating between Commoners and Mageborn had quite possibly passed forever.

And it was that that particularly kept Tagaza awake that long night before Falk's expected summons in the morning. Because whichever way he looked, he saw disaster looming.

If he failed to find Brenna, or if she were dead, Falk's plan would fail, the Barriers would not fall, magic would dwindle away . . . and the Commoners would take their revenge.

If he did find Brenna, and Falk succeeded in his Plan,

and brought down the Barrier, but then pushed aggressively into the outside world, he would soon run into the limits of magic. The Outsiders would defeat the Kingdom . . . and this time, there was nowhere for the Mageborn to flee.

Falk's summons came very early in the morning: the cell's magelight, reacting to the impending day outside the dungeon, had barely begun to glow. But Tagaza was awake. "Hello, Charic," he said to the Royal guardsman who opened the cell door. "Time to attend Falk, I presume?"

Charic had been in the Magecorps before joining the guard; he'd once accompanied Tagaza on his annual inspection trip to the Cauldron. He half-smiled, looking a little shamefaced. "Yes, First Mage," he said. "I'm to put the manacles back on you, if you don't come willingly." He looked down at his feet. "I'd really rather not."

Tagaza sighed. "No need," he assured the guard. "I told Falk I would do what he asked, and so I will. I presume we're going to the Spellchamber?"

"Yes, First Mage."

Tagaza smiled. "Shall I lead the way, or will you?"

Charic laughed. "Perhaps you should, First Mage. So I can follow and make sure you don't run away."

Tagaza chuckled. "Charic, have you ever seen me run *anywhere*?"

"No, First Mage," Charic admitted, still grinning. "This way, then."

"This way" led up stairs, down one of the long corridors running down the middle of each wing of the Palace, to the Grand Entrance, and then up more stairs, climbing, climbing, Tagaza having to stop halfway, puffing. He gave Charic a rueful smile, then resumed climbing.

At last they reached a great hallway, wide and curving, following, he knew, the outside wall of the dome that was the Palace's central feature. Through two doors of beaten silver, and . . .

The Spellchamber. Tagaza, still breathing hard, stood just inside the doors, looking up at the high domed roof, decorated with silver stars and golden comets in a painted sky of deepest blue. Here a mage could draw most easily on the energy of the roaring fires of the MageFurnace far below. Few magics required that much power, but the spell Tagaza would use to locate Brenna certainly did. More typically, the Spellchamber was used when there was a need to fine-tune the weather or the course of the magical sun within the Lesser Barrier, perhaps two or three times a year. The rest of the time it stood empty.

But it wasn't empty today. Falk already stood there, waiting. "First Mage," he said coldly. "How kind of you to come."

"How kind of you to invite me," Tagaza answered, tone equally icy. He looked up at the magelights in the ceiling, and willed them to glowing blue life. Their illumination made the ceiling seem darker and set the silver-and-gold decorations sparkling.

The room was uncomfortably warm. All around the edges of the dome were vents which could be opened to make it hotter still, to counteract the deep chill the magic worked there would produce, even though the bulk of the energy would be drawn from the MageFurnace.

A warning tale told to young Mageborn studying at the College of Mages recounted the fate of a mage who worked a mighty spell in an enclosed space and was discovered in the morning frozen solid. The tale was so well known that a popular students' pub was called The Frozen Mage.

"You may go," Falk said to Charic. Charic saluted and left, closing the silver doors behind him.

Tagaza walked past Falk to the center of the room, where what looked like a circular pedestal emerged from the floor. He could feel heat radiating from it. It was, in fact, a pipe, driven through the heart of the Palace, straight down into the fires of the MageFurnace. A bit of magic . . . a substantial bit of magic, actually . . . kept the exhaust gases from pouring up that pipe into the dome, venting them instead through the Chimneys, located a few miles to the east of New Cabora. All the MageFurnace's wastes were likewise dealt with. After centuries, the Chimneys had become a vast, blighted wasteland of smoke and ash where nothing grew.

A metal cap on top of the pipe gave it its pedestal-like appearance. Sliding open that cap would simultaneously open the hot-air vents along the outer wall of the chamber.

Tagaza turned his back on it to face Falk. "Before I begin this," he said, "it might be helpful if you told me more about Brenna's escape. Do you have any idea where she might be now? So that I know approximately where to look first."

"Northeast of the manor," Falk said. "Quite likely in the vicinity of the Great Lake, or even on it."

Tagaza blinked, startled. "How did she get that far in such a short time?"

"You don't need to know that," Falk said. "Prove your loyalty by finding her, and then, perhaps, I'll tell you. But not yet."

Tagaza shrugged. "All right." He turned back toward the pipe, closed his eyes, and reached inside himself for the immensely complex spell he was about to attempt, made more complex by the fact it had been developed by a previous First Mage, and reflected his personal idiosyncrasies.

Magic of this strength required fierce concentration. A slip of the mind could send the spell awry, and with the energies involved, that could be catastrophic. In fact, one of the functions of the Spellchamber was to contain the damage should that happen.

Damage to the Palace, that was; the damage to those within the chamber would just be too damn bad.

Tagaza had no fear that his spell would go catastrophically awry. Whether it would actually *work*, of course, was a different matter, because he had never attempted it before.

It was a brilliant piece of theoretical work, though, he had to admit, even though it wasn't *his*. First Mage Cassik, who had served Queen Castilla, whose inheritance of the Keys had disrupted the dynasty of Falk's family, had theorized that since the Great Barrier drew a little bit of magic from every Mageborn in the Kingdom all the time, it should be possible to trace those threads of magic to an individual.

In practice, he had found it impossible to differentiate one ordinary Mageborn from another in that vest web of magic: but the Heir was different. Linked as he or she was in two directions, to the Barrier, and to the King, the Heir must, of necessity, be a conduit for a much greater share of the Barrier's energy, and so the Heir's thread stood out like a thick cord among threads of gossamer.

Tagaza finished forming the spell in his mind. To him, spells were like complex patterns of light that he visualized, then let pour out into the world through his hands. This pattern was horrendously complex, and he was hardly conscious of his physical actions as he held it in his mind's eye and stepped up onto the low stair that surrounded the pipe.

Falk reached out and pulled the lever that opened the cap and, with a great grinding noise, all the vents along the wall.

Heat roared out of the pipe into Tagaza's face . . . and vanished as he released the pattern in his mind through the hands he had thrust into the uprushing column of scorching air.

He felt as if he had suddenly grown enormous, as though his body, insubstantial as a ghost, had exploded in size, swelling out through the walls of the Palace, across the city, across the Kingdom, his head soaring higher and higher until he could look down on everything within Evrenfels.

The Great Barrier blazed in his mind, a huge silver circle. Like the circle of the Unbound, Tagaza thought with a remote part of his mind that was not caught up in the power of the spell. But still unbroken . . . for now. The Lesser Barrier, on this scale, was a single white pearl of light at the very center of the Great Barrier's vast circumference.

And then, suddenly, a web of power exploded in his vision, streams of light, all colors of light, red, blue, gold, green, pouring out from the Palace, from the city, from everywhere there were Mageborn, pouring into the Great Barrier: and it no longer appeared silver, but was an ever-shifting, intertwined mass of color, like an impossible bright aurora brought to Earth. *It's beautiful*, he thought, his heart aching with it. *It's so beautiful* ...

But he wasn't there to sightsee. He began searching for the thread of power from the Heir, thicker, brighter than all the others ... and Falk had given him some idea of where to look.

The Great Lake. It was easy to distinguish in his mental view of the Kingdom. He could see no physical terrain, of course. For all it felt as if he were standing high over the Kingdom looking down at it, he was really still trapped in his physical body, and his "vision" was only his mind's way of making sense of the information it was receiving from his magical senses. But he knew the map of the physical Kingdom as well as he knew the layout of his own bedroom, and in his mind, he could superimpose it on the magic he sensed. Toward the northeast, there were very few Mageborn. Those small clusters had to be the villages of Westwind and Pelican Nest on the western shore, the threads of their handful of Mageborn residents adding to the weft and warp of the Barrier.

Go farther northeast, and you were in the Great Lake, and farther northeast still, and there was only wilderness, home to the Minik and no one else, until you reached the Great Barrier again. And it was there, in that great blank expanse, somewhere on the lake but near the northeastern shore, Tagaza judged, that he found one final thread of magic. He peered closer, willing his magical eye to focus as sharply as possible on it ... and saw at once that it was different from all the others: white rather than colored, thicker, brighter.

There could be no doubt. It belonged to the Heir. It belonged to Brenna. And she was on the Great Lake.

And then, as though from a great distance, he heard an enormous roar ... and an instant later was hurled back from the pipe by a screaming blast of scalding-hot steam, erupting from far below.

His mental image of the Kingdom and the Heir's whereabouts vanished, brutally severed from him along with his magical senses. The spell he had carefully constructed, the spell drawing on vast amounts of magic from the magic lode and vast amounts of energy from the Mage-Furnace, collapsed in ruin and blazing agony inside his head . . .

. . . and took his consciousness with it.   •

The pillar of steam erupting from the pipe blew Falk flat on his back, and hurled Tagaza away like a rag doll, to lie in a crumpled heap on the marble floor. The deep chill that had gripped the room as Tagaza worked vanished in the same instant. The temperature began to climb. Falk, staring up at the boiling mass of steam beginning to fill the room, realized that in moments he and Tagaza would be so much cooked meat.

He lunged at the First Mage and dragged him toward the closed doors, throwing his will against them so hard they burst from their hinges and smashed into the far wall, one striking a glancing blow on Charic, spinning him around with a shout of pain, clutching his broken arm. Falk instantly realized his mistake; the steam would soon fill the hallway outside the chamber as well. With another surge of will, he blew out every one of the tall windows set between fluted pillars that encircled the dome. Steam rushed out through the gaps. Coughing and stumbling, Falk dragged the unconscious Tagaza to the stairs, Charic staggering after him, clutching his arm, leaving a trail of blood behind: the bone had punctured the skin.

Leaving Tagaza slumped in the stairwell for the moment, Charic sitting beside him, bleeding, Falk ran down the stairs, emerging into chaos, servants and Mageborn rushing around like frightened quail. Falk grabbed the first servant who passed, a teenage girl. "Get a Healer," he ordered. "Send him up the stairs to tend to the First Mage and the guard he'll find there." The girl gave him a frightened curtsy and hurried off.

Falk ran the other way—to a different stairway whose broad steps descended to the MageFurnace. Mingled steam and smoke poured up those stairs, and before he reached them, men began to boil up them as well: men with reddened skin and terrible burns, coughing, slumping against the white marble walls of the central chamber as soon as they were clear of the stairs.

Falk saw Healers arriving at a run and hoped that fool of a girl had been smart enough to send one to minister to Tagaza. He knelt by the nearest man, who seemed shaken but unhurt. "What happened?" he demanded.

"Water," the man choked. "I don't know where it came from. A flood of water, pouring into the Furnace . . ."

"Sabotage," said a voice from behind Falk, and he straightened and spun to see Brich, grim-faced.

"Sabotage? How?"

"Someone," Brich said, "found a way to direct the waters of the lake into one of the Furnace's air intakes."

"*Who?*" Falk snapped.

"We've had . . . a communication," Brich said. "From the Common Cause. They claim responsibility. They say it's in retaliation for the destruction of City Hall. They say they will do far worse if the 'repression of the Commons' is not eased."

"They don't know what repression is," Falk snarled. "But they're about to find out. I want a platoon of guards ready at the bridge in twenty minutes. We're going back to the Square."

Brich looked like he was about to say something, but, wisely, did not. Instead he just nodded and turned away.

Anger such as he'd rarely felt blazed in Falk's heart. Not only had these Commoner criminals disrupted life in the Palace—temporarily, he thought with a mental sneer; the MageFurnace could not be doused so easily, and would soon be blazing at full power again—but, more importantly, they had disrupted the search for Brenna. And that meant that, once again, they had interfered with the Plan.

Falk was getting very tired of things interfering with the Plan.

He couldn't do anything about locating Brenna . . . but he could do something about Commoner interference.

And he would take great pleasure in it.

He turned his back on the wounded men and the Healers tending them, and headed for the bridge into New Cabora.

CHAPTER 17

AS THE DOGSLED APPROACHED, Brenna reached out and gripped Anton's hand. He squeezed back, and so, hand in hand, they awaited the arrival of their discoverers.

The dogsled told her nothing. This time of year, it was the preferred method of travel, for Commoners, at least, between scattered villages, especially up here, where roads were nonexistent. The three figures on it, two riding, one driving, all heavily swathed in fur, revealed nothing more at first glance. She wished *she* had that much fur to wear; her own winter coat, which she had always thought so warm, had felt like a thin wrap in the airship and felt like nothing at all now they were standing on the windswept ice. *Whoever they are, if they don't help us, we'll freeze to death*, she thought.

Oddly enough, it was the dogs that gave her the first clue as to what sort of people were coming to meet them, and the realization made her squeeze Anton's hand harder.

He turned to look at her. His eyebrows were rimed with ice and his cheeks as red as though they'd been scalded. "What is it?"

"The dogs," Brenna said. "They're wearing jewelry."

It sounded absurd, put like that, but she didn't know what else to call the collars set with bits of silver and glass and semiprecious stones that each dog wore. They made the animals' necks sparkle as, tongues lolling, they raced toward them.

"So?" Anton said.

"Savages," Brenna said, and then said nothing more, because then the dogsled was upon them, the driver shouting to the dogs to stop and pulling a lever that jammed spikes into the lake surface to slow the sled. It ground to a halt in a flurry of snow and ice chips, skidding sideways a little. Even before it quit moving, the two fur-swaddled men aboard it had hit the ice and raised the crossbows they carried.

"Minik," Anton said under his breath, and then, raising his voice, said something in a language Brenna had never heard before, lilting and fluid, like the call of some wild forest songbird.

The crossbows lowered a little, the men's faces, brown and shiny—smeared with some kind of grease as a protection against the cold, she realized—startled and puzzled.

The driver had jumped down from the back of the sled and came forward. The two other men stepped aside so he could stand between them. He gave Anton an appraising look, and said something in the same fluid tongue.

Anton frowned, then replied haltingly.

The man's eyebrows lifted. He spoke to the other two men, who nodded and lowered their crossbows completely.

Then the man turned to Brenna. "I am High Raven, leader of the clan of the Three Rivers." He spoke the common tongue flawlessly, his accent, though odd, easier to understand than Anton's had been at first. "The boy says he is from Outside the Wall of Sorrows. This is a thing I find hard to believe, but we will test him to see if he tells truth. He says you are a great princess of the MageLords. Is this true?"

Brenna shot Anton a look. He blushed. "Not quite what I was trying to say, Chief High Raven."

"I am not a Chief," High Raven said. "I am a clan leader." He regarded Brenna steadily. "Then you are not a great princess?"

"No," Brenna said. "I'm a Commoner. But a MageLord has been my guardian."

"Has been?"

"He is a monster," Brenna said. "I escaped him."

"In this." High Raven indicated the airship, the blue silk stretched out across the ice like a giant snake, here and there rippling a little in the wind.

"Yes."

"It is a thing of the Outside World," Anton said. "It's called an airship."

High Raven turned and looked back at the shoreline, then at the setting sun. "We will have to hurry if I am to send men enough to bring this thing to the camp before darkness. Let us ride the sled together, and when we are warm around the fire in the longhouse tonight, you will tell me what I wish to know."

A few minutes later Brenna found herself seated, more or less comfortably, on the flat wooden base of the sled. Anton sat on the other side, his back to her. High Raven sat on the end, his back to them both. One of the men had taken his place as driver; the other had remained with the airship as a guard.

The roar of the sled's runners on the ice made it impossible to talk, which suited Brenna fine. She stared at High Raven's broad-shouldered back. A savage. A savage chief . . . clan leader, whatever. How many Commoners had he killed, how many farms had he pillaged?

She pulled herself up short. She didn't know he had done anything of the sort. But it was hard to think of him in any other light when all she had to go on were the many tales she had heard as a child of the Minik, the Savages of the North.

In most of those stories they were faceless villains, bloodthirsty denizens of the forests who emerged in the middle of the night to terrorize innocent villagers. Occasionally they were presented more like ghosts, elemental spirits that resented the creation of the Great Barrier and in the guise of men took their revenge. She did remember one story in which a young Commoner girl and a Minik boy made friends, but it had ended badly with the boy reverting to his bloodthirsty nature and a noble MageLord being forced to kill him to save the girl's life—and more importantly, it was implied, her maidenhood.

None of those stories had prepared her to come face-to-face with one of the savages herself. Especially one that didn't sound like a savage at all and spoke her language as well as she did.

And how did Anton know *their* language?

Well, she supposed she'd find out soon enough. And it wouldn't do to assume that High Raven was a murderous, almost supernatural villain like the savages of the children's stories.

No, that wouldn't do at all.

The dogsled fairly flew over the ice, and in short order they reached solid ground . . . as opposed to solid water, she supposed. Frozen reeds sticking out of the ice crunched as they slid over them, then they bounced upon onto the bank and rushed into the forest, flying between tall pines on a barely-there track that the dogs seemed to know well.

Perhaps five minutes later they emerged from the trees into an open area dotted with huts, smoke rising from holes atop their dome-shaped roofs. A tall bluff, its exposed face a pebbly conglomerate, sheltered the camp from the north. A stream, frozen solid, wound along the south edge and bent around the bluff out of sight a short distance to the east.

Most of the huts were made of hides, shaped on a frame, but in the center of the camp rose something much larger and longer constructed of logs, caulked with clay and roofed with pine branches.

"You will wait in the longhouse as our guests," High Raven said. "I must see to the retrieval of your . . ." he nodded at Anton, "airship."

Brenna was glad, as the man who had been driving drew his crossbow and escorted them toward the longhouse, that High Raven had specified that they were guests. Otherwise she would have felt a great deal like a prisoner.

Inside, the longhouse felt deliciously warm. A fire

burned in a pit at its center, fed a new log periodically by a toothless old woman who gave them a hard look as they were brought into the dim interior.

"Wait," their guard said, and went out again. Brenna looked around. Large logs encircled the fireplace, obviously meant as benches, and she sat down on one. Anton sat beside her. The old woman moved to the far side of the fire.

"Why did you—" they both said at once, turning toward each other at the same instant, and Brenna, despite everything, laughed, Anton echoing her a moment later. The old woman leaned over to one side to get a better look at them around the fire, shook her head, then leaned back again . . . which for some reason only made them laugh louder.

The laughter died quickly. Anton, though, still smiled as he said, "You first."

"Why did you call them Minik?" Brenna said. "How did you know that's what they're called?"

"Because I know many of them," Anton said. "Back home, we call this the Wild Land, but it belongs to the Minik. The Union Republic has negotiated treaties allowing us to settle here and there. We conduct a lot of trade with them."

"That's why you know their language?"

Anton nodded. "When the Professor told me we were coming here, he made me learn their language. It's only polite," he said. Sadness briefly clouded his face, then he smiled a little. "I turned out to be a much better speaker than he was. He almost got us beaten up in an inn one night when he garbled a request for cheese toast."

"What did he really ask for?" Brenna said.

Anton shook his head. "You don't want to know. Now, my turn." He met her gaze squarely. "Why did you call them savages?"

"It's . . . what we call them," Brenna said, and suddenly felt ashamed. They obviously weren't savages. That was MageLord talk, treating everyone else as somehow lesser than themselves. Commoners, savages . . . all just subjects to be used and abused at will. "I've never actually seen one before. They were all driven out of the South when Evrenfels was established."

"They have stories about those days, you know," Anton said. "In the Outside, I mean. Stories of the day when 'the sky exploded and the ground burned and the People died.' And then stories about the sudden appearance, between sunset and dawn, of the Wall of Sorrows that separated friend from friend, clan from clan, family from family, children from parents." Anton gazed into the fire. "The Professor made a study of those stories. He thought the Anomaly had some cosmic origin. 'Who knows what strange forms of matter may exist out among the stars?' he used to say to me. 'Who can say what effect such strange matter would have should it contact the Earth?'" Anton shook his head. "But the truth turned out to be far stranger."

Brenna had never thought about what the arrival of the MageLords must have meant to the savages—the Minik. One more black mark to set down against them. The more she learned about Falk and his ilk, the happier she was to be a Commoner.

They talked a little more, mostly in low voices, as they waited for High Raven to return. About an hour later, he did, with half a dozen other Minik in tow, three men and three women, gray-haired and wizened but hale. "These are those whose council I keep," High Raven said. "They will listen with me and help me to make the wisest decision."

"About what?" Brenna asked, tentatively.

"About your fate," High Raven said without smiling. "Minik-na are not welcome here."

"Minik-na?" Brenna said.

"Minik means People," Anton said. "Minik-na means 'not people.'" He shot her a look. "Or, you might say, savages."

"Oh," Brenna said in a small voice.

"But you are most unusual Minik-na," High Raven said. "Were you grown men come to hunt our lands, you would already be food for the scavengers. But you are young, you have come in a most unusual device . . . and this one," he nodded at Anton, "speaks our language and claims to be from Outside the Wall of Sorrows.

"And so we will hear your stories. You will tell us the truth. I will talk with my councillors. And then I will decide what will be done with you."

"We cannot ask for anything fairer than that," Anton said quietly.

"Then let us begin."

For the next hour, they talked. The Minik seemed interested enough in what Brenna had to say, but it was Anton's claim that he had come from beyond the Barrier—the Wall of Sorrows—that really captured their interest. Brenna began to think that maybe everything would work out after all when Anton mentioned the name of a particular clan of the Minik and one of the old women cried out and leaned forward eagerly, wanting to hear more; for she came from the splinter of that clan that had been sundered from the rest when the Barrier had sprung into being. But Anton was unable to answer her furious queries in her own tongue about the families whose names her clan had kept fiercely alive for all these centuries, and she had sat back, scowling and frustrated . . . taking a little bit of Brenna's hopes with her.

"There is a thing I do not understand about your tale," High Raven said to Brenna. "You say your guardian, this Lord Falk, stole Anton's memories, and would twist his mind to make him falsely loyal. But when I lived among the Minik-na as a young man, I learned that among your Mageborn there are two kinds of magic, hard and soft. This Lord Falk is a wielder of the hard magic, but the delving and twisting of minds is a matter for those who wield the soft. How then could he do this?"

"He has help," Brenna said bitterly. "Someone I thought was a Healer. Mother Northwind."

The name had a peculiar effect on High Raven. He froze, very much like the bird that was his namesake, head cocked, hard black eyes studying her. "A Healer named North Wind?" he said at last.

"Mother Northwind, yes." Brenna shuddered. "But she is no Healer. She's as much of a monster as Falk."

High Raven ignored that. "She will be looking for you, then?"

"I don't know," Brenna said. "Falk will be. As far as I know, she was just a . . . tool he was using."

"Hmmm." High Raven exchanged looks with the elders who had accompanied him. "We have heard enough," he said. "We will discuss it. You will continue to wait here. There will be food, soon, for all. And I will tell you your fates before the day is done."

With that, he got up and left the longhouse.

Brenna glanced at Anton for reassurance, but Anton, staring after the departing clan leader, seemed to have none to give.

———

Bucketing along in the horse-drawn carriage—apparently she didn't rate a magecarriage—bearing her from Lord Falk's demesne to the Palace, Mother Northwind felt a kind of . . . poke . . . in her mind. It was a sensation she had crafted to alert her when someone wished to speak to her via magelink.

The two men-at-arms accompanying her to the Palace were literally just inches away, their butts planted on the seat on the other side of the carriage wall, but they would never hear a thing through the noise of creaking wheels, pounding hooves, and rushing wind. She called up the magelink, expecting to see Vinthor or Goodwife Beth—who was neither good, a wife, nor named Beth, she thought with amusement—but instead seeing a face she had not seen in years and had not really ever expected to see again. Startled, she let the magic develop fully, so that her face would be visible, and her voice undisguised. Then, staring at the craggy brown visage, framed by long black hair drawn back in a ponytail, bluestones shining in its ears, she said, wonder in her voice, "High Raven?"

"Healer North Wind," the Minik clan leader said. "Long has it been since we last spoke."

"Long indeed. You left me with the impression that it would be the last time, too, as you withdrew into the wilderness. Yet I see you never discarded the magelink spellstone I left you with, should you change your mind." She felt a spark of curiosity. "So why *have* you changed your mind?"

"I have two Minik-na in my camp," High Raven said.

Mother Northwind frowned. "So?"

"They mentioned your name," High Raven said. "They called you a monster."

Mother Northwind's mouth quirked. "Sounds like they know me, sure enough." And then she sat up. "Two of them. Young? A boy and girl?"

"Yes," High Raven said. "Brenna is the girl's name, Anton's the boy. They arrived in a . . . flying thing. I thought them MageLords and would have killed them on sight— except that the boy spoke to us in the True Tongue."

"He's from outside the Great . . . outside the Wall of Sorrows," Mother Northwind said.

"So he says," High Raven said. "And I find his claim credible." She found his lined, impassive face as hard to read as it had been when she had last seen him, the day she had returned to the shore of the Great Lake to tell the clan that had preserved her life that the MageLord who had massacred their kin had died a fittingly horrible death. High Raven had been the new clan leader them, following the death of his father, who had set her free, but she had known him well for years. "Why did he call you a monster?"

"High Raven, I *am* a monster," Mother Northwind said softly. "I can kill with a touch, twist the minds of men, steal their very souls."

"You can also Heal."

"I can also Heal," Mother Northwind agreed. "And

when I do the other, it is only in the hope that by so doing I can heal the damage done to the world by the MageLords and the Wall of Sorrows." She leaned forward. "I am close, High Raven. Since I left you, I have been working toward the destruction of the Wall and the MageLords who built it, and I am very close now to success. The Minik here and beyond the Wall of Sorrows will be one people again, and the MageLords will be humbled. But I need that girl. I need Brenna, and I need her alive."

High Raven studied her. Mother Northwind was surprised he had actually made use of the spellstone she had left with him. It would be sitting there now on the ground before him, probably, frosted and smoking, her face hanging in midair above it, a terrifying mystery if the Minik were the primitive savages the MageLords believed ... but of course she had lived among them for far too long to believe they were either primitive or savage. They had no magic, that was all, but for the MageLords that alone was enough to render them something less than fully human, just like the Commoners.

"Send someone for her," he said abruptly. "We are at the Camp of the Bear. You remember?"

She remembered it well; she'd wintered there four or five times when she'd lived with the clan. "I remember," she said.

"Have them come north along the east shore of the lake," High Raven went on. "They must bring a large sledge to carry away the flying thing, the airship. So that we may know them, have them carry a banner of blue ... the blue of your eyes, North Wind." Mother Northwind blinked at that. "If they do not do so, we will kill them as we would any other interlopers."

"They will do so."

High Raven studied her in silence for a long moment. "It is good to speak to you again, North Wind," he said at last. "If you do as you say, and the Wall of Sorrows falls, perhaps we may yet meet once more in person."

"Perhaps, High Raven," said Mother Northwind.

The magelink vanished.

Mother Northwind gazed, eyes unfocused, into the empty space where it had been. Sometimes she wondered why no one in the south seemed to register the fact that Northwind was hardly a proper Mageborn name. It was, in fact, merely a translation into the common tongue of a Minik name, given to her by the people of High Raven's clan when she had lived with them and served as their healer and midwife.

If I believed in omens, she thought, *this would be a good one: that the very clan I once belonged to has found the Heir for me.*

When did he notice my blue eyes? she thought a little wistfully, feeling for a moment like a girl a quarter her age.

And then, suddenly, she stiffened. *But this changes everything!* She had thought to let Lord Falk bring Brenna back to the Palace and somehow spirit her away from there before he could take her north to the Cauldron. But now she had, or soon would have, both Brenna and Karl. She had only to have Brenna taken to Goodwife Beth's safe house. Verdsmitt was inside the Palace . . .

After twenty years, the pieces of her grand scheme were at last falling into place.

But they'd quickly fall out of place again if Falk found Brenna. She knew exactly how he meant to do that: knew that he would be calling on Tagaza to go to the Spellchamber and use the powerful spell created to locate the Heir.

Mother Northwind had always had a healthy respect for what the strongest MageLords could do with their hard magic, and so had laid emergency plans to disrupt the use of the Spellchamber.

It is time, she thought, *to put those plans into effect.* She smiled. And by destroying New Cabora City Hall . . . the guards on her carriage had told her of that, their news having come via the magelink that had also provided their orders . . . Lord Falk had even provided the perfect excuse for it, one that would have no one thinking that the timing was anything but coincidental when it stopped Tagaza from locating the true Heir.

And so she summoned one more magelink, and passed a brief message to the Commoner who answered . . . and thus, when she arrived at the Palace in the early morning light, she was not at all surprised to find all in confusion, the MageLords having just been forcibly reminded that they were not totally sufficient unto themselves; that they did, in fact, depend on the Commoners for many things, including stoking the great MageFurnace with the coal that other Commoners dug from under the rolling hills of the southeast.

Three Commoners and one Mageborn had died in the mayhem in the great chamber of the MageFurnace as water had poured onto the hot coals and flashed into scalding steam. A regrettable but acceptable price, Mother Northwind thought.

She felt certain High Raven would agree.

She allowed herself to be helped from the carriage and led to her sumptuous quarters not far from Falk's own, hobbling along with her cane, a harmless and humble old woman.

CHAPTER 18

WHEN LORD FALK RETURNED from the Square, grim-faced, the heart of New Cabora lay in ruins, the Courthouse and the Grand Theater (where many of Verdsmitt's plays had shown in triumph) having both suffered the same fate as City Hall. Falk had made it clear that the fault lay with the Common Cause, "common vandals," he called them, who had murdered other Commoners with their foolish and futile sabotage of the MageFurnace, and who had now brought down just retribution on their city. "Why are you protecting them?" Falk shouted to the white-faced, staring crowds, silent except for sobbing children too young to understand why they had been forced out into the frozen streets at sword point. "Give me their leaders! Give me their Patron! Give me Prince Karl! There is someone within the sound of my voice who has the power to do all these things. There is someone else who knows who that person is. If they will not act, force them to! For the sake of your livelihoods, your homes, your families. Tell me who they are!"

His voice might have been falling on deaf ears, for all the reaction it got, but he knew he was speaking the truth. There were people in that crowd who knew the leaders of the Cause, or knew how to get to them, and Falk was confident they would not let their city be reduced to rubble over some petty concern about so-called freedom. *Freedom to live in squalor and chaos*, Falk thought, looking around at the Commoners in disgust. Poor. Benighted. Powerless. Did they not realize how much the MageLords had done for them? Did they think they would have survived, prospered to build New Cabora at all, if the MageLords had not made it possible to survive in this frozen northland in the first place?

Falk was tempted to leave it at that, but he knew the importance of mixing a little honey with the bitter vinegar. "These buildings can be rebuilt," he said. "Not in one year, or five years, or ten years, but in one day, one week, one month. The magic that destroyed them can build them up again. Your city can be what it was ... if you cooperate with me." He scanned the faces again. "And if it is me you hate," he said, "don't think of it as cooperating with me. I serve King Kravon. Serve him in turn as duty demands, and I will be as pleased on his order to build up your city as I am sorrowful at having to tear it down."

Still nothing. Falk found the crowd's silent, steady regard slightly unnerving, as though they were measuring him against something and finding him wanting. But he shrugged off the feeling, turned, and jumped down from the statue's pedestal. "Get me out of here," he said to the guards. They formed a tight phalanx of blue and steel around him and marched him through the crowd, which parted in front of him and closed in behind him like water passing under a boat.

Back in the Palace, he first checked on the MageFurnace. As he had expected, the Mageborn had driven the water away as clouds of steam, sent out through the Chimneys. The fires were being stoked, the heat returning. The interruption in power had been minute, and if a few magelights had gone out, a few magelinks cut in mid-conversation, a few breakfasts left uncooked, and a few MageLords left unwashed, well, what of it? The Lesser Barrier had not been touched, for like the Great Barrier, it drew its power, via the King's Keys, from the great fiery Cauldron in the north.

Where, if everything had gone as planned, Falk thought

bitterly, he would soon have been traveling with that little vixen Brenna.

Had Tagaza located her? Tagaza couldn't tell him. He had remained unconscious since the eruption of steam from the MageFurnace had interrupted his spell. No Healer had yet been able to wake him, or even figure out why he still slept.

No Healer currently in the Palace, at any rate. But Falk had another Healer to call on. If anyone could Heal Tagaza, it would be Mother Northwind.

And then he turned onto the broad boulevard leading up to the Palace from the bridge, and saw a carriage bearing his coat of arms being driven away from the main entrance, and quickened his pace, knowing that she had arrived.

He found her in the rooms he had set aside for her, not far from his own, sitting by the fire, knitting, as though she had never left her cottage. "Well, Lord Falk," she said as he came in, before he could say anything at all, "I must thank you for sending your men-at-arms for me last evening. It saved me that long walk down to the manor to demand they take me to the Palace."

"Good day to you, too, Mother Northwind," Falk said dryly. "I hope you had a pleasant journey."

Mother Northwind snorted. "Too old for small talk," she said. "We both know why I'm here. You need me to question Davydd Verdsmitt for you. And I want to be here when you find Brenna and the Prince . . . poor lambs."

"You are quite correct in the former," Falk said. "Verdsmitt, if he is not the mysterious Patron, is at least very high up in the Common Cause. He can name names, people we can arrest and question in turn, until the whole foul web unravels. You heard what they did to the MageFurnace."

"I heard," Mother Northwind said sympathetically. "You poor MageLords. No running water for a whole morning!"

"The inconvenience was minor," Falk said, refusing to be baited. "And the only people killed were Commoners.

But as a symbol of rebellion . . . it could not be allowed to stand."

"Rather like the buildings in New Cabora Square?" Mother Northwind chuckled. "I hear you've been making some 'forceful' speeches there."

"Someone will give me information," Falk said. "I don't care how popular the Common Cause, there are those who will betray them to stop the destruction."

"People can be funny about things like that," Mother Northwind said. "Don't count your hawks before they're fledged, as they say." She put aside her knitting, glanced around, and laughed. "I'll be thinking I'm old, next. Here I am looking for my cat to jump in my lap, and I left him behind with one of your scullery maids. Well." She smoothed her dress, then reached for her cane. "Hadn't you better take me to Verdsmitt, then?"

Falk cocked an eyebrow at her. "Why so anxious?"

Mother Northwind sighed. "Lord Falk, I have many friends among the Commoners. If there is anything I can do to stop this destruction of New Cabora, I want to do it as soon as possible." Then she chuckled. "Besides," she said, "a chance to rummage around in the head of the famous Davydd Verdsmitt? How often does a girl get an opportunity like that?"

She struggled a bit getting to her feet—probably stiff after her long carriage ride, he thought—but he made no move to help her; no power on Earth could have compelled him to get close enough to Mother Northwind for her to touch him. As she heaved herself up, he said, "You haven't asked me about Brenna."

"You obviously haven't found her," Mother Northwind said. "What is there to ask about?" She took a deep breath. "Don't ever grow old, Lord Falk. It is a terrible thing."

"Considering the alternative, I think I'd like to risk it." Falk said. "You're right, Mother Northwind, I haven't found her. The last confirmed sighting of the airship was several miles west of the lake. After that, nothing. They had lost a lot of height since fleeing the manor. I don't think they could have cleared the lake. But where they went after that . . ." He shook his head. "We'll find her. That is the other thing I need you here for, Mother Northwind."

She had hobbled closer, and he carefully, while trying to avoid the appearance of haste, backed into the hallway in front of her. "Me, Lord Falk? I have no magic with which to find Brenna."

"No, but Tagaza does," Falk said. "He would have found her already if not for the sabotage of the MageFurnace. And now he is unconscious. The Palace Healers don't understand what is wrong with him. But you . . ."

Mother Northwind sighed. "I will examine him for you, Lord Falk. In both ways, if you like."

Falk was tempted . . . *very* tempted . . . but he had given Tagaza his word that if he cooperated, he would not let Mother Northwind into his mind. For the sake of honor, as well as for the many years they had known each other and whatever friendship that had entailed, he would keep that promise . . . for the moment, at least.

"No, Mother Northwind. Just heal him so he can perform the spell again."

"As you wish." She had stopped, and for a moment he wondered why, until she said, "Well, are you going to take me to Verdsmitt or not? I don't know where he is!"

"Of course." Falk led the way, reminding himself again that Mother Northwind was only a talented soft mage, neither omniscient nor omnipotent . . . and, ultimately, his servant.

Soon, he thought, *to be my subject.*

It was useful to remind himself of those things, because Mother Northwind had a knack for keeping him off-balance.

———

Davydd Verdsmitt sat in his cell, writing. He had asked for, and to his surprise received pen, ink, and paper. The new play was going well, all the mental writing he had done paying off in an almost seamless flow of words onto the page.

Not that it was any more likely than it had been that the play would ever be produced, but that didn't matter. Verdsmitt was a writer, and so, he wrote.

But he was also much more, and even while he wrote, he was aware of what was happening outside his cell. He had felt Tagaza's effort to build some powerful spell in the Spellchamber high atop the Palace . . . and the sudden lessening of power all around as the MageFurnace had been doused with lake water. At that moment, he could have broken out of his cell, instituted his own backup plan, and added to the chaos—but he did not.

He did not, because he knew that the Patron was on her way to the Palace, and that could only mean that her Plan was still in effect.

He felt her arrival and, a short time later, felt her approaching with Falk. As the Minister of Public Safety and Mother Northwind approached his door, he tidied away his manuscript and stood to greet them.

A guard opened the door, and Lord Falk stepped in first. He glanced from Verdsmitt to the stacked papers. "So glad to see your stay with us hasn't been wasted," he said. "Davydd Verdsmitt, allow me to present Mother Northwind, a Healer of great renown. I have asked her to examine you so that we can assure the Commons you are unharmed. It might go some way to lessening tensions brought on by . . . recent events."

He thinks I don't know anything of what has happened, Verdsmitt thought, *that I don't know what he has done in the Commons, or what the Commoners did here. Well, no need to set him right.* "I believe I am quite well, but of course I would be glad of a second opinion." He nodded politely. "Mother Northwind. An interesting name. Do you mind if I use it in some future play? Perhaps you could be a friend to Goodwife Beth."

Mother Northwind's mouth quirked. "I would be honored." She looked at Falk. "There's no need for you to stay. I know how busy you are this morning."

"There are, indeed, things I must attend to," Falk said.

"I'll await the results of your examination in my office." He nodded to Mother Northwind, inclined his head slightly to Verdsmitt, and went out.

The guard closed the door behind him.

"Welcome, Patron," Verdsmitt said.

"Mother Northwind, please," she said. "I realize no one can eavesdrop on us while I wear this," she lifted her arm, showing a silver bracelet fogged with condensation that he himself had enchanted for her some months previously, and whose presence he had sensed the moment she entered, "but it is still best to be discreet. It's simply a good habit. We Healers are very big on encouraging good habits, you know." She looked him up and down, and smiled a little. "In my professional opinion, you look well, Davydd."

"As do you, Pa . . . Mother Northwind."

"Ah, I may look like a young girl still, but my knees are those of an old woman," Mother Northwind said. "Sit with me."

They sat side by side on the narrow bed. "How stands the Plan?" Verdsmitt said.

"Better than I had hoped, when Brenna and that dolt of a boy from Outside took it on themselves to fly away from Falk's manor."

Verdsmitt cocked his head to one side. "That sentence," he said slowly, "almost makes sense . . ."

"Never mind," Mother Northwind said. "Better you don't know of it so you cannot accidentally let slip something about something you don't know about."

Verdsmitt started to protest both her sentence construction and her warning, then thought better of both. "Good habits," he said instead.

"Exactly," said Mother Northwind. "But there are some things by rights you shouldn't know that you *must* know. So: Brenna ran away from home, but I have located her and she is being brought to the city. And Prince Karl, shortly after you were arrested, was . . . kidnapped by the Common Cause."

Verdsmitt shot her a look, an exaggerated "take" that on stage would almost certainly have gotten a laugh. It elicited a chuckle even from Mother Northwind. "A surprise to us all, I'm sure. But not to worry. I know where he is, and he's safe . . . he's at Goodwife Beth's."

Verdsmitt snorted. "Depends on what you mean by 'safe.'"

"Anyway, he's out of the city. No one but the members of Vinthor's cell know where . . . and they're all at Beth's as well. There is no one to betray him in New Cabora, no matter what . . . incentives . . . Falk may provide."

"That is one of the things I should not know, and so I can say nothing of it to Falk," Verdsmitt said softly, "but I know what he has done to my city. He has brought to it what the MageLords always, sooner or later, bring to the lives of Commoners: wreck, ruin, and destruction." He lowered his voice, even though he knew no one could hear. "Give me leave to kill him, too, Patron."

This time Mother Northwind did not rebuke him for using that title. Instead she studied him thoughtfully. "You are remarkably bloodthirsty for a playwright," she said. "And remarkably set against the MageLords for one who is, after all, one of them."

"I haven't considered myself a MageLord since I was sixteen years old," Verdsmitt snarled. "As you well know."

He instantly regretted losing his temper. As a man who had led a double life for a very long time, and as a professional actor, he prided himself on being able to school his emotions. But he hated to be reminded of the accident of birth that had made him MageLord, even though without it he would not have the unique skills that made him so valuable to Mother Northwind's plan now.

And she, of all people, knew that.

He clearly remembered the rainy night, more than two decades gone, when she had presented herself at his door in the slightly shabby-but-still-respectable neighborhood of New Cabora where he had lived at that time. He hadn't been Davydd Verdsmitt, famous playwright, then, but Davydd Verdsmitt, barely-making-ends-meet-by-sweeping-floors playwright.

His first play was just then about to take the boards at the Paragon, whose name was a better joke than anything he'd written. A bat-infested old firetrap that mostly staged ancient farces—interspersed with equally ancient strippers—it had had the undeniable attraction of being cheap to rent.

He'd been so young then. Only half a dozen years had passed since he had so violently removed himself from the ranks of the MageLords, "drowning" in a tragic boating accident on the Great Lake, body never recovered. Not that he supposed his father, Lord Athol, now Prime Adviser to the King, had looked very hard. After all, a few days before he had all but suggested to his son that he quietly commit suicide.

Mother Northwind must have been younger then, too, but in his memory she looked the same as she did now, leaning on her stick, standing in the rain. "Aren't you going to ask an old woman in?" she'd said.

And then she had offered him her grand bargain.

Before he could even ask her who she was or where she came from, she said, "I know about you and Kravon."

He had physically started. "How—?" And then, belatedly, had attempted to recover. "The King? I'm a Commoner. What is there to know about me and the King?"

"Let us dispense with these games right now," Mother Northwind had said. "You cannot deny anything to me, you cannot hide anything; I know everything you and Kravon did together. I know what your feelings for him were, and his for you. And I know how much it devastated you when he renounced you, renounced the love you thought he felt for you, and revealed and reviled you as a homosexual."

Verdsmitt remembered how the blood had drained away from his face and head, making him so dizzy he'd had to collapse into the nearest chair to keep from falling to his knees. "That's—"

"I don't care in the slightest that you prefer your own

sex," Mother Northwind said. "If it would amuse you, sometime, I will tell you just how many of the MageLords who shunned and laughed at you after King Kravon made the truth known are also bedding boys—and each other—in the privacy of their own estates, usually with their poor wives none the wiser." A flicker of anger had touched her face, quickly smoothed away. "But you have something I need, Davydd Verdsmitt: magical ability of a kind that comes just once a century, if that."

He couldn't deny being a MageLord; why deny *that*? "Much good it has done me."

"Your skill as an enchanter, while you were still a boy, awed your tutors," Mother Northwind said. "It was so great, so extraordinary, that had you not chosen so precipitously to drown in the Great Lake, the scandal would soon have been forgotten, papered over as such things are for MageLords." She shook her head. "Well, it is too late for you to return to your father's estate . . ."

"I would die first," Verdsmitt growled. "My father threw me out, told me to—"

"I know," Mother Northwind said, though again, she didn't say *how*. "But listen to me, Davydd Verdsmitt. It is not too late for you to take revenge."

He had stared blankly at her. "Revenge?"

"On your father. On all the MageLords who laughed at you, scorned you, made you an object of ridicule in taverns and manor halls around the kingdom." She poked at him with a bony finger. "But *especially* . . . revenge on King Kravon."

And then she had explained something of her plan, her grand scheme to grow a Magebane—Verdsmitt still found it hard to believe such a thing even existed, much less could be created, like a play or a piece of pottery—and with him bring down the entire rotten edifice of Evrenfels . . . a scheme that required only one thing: a way to kill the King at the precise moment he needed to die.

"An ordinary mage couldn't do it," Mother Northwind said. "The magical defenses woven around the King are too strong. *I* could do it, were I in physical contact with him . . . but I must be elsewhere when the deed is done. A simple physical attack such as Commoners might launch would be thwarted by the same defenses that protect him from a magical one. But an enchanted device, so subtly made, so carefully constructed that it leaks nothing of its magical nature to those searching for such things, one that looks like an ordinary, unthreatening object, something the King might even carry on his person, something that can be triggered at just the right time . . . such a device could do the trick. But to create it would take the greatest enchanter the Kingdom has ever known." She cocked her head, eyes on his, and said softly, "You."

The appeal to his pride had helped to lure him in. The chance to take revenge on the MageLords, and on the man he had once loved but now hated with even more passion, might have been enough for him to agree. But what had really sealed the deal was the final offer from Mother Northwind: if he agreed to help her, she would fill the Paragon with paying patrons for a week.

"A week is all I can give you," she said. "I have contacts enough to arrange for that. After that . . . your play must stand on its own merits."

"It will," Verdsmitt had said fiercely. "It will. Give me an audience, Mother Northwind, and I will do the rest . . ." He'd stood and held out his hand to her. "*All* of the rest."

She'd smiled, and taken his hand. She'd held it for a long moment, squeezed it hard to support him as a brief bout of dizziness made his knees inexplicably sag. "I am confident of it, my boy," she'd said, and as the dizziness passed, she'd disappeared once more into the wet night.

Since then he had never wavered, never doubted that what he and Mother Northwind planned had to be done . . . and never let dim or waver the bright flame of his hatred of his one-time friend and lover Kravon, now King.

Which was why, he told himself, he had reacted with anger to Mother Northwind's naming of him as a MageLord. So he had been, but so he was no longer. And if their plan succeeded, as they both hoped, soon there would be no MageLords or Mageborn: all would be equal, all would have to face the vagaries of the world without magic and the arrogance it bred.

"Sorry, Davydd," Mother Northwind said now. "I cannot help baiting people. It is a bad habit and will land me in trouble someday, I fear."

Verdsmitt snorted. "As opposed to plotting to murder the King, tear down the Great Barrier, and destroy magic forever?"

"I suppose there is some possibility that that will land me trouble, as well," Mother Northwind said serenely. "But it hasn't yet."

She leaned forward. "Listen to me, Davydd. I regret things did not come together as smoothly as we had hoped, but the pieces of the plan are still in play and still under my control. Brenna and Karl will soon be together. The moment for you to strike Kravon is still close at hand ... very close. Can you sense the devices of yours we have smuggled into the Palace?"

"Yes," Verdsmitt said. "I know much of what has been happening in the Palace. And if more disruption is called for ... those devices, too, are within range of my will."

"Not yet," Mother Northwind said. "But the time may come." She studied him. "I did not answer your request for leave to kill Falk. Does he, too, carry one of your devices?"

"No," Verdsmitt admitted. "And he is powerfully protected. I don't know *how* I could kill him, Mother Northwind, but I would find a way."

"Hmmm. Well, I'd rather he stayed alive for now. While he pursues *his* Plan with such fervor, he gives me space to pursue *mine*. But to return to these devices. Can you activate them from within the cell?"

"No," Verdsmitt said. "I can sense them, but these cells carry their own enchantments."

"How close do you have to be?"

"Anywhere within the Palace, as long as I am free of this

cell. The original plan was for me to use the enchantments woven into my clothing to escape when the time comes—"

"There is a better way," Mother Northwind said.

Davydd Verdsmitt waited for her to go on.

She smiled. "Just how good an actor are you, Davydd?"

———

Falk, signing what seemed like the thousandth document in the last hour—the worst part about a crackdown on the Commons was the amount of paperwork it generated— paused to clench and unclench his cramped right hand, and then realized that Mother Northwind had just entered the room.

"Ah," he said. "At last." He gestured to one of the chairs on the other side of his desk; Mother Northwind seated herself with an audible creaking of joints. "Well?"

"Your hunch was correct, Lord Falk," she said. "I did not believe it until I saw it in his mind, but Davydd Verdsmitt . . . is the Patron. Well, one of them."

Falk felt a rush of pleasure. "I knew it!" He leaned forward. "And who was the mage who helped him?"

Mother Northwind shook her head sadly. "Here is another thing I would not have believed, Lord Falk," she said. "His accomplice was . . . the First Mage himself, Tagaza. Who also sometimes acted as the Patron. Again, as I think you suspected."

There was no rush of pleasure at hearing *that* suspicion confirmed. "I am not surprised," Falk said grimly, "but I am pained. What else did you glean from Verdsmitt's mind?"

Mother Northwind laughed. "Much about the sexual proclivities of various members of the acting profession. A great deal more than I wanted to know about the technical aspects of producing a play. But about the Common Cause . . . less than I had hoped."

Falk's eyes narrowed. "Why?"

"Tagaza, again," Mother Northwind said. "He is, of course, a master of hard magic, but he is also not completely unskilled at certain elements of soft . . . or rather, of some of those forms of magic that straddle the realms of hard and soft." She sighed. "His meddling in Verdsmitt's mind was clumsy but unmistakable. He created a . . . wall, a wall that I cannot breach. To do so would kill Verdsmitt, and still I would not gain the information I want. And this wall not only keeps me from accessing information about the Common Cause in detail, it keeps Verdsmitt from consciously knowing it himself."

"And yet you confirmed he gave orders as the Patron."

"Only because my skill exceeds Tagaza's," Mother Northwind said acerbically. "He has built a wall, but it is rough and unfinished enough that here and there light seeps through the cracks."

"If Verdsmitt has no knowledge we can access, if he doesn't even remember that he is the Patron, then he is useless to me except as an example," Falk said. "I will hang him from the statue in the Square so that the Common Cause and all their sympathizers know their leader has been arrested and condemned. Even if no one has come forward by then to tell me where Prince Karl is being held, that will open the store-hold of information on their sinking ship and send the rats scurrying out to save themselves."

"A colorful metaphor," Mother Northwind said. "Have you thought of writing plays?"

Falk was already opening a drawer on the left-hand side of his desk, in which he kept execution forms. He had pulled one out and was reaching for a pen when Mother Northwind's next words stopped him.

"But would it not be better, Lord Falk, to have the Patron alive . . . but loyal to you? To turn Davydd Verdsmitt's gift for propaganda *against* the Common Cause, instead of serving it? The confusion in the ranks of the Cause would be the same, seeing him alive at your right hand, supporting you, as it would be if he were dead . . . no, worse; because if you kill him, he becomes a martyr. Save him, and the leader of the Common Cause, the man most devoted to its perverse ideology, becomes nothing more than a turncoat, a sniveling coward who saved his own skin. How's that for a symbol?"

Falk put down the pen he had just picked up. "You can do this?"

Mother Northwind smiled a little shamefacedly, like a child caught with her hand in the sugar jar. "It's already done. Once I realized how little information I could retrieve from Verdsmitt, I . . . well. I confess I may have acted in haste, Lord Falk. I beg forgiveness if so."

Falk had never heard Mother Northwind beg forgiveness for anything.

"I . . . was angry. And since I could not take what I wanted from Verdsmitt's mind, instead I . . . twisted it. To serve you, and the MageLords, and especially King Kravon." She shook her head. "I should have asked for your permission and advice first, of course. I cannot undo it, but you can still kill him, or I can, if you'd like him dead due to natural causes—"

"Kill him?" Lord Falk laughed. "Mother Northwind, your skills continue to amaze me. Of course I won't kill him." He stood. "I want to see him."

"And he wants to see you," Mother Northwind said. "To beg your forgiveness."

"Which he shall most certainly have, Mother Northwind," said Falk. "Which he shall most certainly have."

Mother Northwind had been as good as her word, Falk thought, as he watched the stiff-necked playwright, so cool and arrogant the last time they had met, kneel before him and beg for forgiveness and mercy, tears streaming down his face: beg to be allowed to make a public statement to the Commons renouncing the Cause. He promised to burn his seditious play in the center of the Square. He offered to write another extolling the grandeur of the MageLords. He pleaded for an audience with King Kravon himself.

He begged so much that Falk soon got tired of it. "Of course, of course," he said. "All of that can be done. But there is no need to make any plans now, Verdsmitt. Come with me, and I'll have Brich find some more . . . suitable quarters for you. And if there's anything you need from your quarters in the city . . ." Which had, of course, already been completely searched and stripped, which meant it was all in Falk's storage rooms somewhere, but no need to tell him that, "just let Brich know."

Mother Northwind had waited in Falk's office throughout the exchange. She raised an eyebrow at him as he came in, and he laughed. "I say it again, Mother Northwind. You are a wonder." He sat down at the desk once more. "Now, Tagaza. The *other* Patron."

"Do you still want me to stay out of his mind?"

"Yes," Falk said firmly; then amended " . . . for now." He spread his hands. "My focus is on his completing the spell to find Brenna. Once he has done that, then I want you to strip his skull of everything he has ever seen, heard, thought, or smelled. Promise be damned. The man is a traitor."

"I take it you *will* be executing *him*," Mother Northwind said quietly.

"I will chain him to the Rock of Execution myself," Falk snarled, "and it will be *my* will that makes it burn hotter than it ever has before."

"Very well. Take me to him, and I will see what I can do . . . as a Healer." She sighed. "I confess I'm a little weary after my dealings with Verdsmitt, but a simple Healing should not take much more out of me."

"You will have the finest dinner the Palace chefs can create after your work today," Falk said.

Mother Northwind laughed. "No, no," she said. "A simple meal is all I ask. A simple meal for a simple woman."

But as she heaved herself up on her cane and made her way out of Falk's office, he smiled to himself. *There's nothing simple about you, old woman*, he thought.

And then the smile faded. *Many have underestimated Mother Northwind*, he thought . . . and wondered, just a little, if there were a risk he had just done the same.

CHAPTER 19

HIGH RAVEN HAD PROMISED TO TELL Brenna and Anton their fates before the day was out, and he was true to his word . . . but only in part.

Their immediate fate, at least, was not to become "food for scavengers," which Brenna supposed was the most important thing. But beyond that, High Raven was not forthcoming. "You will live," he said. "What more do you need to know? Tonight, and perhaps for one or two more, you will be our guests. Then you will move on."

"Move on where?" Brenna asked, but High Raven would not say.

The next two days were the strangest Brenna had ever spent. She had resigned herself to spending the evening sitting around the fire, chewing in silence on whatever gristly game the Minik had managed to scavenge from the Wilderness. Instead, she ate sumptuously: caribou and lake trout, pickled mushrooms, sweet cattail pollen cakes and more, washed down with a powerful drink that smelled and tasted of honey. And when the food had finally quit coming—only because she couldn't eat anymore, not because there was any shortage of it—the music and storytelling and dancing began, and went on far into the night.

The music was strange, and wild, the whistling of high flutes and the singing of a strange single-stringed . . . fiddle, she guessed you call it . . . twining around each other above a constant but complex drumbeat. It made her feel ... different. Wild.

Free.

Free of Lord Falk. Free of the MageLords. Free of Mother Northwind. Free of all the restrictions she had lived under so long, restrictions that seemed all the more smothering now she had escaped them, having literally flown away like a bird fleeing a cage through a suddenly opened door.

Free ...

She began to eye Anton speculatively as she drank more of the mead, listened to the throbbing drums, watched the Minik dance, men and women stripped down to nothing more than loincloths, bodies glistening with sweat ... Anton wasn't watching her, though, he was watching some bare-breasted girl even younger than she was, eyes wide, lips slightly parted, and she felt a pang of jealousy, and suddenly she was up and dancing, too, and then Anton joined in, and for a few moments they were dancing together, though not the kind of dancing she'd thought so exciting at the Moon Ball. This was wild, primeval, sensual ...

Free.

But then, suddenly, it ended. The drums stopped, the flutes sighed their last high notes, the fiddle vibrated into silence. Brenna and Anton suddenly found themselves alone in the space around the fire, as the Minik began gathering their clothes, retrieving plates and vessels they had brought in for the communal meal, and streaming out into the cold air to return to their own huts.

Brenna and Anton were still breathing heavily. Brenna was excruciatingly aware of how close he was. She wanted to get closer. She wanted him to touch her. She wanted ...

She started toward him, but was suddenly jerked back by a strong hand on her arm. The old woman who tended the fire was staring at her. Her look was not unsympathetic, but she shook her head and pointed behind her, where, Brenna saw, a bed of pine boughs had been made on the floor, two red woven blankets spread on top. And then she stepped between Brenna and Anton and pointed at a second bed on the far side of the fire. Anton licked his lips, but nodded and, with a last glance at Brenna, made his way to his own bed ...

... as Brenna did to hers, frustrated and a little angry. *Free*, she though. *Free of everything except chaperones!*

In the morning, though, without the mead adding fuel to the fire in her blood, without the beat of the music and the half-naked bodies weaving in and out on the dance floor, she was more grateful than not. She found it hard to even look at Anton that morning, and the reluctance seemed mutual. The old woman smiled to herself and put more wood on the fire.

Maybe not a chaperone, she thought. *Maybe just wise with age.*

High Raven came to fetch them an hour later, taking them to the large sled which had brought the airship ashore. Anton almost leaped at it, insisting the envelope be stretched out fully, running his hands over every rope, inspecting the burner. "Undamaged, as far as I can see," he said. "Except for some of the wicker." He pointed to a hole that had worn in one corner of the gondola during the slide across the ice. High Raven, who had been watching silently, came closer to examine it. He grunted.

"We can fix that," he said.

While Anton had been examining the airship, he had collected a crowd of Minik, mostly children who laughed and whispered and pointed, but also a few men and one or two women, though in general, Brenna had noticed, the women seemed to be the ones doing all the work around the camp. The men had been very good at drinking and dancing the night before, but she wondered what they did during the day. Hunt, she supposed, though she saw little evidence of it.

Her impression that women did all the work was strengthened when High Raven sent a little boy running off somewhere. He returned with a woman, tall and sturdy, her hair, in a braid reaching almost to her waist, just beginning to gray. "My wife, Sweetwater," he said. Then, in rapid-fire, lilting Minik, he pointed out the hole in the gondola.

His wife replied briefly and, even Brenna could tell, in the affirmative, and went away again.

"She will fix it," High Raven said. He turned to go.

"What should we do?" Brenna called after him.

"Whatever you like," he said, glancing over his shoulder. "You are our guests. But do not leave the camp."

"Why not?" Brenna said, out of some perverse impulse.

"Guests do not leave unexpectedly," High Raven said. "If they do, they are no longer guests." He walked away. The other men followed. The children remained close but not too close, pointing and giggling.

"A very polite way of saying that if we leave, we will be brought back—and no longer treated as guests," Anton noted.

"In other words, we're still prisoners," Brenna said. Her thoughts of freedom the night before came back to mock her.

"But alive. And not in Falk's hands. That's something, right?" Anton made a face at a little girl in a long buckskin coat decorated with colorful but rather clumsy beadwork; it had the look of something she had made herself. She screeched, then ran behind a bigger boy—her brother?— and hid, giggling, peeking out again as if to show she wasn't really frightened.

Brenna again remembered calling the Minik savages, and felt renewed shame. She hid her eyes with her hands then drew her hands back again. "Peek-a-boo!" she said.

The little girl laughed and copied her. "Peek-a-boo! Peek-a-boo!" she shouted, and soon all the children were shouting it, running around and around Brenna and Anton, alternately hiding and showing their eyes and shrieking at the top of their lungs.

A group of passing women gave the children an indulgent glance and Brenna and Anton warm smiles, and she suddenly felt better again about their circumstances. So they weren't allowed to leave the camp; well, so what? It wasn't like they could go anywhere. She wouldn't last a day in the northern wilderness, even with Anton's help—and he, though she was certain he must have far better survival skills than she, wouldn't fare much better with no supplies.

Could you still be called a prisoner when your prison walls were saving you from certain death?

Her improved feeling lasted throughout the day, as they played with the children, sharing their noon meal of fish and bannock, and watched High Raven's wife expertly weave new wicker into the hole in the gondola. That night there was more music and dancing, but of a more sedate kind, and no mead. The previous night, Anton explained to her as they sat watching the women perform a slow, shuffling dance around and around the fire, had been a feast to welcome new guests. Tonight was just an ordinary night.

That night, Brenna went to sleep almost content, not even worrying about what the morrow would bring . . .

. . . which was why what it did bring came as a horrible shock.

———

Anton saw them first. He had gone down to the airship once again, as though to reassure himself that it still was all right and hadn't been "eaten by wolves or something in the night," as Brenna teased him. She stayed behind in the longhouse, where the old woman seemed to have taken a liking to her and was showing her how to string beads together, then sew them onto a piece of buckskin.

Anton didn't mind the teasing. He found he didn't mind much of anything where Brenna was concerned. He'd found it very hard . . . he winced; bad choice of words . . . difficult to go to sleep after that first night's feast, his blood, like hers, he suspected . . . hoped? . . . inflamed by the mead and the music and the bare, glistening flesh in the firelight . . .

He sighed and tried to put the image out of his mind. He took another look at the envelope. He'd asked that it be rolled up and tied in a round bundle, and the Minik had done a neat job of it, much neater than the job they'd done when they'd first transported it to the shore from the ice. That was why he'd examined it so carefully than first time. It was one thing to mend wicker, quite another to mend the thin silk of the envelope without sewing machines or . . . magic.

He shook his head. Here, with magic no more in evidence among these Minik than those he knew on the Outside, it was hard to believe that he had truly seen the things he had seen back in Lord Falk's estate. But he *had* seen them, and the fact they had successfully flown across the lake at all was proof of it. Those mageservants . . .

And then his thoughts were interrupted as two sleds came roaring up the trail from the lake, both pulled by panting dogs whose breath sent huge clouds of steam into the air. The one in front he recognized as the one that they'd ridden in from the crash site. The one in back . . .

He straightened.

It was larger than any of the Minik sleds; larger, and with a very different look. The dogs were different, too, larger but somehow not as tough-looking as the Minik dogs. There were more of them, though.

The sled had a kind of flagpole attached to it from which hung a bright blue banner, very nearly the same color as the airship. And on it were . . . Minik-na.

There were four men, wearing coats that looked both bulkier and not as warm as the furs of the Minik, and hats with large earflaps that were almost comical . . . not that Anton felt like smiling. He could think of only one reason the Minik would suddenly allow Minik-na into the camp, and he didn't like it.

High Raven was talking to the men; he turned suddenly and came walking toward Anton. "Where is Brenna?" he said.

"In the longhouse," Anton said. "I'll get her."

"Stay where you are," said High Raven. "I will get her."

He went into the longhouse and emerged a moment later with Brenna, who was tugging her coat on as she came. She reached Anton and stopped. Her eyes widened as she took in the new arrivals.

"Your time as our guests has ended," High Raven said. "You will go with these men."

"Who are they?" Anton said.

"They are servants of North Wind," Raven said.

Brenna gasped. "You can't mean . . . you're not sending us back to that . . . that witch!"

"That 'witch,'" said High Raven softly, "lived with this clan for ten years. That 'witch' saved the life of my wife and the life of my firstborn son, turned the wrong way in the womb. That 'witch' avenged the massacre of Minik by the MageLord Starkind, securing the honor of this clan and her place in it. That 'witch' is, and always will be, a friend of the Minik, a friend of this clan, and a friend of High Raven. She tells me she has need of you. I will send you to her."

Anton knew there was nothing they could say against such an argument from a Minik clan leader, but Brenna tried anyway. "But I told you what she wanted to do!" she cried. "She reached into Anton's mind, stole his thoughts . . . she will twist his mind until he is no longer himself, but a mere puppet of Falk's. If you give us to her, you are giving us back to him. You are giving us back to the MageLords you claim to hate!"

Most of Brenna's words seemed to roll off the implacable Minik like water from a smooth stone, but her last outburst caused his eyes to narrow. "I am giving you to North Wind," he said. "If you think that is the same as giving you to the MageLords, then you know nothing about North Wind." He made a chopping gesture with his hand, as if it were a knife severing a rope—severing the thread of conversation, Anton guessed. "It is done. They will take the airship, and they will take you, to where North Wind wants you to be. The Minik are done with you. You are no longer guests. You are no longer welcome in our camp. Do not come here again." And then he walked away without looking back.

A soft sob escaped Brenna. Anton, feeling drained and helpless, reached out and took her gloved hand. Then he led her toward the waiting sled.

Karl woke on his third day as a captive of the Common Cause to the sound of arguing.

He rolled over and sat up. Gray light seeped through the curtained window; midmorning, then.

He could make out Vinthor's voice, and Beth's, but the loudest voice . . . was that Jopps'?

Intrigued, he rolled out of bed, pulled on the warm dressing gown Goodwife Beth had provided, slipped his feet into the slippers she had given him, went out, and descended the stairs.

He had rather hoped to do so silently, but he was defeated by the slippers, which flapped against the bottom of his feet like the warning tail slaps of a beaver in a pond. Rather than creep down unobserved, he found himself being stared at by Vinthor, Goodwife Beth, and Jopps as he entered the kitchen. There was no sign of Denson.

"Your Highness," Vinthor said.

"What's all the noise?" Karl asked.

"None of your concern," Jopps said gruffly.

But Goodwife Beth seemed to have no qualms about telling him. "Oh, it's a terrible thing, duckling," she said. He found the comic-character act a little creepy, having seen what lay behind the jovial mask, but she hadn't shown the hidden steel since. "Lord Falk has been blowing up buildings in New Cabora, he wants you back so bad. First City Hall, then the Grand Theater and the Courthouse. He must love you a whole bunch, sweetie."

Karl gave her a hard look, but she returned it blandly.

"Yeah, he loves you so much he's left my parents homeless," Jopps snarled. "When the Courthouse came down, it took a street of apartments with it." Jopps turned to Vinthor again, voice pleading. "Sir, I have to go to them. They need my help. You don't need me here . . ."

"What if Falk finds us and attacks?" Vinthor countered. "I'll need every man."

"If he attacks, you'll slip out the back door and escape while he's knocking down the front," Jopps said. "Whether I'm here or not won't change that."

"It's a matter of duty," Vinthor said. "You swore an oath . . ."

"Oh, let him go, there's a good cell leader," Goodwife Beth said. "One man won't make a difference. And you're the only man here with any family, aren't you, poor dear?" she said to Jopps.

He nodded. "Denson's got no one. None of the others, either."

Vinthor frowned, but Goodwife Beth's gaze had become . . . penetrating. "All right," he said at last, almost explosively. "All right," he repeated, and this time he just sounded resigned. "Permission granted. Look after your parents. And then come back here."

"Yes, sir, thank you, sir!" Jopps said, and almost ran from the room.

"You did the right think, cupcake," Goodwife Beth said warmly to Vinthor, and then she looked up at Karl, who still stood on the stairs. "I'm afraid you're not the most popular person in New Cabora right now, Your Highness, love," she said. "Old Falk is making sure of that."

"I would stop him if I could," Karl said. "If you returned me to the Palace—"

Vinthor let out a laugh that sounded more like a snort, and Goodwife Beth smiled hugely. "I'm afraid we can't do that, precious. Patron's orders." She cocked her head to one side. "Come here and let me see how that dressing gown fits, there's a lamb."

Wishing he'd never come down, Karl flip-flopped over to her.

"Turn around, chickadee," she said. He did. "Come closer." He took a step in. "Let's just check the size," she said, and before he could react, had opened the dressing gown wide. "Oh, my," she said, "I guess I should have given you some pajamas, too!" And then she flicked the dressing gown closed again. "Looks like everything is sized just fine, ducky!" she said cheerfully. "Toddle off now and get yourself dressed, if you're up for all day."

Cheeks burning with shame, Karl turned and headed

toward the stair, exchanging a look with Vinthor, who wouldn't meet his eyes.

From his bedroom window, Karl watched Jopps mount up and ride out of the farmyard, heading back to New Cabora.

What else has Falk done, trying to find me? he thought sickly. *What other atrocities have I brought down on the Commoners' heads by my stupid, childish behavior?*

None of this would have happened if he hadn't decided to follow the two men he had seen out his Palace window. City Hall would still stand. The Grand Theater. The Courthouse would still be there, and the apartments behind it.

And Falk wouldn't stop. He would keep up the pressure on the Commoners, pushing harder and harder until someone broke and told him where Karl was hidden.

And then what? An armed assault against Goodwife Beth's farmhouse?

If that happened, magic-wielding guards against Commoners armed with swords and crossbows—sticks and stones, for all the good they would do without magic—then how many more would die? How many more would die because of Prince Karl, the man who had promised to the Commoner in the Council Chamber that he would be a better king than his father, that he would bridge the gap between Commoners and Mageborn?

It would be better for everyone if the assassin had killed me, he thought darkly. *Better if I had never been born*.

Jopps disappeared in a cloud of snow down the road leading out of the little valley, and Karl flicked the curtain closed and turned, pointlessly, to getting dressed.

The cloaked man on horseback watched from a hillside as, out on the ice of the lake, two dogsleds hurried south. He had been very careful to position himself below the hill's crest, to avoid silhouetting himself against the bright morning sky.

There was little chance he would be noticed now, with

the light behind him turning the hill into a giant lump of shadow, while illuminating the two dog sleds—and especially the bundle of bright blue that seemed to form a large part of the second sled's cargo.

Like all members of the King's Mounted Rangers, Constable Orlam was Mageborn, and though his own magic was slight, it was sufficient for his needs. All of the "Mounties" were trained in the construction and operation of certain enchanted objects to help them in their duties. Orlam took one of them now, a magniseer he had crafted himself, from a case hung on his saddle. Though the air was already frigid, sparkling with ice crystals in the westering sunlight, the magniseer frosted over . . . and to Orlam, it appeared the dogsleds on the lake leaped a dozen times nearer.

Of course, Orlam had never seen an airship, as the orders from the Palace telling him what to look for had termed the object of his search. He didn't really believe the rumors flying through the ranks of the Rangers that this airship was a kind of flying carriage from beyond the Great Barrier. But there was no doubt that the thing on the second sled, one of the big sixteen-dog freight sleds that carried cargo to communities all along the shoreline in winter, matched the description. The dogs were pulling it well enough, but Orlam could tell it was a heavy load. Two men rode with it, one driving, the other resting.

The smaller eight-dog sled in front carried supplies wrapped in hides and tied down with ropes, and four people. Bundled against the cold as they were, it was difficult to tell much about them, but it looked to Orlam very much as though one of them was smaller and more slender than the others . . . and the coat she wore matched another part of the description he had been given.

He lowered the magniseer and tucked it away again. It was pure happenstance that he had come close enough to the lake to see them down there, running that close to the shore. Normally at this stage in his patrol he would have been miles away to the east; but he had been summoned in his capacity as a dispenser of the King's Justice to rule in a land dispute near Birchwood that had grown heated enough to come to violence, and from Birchwood it had made more sense to reverse his usual patrol pattern.

Which had put him here and now.

Praise to the SkyMage, Orlam thought, and felt a thrill of pride that he had been the one chosen to discover the girl that Lord Falk said was so important to Unbinding the Mageborn at last, freeing them from the prison of the Barriers.

Careful never to crest the top of the hill, he moved out of sight of the lake, and then opened a magelink to the Palace.

CHAPTER 20

FALK STOOD ONCE MORE BY THE STATUE in New Cabora Square, guards surrounding him, soldiers forming a white line all around the square. Both guards and soldiers were heavily armed, not just with pikes, shields, swords, and clubs, but also with less-visible and yet far more deadly enchanted weapons: flamesweeps, breathstoppers, the euphemistically named meloncrushers. The guards and soldiers had enough power at their disposal to slay every person in the Square in seconds—and the Commoners knew it. Falk smiled. Hell, *he* could have killed most of them singlehandedly.

MageLords ruled by divine right and with divinely bestowed power. The Commoners' place was to serve. If they served well, they might be rewarded. If they rebelled . . . well, the ruins of City Hall, the Courthouse, and the Grand Theater were testament to what would happen.

But though Falk was perfectly willing and able to continue using force to keep the Commons in line, he didn't want to have to. He wanted this unrest quieted, so he could focus on finding Brenna and finally . . . *finally* . . . bringing his great Plan to fruition.

And, thanks to Mother Northwind, he thought he had found a way.

He was not the one making a speech today in the center of the Square. He stood on the lower level of the statue's great pedestal. Above him, looking out over the crowd, stood Davydd Verdsmitt.

"He will do whatever you ask of him," Mother Northwind had assured him, and indeed, Verdsmitt had agreed at once to come to the Square and make the speech he was about to deliver, one that had been written by Falk and then "improved" by Verdsmitt. Falk's mouth twitched. Whatever else Mother Northwind had done to the man's mind, it hadn't stopped him from thinking like a writer.

He glanced at one particular guard who, rather than watching the crowd, was watching Falk. If Verdsmitt's speech was not *exactly* what Falk had asked for, Falk would signal that guard, and the speech—and Verdsmitt—would both be cut short.

But Verdsmitt did not stray from the text. "Fellow New Caborans!" he shouted. "You know me. You know who I am. You know my skill with a pen. And you know I have sometimes turned that skill against the rule of the MageLords."

A murmur swept through the crowd. *They'd known*, all right, Falk thought, *but they're uneasy that he's admitting it in front of me.*

Well, they're about to feel a great deal uneasier.

"I come before you today to tell you . . . I was wrong to do so."

The murmur swelled to something louder. "Davydd, no!" someone shouted. Falk hoped the guards had noted whoever it was; he might be worth talking to privately later.

Verdsmitt held up his hand. "I was wrong, because I did not realize where it could lead," he shouted. "Look around you. We cannot defy the MageLords. They alone have magic, and that magic gives them the power—and the right—to rule those of us to whom it is denied. It is the natural order of things, and we cannot change it. Nor should we attempt to do so."

The murmur in the crowd had a nasty edge to it, and the guards were fingering their weapons. Falk frowned. Had he misjudged . . . ?

But Verdsmitt's speech wasn't finished. "We cannot change it, but we can improve on it," he said. "I have had consultations with Lord Falk since I was arrested—as I most definitely deserved to be!" (Here he gave one of the wry grins that made him so appealing on stage.) "We have reached an understanding. Prince Karl must still be returned: there is no question about that. But once he is returned, and as long as there are no more acts of open rebellion, sabotage, or defiance, Lord Falk has agreed to an extraordinary meeting of the MageLord Council and representatives of the Commoners, to find ways that Commoners can exercise more self-rule . . . within the limits set by the King, of course. And I remind you that Prince Karl has long been a friend to the Commons, and will surely do everything he can to address our grievances.

"Therefore, friends, especially my friends within the Common Cause, I call on you to put thoughts of rebellion behind you, for the greater good of all. To prove his good faith, Lord Falk has agreed to magically rebuild the Courthouse within the week. If there are no more incidents, he will rebuild the Grand Theater the week after that." Another grin. "Where, I remind you, there is supposed to be a remount of my mystery *The Light in the Sky* in a month's time, so, if you love me . . ."

Astonishingly, that evoked a few chuckles.

"Finally, City Hall will be rebuilt as soon as Prince Karl is returned," Verdsmitt continued. "It is a fair offer, a magnanimous offer, and one that proffers hope for a new era of better relations between Commoners and MageLords." That wry smile once more. "As someone once wrote, 'Mount Perfection cannot be scaled, but you have a fine view of its peak from Mount Good-Enough.'"

The smile and the well-known line—from *Up and Down and 'Round the Town*, one of Verdsmitt's popular comedies—both perfectly delivered, elicited outright laughter, and Falk saw the guards relax a little.

"One week of quiet," Verdsmitt said. "One week, and our beautiful Courthouse will be restored. The curfew will be lifted, the number of guards patrolling our streets reduced. One week. Two weeks, and the Theater returns. As soon as Prince Karl is released, City Hall. And then . . . the Unity Convention.

"We all hope for a better life for our families and children. I offer you a way to make that hope reality. Please don't steal it away from all the frightened fathers and mothers and children, grandfathers and grandmothers, by launching more attacks on the MageLords, attacks that are as doomed to failure as the attack on the MageFurnace. And to those who are holding the Prince, I say, you are holding our future captive, as well. Free him, and free us all.

"Let us all join together in hope, let us all hope together for change, let us together change our ways to ways of peace, and together, we will all give hope and peace a chance.

"Thank you." And Verdsmitt bowed, a deep actor's bow.

The applause started slowly at first, then swelled, then grew to a great roar of approval. Falk saw tears on the Commoner faces below him, people holding up their children to see Verdsmitt as he waved and bowed again, and was surprised to feel . . . well, jealous, he supposed, jealous that Verdsmitt could rouse that kind of emotion, that kind of adulation, even while announcing what was essentially a surrender of everything the Common Cause claimed to stand for.

Verdsmitt has his own magic, Falk thought. *The magic of words. In some ways, it may be stronger than mine.*

But then, just as a reminder to himself, he deliberately looked past the feet of the bowing Verdsmitt at the ruins of City Hall. *And in a great many other ways*, he thought, *it is not.*

Their return trek to the Palace was considerably different than their approach to the Square had been. The guards had to stay close around Falk and Verdsmitt, but it seemed to be mostly because so many people wanted to see Verdsmitt, even reaching out hands they had to know would be slapped away, trying to touch him or get him to touch them.

"That was well done," Falk said to Verdsmitt when they had finally left the press of the crowd behind and were approaching the gate. "It was everything I had hoped for, and it may indeed return peace to the streets." He studied the playwright. Mother Northwind insisted the man did not know he was the Patron, and neither did the rebels of the Common Cause, that he always issued orders indirectly, or through a Mage link and that Tagaza disguised their identities. *Too bad*, Falk thought, *or I could have just made him order the release of Karl and had him give me the names of all the Cause's leaders, without any of this "Unity Convention" nonsense. But if he doesn't know he is the Patron . . . what does he think he just accomplished?* "Do you really think the members of the Common Cause will listen to you?"

"I think there is a good chance of it, my lord," Verdsmitt said modestly. "If I have made them understand how wrong they are—how wrong *I* was—to raise voices and hands against good King Kravon and Your Lordship, then they most certainly will. And if they do not, my lord, I beg you to be magnanimous and not let one or two minor harassments by overzealous Commoners derail your promise to rebuild and to hold the Unity Convention. After a major attack, of course, you must take firm action, as I'm sure every reasonable person will agree, but if little real harm is done . . . if you condemn it but refuse to allow it to derail your plans for rapprochement, it would go a long way toward improving Your Lordship's standing in the eyes of New Cabora's Commoner citizens."

Falk nodded thoughtfully. "I believe you are right, Verdsmitt. Of course, I will have to weigh carefully the seriousness of any such attack, but if it is minor . . . well, as you say, I can afford to be magnanimous in pursuit of the greater good." He clapped Verdsmitt on the back. "And may I say, Davydd," he said, using the playwright's first name for the first time, "how wonderful it is that you have come to understand how foolish all of this Common Cause business has been." *Not that you had any choice in the matter.*

"Thank you, my lord." Verdsmitt bowed his head as though to hide how touched he was by the praise.

SkyMage, Falk thought with admiration, *Mother Northwind outdid herself.*

His pleasure faded, however, as he contemplated the reason she had been unable to make Verdsmitt even more useful: Tagaza. Even now, he knew, Mother Northwind was with the First Mage, trying to put him back together so he could re-create the spell that would find Brenna . . . *and then face his just punishment*, Falk snarled silently.

"My lord, a word," said a voice from his other side, and Falk turned to see Captain Fedric. "My lord, a Commoner approached us in secret as the crowd dispersed, with an urgent request to speak to you." Fedric lowered his voice. "He says he knows where Prince Karl is . . . said that if Verdsmitt is giving up, then so is he."

Falk glanced at Verdsmitt, who gave no sign of hearing anything that had been said, eyes focused on the gates inside the archway of stone that marked the opening through the Lesser Barrier. In calmer times, those gates stood open, though guarded. Since Karl's disappearance, they had been kept magically sealed, opened grudgingly only to those with urgent business in the Palace.

Like barn doors shut after the cows have escaped, Falk thought cynically, which he thought he was entitled to, since it was, after all, his belated and useless command that had shut them. Still, some things you did just for appearances.

He looked back at the captain. "Where is this man now?"

"In the guardhouse of the gate," Fedric replied. "Awaiting your wishes."

"Take him to the Palace," Falk commanded. "But don't take him down to the dungeon—no need to terrify him back into silence. Take him to one of the small conference rooms . . . the Blue Lounge, I think. Provide him with refreshment. A full flagon of really good wine. And when I am unfortunately delayed, offer him a second flagon, and tell him I will be along shortly . . . just as soon as my pressing schedule allows."

Fedric smiled. "Yes, my lord," and peeled off toward the guardhouse.

The gate swung open, and Falk and Verdsmitt, accompanied by a remaining quartet of bodyguards, started across the cobblestoned bridge. "In your most recent play, Davydd," Falk said conversationally, "you had a line—a rhyming couplet, no less ... let me see if I can remember it ... ah, yes. 'How people cheered when that cursed arch and gate/were thrown to ruin, nine hundred years too late.'"

Verdsmitt winced. "Don't remind me, my lord. I wish that play had never left my pen."

"Well," Falk said judiciously, "I'm no critic, but I thought it had its moments. Perhaps it just needs rewriting. I could offer you my thoughts ..."

"My lord," said Verdsmitt. "I wish you would. It pains me to think how until now I have stumbled through the dark thickets of verbiage without your shining insight to light my way."

Just for a moment, Falk thought Verdsmitt was mocking him. But the playwright's face remained so sincere he dismissed the notion as ludicrous. Still, perhaps Mother Northwind had gone a little overboard in turning Verdsmitt loyal. Falk would have to remember that. Sometimes those who only said yes were far more dangerous to a ruler ... *Would-be ruler*, Falk thought, *you're not there yet*, but still, he cherished the thought ... than those who dared to tell him no.

Once across the bridge, Falk took a deep breath of the balmy air, thick with the smell of green growing things, and began shedding his coat. "Well, again, Davydd, excellent work today. Now that you are at liberty to move around, I hope you'll take time to enjoy the Palace grounds. The ornamental gardens are really quite beautiful."

"Thank you, my lord, I have been hoping to do so." Verdsmitt bowed low, then turned and angled away, pulling off his own coat as he did so. One of the servants, who had scurried up as they had stepped off of the bridge, took it and strode off toward the Palace as Verdsmitt disappeared around a flowering bush.

Falk walked slowly on toward the Palace himself. He would wait two or three hours before questioning the informant who had approached the captain, plenty of time to let the wine work on him. It was one of the softer interrogation techniques, but sometimes remarkably effective. Even if the man were dissembling, he would be more likely to betray himself with a flagon of wine . . . "really good wine," as he'd told the captain, which would be understood to mean the wine that they heavily fortified just for these occasions, the taste of the extra alcohol magically removed.

In the meantime, there was Mother Northwind's progress with Tagaza to check on.

But on his way to Tagaza's quarters, he was met by Brich, who for once—*And a nice change it makes, too,* Falk thought—looked pleased by the news he carried. "Yes, Brich?"

Brich smiled. "My lord, a message came in this morning from a Mounted Ranger on the east side of the lake. He has spotted Brenna, Anton, and the airship being pulled south by dogsleds. The Mountie is shadowing them from the shoreline."

I have her again! Falk thought, and it felt like a huge weight had been taken off his shoulders. "I would issue orders to immediately dispatch a sizable contingent of soldiers to seize them as soon as an opportunity presents itself, but I suspect they would be redundant," Falk said.

Brich's smile widened. "The orders were issued the moment the message came in . . . in your name, of course."

"Excellent." Falk trusted Brich—about the only person he could say that of, now that Tagaza had betrayed him—and had made it clear to his secretary that he could, within reason, issue orders on Falk's behalf if time were of the essence. "They will seize them tonight, and have them back here . . . ?"

"Within two days."

"Excellent," Falk repeated. "Well done, Brich."

"Thank you, sir." Brich looked almost as pleased by the praise as Verdsmitt had. *And Mother Northwind*, Falk thought rather smugly, *didn't have a thing to do with it.*

With Brenna having been found by ordinary means, it was no longer urgent that Tagaza be healthy enough to try his Heir-finding spell again—but when Brich intercepted him, Falk had been on his way to see how the First Mage was coming along under Mother Northwind's ministrations, and now he let inertia carry him the rest of the way . . .

. . . to be met, outside Tagaza's quarters, by a grim-faced Mother Northwind, just closing the door behind her.

"Ah, Mother Northwind. How goes it?"

"I'm sorry, Lord Falk," she said. "I did my best, but . . . he died ten minutes ago."

With Brenna found, he felt little but relief at the news; and feeling a little impish, knowing it would shock her, he simply shrugged and said, "Oh, well. These things happen."

This was so obviously not at all the response she had expected that she actually seemed speechless for a moment, much to his delight. For once, knowing Brenna and Anton had been found, he was a step ahead of her.

She'll find out when they're brought here and not a moment sooner, he thought. *A valuable reminder that, useful though she is, the Plan we are both working for is mine, and I can achieve it even without her help.*

"Although I'm very sorry to hear it, of course," he continued. "What happened?"

"His own spell happened," Mother Northwind said, her dark eyes narrowed as she searched his face. "It was interrupted just as he was gathering the energy he needed . . . and that energy had to go somewhere. He tried to throw it off into the steam, but he was being hurled backward and scalded at the same moment, and lost control. Some of the energy burned through him. His brain was so badly damaged I could not heal it. And even as I tried, the last thread holding him to life snapped. I chased after it, trying to keep his heart beating, keep him breathing, but every Healer has limits, even I, and . . . he slipped away." She sighed. "It may have been for the best. Even if he had lived, I do not think he would have been more than a ... lump. His mind, I think, was destroyed at the moment of the accident. Even his memories were lost." She spread her hands. "I have failed you this time, Lord Falk."

"Through no fault of your own, Mother Northwind," Falk said. He smiled, thinking of Verdsmitt. "And you have succeeded spectacularly for me so many other times. Now, go and rest. You have done all you can for me for now."

"Thank you, Lord Falk," Mother Northwind said. "I *do* feel fatigued." She made her slow way down the hall, and Falk watched her go, feeling like a little boy who had just put something over on his mother.

His own mother was long dead and hadn't wasted a lot of affection on him when she was alive, and he would never mistake the "Mother" in Mother Northwind as anything more than an honorific the Commoners applied, but still, the feeling was the same.

His smile widened as she turned the corner and went out of sight, and he thought about the informant waiting in the Blue Lounge. If the man really did know where Karl was—and Falk had high hopes—then Falk would know *two* things Mother Northwind did not, and presenting her with the *fait accompli* of both Karl and Brenna back where they belonged, under his thumb and in the Palace, would send an even more forceful message to her not to underestimate *him*.

It was still too early to go to the Blue Lounge, so Falk directed his steps instead toward his office, where the damnable paperwork had no doubt climbed to alarming new heights during the course of the day. He stepped aside with a smile—much to their surprise—for the servants hurrying to Tagaza's room to take charge of the body. There would have to be a state funeral, of course, but it would fortunately fall to the Prime Adviser, Lord Athol, to arrange it and to give the eulogy. *I'll get Verdsmitt to write it for him*, Falk thought. *There won't be a dry eye in the Great Hall.*

His smile faded as he thought of the one thing Tagaza's death *did* cast uncertainty on: the spell that would break the rules governing the succession of the Keys and transfer them to him in the moment of the simultaneous deaths of King and Heir. But then, after recent events, he would not have trusted Tagaza to perform the spell even if he had lived. The other mage who had learned the spell was a staunch member of the Unbound, and almost as skilled as Tagaza.

He'll suffice, Falk thought.

And the time was drawing oh-so-near.

There was one other thing to think about, though. Falk made his way through the magically sealed door and guard station ("Marigold." "Cornflower.") to his office, nodding to Brich, text-stamping away once more.

The Outsider boy, Anton, Falk thought, sitting at his desk. *There's where Mother Northwind can help once more. Make him as loyal to me as Verdsmitt, and he will teach me how to operate his airship. Send him back over the Barrier with someone I can trust . . . he can be my ambassador to the Outside, assure them we only want peace, that when the Barrier falls there will be no cause for alarm . . .*

. . . and then the Outsiders will be all the more unprepared as we annex all the villages along the Barrier and prepare to move inexorably into the rest of the world.

Yes, Falk thought. *That is what I'll do.*

Satisfied, he pulled the nearest stack of paper toward him and reached for his pen.

Mother Northwind was thinking furiously as she walked away from Falk, but though she racked her brain, mentally reviewing everything she thought she knew about the current state of play, she could think of no reason why Lord Falk should have reacted with such equanimity to the news of Tagaza's death. *These things happen?* What kind of way was that to respond to the death of your oldest friend . . . not to mention the architect and planned-for-executor of a major component of your two-decade-old plan to seize the Kingdom and destroy the Great Barrier?

Mother Northwind had been prepared for consternation,

fury, accusations of incompetence . . . anything, really, except for this calm, almost jovial acceptance.

She reviewed what she knew. Prince Karl was safely ensconced at Goodwife Beth's. Brenna and Anton by now had been retrieved by the dog teams sent north from Foam River. They would soon be delivered to a rocky bay, safe from prying eyes, on Foam River's outskirts, and from there taken to join Karl.

The only thing . . . the *only* thing . . . she could think of that might have made Falk so accepting of Tagaza's death was the speech Verdsmitt had been expected to deliver. *He must have done himself proud*, Mother Northwind thought. *People forget he can act as well as he can write. And it must have been difficult for him to portray himself as suddenly rejecting the claims and ideology of the Common Cause.*

Well, she thought, the Common Cause had always been a sideshow for him, really. Verdsmitt's true driving purpose had always been revenge on his ex-lover, King Kravon . . . not surprising, since when she had touched him on the night she enlisted him, she had ensured that time would do nothing to dim the bright, shining pain caused by Kravon's betrayal, or Verdsmitt's burning desire to retaliate.

That must be it, she thought. Verdsmitt's speech had gone so well that even Tagaza's death could not shake Falk's renewed confidence. Perhaps he had already resigned himself to not being able to use Tagaza to find Brenna, assuming he would eventually find her through nonmagical means.

She paused for a moment as she climbed the stairs one floor to the level of her apartment. She did feel fatigued; she hadn't been lying about that. Healing a man was tiring, but killing one was exhausting . . .

. . . especially when you first had to systematically search for and destroy his memories so that no other Healer could reach inside and find some fading evidence of his complete innocence. Not that it hadn't been interesting to rummage in Tagaza's mind, especially those parts that had to do with the Great Barrier. Tagaza really did believe that magic would fail on its own in a few years if the Barriers were not brought down. More, though he had never told Falk—and now never would, Mother Northwind thought with relish—he believed that Falk's dreams of conquest were futile, since the farther Falk's forces got from the lode of magic on which Evrenfels was built, the weaker their magic would become, until it didn't work at all.

He was never really on Falk's side, either, Mother Northwind thought. *Three of us working to bring down the Barriers, and none of us for the same reason.*

And if I fail, and Falk succeeds, little good will it do him if Tagaza was right. He will never be able to expand his kingdom, and when the weapons Commoners have created in the Outside that I saw in Anton's mind are brought to bear, I doubt he will even hold Evrenfels.

She did not expect to fail. But she took some comfort in the thought that, even if she did, the MageLords would still be destroyed.

Breath coming a little easier, she finished climbing the stairs and headed to her room for what she felt was a well-deserved rest.

———

Two hours later, Falk finally went down to the Blue Lounge. The two Royal guards at the door saluted and held it open for him.

The man seated at the head of the long table of dark wood beneath the blue walls had not only drunk all of the wine provided him, he was well into a second flagon. He stood up when the door opened, but Falk noted with satisfaction that he put out a hand to steady himself.

Falk studied the man without saying anything for a moment. For his part, the man stood with his head cast down, that one steadying hand still on the table. He was breathing unusually hard, as though he had just been running instead of seated in a comfortable chair enjoying cheese and bread and lamb-stuffed pastries. He was also one of the most nondescript men Falk had ever seen, round and somehow soft around the edges, as though only half-formed.

"I am Lord Falk, Minister of Public Safety to His Majesty King Kravon, Keeper of the Keys and the Kingdom," Falk said at last. "I hope you found the wine and food to your liking."

"Yes, my lord. Thank you, my lord," said the man.

Falk sat down at the far end of the long table from the Commoner. "And your name is . . . ?"

"They call me Jopps, my lord," he said, his face glistening with perspiration, though the room was cool.

"Not your real name?" Falk said.

Jopps said nothing.

Falk shrugged. "No matter. Very well, Jopps. You told my Captain of the guard that you know where Prince Karl is."

"I do," Jopps said. "My lord. But I want some guarantees before I tell you."

Lord Falk's eyebrows rose. "I am not in the habit of negotiating with those who hold information it is their duty as loyal subjects of King Kravon to share," he said.

Jopps shook his head. "Don't care. No guarantees, you get nothing from me. My lord."

Mother Northwind could get it from you, Falk thought, and immediately rejected the thought. It was too easy to rely on her for gathering intelligence—and that was dangerous. For one thing, she was old, and he wouldn't have her skills to draw on forever. For another, relying too much on her would mean his own not-inconsiderable skills at acquiring information could wither. And for a third, he preferred to keep some secrets for himself.

"What guarantees?" Falk said.

"My parents, my lord," Jopps said hoarsely. "They lost their home, and the shop, when you destroyed the Courthouse. They need a place to live. They need money." He licked his lips. "And Healers. They're sick, Mom especially. You promise to look after them properly, like they . . . like they were Mageborn . . . and I'll tell you where Prince Karl is."

Falk studied him. "You want nothing for yourself?"

"No, my lord," Jopps said. "Nothing."

How unusual, Falk thought. *And refreshingly straight-forward.* He shrugged mentally. Well, why not? It would cost next to nothing. And if the man's information turned out to be bogus . . . well, it would give him a lever to use to pry the truth out of him. "Agreed. Where is the Prince?"

Jopps took a deep, shaky breath. *He looks*, Falk thought, *like he's going to be sick.* But though it might have been close, Jopps did not spew the contents of his stomach across the shiny surface of the table. Instead he said, "Goodwife Beth's, my lord."

Falk cocked his head. "Goodwife Beth," he said carefully, letting a little sharpened steel show in his voice, "is a character in a Verdsmitt play."

"Also the name of a woman . . . very tough woman . . . high in the Cause," Jopps said. All of a sudden words came rushing out of him, a different kind of spew as though, now that he had begun to talk, he might not be able to stop. "I don't know where she came from originally. She puts on this whole 'Goodwife Beth' act but underneath she's hard as nails. Slice your throat in a second if she thought you deserved it. She's got this farmhouse, well, that's what it looks like from the outside, out in a little valley west of New Cabora—closest town is a place called Quillhill. I can show you the exact spot. Thing is, it's not really a farmhouse . . . or I guess it is, but it's set into the hill . . . and there's more house inside the hill than you see on the outside. Got a secret exit up on the hilltop. Got to know that if you're going to go after the Prince. They'll try to take him out that way. I can show you where that is, too."

He stopped, suddenly; either he was out of breath or a second thought had finally chased down his runaway first one.

"Very complete," Falk said. "Perhaps you could show us on a map . . . ?"

Jopps nodded.

"And how do you know this, Jopps?" Falk said softly. "Why should I believe you?"

"Been in the Cause a long time," Jopps muttered, not meeting Falk's eyes. "Verdsmitt's doing. Heard him speak once, secret meeting . . . convinced me we had to fight back, had to try to make things better for Commoners, that King Kravon doesn't care about us, people freezing to death in the streets of the city every winter. . . it's obscene.

"Anyway, I joined up. Did odd jobs, nothing major. Then I met this girl called Jenna. Beautiful, young . . . I think I was half in love with her. We all were." He swallowed hard and dashed his hand across his eyes, quickly, as if chasing away a fly.

"We got word from the Patron. Something special planned. Biggest thing the Cause had ever done. The Patron needed a volunteer . . . needed a young woman . . . and Jenna stepped forward. She must have known she'd never get away with it, even if it worked . . . but she volunteered anyway."

"Volunteered for what?" Falk asked.

Jopps looked up for the first time. "To kill the Prince," he snarled. "She hid in the bubble under the water where he liked to swim, waited for him. But something went wrong. The Prince wasn't hurt, and Jenna . . ." He shook his head, then went on with a voice grown suddenly hoarse.

"And it didn't do a damn bit of good. All it did was bring the guards into the streets, rounding up people. Made things worse, not better. Jenna died for nothing. The Common Cause . . . the Patron . . . killed her for *nothing*." His voice was rising now. "I think the Patron *knew* it wouldn't work! I think the Patron threw away Jenna's life for nothing, just to cause a little trouble . . . and the only trouble she caused was for *us*!

"And then Verdsmitt got himself arrested. That was on the Patron's orders, too." *That* got Falk's attention. *Verdsmitt had* wanted *to be arrested?* "Patron wanted him in the Palace, for some reason. I don't know why. Me and Denson, we were sent in through the Barrier . . ."

"How?" Falk demanded, leaning forward.

Jopps shrugged. "I don't know. Little stick of a thing,

colder than an icicle. It cut an opening in the Barrier, like a knife cutting a wax-paper windowpane. Then you had a few seconds to get through before it closed up. Would only work twice, we were told; once in, once out, then it would just be a stick again.

"Well, we got in with our folding boat, came over to this side of the river. Then . . ." He took another deep breath. "My lord, we put some . . . things. Here and there around the outside of the Palace. Stones, sticks, they didn't look like much, but they had that chill, you know, that magic thing."

"You'll show me exactly where these things are?" Falk snapped.

Jopps nodded rapidly. "Of course, my lord."

Enchanted objects for eavesdropping . . . or murder, Falk thought. *Tagaza's doing. And that's why he was so willing to do the spell to find Brenna. He had other ways to disrupt the Plan, even if I got her back.*

Hell, he was head of the Magecorps. The whole Palace may be full of his devices!

Well, no matter. *Tagaza's dead*, he thought fiercely. *Whatever those devices were intended to do, he's not around to trigger them. We can collect them at our leisure.* He made a mental note to interrogate the Magecorps mages responsible for Palace maintenance. "Carry on."

"Then we hid and watched to see what happened when Verdsmitt was taken. We thought he was going to do something spectacular, thought he was going to escape and come running out to us, something . . ."

"But it was Jenna all over again. Nothing happened, except we didn't have Verdsmitt anymore." He sounded bitter. "So we rowed back across the lake. Got through the Barrier all right, were packing up to head into the city . . . and out of nowhere, here comes the rutting Prince. He ran right through the Barrier. I could have sworn it had already closed, but . . . there he was!"

He shook his head. "We didn't want him. Could have killed him, but we didn't want to do that without orders from higher up. I figured we were just delaying the inevitable. The Patron had already tried to kill him once, after all. But next thing you know we're dragging the Prince's sorry ass out to Goodwife Beth's."

"So why did you decide to come to me?" Falk said.

"I heard about what happened to the Courthouse, what happened to Mom and Dad," Jopps said. "I came back to help them, didn't come back to betray anybody. But then I saw everything that had happened just because the bloody Patron decided to try to kill the Prince and then keep him when he jumped into our hands, and I thought, 'This ain't worth it.' We're supposed to be about making things better for the Commons, and instead we've done nothing but make them worse.

"And then Davydd Verdsmitt himself, today, telling us to give up . . ." Jopps swiped his hand across his nose. "If he's done with the Cause, then I am, too. That's the simple truth. And so is what I've been telling you about the Prince. You go where I show you, you'll find him, my lord."

"We'll find your friends, too," Falk said.

"They ain't my friends. Not anymore."

Falk considered. "All right, Jopps," he said, "I'm going to trust you. But you're coming with us on the raid. If things aren't exactly as you told us . . . if you've set us up for some kind of ambush . . . you'll wish you were never born—" he turned his voice ice cold, "—and so will your parents in the few short, miserable days they have left to them."

Jopps paled, but he nodded once. "I told you the truth," he said. "You go there, you'll find him."

Falk smiled. "Well, then, let's go there, shall we?"

CHAPTER 21

FOR BRENNA, the ride south on the dogsled was like a nightmare from which there was no waking, one of those nightmares in which a monster was chasing her and no matter how fast she ran she couldn't get away ... except in this dream they were chasing the monster, and getting closer and closer to it far faster than she could have run.

She couldn't believe that all their efforts to make the airship flyable and escape from Falk's manor had been for naught. She couldn't believe that High Raven—who she had decided was a fair and honorable man who would not turn Anton over to the fate that Falk and Mother Northwind intended for him—would betray them to the witch just because she used to heal broken bones and chase away fevers for the clan. The Commoners in Falk's demesne also praised her healing abilities, but that didn't make what she intended to do any less evil!

But here they were, sliding across the ice pulled by the panting dogs whose breath-fog swept across them, as though to emphasize just how fast they were moving toward the one place they didn't want to go.

The first night they made use of a rough stone building nestled against a hillside, all of them, men and dogs and Brenna alike, sleeping around a central fire pit, the men taking turns watching through the night. There was little talking.

After another day's miserable travel, they made camp in

a sheltered cove, where piles of boulders formed a kind of protective embrace around a curved beach, and the ground inside sloped up sharply into trees. You couldn't say it stopped the relentless, bitter wind entirely, but it reduced it to fretful, swirling breezes that, unlike the wind on the lake, didn't feel like a sharp knife cutting deeper into any exposed flesh ... until you couldn't feel the flesh at all, of course. Before they had left the Minik camp, their new captors had insisted that both she and Anton spread protective animal grease on their faces and any other skin left exposed by their coats and gloves, augmented by the additional clothing their new captors had brought with them. They hadn't suffered frostbite, but they smelled like last week's breakfast.

A ring of fire-blackened stones on the beach mutely testified that the cove had been used for camps before. As tents were hauled out and set up by one man, fire and food were arranged by another, and the other two tended to the dogs, giving them food and water and thoroughly examining ther feet—two were already wearing little leather booties that Brenna might have thought cute if the dogs wearing them didn't weigh better than half as much as she did and had fangs roughly the size of her little finger, which they enthusiastically showed whenever she got too near.

Brenna and Anton sat on rocks as close to the fire as they could get once it was lit. Brenna had been cold the day before; after a second day on the ice, she was beginning to think she would never be warm again. But she'd heard their leader say they would be off the ice some time tomorrow, and now she dared to ask him about it as he hung a stewpot from the metal rod suspended over the fire by two forked sticks.

She didn't really expect him to answer, but he surprised her. "Before noon. Foam River. Not that we're going into the town. But that's where the next lot'll take over." He spat into the fire, which sizzled. "Good riddance, I say. Don't know what you're wanted for, but I'll be glad to be—"

He stopped in mid-sentence, looking puzzled, then his

eyes rolled up into his head and he fell face forward into the fire. Brenna screamed and jumped up, and only then, as his clothes began to smolder and the smell of cooking meat rose into the still night air, saw the feathered shaft protruding from his back.

The other three had spun as one at the sound of their leader falling into the fire, and as one they fell, two killed instantly, the third screaming in agony as a shaft shattered his knee. Blood fountained from a severed artery, and his screaming was short-lived.

The screams had set off the dogs, which howled and barked and ran wildly back and forth. Anton ran to Brenna, who grabbed him and hugged him tight, pressing her face into his shoulder, trying to close her ears to the horrible sizzling of the man in the fire, to the noise of the dogs . . .

. . . to the crunch of running footsteps in the snow. Her head shot up as six men burst into the light, the naked swords in their hands glittering with frost. *Enchanted,* she thought.

The new arrivals were dressed all in white: white coats, white trousers, white boots. Even their helmets were painted white. But on their shoulders were round blue patches slashed across with a streak of red.

Army soldiers, Brenna realized. The first, a tall man with a large, beaked nose and a bushy mustache rimed with frost, strode over to them. "I am Sergeant Meerk," he said. "By order of Lord Falk, I arrest you. You are to be returned immediately to the Palace."

Brenna exchanged a startled look with Anton. It made no sense! The men who had just died had already been taking them to Falk . . . well, Mother Northwind, but that would have been on Falk's behalf . . .

. . . wouldn't it?

But if these men were acting on Lord Falk's orders, maybe . . .

"I am Lord Falk's ward," she said. "I thank you for your rescue, but I must demand that you—"

"I know who you are," the guardsman said. "And my

orders are to arrest you for certain, him," he nodded at the boy, "if at all possible . . . and do what we liked with the others." He took a couple of steps to the fire and kicked the body off of it. "Commoner trash!" Brenna hid her face against Anton's shoulder again, but not before she'd had one horrible glimpse of what was left of the dead man's face.

"I think I'm going to be sick," she mumbled to Anton.

"Not on my shoulder," he whispered. "Although I guess it would be fair turnabout for what I did to you the day we met . . ."

Despite everything, that made her chuckle. It threatened to turn into hysterics, though, so she bit it off. "There's something strange here," she whispered. "The dogsledders were taking us to Mother Northwind, who Falk told to twist your mind to make you loyal to him. These guards are taking orders from Falk, too . . . and yet they killed Mother Northwind's men."

"I know," Anton murmured. "Maybe—"

But Sergeant Meerk was pulling him away. "Enough of that," he snapped. "There's a carriage waiting to take us to New Cabora, but we have to get to the road and it's a long walk."

He snapped orders, and while two men stayed behind to deal with the cleanup, he and the other three formed a square around Anton and Brenna and marched them up the hillside into the snowy forest.

There was no chance to talk again during that hours-long hike, no chance to talk in the carriage with two guards keeping them silent.

As it turned out, there would be no chance to talk again for a very long time.

Karl jerked awake, not sure why. He lay in darkness for one long breathless moment, then heard the noise of splintering wood downstairs, followed by shouts and the clash of steel on steel.

His bedroom door crashed open, letting in red light and acrid smoke. Denson, sword in hand, shouted, "Get up!" Karl, naked, scrambled out of bed and grabbed the dressing gown Goodwife Beth had given him, but he barely had time to slip his arms into it before Denson grabbed him and shoved him toward the far end of the hallway, where the false wall hid the extended corridor built into the hillside. Karl managed to get the dressing gown cinched as they skidded to a halt at the wall. Downstairs there was a flash of blue light and a man screamed, the sound ending abruptly. Denson had opened the panel in the left wall that hid the lever to open the door; he pulled it hard.

"What's going on?" Karl said. His heart pounded in his ears. Two minutes earlier he had been fast asleep and his brain was playing catch-up to his frightened body. "An attack?"

"Falk's rutting guards," Denson snarled. "Jopps must have sold us out. Open, damn it!" he shouted at the wall, which was slowly starting to slide aside.

More shouts, the clash of swords, on the stairs now. Karl, glancing back, saw Vinthor's head appear. Then Denson grabbed him and dragged him into the hidden hallway, turned and grabbed another lever on that side. As the door began to close, Karl saw Vinthor drop from sight. An instant later two men in the blue-and-red uniforms of Royal guards stormed up the stairs and went straight into Karl's room. Finding it empty, they turned the other way—just in time to see the door to the secret passage closing, but with no time to reach it before it sealed.

Denson twisted the door lever sideways, and something heavy thudded into place inside the door. "Out the back door," Denson said, hurrying on down the corridor. "Horses up there."

"I'll freeze," Karl said, remembering the last time he had been marched barefoot through the snow. "I need boots at least, a coat—"

"You'll be lucky if I leave you your head, you mewling piece of MageLord filth," Denson growled. "I don't care if your balls freeze off." They'd reached the end of the hall-way. Denson pulled open that door, revealing the room where Karl had found him playing cards with Jopps the day he'd arrived. A man Karl hadn't met stood behind the overturned table, a crossbow leveled at the door. He low-ered it at the sight of Denson and the Prince. "What's—" he began.

"Royal rutting guards," Denson said. He turned and slammed the door shut, then lowered a heavy oak bar across it. "Time to get the hell out. Where's Spilk?"

The man with the crossbow jerked his head up. "Went up to watch the exit. Haven't heard anything."

"Then there's still a chance. If you have to fight," he said to the man with the crossbow, "watch for spells. Someone stops moving, gets a distant look like he's taking a shit, shoot him. They got Lazy with a melonbreaker. Head came apart like rotting fruit." He stared up the ladder leading to a hidden exit high above on the top of the hill. "If it was Jopps," he said almost to himself, "they're going to be wait-ing up there. Waiting for the first head to show itself . . ." He turned to the crossbowman. "Give me your helmet."

"What—?"

"Give it to me!" Denson barked. The crossbowman hes-itated, then slipped it off and handed it to him. Denson turned and jammed it onto Karl's head, almost taking his right ear off. Breaking noises came from the other side of the barred door. Denson grunted. "Didn't take them long." He pointed up. "Climb. You stick your head out first and we'll see if you keep it."

"But—"

"If they're out there, you royal turd, then Spilk is al-ready dead and me and Riddler here ain't long for this world. But I'll still count it a good night if they kill their precious Prince trying to rescue him. Now climb, or I'll shove this sword up your lily-white ass so far it'll snick out your tonsils. Go!"

Terrified, Karl turned and started to climb.

The rusty iron rungs were cold beneath his feet, and

once he had climbed a half dozen, he'd left the dim light of the guardroom behind him and moved upward through total darkness. The helmet, a size too small, squeezed his head so that he could feel his pulse pounding in his temples. The nightgown had come untied and flapped open around him, and the cold and the prospect of what lay ahead alike had his testicles trying to crawl inside his belly.

But he could do nothing but climb. Denson was behind him with sword in hand.

Suddenly he saw, over his head, a slightly less-dark circle within the black of the tunnel, a tinge of red to it. He slowed, then gasped as something sliced his heel, warm blood trickling from the wound. Denson wouldn't let him stop. He could only go on.

With a deep breath and a prayer to the SkyMage he didn't believe in, he poked his helmeted head up into the gray light, and suddenly everything happened at once.

He glimpsed half a dozen men, all guards, encircling the opening, saw a body lying in bloody snow just a few feet away—and then heard "Don't! It's the—" screamed at the same instant that blue light exploded all around his head, blinding him. There was a wet popping sound, and pieces of something wet struck his face and slid down it. He blinked, dazed but unhurt, then hands seized his shoulders and pulled him from the tunnel into the bitterly cold air.

"Down!" he heard Denson shout in the tunnel, then Riddler's voice, "They're underneath us, too!" and then an inferno of blue flame roared up from the tunnel behind him, followed by a plume of greasy black smoke . . . and then silence.

Someone was putting a heavy fur-lined leather cloak around Karl's shoulders, someone else had found him boots, but Karl barely noticed. All he could see was the dead guard lying in blood-soaked snow just the other side of the secret exit, his headless body encircled by grisly bits of red, white, and gray.

Mother Northwind spent the day after Tagaza's tragic death in her quarters, pleading fatigue. In fact, she was waiting: waiting for the magelink to come to life, with news of Brenna's progress toward Goodwife Beth's. Once Brenna was in the safe house, Mother Northwind thought with something approaching smugness, she could at last bid farewell for good to Lord Falk. After Kravon was dead, Verdsmitt was welcome to kill Falk, too, if he still wanted to—and she was pretty sure, after the speech Falk had "made" him make, that he still wanted to. Of course, by that time, if all went well, the Barriers would have collapsed and magic with them, and without his enchanted toys to help him, Verdsmitt would have to strangle Falk with his bare hands, but again, she thought he'd be willing to try.

As night fell, she began anticipating the call from the team collecting Brenna and Anton at Foam River. But the magelink did not activate.

Midnight came and went with no word, and at last, reluctantly, she decided she would risk magelinking to Goodwife Beth directly. She summoned the glowing blue globe, sent out the call . . . and got nothing in return. No link could be made.

She left the globe active so long that the temperature in the room dropped noticeably; then, shivering a little, she snapped it out of existence and moved closer to the fire.

What could have happened? Had they been forced to flee, move to a different safe house, Beth somehow prevented from taking the magelink-bracelet provided by Verdsmitt with her?

If that were the case, she might not hear anything for days, until someone managed to get a message to her through the Common Cause network of cells and sympathizers. She might get a knock in the middle of the night, a scrawled note slipped under her door . . . or she might not, if the message or messenger went awry. She'd be right where Falk was, wondering where Karl and Brenna were.

Frustrated and beginning to be worried, she went to bed. In the morning, there did indeed come a knock on the door.

She hobbled to it and opened it to find a liveried servant holding a silver tray with a card on it. "Your pardon, milady," he said formally. "The Honorable Lord Falk, Minister of Public Safety, requests your presence at dinner tonight in the Prince's Banquet Hall. I am to tell you that the entire King's Council will also be present."

Mother Northwind was astonished, and a little horrified. *What on Earth can Falk be thinking?* she thought. *He's always kept me in the shadows. Why is he dragging me out to a formal dinner with the King's Council, of all people?*

Her first instinct was to say "No." But . . . until she knew for certain where Brenna and the Prince were, she needed Falk, which meant putting up with his arrogance, his assumption that she was just a useful tool—a powerful, dangerous tool, but still a tool. *A tool*, she thought, *does not refuse to be used.*

And then she smiled a little. Besides, it *would* be interesting to see the Councillors. They wouldn't recognize in her the much younger Healer Makala, who had once lived in the Palace and tended all of them at one time or another. She imagined herself, in the middle of the dinner, shouting, "I've seen you all naked!" Her smile turned to a chuckle. "Tell Lord Falk," she said, still chuckling—the servant very carefully not reacting to that no-doubt unexpected response—"that I am honored by the invitation and will attend with pleasure."

"Yes, milady."

"And don't call me milady," Mother Northwind said. "I'm not yours, and I'm definitely not a lady." And then she shut the door on the servant's bemused face.

She knew a lot about those Councillors. It was while healing Lord Athol's hemorrhoids that she had found out about his son's "perversion" and supposedly tragic but actually most welcome suicide, and begun putting together the pieces that had led her to the oh-so-valuable Verdsmitt a few years later. She'd known enough about Lady Estra's under-the-table deals with merchants and suppliers to blackmail several dozen people, had she just wanted to be

rich, and knew about the idiot, illegitimate son that Lady
Vin kept locked in a basement room in her manor up by
Berriton. But of course, all that information was long out of
date now. Shaking a few hands, being helped to her seat
and out of it again . . . she couldn't glean much in such short
moments of contact, but she could probably at least, if she
were to use Falk's terminology, "update her files" on them.

If her plan proved out, none of that information would
likely matter, but you could never have too much information, Mother Northwind thought. Falk had once told her
there was a saying in his trade that "ninety percent of the
intelligence you collect is useless; the trouble is, you never
know which ninety percent it is."

And so it was that Mother Northwind allowed a young
man—very interested in (much younger) ladies, but without much of anything else in his head—to take her arm and
escort her to the Prince's Banquet Hall, a relatively small
dining area near Karl's quarters on the fourth floor of the
west wing. It was surprisingly tasteful for a formal Palace
room: black-and-white tiled floor, white walls, a black fireplace, a long black table spread with snowy white linen,
black sideboards with white marble tops. A silver chande-
lier sparkled overhead. They came in through large side
doors; a swinging door at one end of the room led to a
kitchen, from which good smells were emerging, while a
closed door at the other end of the room led, she supposed,
through a hidden hallway to the empty quarters of Prince
Karl.

The Councillors milled about, talking in low voices, sipping from the glasses of sparkling wine and nibbling the
appetizers the servants circulated among them on silver
trays. Mother Northwind recognized all of the Councillors
at once, though they hadn't, for the most part, aged well;
too much time in the Palace, too many dinners like this
one, had put too many pounds on some of them and gave
the others a kind of . . . preserved look, like a corpse in
stasis.

Of course, one Councillor was *literally* a preserved

corpse: Tagaza, the First Mage, who would remain in stasis until a state funeral could be organized, after travel became easier in the spring. His death might have contributed to some of the somberness Mother Northwind detected in the room, but she suspected what contributed to it a lot more was the trouble in the Commons: the attack on the Prince, his disappearance, Falk's destruction of the Square, the sabotage of the MageFurnace. *The MageLords*, Mother Northwind thought with some satisfaction, *are feeling a lot less sure of themselves than they are accustomed to.*

She smiled. *Just wait until I'm finished with them.* She turned that smile on a servant who had approached her with wine. "Why, thank you, I believe I will."

Falk was engaged in conversation with Lord Athol in the corner by the kitchen door; he saw her came in and detached himself from the Prime Adviser to greet her.

"Mother Northwind," he said. "How good of you to come." He nodded to the Councillors. "I told the King's Council of your tremendous, though sadly unsuccessful, attempt to save Tagaza's life, and they all wanted to meet you."

"Well, I'm honored, my lord," Northwind said, a little too loudly, as though she were slightly deaf. "It's not often a simple country Healer like me gets to hobnob with the great and powerful."

Falk's smile seemed genuine, and she suspected she knew why. "Well, then," he said. "Allow me to introduce you."

She resisted the impish impulse to ask him to take her arm, knowing full well why he never had and never would, and instead hobbled on her own over to the first of the Councillors.

Half an hour later, as she sat down to dinner on Falk's left hand—Falk himself, as host, sitting at the table's head, and Lord Athol on his right—she knew a lot more about the Councillors, but none of it seemed very important. Lady Vin's idiot son had died, "cause unknown," and been quietly buried on her estate. Lady Estra was still corrupt. Lord Athol had pretty much forgotten about his long-dead first son and was much more focused on his now ten-year-old replacement, although slightly worried by the boy's recently displayed tendency to torture small animals.

When they were all seated, one chair remained unfilled, between Athol and Falk. As the servants stepped back into their assigned places along the walls, ready to pour and serve and tidy away as required, Lord Falk tapped his glass with his spoon for quiet, then got to his feet.

"Lords and Ladies, Mother Northwind," he said, "I know you must wonder why I have invited you to such a banquet after so many disturbing events. I'm sure you have said to each other, 'What is there to celebrate?'

"To which I reply . . . this!" He turned toward the closed door Mother Northwind had assumed led to the Prince's quarters. It swung open . . .

. . . and Prince Karl, in full Royal finery, limping a little but otherwise apparently unharmed, stepped into the room.

The Councillors surged to their feet. Mother Northwind did not. She felt as though she'd been slapped. She glared at Falk, and saw him looking straight at her. *The bastard*, she thought. *Making a point that he knows a few things I don't. Putting me in my place.*

She couldn't stay seated while the Prince made his way to his chair at the far end of the table. Protocol and prudence alike dictated that she climb to her feet. And so she did, while the Councillors applauded—actually applauded!—Prince Karl as he limped to his place.

Verdsmitt gave you a few pointers on stage-managing this, didn't he, Falk? she thought.

Once the Prince sat down, Falk gestured for the others to do likewise, but he wasn't done yet. "My Lords and Ladies, Prince Karl was rescued from the Common Cause thugs holding him prisoner near Quillhill early this morning. We have captured the woman who ran what proved to be a quite substantial hideout and staging area for the Cause, and are questioning her.

"But that is not the only good news I have to share with you this evening. For obvious reasons I have not made it widely known, though some of you may have heard rumors, but my young ward, Brenna, whom many of you have met on her annual visits to the Palace, was also kidnapped . . . kidnapped from my manor and taken cross-country to the Great Lake, where she was temporarily held by savages. They sold her to the Common Cause, who perhaps hoped to blackmail me in some fashion. Fortunately, a Mounted Ranger spotted them, and she, too, has been rescued.

"She will not be joining us this evening, as she recovers from her ordeal, but it is also her return to my love and care that I wish to celebrate tonight." He paused and looked around the table, smiling a smile Mother Northwind dearly wished she could personally rip from his face. "There is one more exciting development to report, but for that, I will wait until tomorrow morning's formal meeting. For now, let us eat and drink and enjoy ourselves in celebration of the safe return of both the Prince and my dear ward Brenna. Lords and Ladies, Mother Northwind, I give you a toast: Prince Karl!"

"Prince Karl!" the Councillors said, and then began talking in much more animated voices than before while the servants brought the onion soup.

It smelled wonderful, and Mother Northwind had eaten little all day, but after what she had just heard, she wanted nothing to do with it. Lord Falk continued to watch her, however, and so she forced herself to eat it, every spoonful, though each one tasted like sawdust, and slid down her throat and rested in her stomach like lead.

Karl ate mechanically, mouthed pleasantries to the Councillors, smiled, and felt dead and confused inside. Was it all over, then? Had everything that had begun with the assassination attempt by the lake boiled down to those few moments of bloody terror at Goodwife Beth's farm? The Common Cause, or at least their mysterious Patron, had at first wanted him dead. Then, fortunately, they had decided he might have some value alive after he obligingly handed himself over to them.

But now, just like that, he was back in the Palace. Goodwife Beth was in prison. Most of those who had held him were dead. And it sounded like Davydd Verdsmitt himself had pulled in his claws and was rubbing up against Falk like a house cat, purring and mewling for scraps from the MageLord's table.

His own vehemence surprised him. The Cause was his enemy, and now it had been removed. He had been returned to his former life of indolence and indulgence, awaiting the sad demise of his father some unguessable number of years in the future. He should be pleased; hell, he should be ecstatic.

And yet . . . the people he'd met in the Cause had seemed more real, more alive, more *important*, in fact, than the lords and ladies at table with him.

Except . . . *her*. He gazed down the length of the table at the strange old woman seated at Falk's left hand, across from Lord Athol (who had hurried down to offer his unctuous welcome as soon as the toast was finished). "Mother Northwind," Falk had called her, some backcountry Healer from near his manor. He had offered no explanation as to why she was invited, when the First Healer himself had not been. But the dark eyes that peered back at him on either side of the prominent, blade-sharp nose did not seem to match the bent and wizened exterior. They did not look like the eyes of an old woman, they looked like the eyes of a hawk that had seen its prey, and Karl found himself profoundly uncomfortable under that gaze.

The other person notable by his absence was the First Mage, Tagaza. Karl wondered about that, and when Falk got up from his place at Karl's right side to have a word with the head server, Karl leaned over to Lord Athol, seated at his left, and said in a low voice, "Lord Athol, where is Tagaza? Surely the First Mage should be here."

Athol's eyes widened. "Did you not hear, Your Highness?" he said, and perhaps he had had one too many glasses of wine, for his voice was loud enough that heads turned to look at him—including Falk. "The First Mage is dead. When the Common Cause sabotaged the MageFurnace, the spell he was attempting went fatally awry."

Karl stared at him, shocked. Tagaza, dead? But— "What kind of spell?" he said. "What sabotage?" He felt anger rising in him, and turned his head toward Falk, now striding back in his direction. "Lord Falk, why was I not informed of these developments?"

"Your Highness," said Falk, "you have barely been returned to us after a traumatic experience. I did not wish to trouble—"

"But I *wish* to be troubled, Falk," Karl said, his voice rising. "I wish to be troubled with the affairs of the Kingdom I will one day rule!" He slammed his fist down onto the table. "You will not treat me like a child, my lord. You will treat me like the Prince and Heir I am, or when I am King, I assure you, *you* will no longer be Minister of Public Safety!"

All the Councillors were staring at him, almost comically frozen in place by his outburst. Mother Northwind's expression remained unreadable. Nor was she watching him: she was watching Falk, and a moment later, every head turned in his direction as the Councillors awaited his response. *They're all terrified of him*, Karl thought. *He probably knows things about all of them that would prove embarrassing or worse if he released them. They will never support his ouster, if it really comes to that.*

But at that moment, Karl didn't care—didn't care that all the careful political instruction Tagaza had given him over the years told him he was being a fool. He had been attacked, kidnapped, imprisoned, and almost killed by one of his own guards. Either he was the Prince, or he wasn't: and if he was, then it was about damn time he acted like it.

Falk's face was doing a very credible imitation of a thunderstorm. "Your Highness, this is neither the time nor the—"

"Then we will discuss it immediately following this

dinner, Lord Falk," Karl said with all the hauteur he could manage. "We will discuss it in detail. I want to know everything that has happened since I was kidnapped. I have heard some of what you have done in the Commons, and I have many questions about that, as well: such as how you expect me to rule a kingdom you seem determined to plunge into civil war, Mageborn against Commoners." He gave Falk his coldest stare, though his heart was racing in his chest and he knew if he took his hands off the table they would be trembling. "I hope you have answers." And then he turned his head away from Falk to Lord Athol, and said, "And how has the ice-fishing been this winter, my lord?"

It had to be his imagination, but he could almost swear he felt Falk's gaze burning into him like a pair of hot pokers.

CHAPTER 22

ANTON KNEW MOTHER NORTHWIND had done something terrible to him the first time they met, and he knew Brenna thought Lord Falk wanted Mother Northwind to do something more terrible yet, but though he was getting better at accepting the impossible things he saw everywhere around him in this strange country, the notion that someone could reach inside his brain and change everything he believed was so far outside his experience that he couldn't take the threat as seriously as Brenna obviously wanted him to.

Like her, he had been shocked when High Raven handed them over to the Commoners who had come north to return them to Mother Northwind, but he understood Minik culture better than Brenna and knew that High Raven literally had no choice: Mother Northwind was obviously considered a member of the clan for all she had done for them years earlier, and the request of a clan member would always outweigh the needs or desires of someone outside the clan—another Minik, even, let alone Minik-na.

The ride south on the dogsled had been unpleasantly cold, and the sleds on the ice had made too much noise for easy talking—not that the men who had taken them showed much interest in playing tour guide, and Brenna had no more been to this part of the Kingdom than he had—but even without knowing what he was seeing, he had found it fascinating, watching the changing shoreline to his left and the unchanging ice to his right: not for the scenery, which after all wasn't much, but simply because he knew he was the first person from the Union Republic to see it. *The Professor would have loved this*, he thought sadly.

The sudden violence on the shoreline horrified him as it had Brenna, but maybe not quite as much—it had been a while, but he was not exactly a virgin when it came to violence. You didn't live as long as he had on the streets of Hexton Down without seeing things that Brenna had no concept of in her sheltered existence. It was so obviously terrifying for her, though, that almost without thinking he drew her to him for comfort—and was inordinately pleased when she returned the embrace.

But then had come her cryptic warning about the men who had been killed being Mother Northwind's, and the men who had killed them being Falk's, even though Falk and Mother Northwind were supposed to be allies in a plan to bring down the Anomaly . . .

Anton was way out of his depth. He didn't know enough about, well, *anything* to guess who could be an ally and who an enemy. And since that hurried exchange in the blood-soaked camp, he had not even been able to talk to Brenna.

The carriage they had climbed aboard near the village of Foam River had its windows sealed against prying eyes, and so Anton had seen nothing of their approach to New Cabora. Now he heard the rumble of wheels on dirt change to the clatter of wheels on cobblestones, and felt the accompanying change in motion. He smelled smells he knew from cities back home, horses—lots of horses—wood smoke, coal smoke, outhouses and bakeries, frying meat and rotting meat, sweat and sweets, a cacophony of odors that suddenly made him feel homesick for the crowded, dirty streets where he had grown up.

There was something different about the sound that made him think they were crossing a bridge, and then . . .

The smells changed. From city to country, and even more astonishingly, from the cold, harsh smells of winter to the warm, soft smells of spring: water, and marshland, green growing things, flowers.

At the same time, he realized it was warming up. Not just a little, either, but a lot. In moments he felt far too warm in his heavy winter clothing.

And then they rolled to a halt, and an armed man in a blue uniform, wearing a silver breastplate and helmet, opened the door to the carriage, and Anton stepped out into a whole new world.

It had been cloudy when they'd been loaded on the carriage, and looking up, he could still see the clouds, but they were *behind* the sun, or, he supposed, some magical facsimile thereof, a brilliant beacon that cast bright sparkles off the lake he was facing and brought the greens and reds and yellows and purples and whites of the ornamental garden that stretched between him and the lake into vibrant, glowing life.

Beyond the lake . . . snow. And, shimmering strangely as though seen through heat haze, though surely it wasn't that warm, the city of New Cabora, stone buildings black from burning coal, smoke rising from a thousand fires . . . a proper city. *A real city. Almost like home.*

His new guard pulled him around the corner of the carriage, and he stared up in awe. *Unlike this!*

Stretching more than a hundred yards in both directions from the central block, itself at least a hundred feet wide, a palace glowed in the false sunlight. Sheathed in white limestone, four stories high on each wing, with six stories on the central block and a giant dome above that, it wasn't the largest building he'd ever seen—the railrunner station in Hexton Down was probably bigger—but it was easily the most beautiful.

Again, he wished he could have asked Brenna about it, but though she was not far away, their paths were already diverging. She, too, had a blue-uniformed guard, who was handing her over to two women, servants by the look of them. He only had time to exchange the briefest glance with her (and not a very meaningful one, at that) before she was taken away, once more the ward of Lord Falk, and Anton was taken in the opposite direction to ... what?

A cell, it turned out. In the same cell where, though Anton didn't know it, Davydd Verdsmitt had sat just three days earlier, he sat on the bed, stared at the wall, and waited for Lord Falk to decide his fate.

I hope, he thought, *that at least he takes good care of the airship.*

———

Brenna's quarters were more palatial than, but every bit as much a prison as, Anton's cell. As usual when she came to the Palace, she was placed in a guest suite next to Lord Falk's apartment, with a luxurious four-poster bed, a bathroom with hot and cold running water, a toilet with a constant stream of water running through it to whisk away any waste, a sumptuously furnished private living/dining room with an enormous fireplace and ceiling-high windows overlooking the lake ...

... and a few things that had not been there on her previous visits: a magical lock on the door and windows, two Royal guards outside the door, and a maidservant named Hilary whose nervous demeanor made it clear to Brenna she had stringent instructions from Falk to keep an eye on her as well as help her dress and bathe.

Brenna never would have believed it, but she thought she would have preferred a mageservant. She had asked another maid about the lack of mageservants in the Palace on her first visit, when she was just ten years old, and the girl had explained that most MageLords didn't like them. "They prefer to hire Commoners," the girl had said. 'They're everywhere, might as well make use of them' is what my previous employer said to me once."

Remembering that now, Brenna thought how much of the MageLords' contemptuous attitude toward Commoners— Commoners like me!—was summed up in that phrase. And she knew well enough that there were some MageLords who treated their human servants with exactly the same amount of respect they would show to a mageservant—none.

With no indication of when, or if, she might be summoned to talk to Falk, or he might come to talk to her—though surely that would happen—and unable to leave her prison, she decided to make the most of it and do something for which she'd been pining for days:

She took a long, hot bath.

Lord Falk kept his fury at Prince Karl's public insolence tamped down well beneath the icy crust of his exterior as he showed the members of the Council out one by one. *It doesn't matter what the brat thinks or says*, he reminded himself. *Everything is in hand.*

It galled him, all the same. Tonight had been intended as his opportunity to reinforce in the Councillors' eyes just how effective and, indeed, dangerous a Minister of Public Safety he was; to remind them who was the real power in this kingdom. After all, in the course of a few days he'd defused a Commons rebellion, rescued his ward, found out who was responsible for the attempt on Prince Karl's life, and returned the Prince to his rightful place in the Palace.

The Prince—*the false Prince*, Falk thought savagely—had taken some of the bloom off of that rose—but again, it didn't matter. Because the accomplishments the Councillors did not know about were even greater. He had also lucked into information about the outside world, retrieved an amazing flying device, and finally put all the pieces together for the great moment when he would seize control of the Keys for himself.

Soon now, he told himself as he smiled at Athol and sent the Prime Adviser on his way, *the wrong done to my family will be righted, and I will return the Kingship to our line. And I will be a King such as Evrenfels has never had, freeing us from our self-imposed prison, eventually reclaiming the Old Kingdom stolen from us by Commoners.*

Commoners. They would fall in line. They had no choice. He had decapitated their precious Common Cause. Their attempt at sabotaging the MageFurnace had been futile (even the coup of killing the First Mage had ultimately meant nothing), and he had already demonstrated to them, as should have been done long since, what it really meant to defy the MageLords: that what they claimed was oppression and exploitation was nothing compared to what could be done to them if the MageLords chose to do it.

Not bad for a few days' work, he thought. *Not bad at all*.

Prince Karl had been the first to retire, as protocol demanded, and Falk had promised to come to his quarters later to provide him with a full briefing of everything that had happened in his absence. *It doesn't matter*, he told himself again. *It costs nothing to keep him thinking he's really the Heir for the short time he has left, and if it keeps him placated, it's worth the effort.*

However humiliating it felt.

The other Councillors had left one by one after Karl's departure, most congratulating Falk on his success in finding the Prince and his ward, and hoping that Brenna would soon be up to social calls so that they could renew her acquaintance. Falk was polite but noncommittal on that point.

Finally, only Mother Northwind was left, ostensibly remaining behind to ease the pain of a strained shoulder "suffered pulling poor Tagaza from the Spellchamber," Falk said, which earned him, he hoped, at least a couple of sympathy points from the one or two Councillors who had actually *liked* Tagaza.

Mother Northwind had gotten up from her chair while he was saying his farewells, and was staring into the fire when he returned. He studied her, wondering what her reaction would be to the evening's events. She had obviously known nothing about either Brenna or Karl being found, for all her vaunted connections among the Commoners. If their relationship were the chess game it sometimes felt like, he had just stolen a piece.

But when she turned to face him, she was smiling. "Well,

my lord. That was a pleasant surprise, without a doubt. I'd made up my mind the whole lot of them was gone for good: Brenna, the Prince, and Anton. However did you find them?"

"Just luck," Falk said. "A Mountie spotted Brenna and Anton on the ice of the Great Lake, riding dogsleds, no less. Seems they fell in with some savages who sold them to the Common Cause, probably for a handful of beads. He mounted a rescue."

"What happened to the Commoners?"

"All dead," Falk said. "Just the way I like them when they've been involved with something like this. It's amazing how much less trouble dead Commoners cause me than live ones."

Mother Northwind turned her head suddenly toward the fire. "Then I suppose the same is true of the Commoners who held the Prince."

Falk shrugged. "Most of them. One or two escaped. But as I said, we do have the woman who calls herself Goodwife Beth. She's in a cell awaiting my interrogation."

"Hmmm." Mother Northwind picked up the poker and stirred the coals of the fire. They flared briefly, but the wood was long gone and they quickly settled back to a red glow. "She may be quite high up in the Common Cause," she said, as if thinking out loud. "Perhaps . . ." She looked up at him again. "Lord Falk, I feel badly for failing with Tagaza. Perhaps I can help with this woman's interrogation."

"I can get information on my own, Mother Northwind," Falk said softly. "As I believe the presence of the Prince, Brenna, and Anton in the Palace tonight demonstrates."

"I never said you couldn't," Mother Northwind said, voice cheerful. "Always said you were the best at what you do. But there are some kinds of information it takes a long time to get out of people *your* way. Like the other leaders of the Common Cause. Verdsmitt and Tagaza were the Patrons, sure enough, but just because you have the one and the other is dead, it doesn't mean the whole Cause will collapse. There will be other leaders. They'll be trying to regroup. Seems to me a true believer in the Common Cause like this Beth woman could stand quite a lot of your kind of interrogation before giving away that list of names. But if I were to go in there, give her an 'examination,' just to be sure she hasn't been injured ..."

"You can come out with the information within a couple of hours," Falk finished for her. He felt an odd reluctance to take her up on her offer, but that made no sense. He knew what she could do—*had* done—for him. And certainly today he had reestablished his independence—and preeminence. Maybe this was her way of reassuring herself, and convincing him, that he still needed her.

He could afford to be magnanimous, he decided. He had made his point.

"Very well," he said. "Please 'examine' her at your convenience. And then ... there's still the matter of Anton."

"You still want him ..." Mother Northwind smiled. "...Verdsmitted?"

Falk barked a laugh. "Ha! Verdsmitted. I like that. Yes, I think I do. But for a different reason than before. Now that we know this airship of his can fly, I've got a better idea for using him. I want to send him to the Outside as my emissary."

"Isn't the sending of emissaries usually the prerogative of Kings?" Mother Northwind said, her voice dry.

"Which I will be by the time he returns," said Falk, shrugging. "I'm only jumping the flag a little bit."

"And what message will you send with this emissary of yours?"

Falk spread his hands. "That we are a peaceful people, that we mean no harm to anyone, that we look forward to a long and profitable trade relationship as equal partners ... that sort of thing. I want them absolutely convinced that we are no threat to them ..."

"Until you prove it otherwise."

"Exactly. Think of it as softening up the battle space."

"And magic? What will he say of that?"

"Magic?" Falk gave her a blank look. "There's no such thing as magic. The Great Barrier is a natural phenomenon our ancestors were unfortunate enough to be caught on the wrong side of, but our extensive studies of it over the years have convinced us it is weakening and will soon collapse altogether."

Mother Northwind laughed. "Clever, Lord Falk. One might even call it, if one were a wholehearted believer in the myths surrounding the SkyMage, diabolical."

Falk felt a flash of anger at that, and then another flash of anger at himself for letting her get to him so easily. *She's trying to regain lost ground in our little power struggle*, he thought. And so though he was on the verge of snapping at her, he instead limited himself to a mild, "I'm not the Dark One, Mother Northwind. Not even a minor demon."

"Not sure the Commoners would agree with you," Mother Northwind said, "but as they say, if you have to choose between being feared and being loved, it's always better to go with being feared."

"In any event," Falk said, seizing firm control of the conversation again (he hoped), "the sooner you sway young Anton fully to my side, the better. I'd like to send him Outside as soon as possible."

"*Is* it possible?" Mother Northwind said. "The airshipthing has so far traveled only with the wind, and the wind will take it east, not west."

"It is possible," Falk said. "By the boy's own testimony. We need only provide the right kind of fuel for the . . . engine, I think he called it . . . and that burner-thing. Once he is twisted to my ends, he will be able to tell me how to find or create this fuel." Time for a little dig. "You *can* still do it, can't you? Attempting to heal Tagaza seemed to take an awful lot out of—"

"I can still do it," Mother Northwind snapped, and Falk smiled inwardly. "In fact, I'll do it right after I examine this Goodwife Beth person. That way I don't have to drag my poor old-woman's knees down those stairs to your damnable dungeon twice."

"We don't call it a dungeon, Mother Northwind," Falk said. "We call it the Center for Extended Detention."

"I'm sure you do," said Mother Northwind. She had hung her cane from the back of a chair while she poked at the fire; now she turned and picked it up. "Now, if there's nothing else, my lord, I am getting increasingly anxious to see my bed . . ."

"One more thing," Falk said. "Brenna."

Mother Northwind sighed. "You want me to interrogate *her* for you, too?"

Falk laughed. "Of course not. She's been a pawn in all of this; my pawn, admittedly, then Anton's, to help him escape—he took advantage of her more ways than one, I'd wager. She'd have no knowledge of any interest to me, unless one of my human servants has been stealing silverware. And there is still the risk that any . . . manipulations . . . of her by you could disrupt her status as Heir."

"Then why do you mention her?"

"You know why." Falk's eyes bore into Mother Northwind's. "Everything is in place, Mother Northwind. My man is in position within King Kravon's inner circle. I have Brenna. The mage who will replace Tagaza in carrying out the spell of transference is standing ready in Berriton— we'll collect him on our way to the Cauldron. So now I ask you, as one who has been involved in this great Plan from the very beginning, as one who in large part made it possible, by switching the Heir with our fake Princeling at birth, as one who has, in your own way, worked as hard toward its success as I have: is there any reason of which you are aware that I should not proceed?"

Mother Northwind was silent for a long moment. "This man of yours, in place to kill the King," she said. "You trust him?"

"As much as any man can trust another, yes," Falk said. "He has aged parents. They are currently living in a cottage on my demesne, under the protection of my men-at-arms."

"Even so," Mother Northwind said. "If there is a weak link in your plan, surely it is there, in this Commoner . . . I presume he's a Commoner?"

"Of course. Mageborn must account for their presence.

Commoners . . . who notices the servants? And in any event, the King is well protected against magic. The assassination must be done by physical means."

"Well. This Commoner. You cannot know if he has what it takes to strike down the King in cold blood until he does so."

"If he does not, he knows what will happen," Falk growled.

"But when the moment comes to strike the necessary blow, he may still falter. I would feel better if you would let me examine him—make sure he is the man for the job."

Now that, Falk thought, *is an excellent idea.* "Please do, Mother Northwind. I should have thought of it myself. I confess I, too, would rest easier knowing our assassin is absolutely reliable."

"So," said Mother Northwind. "Three 'examinations' I must perform, not to mention this problem with your sprained shoulder." She sidled closer. "If you'd just let me take a look at it, I'm sure—"

Falk, trying not to look as though he were in a hurry, stepped back. "Thank you, but I find it much improved."

"It's a miracle," Mother Northwind said. "Praise the SkyMage!" She laughed. "I'll show myself out."

And after she was gone, Falk once more thought, *That went well . . .*

. . . although as always, after he'd spoken to Mother Northwind, his confidence was seasoned with the tiniest dash of doubt.

CHAPTER 23

THE MORNING AFTER HER CHAT WITH FALK, Mother Northwind once more made the torturous descent to the please-don't-call-it-a-dungeon. She asked to be let into Goodwife Beth's cell first.

It was not a meeting she'd been looking forward to.

Beth, lying on the bed in Tagaza's former cell with her arm thrown over her eyes, moved her arm as the door opened, then scrambled to her feet as the door closed.

"Hello, Beth," Mother Northwind said. "Long time since we were last both in the Palace together, isn't it?"

Beth blanched, and even put a finger to her lips, but Mother Northwind shook her head. "We are protected," she said, holding up her left arm to show Verdsmitt's anti-eavesdropping bracelet, "while I wear this."

And suddenly Beth relaxed. "If you say so . . . Patron." And then her face clouded. "I failed you, Lila," Beth said. It was the first time Mother Northwind had heard her birth name spoken in more than twenty years. She was quite surprised by the pang she felt in response. "You sent the Prince to me for safekeeping, and I—"

"Not your fault, Beth," Mother Northwind said. "Jopps betrayed you."

"Jopps?" Beth's brow furrowed. "He wasn't even . . . oh!" And then her face changed again, went hard. "If I get hold of him, his nuts are paste."

Mother Northwind chuckled. "You always did have a way with words, Beth."

She and Beth went back a long way. When she had been an anonymous Palace Healer, Beth had been a serving girl. Their schedules had overlapped so that they were often eating in the kitchen together, and they'd struck up a friendship, Mother Northwind hearing everything about Beth's family, about the young man she hoped to marry, about—

Well, it didn't really matter what else she'd spoken of, did it? None of it had happened. Beth had developed a bad case of acne, something even Mother Northwind could not cure quickly, though she tried. Finding her face unappealing, the Mageborn chef had simply told her one morning to get out: out of the kitchen, out of the Palace. She'd been owed a month's wages. She didn't get them.

Beth's husband-to-be had been furious at her for losing her precious job in the Palace, and had dumped her. She'd moved back in with her parents, but that had been short-lived. Within six weeks her father ran off with a woman from Berriton, taking the family's small store of savings with him. Her mother wound up in a debtor's prison shortly thereafter for failure to pay the rent to their Mageborn landlord.

The only reason Mother Northwind knew about *those* things was because the next time she'd met Beth, after she'd left the Palace and set up shop as a Healer in New Cabora, was at Tallule's House of Perfumes, one of the busiest brothels in the city. Beth had been entertaining as many as ten customers a day (Mageborn as well as Commoners) in a desperate (and doomed, considering how much of her earnings went to Madame Tallule) effort to pay her mother's debts, and not surprisingly had picked up an infection.

Mother Northwind soon chased that out of her body, but knew it was just a matter of time before something worse would claim Beth, or more likely that some customer, probably a drunken married Mageborn slumming in the Commons, would do something to her that couldn't be set right . . . and she couldn't let that happen. So she had hired Beth as her assistant. When it came to the kind of bawdy flirting that kept a man off-balance and less careful about what they said, Beth was a master, and ultimately Mother Northwind had set her up as a barmaid in a tavern inside the Mageborn enclave. If she chose to sell some of the traveling marketmen more than just beer and steak in order to help her mother, Mother Northwind didn't care, as long as she got information from them as well as tips.

As Mother Northwind had begun to shape the Common Cause, trying to make it a solid foundation on which a new and more equitable order could be founded when she succeeded in destroying the MageLords, she had needed someone to serve as her second-in-command, someone she could trust explicitly, and Beth had met that need. Beth was the only person within the Cause to know that the sometimes-helpful Healer/Witch and the secretive mastermind Patron were one and the same.

Which made her doubly dangerous now . . . and what Mother Northwind needed to do doubly anguishing.

But Beth surprised her. "I know why you're here," she said bluntly.

Mother Northwind studied her. "You do?"

Beth made an impatient gesture. "I'm not stupid, Lila. I know the kind of powers you wield—I've seen you use them often enough. Falk is going to interrogate me. He's going to *torture* me. And he is a master at it. I know, no matter how much I might try to fool myself, that I will tell him everything I know. And if I know the true identity of the Patron, if I retain any memory of our years at the Palace together, or how you got me out of Tallule's or . . . or any of that stuff, he *will* get it out of me. So . . ." She swallowed. "So it's important I don't remember. Any of it. Not even . . . not even the good times." A tear glistened at the corner of her eye, then traced a gleaming track down the curve of her cheek.

Mother Northwind sighed. "I'm so sorry, Beth ... but yes. I'm close, so close to my goal ... but I'm not there yet. And I'll never get there if Falk starts to mistrust me. So ..."

"All right," Beth said. "All right."

Taking a deep breath, Mother Northwind reached out her hand. But Beth pushed it away. "Don't just touch me, Lila," she said. She began to sob, great, wrenching sobs that shook her whole body. She moved closer and wrapped her arms around Mother Northwind. "Hug me, Lila. Hug me!"

Her own heart breaking, Mother Northwind gathered Beth in her arms ... and did what she had to do.

For several minutes they clung to each other. Then, exhaustion blackening the edges of her vision, she pulled away. Beth looked at her, puzzled. "Who are you?" she said. "Do I know you?"

"Just a Healer," Mother Northwind said around the lump in her throat. "Just a Healer."

"A Healer? But I'm ..." Beth looked down at herself. "I'm not hurt. Am I? I mean ..." She held up her hands, turned them over. "I feel all right."

"You're fine," Mother Northwind said. But as she got up to cross the hallway to Anton's cell, she thought, *I, on the other hand, am not.*

She paused in the corridor, taking a few more deep breaths, feeling some of her strength returning, but slowly, so much more slowly than it once would have. *Age,* she spat silently. *Pah!*

In her pouch she had four vials of a precious restorative she could use in an emergency. Difficult to make, dangerous to use, it would restore her strength for a time, but when it ran out, she might well collapse for a week.

She leaned against the wall. *Not yet,* she thought. *I may still have need of it, but not yet.*

She straightened at last and made her way to the cell where Anton was being held: the same cell previously occupied by Verdsmitt. The neat symmetry of that, considering what she intended, was not lost on Mother Northwind.

The Outsider boy jumped up from the narrow cot as she

came in. "You!" he said. "Brenna told me what you did. You stole my thoughts. You . . . Brenna calls it rape!"

"Did it feel like rape?" Mother Northwind said tartly. "It's not like you struggled. I was in and out of you as quick as you were in and out of that tavern maid in Wavehaven."

Anton turned bright red. "Brenna told me what you want to do to me next. She overheard Falk talking to you about it. I—I'll kill you if you try it."

Ah! thought Mother Northwind. *So that's what precipitated all this.*

"Proud words for someone in an eight-by-ten cell," Mother Northwind said. "And I assure you, I'm harder to kill than I look. You'd do that with your bare hands, would you? Grab me and . . . ?" She paused, letting that sink in, then made a dismissive gesture, as if she were brushing away an annoying insect. "Well, don't go filling your drawers, boy. I'm not here to twist your mind."

Anton's eyes narrowed. "Even though Falk wants you to?"

"My interests and Lord Falk's are not always in perfect alignment," Mother Northwind said.

"You're after something different than him," Anton said slowly. "Brenna told me . . . the men on the dogsled were taking us to you, but Falk's men killed them. That means he didn't know you had us. And that means we were being taken to you, not him, and probably not here. So why did *you* want us?"

"Oh, you're a clever one, aren't you?" Mother Northwind cooed. "Smart and pretty. No wonder Brenna's so hot to let you under her skirt."

Anton blushed again. "I don't . . . we haven't . . ."

"You do," Mother Northwind said. "And given half a chance, you will. I've watched too many rounds of the boy-girl dance to be fooled by claims of innocence, boy."

"What do you want from me?" Anton exploded.

"I need you to disrupt Lord Falk's plans in favor of my own, of course," Mother Northwind said. "And help me lay contingency plans against the possibility he succeeds at what he's trying to do."

"Bring down the Anomaly . . . the Great Barrier?"

Impressed again, Mother Northwind nodded. "Exactly. Falk's plan, in case you haven't figure it out yet, is to seize the Kingship, which means control of the Keys, and then bring the Great Barrier down and launch his army into the outside world. His *magically armed* army. He wants to return to the long-gone days when everyone bowed to the MageLords, and through them to the King—him."

"Can he do that?"

"Yes," Mother Northwind said, though since she'd been in Tagaza's mind, she doubted it. But no need to tell Anton that. "He can. But he won't. Because I have a different plan. I, too, wish to destroy the Great Barrier, and the Lesser, too—but I will do it by destroying magic. Destroy magic, and you destroy the power of the MageLords . . . and the Evrenfels that will then face the Outside world will be one where the Commoners hold sway, ready to take its place in whatever community of nations has grown up outside the Barrier over the centuries."

"More like a bear pit than a community," Anton muttered.

"Perhaps. Nevertheless, it is time we rejoined it." Mother Northwind studied the boy. He had a head on his shoulders, and a cynical view of the world rare in one so young . . . but from what she had gleaned of his rough upbringing, perhaps that was to be expected. It should serve him well now, in any event. "Falk's plan is to send you over the Barrier again to 'soften the battle space.' He wants you to tell your people there's no such thing as magic, that this is a peaceable kingdom that only wants to play nice with everyone. All lies, but you won't know that."

"But you just told me," Anton said.

Mother Northwind sighed. "But you won't know that *if I twist your mind to absolute loyalty to Lord Falk*, which is what he's requested."

Anton swallowed. "Ah. Of course. But you're not going to do that . . . are you?"

Mother Northwind smiled. "No. *I* like the idea of you

flying home, just as Falk plans . . . but then telling the truth of what you've found here, so that your people are prepared for the moment when I, not Falk, bring down the Barrier, and the Commoners take the government. Then you can fly back and tell me about it, so I can make even better plans for the immediate aftermath of the Barrier's collapse."

Anton studied her. "There's nothing I would like better than to fly back over the Anomaly," he said. "But without compulsion . . . what makes you think I'll come back?"

"Brenna," Mother Northwind said succinctly.

Anton said nothing. Then, "All right."

"Good," Mother Northwind said. "Then let's talk specifics." She smiled, amused as she remembered her conversation with Verdsmitt. "Tell me," she said, "how good an actor are you?"

The next day Anton faced Falk in his office, and hoped the answer to Mother Northwind's question was, "good enough."

Falk studied him. "Do you remember me, boy?" he said.

Anton did his best to look puzzled. "Of course, my lord. You saved my life. How could I forget the warm welcome you provided when I turned up so unexpectedly on your doorstep?"

"And yet you fled my manor."

Mother Northwind had told Anton that she would tell Falk she had altered his memories of that event, so that he no longer remembered Brenna's sabotage of the mageservants or her warning to him about what Falk intended for him. "Here's what you say . . ." she told him, and now, a dutiful actor repeating his lines, he said, "I must apologize, my lord. I did not secure the tie-down ropes as well as I could, and I was anxious for you to see the airship fully inflated and ready to go when you returned to the manor, so I thought I should fill the envelope to make sure it had no leaks. Brenna and I were both quite horrified when the ropes let go. And, of course, with no fuel for the propeller engine, after that we were at the mercy of the wind and weather." He smiled. "And yet somehow you found us and rescued us from those ruffians. So I am doubly grateful to you, my lord. I hope there is something I can do to show my gratitude."

He kept his smile, though inside he felt sick. *That sounded like a lie. It must have!*

But Falk smiled. "As a matter of fact, my lad, there is. Here's what I want you to do . . ."

It was all exactly as Mother Northwind had said. Falk wanted him to make the airship fly once more, but this time to take it over the Barrier, back to the Outside.

"No doubt your return will cause a sensation," Falk said.

It surely will, Anton thought, remembering the crowd of people, even if most of them thought he and the Professor were suicidal lunatics, who had gathered for their launch. He hoped, given the difficulty of arranging transportation to and from the town, that the reporters who had covered their departure would still be waiting, for a while longer, at least, to see if they returned. If they were, he would definitely have a story to tell them . . . but not the one Falk was feeding him now.

Falk wanted him to tell the Outside that all he had found were scattered, peaceful villages, cut off long ago by the mysterious appearance of the Anomaly. He was to say that the Anomaly had been a great subject of study for the people of Evrenfels for centuries, and at last they had found a way to bring it down. He was to say that they posed no threat to anyone, and only wanted peace, trade, and exchange of knowledge.

"Best not to say anything about 'magic' or 'MageLords,' " Falk said. "A little too out-of-the-ordinary for the Outside world. We'll let that knowledge out carefully, perhaps with a demonstration of how our magic can be used to help your people . . . as it has helped us . . . build a better society."

Anton kept an expression of intense, excited interest on his face, and boiled inside. From the stories of the Minik and what he had heard from Mother Northwind and Brenna, he knew exactly what kind of society the MageLords had built with their unique abilities: one of absolute privilege for a few, who held the power of life and death over the many.

At least, he thought, as Falk continued talking, *I don't* actually *have to remember any of this.*

He would deliver a message, all right, but the message would be, "Be ready. The Anomaly is falling. And not everyone on the other side wishes us well."

"Tell them to send for your military, or take up arms themselves, or make whatever preparations they need to defend themselves," Mother Northwind had told him. "I hope it won't be necessary. If my own plans are successful, the MageLords will be powerless, the magical weapons their army depends on disabled, and the Commoners in revolt against them. If the Barrier falls within the month, Anton, that is what will have happened."

"And if it doesn't?" Anton had asked.

"If the Barrier is still in place within a month, I will have failed," Mother Northwind had said, her voice harsh. "The next thing to watch for will be the Barrier falling in the spring. If that happens, then the MageLords retain power, Falk is King, and an army will ride out of Evrenfels intent on conquering every community close to the Barrier, as a first step to sweeping across the world in the years to come."

"We have weapons they don't know anything about," Anton had said.

"And they have weapons you can't even imagine," Mother Northwind had countered. "Falk destroyed City Hall in New Cabora with a flick of his hand. The army is equipped not only with swords and spears and bows, but enchanted weapons that can throw flame, crush skulls, and spray killing needles of ice."

Anton pictured an army of magicians advancing, striking down their enemies with lightning from on high ... could the Union Republic's army stand against that? The sheer impossible terror of it would wreak havoc. Men would break and flee. And once Falk's army had faced the weapons the Outsiders could bring to bear, they would know how to counteract them next time.

"I'll warn them," he had said, and so he would. *But will they believe me*?

"Good." Mother Northwind had paused. "There is one other possibility. If my own plans go awry, I may still be able to thwart Falk's. In which case the Barrier will remain in place, with the MageLords safely locked behind it . . . for now. Eventually, someone may rediscover what Falk and I have learned, but I do not think that will happen soon. And the Barrier won't fall on its own for another two centuries."

"Just what *are* your plans, and Falk's?" Anton had asked. "Brenna seems to be crucial to them both. What are you going to do to her?"

"I?" Mother Northwind had raised her hands, palms out. "I mean her no harm at all. Far from it. For my plans to succeed, she must remain unharmed." She'd leaned closer. "But let this drive you even more to get the Outside world ready to stand against Falk if he succeeds. For *his* plans to be fulfilled . . . Brenna must die."

"What?" Anton had found himself standing, with no memory of having jumped up. "He can't—you have to stop him!"

"What do you think I'm trying to do, boy?" Mother Northwind snapped. "I told you, I need her alive. Of course I'll stop him, if I can. There's nothing you can do about it, at any rate. But just keep that little fact in mind should you be tempted to betray me to him!"

"Not a chance in hell," Anton had said, and meant it.

". . . think you can do that for me, my boy?" Falk said, finishing his instructions.

"Yes, my lord!" Anton said. "It will be a great pleasure."

"Good. Well, then, the first thing is to make sure that this airship of yours is still working. And this time we'll see about finding you whatever it is you need to get these propeller engines of yours working . . ."

The next couple of days went by in a blur as Anton

supervised the process of getting the airship airworthy once more. He had thought rock gas might be impossible to get, but in fact it was used for heating in the wealthier parts of New Cabora, where some Mageborn lived in their own walled enclaves. No pipeline brought it. The well it was drawn from had been drilled by magic a hundred miles to the southeast, and the enchanted wellhead magically transported the gas from there to the homes that burned it. Anton shook his head at that, but it was only one wonder among many he had seen, and hardly the greatest. As long as the gas was there and could fill his fuel tanks, he didn't care how they got it.

The airship could not be launched from inside the Lesser Barrier, obviously, and Falk, equally obviously, did not have any interest in letting it be widely known that he was in contact with the Outside. And so the repair work had all been done five miles outside the city, in the walled yard of a Mageborn-owned horse farm. Every morning Anton rode out there in a horseless magecarriage with two Royal guards. Every evening the magecarriage returned him to the Palace.

Until, on a still, bitterly cold morning three days after his interview with Falk, Anton stood in the gondola once more, the envelope filled with hot air, burner and propeller engine fully fueled, a full complement of sandbags strung along the gondola's rim.

He was not alone. Falk had insisted on sending an "assistant" with him, a Mageborn guard named Spurl who, Anton suspected, was proof that Falk did not quite trust him as much as Mother Northwind had assured Falk he could be trusted. *Well, let the guard come*, Anton thought. *Once we're Outside, I'm quite sure I can handle a single guard, magic or not. If magic even works outside the Anomaly.*

They'd soon see.

The airship, fully inflated, tugged restlessly at the ropes belayed to four posts around the courtyard, watched over by guards who stared uneasily up at the huge blue balloon as though afraid it might topple over on them at any moment. Spurl, in full uniform with a heavy blue cloak added for warmth, clutched the edge of the gondola, already looking as though he was thinking about being sick.

Falk stood a few feet from the gondola. "The SkyMage protect you," he intoned. "Carry out my wishes, Anton, as you love me."

Keep acting, Anton thought, although after *that*, he thought he was closer to throwing up than Spurl was. *Keep acting*. "I don't know if I can ever repay you as you deserve, my lord," he said, and *that*, at least, was truth. "But perhaps this will be a start."

He leaned out of the gondola and shouted to the men standing ready by the ropes, "Cast away on my mark! One . . . two . . . three . . . mark!"

The ropes were let slip. The airship began to rise. Spurl gasped and gripped the edge of the gondola so tightly his gloved knuckles audibly popped.

Coward, Anton thought contemptuously. *Brenna was less frightened than that.*

Brenna. He wished he'd had a chance to talk to her. What would she think when she found out he'd gone back Outside? What had she been told? Did she think Mother Northwind had *really* twisted his mind to make him Falk's puppet?

Did she know that Falk meant to kill her?

Anton felt helpless . . . but that would change. He would deliver his message to the Outside world, but he wouldn't stay to see how that world reacted to it. As soon as he could, he would be coming back across the Barrier . . . *without you*, he thought with a contemptuous glance at Spurl . . . and he would find a way to protect Brenna.

He had never been in love. He didn't know if he was now. All he knew was that he was willing to risk his life to do everything in his power to keep Brenna from being hurt.

Sounds like a good working definition of love, he thought. He seated himself in the pilot's seat, took the wheel, and opened the throttle of the propeller engine. The big blades began to spin, and the airship began to move. Spurl gasped again and sat down hard in the bottom of the gondola, hiding his face.

Anton ignored him, and set a course for the Anomaly . . . and the Outside.

CHAPTER 24

LOCKED IN HER PALATIAL PRISON, Brenna waited for Falk to come interrogate her, both fearing it and wishing he would get it over with. She went back and forth on the question of telling him that the men his guards had killed had been taking them to Mother Northwind. On the one hand, it might sow confusion between the two of them. On the other hand, why should she help Falk? If Mother Northwind were working at cross-purposes to Falk, why not let her work?

But in the end, it wasn't Falk who came to see her, but Mother Northwind.

Brenna had wakened early that morning, she wasn't sure why; something in a dream, she thought, though all she remembered were confusing images of Falk and Anton and the dead man sizzling in the campfire. That image came back far too often in her dreams, and usually cost her the next hour's sleep. This time it had come so close to morning that she gave up going back to sleep at all, and instead got up, found the book she had been rather unsuccessfully trying to read, and settled down next to the lantern. Magelight would have been better, but she had no way of turning them on.

Hilary came in at the usual time, seemed startled to see Brenna awake, but said, "Good morning, miss," and went about her usual tasks of building up the fire and setting the table in the antechamber for the breakfast that would arrive shortly.

Brenna discovered she had read the same page four times without once remembering what it had said, and tossed the book aside. She went out into the antechamber. "What's the weather like, Hilary?" she asked. "I've been locked up in her for so long now I'm beginning to forget what fresh air feels like."

"Outside the Palace, miss? Warm as always."

Brenna grimaced. "No, I mean the real weather. Is it still bitterly cold? Has there been a meltwind?" Once or twice a winter, a great warm wind would sweep in from the west, causing the temperatures to rise so rapidly you could go from winds that would flay the skin from your bones to water running from the roofs in the space of a day.

Hilary shook her head. "No meltwinds, miss. Cold and still." She lowered her voice. "Perfect for launching that flying machine of Falk's, I hear."

Brenna felt a chill that had nothing to do with the weather inside or outside of the Barrier. "Flying machine?"

"That's the rumor, miss." Hilary adjusted the silverware on the snow-white tablecloth on the little table beside the fire. "Shall I have someone light the magelights, miss?"

"What? No, the lantern is fine. Besides, it's getting light outside." She glanced back at the tall windows, which had turned to gray from black sometime in the last few minutes. "What about this flying machine?"

"Well, it's supposed to be a big secret, but of course there are guards involved and they tell the maids all kinds of things, especially when they're . . . well," she blushed, "anyway, the story is that it's a flying machine from outside the Barrier, if you can believe it." Hilary shook her head. "I can hardly credit it myself. What is there outside the Barrier but wilderness and savages? But that's what they say, all the same."

"Did they . . . describe it?" Brenna said, trying to will herself to believe that there could be a flying machine other than Anton's airship.

"Well, miss, the guards say it's big, big as a house, shaped kind of like a loaf of bread, with a big wicker basket under it and this thing inside it like a little MageFurnace that shoots fire up into it until it's all puffed up. A whirligig thing on the rear of the basket—don't know what that's for—and a rudder like a ship.

"There's a strange boy been making sure it's all set to go, and they say that this morning he's launching it on a test flight. Wish I could be there, too, miss," she added. "I would dearly love to see a flying machine. Not a bit of magic about it, the guards say. Commoner through-and-through."

Anton? Brenna felt sick. *Launching the airship . . . with Falk's help?*

Cold fury flooded her. *Mother Northwind did it. She stole his thoughts, now she's twisted his mind. All to help Falk!*

And a test flight? Not a chance. Falk was sending Anton back into the Outside to serve his own ends . . . no doubt to lie to the Outsiders about how harmless the Kingdom of Evrenfels was.

And there was nothing she could do about it.

She wanted to scream and throw things, wanted to sweep the carefully arranged breakfast dishes off the table and into the fire, but she couldn't frighten Hilary that way, and so all she said was, "How . . . interesting."

Hilary brightened. "It is, isn't it, miss?" She looked around to make sure all was set, then curtsied and said, "I'll just fetch your breakfast, miss," and went out.

Brenna went to the window and gazed across the lake toward the center of New Cabora. The real sun was just coming up, washing pale pink across the sky, hazed by the smoke and ice fog rising from the city's chimneys. Brenna reached out and touched the cool glass pane. "Anton," she whispered. She looked up at the sky, as if she would see the airship flying by, a tiny blue dot high in the sky.

But, of course, the sky was as empty as always.

He's Falk's man now, she thought with sick rage. *Falk's man, thanks to that witch!*

She was still staring at the sky when she heard the door to the antechamber open. "Just put the breakfast on the table, and then you can go, Hilary," she said.

"I'm not going to go so soon after working my poor knees so hard climbing the stairs."

Mother Northwind! Brenna spun around. There stood the old crone, hunched over her cane by the fire, beady black eyes staring at her. Brenna's breakfast was on the table, but there was no sign of Hilary.

"You!" Brenna strode toward her, not sure what she intended to do. "Get out of here, you witch!"

"Good morning to you, too, Brenna," Mother Northwind said calmly.

"Don't talk to me. Get out!"

"No, I don't think so."

Brenna wheeled toward the door, but Mother Northwind said, "And there's no use calling for the guard. He can't hear you right now, and he'll have no memory of my having been here. Nor will your maid. She knows she delivered your breakfast, but somehow it didn't register on her that I came into the room with her and remained after she left."

"You *are* a witch!"

Mother Northwind sighed. "No, just a Mageborn with a knack for soft magic who has picked up a few tricks in a long life."

"Falk will know you've come," Brenna said. "He can probably listen in on everything you say here. You should—"

Mother Northwind held up her wrist, showing a glistening silver bracelet. "While I wear this, Falk knows nothing of what I do or say. Now, enough! I have things to tell you that you must know."

"There is nothing you can say that I need to know," Brenna spat. "You mind-raped Anton, and now you've twisted him so that he serves Lord Falk, you damned—"

"Enough!" Mother Northwind's voice, cold and sharp as a frozen dagger, sliced her voice to silence. "You know I do not serve Falk. *His* guards stole you from *my* men ... and murdered them."

"But Anton—"

"Your lad Anton has not been 'twisted.'" Mother Northwind showed her teeth in a catlike grin. "But Falk thinks he has."

Brenna blinked. "I don't understand."

"Then you might try being silent for a few minutes!" Mother Northwind nodded at the door. "Or I can leave now ... and leave you in the dark."

Brenna pressed her lips together, but nodded, once.

"Good." Mother Northwind pulled the chair out from the breakfast table and eased herself into it. "Ah," she said. "That's better." She lifted a silver lid to reveal two slices of buttered toast. "May I?"

"Help yourself," Brenna said between clenched teeth.

Mother Northwind lifted out a piece of toast, replaced the lid, and took a bite. "All right, then," she said. "Anton is going Outside. Falk thinks he's going to soften up the battle space, tell them they have nothing to worry about from the Barrier coming down ... so that when the Barrier does come down, his army will face less opposition. In reality, Anton is going to warn them to bring up their military and be ready to fight if Falk brings the Barrier down in the spring.

"And I'm here to warn you." Mother Northwind finished the piece of toast, and wiped her buttery fingers on Brenna's napkin. "Much better. I was feeling peckish."

"Warn me about what?" Brenna said.

Mother Northwind studied her. "Do you have any idea why you are so crucial to Falk's plans? Or to mine?"

"No," Brenna said bitterly. "I'm just a Commoner girl, nothing special. I don't even know who my parents were, except that they worked for Falk."

"Well, I can set you straight on all that." Mother Northwind leaned forward. "You are not a Commoner. Far from it. Your mother was Queen Aldona. She died when you were born. And your father ... is King Kravon."

Brenna gaped at her. The words made no sense. "But the King only has one son . . . Prince Karl."

"One *child*," Mother Northwind corrected. "No sons. One daughter. You."

"But Prince Karl . . ."

"Prince Karl is not the King's son. He's not even Mageborn. He truly *is* a Commoner."

"But he's the Heir!"

"No," Mother Northwind said softly. "You are."

Brenna seemed to hear a distant roaring. There was a chair against the wall close behind her; she found it with a reaching hand and sat down in it, knees suddenly rubbery. "I don't believe you."

"Then why did your knees just fold like broken twigs?" Mother Northwind snapped. "Of course you believe me. You believe me because it makes sense of your whole life. Falk stole you . . . with my help . . . when you were born. Karl took your place in the Palace, and you became the poor orphaned Commoner girl that Lord Falk took in out of the goodness of his heart."

"But . . . why?" Brenna whispered.

Mother Northwind's eyes were like buttons of black polished stone. "Because to bring down the Barrier requires having the Heir in the right place at the right time— and the best way to do *that* is to keep the Heir close to you without anyone else even knowing she's the Heir."

"You . . . stole me? For Falk?"

"No," Mother Northwind growled. "For myself. Falk just *thinks* it was for him. He thinks I'm just a tool he can use, then discard. Just like all other MageLords think they can use and discard whomever they please!"

"Falk wants to bring down the Barrier so that MageLords can rule the world," Brenna said. "If you feel that way about MageLords, why are you helping him? Why do *you* want the Barrier to fall?"

Mother Northwind's eyes gleamed in the growing morning light. "Because if *I* bring it down—and I will—then I will destroy magic along with it."

Brenna's eyes widened. "Destroy magic? That's impossible!"

"Is it?" Mother Northwind said. "Then I guess I've been wasting my time these last thirty years or more." She shook her head. "No. It isn't impossible. The Outsiders found a way to counter magic eight centuries ago, Brenna. That's why we're here. They had the help of a Healer who, despite being Mageborn, was revolted by the tyranny of the MageLords. He discovered how to craft a weapon to use against the MageLords, a weapon that rendered their magic useless. He created the Magebane: a man impervious to magic, a man who could turn the MageLords' own power against them." She frowned. "I still don't know everything he could do. I have some records of his ... and I've found out some things myself ... but he must have been an even more powerful soft mage than I, for the Magebane he created could extend his protection over an entire army. The spells of the Mageborn fell on that army ... and bounced, falling instead on the Mageborn themselves. They died by the hundreds, and the Commoners vastly outnumbered them to begin with. Without their magic, they were routed. Many MageLords died. Twelve survived. And those twelve brought the surviving Mageborn ... and as many Commoners as were trapped in their service ... here."

Brenna found she hadn't been breathing. She gasped in air, then said, "Are you saying *you've* made a new Magebane?"

"Yes," Mother Northwind said. "Not as powerful as the one of long ago, but powerful enough to do what I need done."

"Which is?"

Mother Northwind spread her gnarled hands. "Break the Keys. Destroy the Great Barrier ... and because it is tied to every Mageborn in the Kingdom, destroy magic along with it. The Mageborn will become ordinary men and women, powerless, no different from the Commoners they have oppressed in ways large and small for centuries. *And the Commoners outnumber them*."

Brenna thought of Falk, and what she had learned from the Minik, and a fierce delight washed through her. "I'd like to see that!" she said.

"You will . . ." Mother Northwind said. "If you survive the next two days."

"What?"

"Lord Falk will come to you later today," Mother Northwind said. "He is going to take you north . . . to the Cauldron."

Brenna blinked. North to the great lake of fire that powered the Barrier? "Why?"

"Falk's plan," Mother Northwind said carefully, "is to destroy the Barrier but leave magic intact. The only way for him to do that is to first seize the Keys for himself."

"Seize the Keys? How is that possible?"

"There's only one way." Mother Northwind gazed intently into her eyes. "It involves a complex spell, the energy of the Cauldron, and the simultaneous deaths of two people: King Kravon, and in that same instant, as the Keys are being transferred, the Heir." Mother Northwind jabbed her cane at Brenna. "You."

Brenna sat frozen, trying to comprehend what Mother Northwind was saying. "Falk means to kill me?" she whispered. "At the Cauldron?" All those years, growing up in Falk's manor, trying to get a spark of affection from him, longing for the parents she had never known, begging anyone she met to tell her about them but learning nothing . . . because there had been nothing to learn. The parents she'd thought she'd lost as a child had never existed. Her real father didn't know *she* existed. She wasn't even a person in Falk's eyes. She was a . . . sacrifice, raised from childhood for no other purpose but to die at the right time in the right place.

She went from frozen to furious in an instant. She jumped to her feet. "You have to get me out of here! You can't just—if he takes me there with him, how can I stop him? He'll have guards, he's stronger, he has magic. I can't fight him—"

"No, you can't," Mother Northwind said. "But I need you alive and unharmed, and I *will* keep you that way. So. You go with Lord Falk. Be aware of what he has planned for you. But I will see that he does not go through with it."

"How?" Brenna demanded.

"Sit down and I'll explain."

Brenna remained standing.

Mother Northwind pounded her cane on the floor. "Sit down! I'll get a crick in my neck with you looming up there like that."

Brenna sat, but not comfortably.

"Although I understand that hearing that someone intends to kill you tends to drive everything else out of your head, you seem to have forgotten that you are not the only one who is to die," Mother Northwind continued acerbically.

"You said . . . he's going to kill the King, too? My . . ." she still couldn't believe it." . . . my . . . father?"

"Your father. Not that he knows it. And not that you could expect much fatherly affection if he did. He thinks Karl is his son and he hasn't spoken to him yet this year that I'm aware of. In any event," Mother Northwind went on, "if the King does *not* die, then you must not die either. And the King will not die. I have seen to it. Falk will take you to the Cauldron . . . but he will bring you back again, alive. And once you have returned, then I will execute *my* plan, and magic . . . and MageLords . . . will be a thing of the past."

"But . . . how?"

Mother Northwind heaved herself to her feet, leaning on her cane. "That's my business for now. But it won't harm *you*, lass. And once it is done, you'll be free to do what you like . . . with whomever you like." She managed a leer. "Anton, for instance."

Brenna blushed. "We haven't . . . we didn't . . ."

"Yes, that's what he claims, too." Mother Northwind cackled, but then turned serious. "You do what you can to *stay* alive, Brenna, and I'll do what I can to *keep* you alive.

And soon we'll both see brighter days." She studied Brenna. "I don't suppose you'd care to shake on it?"

Brenna jumped up and backed away until she felt the wall pressing against her spine. "No," she said.

Mother Northwind sighed. "I do wish," she said, "that soft magic did not require touch. It would make my life so much easier. Well, then, I guess I'll show myself out." She went to the door.

"Wait," Brenna said.

Mother Northwind glanced back. "What is it?"

"Why are you telling me this? Why not just . . . do whatever it is you need to do and leave me none the wiser?"

Mother Northwind smiled. "Smart girl." The smile faded. "Two reasons. For one thing, when the time comes to carry out my scheme, it may be easier if you know the truth. But the immediate reason? Anton told me you know that the men Falk's guards 'rescued' you from were bringing you to me. Falk does *not* know that. I'd rather you didn't tell him. And since now, if you tell him, you will no longer have me to stand between you and certain death . . . you're not going to tell him, are you?"

Brenna swallowed. "No," she said.

"I thought not." Mother Northwind opened the door, passed through it, and closed it quietly behind her.

Brenna stared at that closed door for a long moment, then went back into her bedroom. She pressed her right cheek against the window glass so she could look west, to her left, in the vain hope she might see the airship that must even now be carrying Anton toward the Great Barrier and the strange world beyond it from whence he'd come.

Brenna wished, more than anything else in the world, that she were with him.

———

Falk, with great satisfaction and not a little wonder, watched the airship sail away, the strange chopping sound of its engine and propeller echoing back from the walls of buildings around the horse farm's cobblestoned yard. Anton's mission was hardly crucial, but Falk prided himself on making the best possible use of every tool that came his way, and now felt he had done so with the Outsider boy . . . thanks to Mother Northwind.

The Council had been astonished when he had reported to them the boy's provenance—and revealed the existence of the flying machine. The Commoner in particular had sat up and taken notice, though of course he hadn't been allowed to speak in the ensuing discussion.

They had all agreed that the situation needed careful consideration, but admitted the prospects for communication and trade with the Outside were exciting. "I suggest," said Lord Athol, "that we begin assembling a diplomatic team to be flown over the Barrier, to open formal negotiations with whatever government we may find there." This was duly agreed to, and the rest of the meeting had passed in discussion and argument about the makeup of the team and who should lead it, as the first ambassador the Kingdom of Evrenfels had ever, obviously, had to appoint. Along the way, they agreed to Falk's suggestion that the boy begin training one of his own men to serve as its pilot. Falk had even invited them to see the start of the test flight. None of the MageLords had actually come, of course; none of the Councillors, especially after the recent unrest, had any intention of passing through the Lesser Barrier in winter— certainly not to stand around a manure-strewn farmyard!

The Commoner *had* come, though. Falk had been surprised to see him, but the invitation had been extended to all the Councillors, so he certainly had the right to come. He stood in a corner of the farmyard, his personal guard standing stoically next to him, watching preparations.

Prince Karl had expressed an interest in attending, of course, but despite Karl's annoying new tendency to attempt to throw his weight around, Falk had been completely within his authority to refuse that request. "With tensions so high in the Common, absolutely not," Falk had told the Prince when asked.

Since that night of the welcome-home dinner, he had scrupulously briefed the Prince on everything he had been doing in the Commons: rebuilding the shattered buildings, continuing to seek information about the Common Cause, maintaining enhanced patrols, placing enchanted watchstones all around the Barrier's perimeter in case the Cause had more of the devices Tagaza had given them to slip through the Barrier.

Meanwhile, Teran was once more shadowing the Prince everywhere, and reporting to Falk on who he spoke to and about what. Teran had provided no information of any interest; nor did Falk expect any. The fake Prince was so peripheral to his plans now that the endgame was in sight that he was almost beneath notice. *In a few more days*, Falk thought, *I will take great pleasure in telling that "Prince" exactly what he is . . . then tossing him out into the snow myself.*

Neither Karl nor the Commoner nor any of the other Councillors suspected that the test flight would take the airship, and the now fanatically loyal Anton, on a preemptive diplomatic mission of Falk's own. If asked why the airship had not promptly returned from its test, he would claim there had been a malfunction, that the craft had come down out in the wild somewhere, and that it might be some days before it could be returned to New Cabora.

And if somehow passing beyond the Barrier made Anton less than fanatically loyal . . . well, the guard he had sent along would see to it that any damage was minimal. Spurl knew well that he could be on a one-way mission, but he was one of Falk's most trusted guardsmen, because he was also one of the Unbound.

The airship vanished into the distance, and the guards who had served as the ground crew clustered together, talking in excited voices. Falk watched them, a half-smile playing around his lips. *Things are going to get a lot more exciting in a few days, boys,* he thought.

The next morning, Falk waited again under the western portico of the Palace for the arrival of his magecarriage, as he had less than two weeks earlier, when he had taken the body of the failed assassin to his manor for examination by Mother Northwind. Today there were no clouds in the sky of the outside world, so the dawn sunlight turning the bridge pink was the real thing.

And here came his carriage, Robinton once more at the controls, wearing the enchanted warmcoat his wife had purchased for him. As it approached, Falk contemplated the journey ahead.

Only one road stretched the length of the kingdom north to south. Centered on New Cabora, as everything was inside the circular Barrier, it ran south to the Barrier cattle town of Smallcreek, and north from New Cabora to Berriton, a hundred miles distant, and from thence to the Cauldron, more than a hundred and fifty miles farther yet. From New Cabora to Berriton, and perhaps fifty miles farther north, a few villages were strung along the road, but as it passed from the rolling farmland of the central part of the kingdom into the trackless forests of the north and then into the foothills of the Barrier-bisected mountain range that marked Evrenfels' northern boundary, there were only a couple of army outposts.

Still, even at the modest pace necessary on uncertain winter roads, the magecarriage could take him, Brenna, and the guard a full hundred miles in a day. They would spend the night in Berriton, and there collect the mage from the College who would be standing in for the late Tagaza. They would spend the second night in a Royal shelter, and reach the Cauldron by midafternoon on the third day. There was another shelter there where they would wait until just before midnight, at which time they would go to "inspect" the Cauldron.

When they returned, regrettably without Brenna, Falk would be King.

The spring equinox, when he had originally planned to take this final step, simply because that was the usual time for the inspection of the Cauldron, was still a month away. But in light of recent events, he'd decided to advance the schedule. Even with Verdsmitt now working against the Common Cause, he didn't believe for a moment that the back of the rebellion was broken, though all had been quiet for a few days and he had already begun the magical rebuilding of the Square's shattered structures. *Best to seize complete control of the Kingdom as soon as possible.*

The word had gone out to the army. Troops were already moving out on "winter exercises" that would ensure they were in position to quell any unrest that might follow the King's death. Unbound within the Barrier, in the Colleges of Mages and Healers and elsewhere, were ready to act forcefully against those Mageborn—and even MageLords— who might balk at his ascension to the Throne. Everything was ready.

He took a deep breath, savoring the imminent completion of his Plan. Twenty years. And now, just a couple of more days . . .

Brenna emerged from the door behind him, accompanied by her guard. Wearing a white fur coat and hat with black fur trim, she looked very young. Falk knew her imminent fate was entirely unfair, not her fault, etc., and if there had been any other way for him to bring down the Barrier, he would have taken it. He was no monster, taking pleasure from the murder of innocents, whatever the Commons and certain disloyal Mageborn might think. But in this case, as in so many others, there was simply no alternative. Brenna was the Heir, and the Heir had to die so he could seize the Keys and free the MageLords from their prison. It was the SkyMage's will, and that was that.

Still, he thought he would prefer not to talk to her, and so as she and her guard got into the main body of the carriage, he climbed up beside Robinton.

"Going to be cold up here, sir!" Robinton warned. "Are you sure don't want to ride inside where it's . . . well, I wouldn't want to say, 'warm,' but I might be willing to go as far as 'warmer.'"

"I'll be fine," Falk assured him. "I may not have a warmcoat like the one your wife gave you, but I can shield myself. But thank you for your concern." He grinned. "Anyway, Robinton, we'll all be warm soon enough, won't we?"

Robinton shuddered. "The Cauldron. Been there twice now. Don't think I'll ever get used to that little piece of hell on Earth, though."

Falk laughed. "Personally, I find it quite scenic." He turned and banged on the roof of the carriage, then shouted, "All set in there?"

"Yes, my lord," came the guard's voice.

"Excellent!" Falk said. "Then . . ." He nodded to Robinton. "At your convenience."

"I think now is quite convenient," said Robinton, and the carriage trundled away from the Palace, across the bridge, through the Gate, and into the streets of New Cabora, their road taking them through the Square, where the Courthouse was once again taking shape, mages lifting the fallen beams and stones into place. The Commoners there took one quick look at the magecarriage, saw who was riding it, and either looked away or found sudden pressing business down alleys and side streets. Falk smiled to himself. A cowed population was a quiescent population, and quiescence in the Commons suited him perfectly just now.

Twenty minutes after driving through the Gate, they trundled past the final outlying buildings of the city and onto the road north. Drawing just enough energy from the coal burner to keep himself comfortably warm, Lord Falk gazed down the road stretching straight as an arrow from their rolling wheels to the flat, distant horizon.

As far as he was concerned, they couldn't reach its end fast enough.

CHAPTER 25

MOTHER NORTHWIND REALLY HADN'T IN-
TENDED to tell Brenna the truth...or most of the
truth...until she'd learned that Brenna and Anton knew
that the men who had been dragging them across the ice
were hers, and not Falk's. If Brenna let out *that* bit of information to Falk...well, she'd deal with it if she had to, but
better not to have to. So Mother Northwind had told
Brenna the fate Falk intended for her, and made sure the
girl knew that only she stood between Brenna and certain
death at the end of the journey.

Afterward, though, she thought it might have been the
best thing to do even if Brenna hadn't known that the dogsled drivers had been hers. Perhaps, she thought, the easiest
way to get the Magebane and Heir to do what she needed
them to do was not to *force* them to it—though she certainly could and would if she had to—but convince them to
cooperate voluntarily. Which was why, even as Falk's magical carriage rolled north toward the Cauldron, she was
forcing her aching knees up the Palace stairs to the very top
floor...to the quarters of the Prince.

Karl's bodyguard Teran stood outside. He nodded and
readily admitted her when she told him she had been asked
to check up on the Prince after his recent ordeal. *And why
shouldn't he?* she thought. Everyone knows by now that
I'm Falk's pet Healer from his own demesne. She contrived
to stumble as she was passing Teran, so he would put out a

hand to steady her, which he did; then she smiled, and thanked him, and went inside.

The Prince seemed to have just come out of the bath and, wrapped in a fluffy white dressing gown and fuzzy slippers, was reading a book by the fire. He raised his head as she came in, and got to his feet. "Mother Northwind? What are you—"

Mother Northwind waited for the door to close behind her. "Are we alone?" she said.

The Prince blinked, then glanced around the otherwise unoccupied room. "Um, yes . . . obviously."

"No Commoner maid warming your bed in the other room?"

The Prince's face flushed. "No," he said shortly. "And I think you forget yourself, Healer."

"Don't try to awe me with your Princely high-and-mightiness, Your 'Highness.' " Mother Northwind sat down in one of the chairs by the fire. "And don't stand there like some gawky scarecrow. Sit down. I have things to tell you that you may find upsetting."

The Prince sat, but his face remained clouded with annoyance. "What's this all about?" he snapped. "Why shouldn't I call Teran in here to have you thrown out?"

"I'd like to see him try it," said Mother Northwind. "But you need to hear what I have to say, Your Highness, and what I have to say is for your ears only. In particular, it is not for those ears," she nodded toward the door, "when those ears are pretty much a direct conduit to Lord Falk."

Karl frowned. "Teran? Are you suggesting he's a spy for Lord Falk?"

"It's not a suggestion, you innocent fool, it's a straight-out statement of fact," Mother Northwind said. "Of course he's a spy for Falk. Not only is he a Royal guardsman, which makes Falk his commander, but Falk is holding his mother and sister hostage. So even though he's fond of you, your 'friend' Teran would kill you in a heartbeat if Falk told him to."

Karl's eyes narrowed. "And this is what you think it is so important to tell me?"

"No, but it's part and parcel of it. You are not your own man, Prince Karl. You never have been. You are the creation of Lord Falk. And very soon, he plans to un-create you."

The Prince's annoyance was visibly sliding toward fury. "Enough of these riddles, old woman. Tell me what you have come to tell me, then get out."

"Very well," said Mother Northwind. "You may find it hard to believe. But it is the truth, and you would do well to heed it."

And then she told him exactly what she had told Brenna . . . exactly, right down to leaving out the one little detail she had not shared with the Heir: that her plan, too, required the death of King Kravon . . . but at a time of her choosing, not Falk's.

Karl's face went from red to almost as white as his dressing gown in the course of that telling. "What madness is this?" he whispered when she was done. "You're telling me I'm not the Heir? Not royalty at all? Not the son of King Kravon?"

Mother Northwind shook her head. "No, I'm afraid not, Your Highness." She laughed, amused at her own inconsistency. "Karl, I mean. But you are something far more important."

"More madness," Karl said. "The Magebane is a myth."

"You are not 'The Magebane,'" Mother Northwind said. "You are *a* Magebane. And you are my creation."

Karl got up and went to the window, pulling back the curtains to look out, she surmised, at the place where he had almost been assassinated. "So when the assassin struck, there was nothing wrong with the enchanted weapons."

"Nothing at all," Mother Northwind said. "Your power woke fully with that attack, and hurled it back on the attacker." She studied the back of his head. "Let me guess," she said. "You had already had a hint that that power existed."

"Since I was a boy," Karl said. "Small things ... magic has always tended to go awry near me. Enchanted objects lose their enchantment. Magelights die. And magically locked doors ... can be opened."

Even in her very brief contact with Teran outside, Mother Northwind had seen the memory of the time when one locked door in particular had opened, greatly pleasing two young boys. "Has Falk taken notice?" she asked.

"He's never asked me about it. Tagaza ..." He paused, looking sad. "Tagaza once told me the Magecorps were always struggling with magelights and such near my quarters, but I don't think he ever thought I had anything to do with it." He turned to look at her. "What would Falk do if he knew? Knew I might be a Magebane? Kill me?"

"No," Mother Northwind said. "At least, not until he was certain he could not use you instead."

"He must know what happened at Goodwife Beth's," Karl said.

Mother Northwind's eyes narrowed. "I don't," she said. "Tell me."

"During the attack, Denson ... one of my captors ... wanted me to stick my head up first to draw any fire that might be aimed at him and his friend. A soldier threw a ... I think they call it a melonbreaker ... spell. All I saw was a flash, but the soldier who threw the spell ..."

"Let me guess," Mother Northwind said. "No more head."

Karl shuddered. "Yes."

Mother Northwind noted that shudder. *A soft heart, to go with that soft exterior*, she thought. *I can use that.* "You have it in your power to do away with abominable spells like that," she said gently. "If you do as I ask, you can do away with *all* spells."

Karl glanced at the antechamber window. "That will do away with all that, too," he said, nodding at the bright blue sky the window framed. "Eternal spring in the middle of winter. Sunlight on the darkest day." He paused, then looked back at her. "And Healers?"

Mother Northwind hesitated. "I hope not," she said at last. "Soft magic is not part of the Keys or the Barriers. I do not believe that it will be affected. Not, at least, to the same extent."

Karl studied her. "Meaning you will still have the power to twist men's minds to do your will."

Why deny it? "I believe that I will," she said. "But I will use the power judiciously."

"Will you?" Karl said. "Or are you asking me to throw over one Mageborn-led tyranny for another?"

"No!" Mother Northwind said sharply. "I want only to remove the MageLords from power. Not seize it myself."

"Except when, in your *judicious* opinion, it needs to be seized."

Mother Northwind studied the Prince with new respect. Karl had always been, in her mind, simply the tool she had forged to bring down the MageLords. Falk had always dismissed him as a feckless, immature boy with little interest in politics or anything beyond his own comfort and amusement. But that was *not* the Prince who stood before her now, nor the Prince who had stood up to Falk at the dinner a few nights before.

Well, she thought dryly, *having someone try to kill you, rebels capture you, and a platoon of guards violently rescue you is probably a very effective program for growing up in a hurry.* "I do not seek to rule," she said again.

"Then who will, Mother Northwind? When you throw down all this," his gesture took in the Palace, the Lesser Barrier, the Kingdom as a whole, "What will replace it?"

"Commoners," Mother Northwind said. "Rule by the common people."

"And are the common people ready to rule?" Karl said softly. "Or are you simply paving the way for chaos?"

Mother Northwind felt the first stirrings of real anger. Enough was enough. "The Kingdom is corrupt. The MageLords are brutal tyrants. They oppress and exploit the Commoners, and massacre the Minik at will, as though they were nothing but animals. Chaos would be *preferable*!"

Prince Karl studied her for a long moment. "I'll think about it," he said at last. "I'll think long and hard about whether I want to help you or not."

"Think about it?" Fury suddenly roared through her veins. After all these years . . . ! "You're *my* creation," she snarled. "I changed you in the womb to make you what you are. You will do what I wish!" She got to her feet and stepped toward him. "Or—"

"Or what?" Karl said coldly, not moving. "You'll twist my mind?" He suddenly stood and took a step toward her, within easy reach. "I'm the Magebane, if you tell the truth," he said. "Care to try it?" He held out his hand.

Mother Northwind reached for it—then snatched it back. *SkyMage!* she thought, and *that* was an oath she rarely used.

She was ashamed to admit it, but she had never realized until that moment that she could no more influence the Magebane than Falk could slay him with magic. If she reached inside his mind, would she reach inside her own, instead? If she tried to twist him, would she instead twist herself . . . into madness?

Karl drew his hand back. "I said I will think about your request to help bring down the MageLords," he said, voice calm. "And I will also think about the fact that you 'changed me in the womb.'" His voice dropped to an intense whisper. "Whose womb was that, Mother Northwind? And what became of its owner? *What became of my mother?*"

Mother Northwind remembered a stormy night, a woman in pain, blood, the cry of a healthy baby boy . . . the woman begging to hold the child . . . a soothing hand on the woman's brow . . .

. . . labored breathing that slowed, stopped . . .

It had to be done, Mother Northwind thought. *It had to be!*

But now, faced with that babe grown to a man, forged by her own efforts into someone she could not manipulate as she had manipulated so many others over the years, she was helpless before the memory. "She died when you were born."

"You murdered her," Karl said flatly. "As you murdered the Queen, Brenna's mother . . . and how many others? How many others have you killed or caused to be killed so that your great Plan could go forward, so you could overthrow the MageLords. *In what way does that make you better than them?*"

Mother Northwind trembled with rage. She wouldn't stand there any longer, to be lectured and accused by this beardless boy who owed his very *existence* to her. She had wrestled with and made her choices long ago, and she stood by them. "Those I have slain were few, those I have saved are many," she grated. "The MageLords have slain tens of thousands, here and before this Kingdom was established. If Falk has his way—and if you will not help me, and my plans crumble to dust, then he most assuredly will—thousands more will die in the war that will erupt when he brings down the Great Barrier.

"So. Take your time, *Prince* Karl. Make your own calculations. Decide your own level of acceptable sacrifice. I have worked my whole life to give you that power and put you where you could use it. You once thought you would be King, and wield great power. Now you know you never will . . . but you have more power than you would ever have had as King.

"Whatever choice you make you will have to justify to yourself . . . as I have justified mine."

Without another word, she turned, hobbled to the door, and let herself out.

He'll do as I ask, she thought as she made her painful way down the hallway. *He has to*.

But in her heart she knew that he really had to do nothing of the kind . . . and that the plan she had worked so long to bring to the edge of fruition now depended entirely on another.

I created him, she thought, *but I had no part in molding him, and now, like a mother who gave up her son for adop-*

tion at birth and is now destitute, I have come back to him begging for his help.

Suddenly feeling very old and very alone, Mother Northwind made her way back to her empty rooms.

Karl stared at the closed door, his body still, but his mind in turmoil.

He believed Mother Northwind; how could he not, when he had seen magic literally bounce off him and rebound on its wielder, twice, and when what she had told him so well explained the strange ability he had been aware of since childhood. And he would *gladly* believe he was not the Heir, that King Kravon was not his father . . . though he still had memories, from when he was little, of Kravon showing him affection, and of loving the strange man he saw only on rare occasions.

His real father, his real mother, he would never know. Mother Northwind had chosen them as nothing more than a . . . a breeding pair. She needed an infant she could substitute for the true Heir at birth, an unborn child she could mold into the Magebane, and it could have been anyone . . . it just happened to be him.

She stole my parents from me, Karl thought coldly. *She stole my childhood. She cares nothing about me; I'm just a sword to wield against the MageLords.*

But she had also left him with nothing else to be. He was not the Heir, and Falk had always known it. He would never be King, and Falk might well kill him once he was no longer needed.

And Teran, the bodyguard I thought was also my friend, will help him, he snarled silently, remembering what Mother Northwind had said about *him.*

I could flee, he thought. *Flee through the Lesser Barrier, just walk right through it and disappear into the Commons . . .*

. . . bringing down the wrath of Falk once more on the city of New Cabora, he realized sickly.

How many innocent people would suffer then because of him?

Suddenly Karl couldn't stand still any longer. He turned and strode back into his bedroom, dressed in a hurry, and went out, Teran leaping to attention and following him as he passed through the hallways of the Palace almost at a run.

At the top of the Palace steps, Karl paused, staring down at the ornamental gardens, the statue of Queen Castilla, the lake, and the Barrier, and beyond the lake at the snow-choked, smoky city of New Cabora.

"I'm going across the lake," Karl said to Teran, without looking at him, as the bodyguard caught up to him. "To the place where I like to swim."

"Your Highness? Where the assassin—"

"Yes, where the assassination attempt was made," Karl snapped. "Come." And without another word he strode down the steps, toward the boathouse at the far end of the gardens.

There, he climbed into the same white-and-gold boat he had used to follow Jopps and Denson in the dark the night of Verdsmitt's arrest. Teran climbed in behind him, picked up the oars, and began rowing them steadily, mechanically, across the lake. With only one or two glances over his shoulder, he drove the boat to within a few feet of where the assassin had died.

Karl jumped out, and strode up the grass to the Lesser Barrier. There he stopped. He reached out a hand to the barrier.

"Careful, Your Highness," said Teran.

Karl ignored him. He leaned in with his outstretched hand . . .

. . . and it passed through shimmering Barrier as though it wasn't there. He felt the icy nip of the outside air on his fingers.

Behind him, Teran gasped. "How . . ."

Karl withdrew his hand and studied New Cabora. Sunshine streamed down on the snow in the park today, which cast it back in a million diamond sparkles. The city, buildings black from decades of smoke, squatted on the other side of the parkland beneath a pall of ice fog, the contrast between its dark structures and the pure-white parkland making it look a dark and dangerous place indeed.

He turned around and studied the Palace. It shone like a jewel, white against the green of the lawns, windows sparkling, gardens awash in riotous flower colors. Karl listened. He could hear birds singing, insects chirping in the grass, even a distant, haunting snatch of music, though whether it came from living musicians or enchanted instruments, he had no way of knowing.

A butterfly, its wings iridescent blue, rested on the bright-red petals of a waist-high flower a few steps away. Karl knelt and examined the insect. It reminded him of the Palace in its beauty. Crushing such a thing would be an act of senseless destruction.

But there was one difference between the butterfly and the Palace. The butterfly was natural. Though it was out of season, in the real spring that would soon break winter's grip on the world outside a million more just like it would appear. Its beauty owed nothing to magic.

Karl stood and gazed at the Palace again. Unlike the butterfly, there was nothing natural about it at all. It would not exist if not for magic. And yet, it too was beautiful.

Did he destroy it? Destroy all the wonderful things magic could do because some of those who wielded it used it for evil?

He turned and gazed at the Barrier again, and New Cabora beyond it. The city, black and ugly, was no more natural than the Palace. It had been built by men bending Nature to their will, just as the Palace had been, the only difference being the tools used. The Commoners' tools were crude. Therefore, the city was crude and ugly. The MageLords' tools were refined and powerful. Therefore, the Palace was refined and beautiful. But Commoners and Mageborn alike strove to impose their will on Nature.

The difference, Karl thought, *is that the MageLords also seek to impose their will on others. But would Commoner rule really be any better?*

Turning his back on the Palace, he stared out at the city again, pulled at by the desire to flee, to deny what he was—what Mother Northwind had made him—and simply refuse to act . . .

. . . except that by refusing to act he *would* be acting, and those actions would have consequences: for the Commoners, among whom Falk would surely seek him; for the MageLords, who would find Falk their King; and for the Outsiders, who would soon find themselves fighting the MageLords for their own freedom.

He remembered standing in this place the day of the assassination attempt, thinking how much he longed to be free of his imprisonment in the Palace. Now he *was* free; he could walk out on everything . . .

. . . and yet he felt less free than ever, for he had been given the unwanted power to decide the future of the Kingdom and the world.

It was too much. He put his hand through the Barrier again, held it there so long his fingers stung with cold by the time he pulled them back; but when he turned back toward the boat, he still had not made up his mind what to do.

But he did know one thing he had to do. Teran was staring at him, hand on his belt: not on his sword, but on one of the enchanted spellstones set into his guard belt. Karl glanced down, then up at Teran's pale face. "Were you planning to use that on me?"

"Your Highness . . ." Teran licked his lips. "I thought . . . you put your hand through the Lesser Barrier . . . I . . . *how?*"

"I could walk through it right now, Teran," Karl said. "The Lesser Barrier is no barrier to me. It's as open as that door into the maids' bathing chambers." He softened his voice. "Do you remember that door, Teran?"

A flicker of a smile on Teran's face. "Of course I do." The smile faded. "But I can't let you do that, Your Highness."

"Why?" Karl said.

"I am sworn to protect you—"

"Sworn to protect me?" Karl took a step closer to him and spoke his next words as though he were snapping a whip. "Or sworn to spy on me for Falk?"

Teran stepped back. "Your Highness—"

"Don't bother protesting," Karl said. "I know the truth."

"You don't understand," Teran said. "Your Highness . . . Karl . . . Falk . . . he's got my mother, my sister, they're prisoners in a house in the Mageborn enclave . . ."

Karl remembered Teran's sister, three years younger, as a laughing child with golden hair, playing with a ball in the Fountain Garden, and the hatred he had begun to feel for Falk flared higher. "Teran," he said. "Falk's days are numbered. You won't need to fear him much longer."

"Your Highness . . ."

"Don't call me that," Karl snapped, surprised by his own vehemence. But he didn't deserve the title, had never deserved the title. He was not the Heir. He wasn't even Mageborn. He was Commoner: Commoner, and something more.

Magebane.

"Forget I'm the Prince," he said. "Forget you are a guardsman. Forget Falk. I'm Karl. You're Teran. I've always counted you as my friend. I hope you have counted me as yours."

Teran licked his lips, but his voice was steady as he said, "I have . . . Karl."

"Then I ask you, as a friend, not to tell Falk what you just saw me do." Karl nodded at the Lesser Barrier. "And to remember our friendship when next Falk gives you orders."

Teran licked his lips again. "But, Your Highness . . . Karl . . . my mother, my sister . . ."

Karl smiled. "I am still the Prince. Falk is not in the Palace. Do you know where in the enclave they are being held?"

Teran nodded.

"If I order them freed from the house, can you get them out through the Barrier to somewhere safe, somewhere Falk can't find them?"

Teran nodded again.

"Consider it done." Karl held out his hand. "Now, old friend . . . will you keep my secrets? Will you serve me as loyally as I've already thought you were?"

Teran looked at the hand for a long moment, then turned to look toward the roofs of the Mageborn enclave, just visible through the trees past the bridge. He gazed in that direction for a long moment, then snapped his eyes back to Karl, grabbed his hand, and shook it. "I will, old friend. And beg your forgiveness that I have ever done anything else."

Karl clapped him on the shoulder. "Then let's go back to the Palace. I have orders to give."

He looked back at the city himself one last time. *And then*, he thought, *I have a decision to make.*

CHAPTER 26

FOR MOST OF THREE DAYS Falk's magecarriage rolled northward, and Brenna sat in silence within it. Her guard was obviously under orders not to talk to her, and when they stopped along the way for meals, at first at towns, then, as they rolled into the northern forest, at the Royal way stations built at regular intervals, Falk did not speak to her, either. The driver, Robinton, would give her a "Good morning, miss," and even a "Good night," but that was the most conversation she had over the course of the journey.

The first night they spent in an inn in Berriton, the largest town in the Kingdom outside New Cabora, where the Colleges of Mages and Healers seemed to frown at each other on opposite banks of the North Evrenfels River. In the morning they were joined in the inn common room by a thin, sallow-faced mage, who climbed into the cabin of the magecarriage with her and the guard. He gave Brenna an appraising look, as though she were an unusual species of beetle, then pulled the hood of his coat around his head and promptly fell asleep.

Left with nothing else to do, Brenna stared out the window.

She had never realized, before flying across much of it west to east and now riding through it from north to south, how truly huge the Kingdom of Evrenfels was.

Huge—and underpopulated. The towns, except for New Cabora and Berriton, were very small. Each would

announce its presence by the sudden appearance of culti-
vated fields instead of virgin prairie, and the occasional
farmhouse, which ran from the snug to the ramshackle to,
rather frequently, nothing more than rude sod huts. Brenna
tried to imagine living for a winter in a house made of nothing but dirt, and shuddered. Those would be Commoners,
of course, and they were typically only tenants of a Mageborn landlord, whose much bigger house of stone or wood
would soon enough roll by. South of Berriton they had
passed through Lord Athol's land, and Brenna, spotting his
manor in the distance, had seen that it rivaled Falk's in size.
I wonder if he's got a singing fountain, too, she thought bitterly, as, with the multiple chimneys of the manor visible in
the distance, they passed a sod hut where an old woman
struggled through the snow carrying a load of firewood on
her back.

On the second day, well north of Berriton, they left all
signs of humanity behind except for the road and the Royal
shelters. Flat, tall-grass prairie gave way to rolling hills covered with naked aspen, poplar, and birch; gradually, dark
spruce became more abundant; and finally there was only
black evergreen forest all around, stretching to the horizon,
punctuated by the white sheets of frozen lakes that were
visible whenever they topped a rise high enough to give a
view over the treetops. Then they would plunge back into
the forest again, and into cold, gray gloom.

On the second night, as Brenna climbed wearily down
from the carriage, glad to stretch her legs, she noticed
something. About noon the cold blue skies had given way to
gray cloud; and now, as she gazed around her, she saw
that the shelter they were to spend the night in, a large
cabin made of unpeeled logs, stood on a bit of a hill; and
that to the north, the cloud cover glowed a fitful red, wax-
ing and waning in a slow, erratic cycle.

Brenna didn't have to ask what it was. There could be
only one thing this far north that could give the clouds that
bloody tint: the Cauldron. If not for the cloud, she would
surely be able to see the Barrier Range, and despite every-

thing, she felt a pang of sorrow that it was hidden. She had always wanted to see mountains.

Brenna spent a restless night, that red glow finding its way into her dreams even through the sealed shutters. In the morning they were on their way again before any light crept through the lowering clouds, which now hung so close overhead that the glow of the Cauldron could no longer be seen. Robinton gave those clouds a worried look, and made certain that the coal furnace on the back of the carriage, which both heated the interior and provided energy for the spell that drove the carriage, was fully stoked—and the big coal bin below it packed to the brim—from the Royal shelter's stores.

The terrain changed again, from flat forest to rocky hills and sudden cliffs, and even more lakes. The road wound and dipped and rose again, rounding vast sheets of ice, running alongside rivers, climbing hills, plunging into dark valleys. About noon it began to snow, at first lightly, but more and more heavily as they drove.

Brenna began to see bright flashes of blue light reflected off the snow outside. "Lightning?" she said out loud.

The cadaverous mage they had collected in Berriton, whose name she had gathered was Anniska, grunted. "Lord Falk clearing the way," he said.

Brenna glanced over her shoulder at the wall, covered in plush red velvet, from which the carriage's welcome warmth radiated. "Will the coal last?"

Anniska laughed. "I doubt he's drawn on it at all. I know you can't feel it, but we can." He inclined his head at the guard, who nodded back.

"Feel what?" Brenna was just glad to finally have someone who would talk to her.

"The Cauldron," Anniska said. "We're close enough to draw on it directly. We can save our coal for the return trip."

"Oh." Brenna felt a chill that the warm wall behind her could do nothing to lift, and hoped she would be making that trip with them.

The snow slowed their travel, so that it had grown dark

again by the time they reached the last shelter; dark, but not as dark as it would have been anywhere else, because now even the snow could not hide the glow of the Cauldron. When Brenna got out, the whole sky was red, a sullen, sulky red that flickered and flowed disturbingly.

She looked north. The road climbed, zigzagging, up a steep ridge. At its crest, the spruce trees were black cutouts against the bloody glow.

Inside the shelter, the driver and guard busied themselves with making food. Falk and Anniska sat talking together in low voices in one corner of the high-ceilinged main room, in chairs made of branches lashed together, upholstered in deerskin. Brenna sat in another near the huge fireplace, staring at the flames. No one made any move to prepare sleeping quarters. Instead, they waited.

Brenna could only pick at the plate of venison, potatoes, and carrots put in front of her. She managed to eat a little bread and drink a little water, but that was all her stomach would allow. The two mages seemed no more interested in eating than she did, and even their conversation died away as the evening dragged toward midnight.

But finally Falk said, "It's time," and got to his feet. Anniska followed him to the door and joined him in pulling on coats and boots once more. The guard materialized behind Brenna's chair. "Miss," he rumbled.

Brenna wished she hadn't eaten even the little she had. Her insides felt like water and her knees like green twigs, but she managed to stand and pull on her own coat, hat, gloves, and boots.

Mother Northwind, she prayed, *I hope to the SkyMage you were telling me the truth.*

If the witch hadn't told her what Falk intended for her, how would she be feeling now, she wondered? Just as terrified by the strange silence that gripped everyone as they once more climbed into the magecarriage?

No, she thought. Worried, puzzled, but without this gutwrenching terror, because she would never have thought that Falk meant to kill her.

And suddenly over top of the fear came a surge of anger at the witch, always manipulating, telling her what she had told her just so she wouldn't tell Falk that Mother Northwind was not the ally—or tool—he seemed to think her.

If I live through the next hour, she vowed to herself, *I will tell Falk what I know, and to the Cauldron with the consequences!*

Then she winced at that common but, given the circumstances, unfortunate oath. It might not be consequences that were consigned to the Cauldron this night.

The magecarriage surged forward, up the hill, toward the lowering red clouds. Brenna gripped the hanging strap dangling by her head so tightly her knuckles popped, and held on.

They climbed, switching back and forth, up the steep slope. The clouds drew closer and closer until Brenna was convinced they would plunge into them before they finally crested the ridge, but suddenly they were over the top and switchbacking down the other side . . . and as the path of the magecarriage turned her window toward the north, she caught her first glimpse of the Cauldron, and thought her heart would burst through her chest as it began to race in terror.

A vast lake of molten rock stretched into the snow-veiled distance, its crust of black shot through with lightninglike red cracks and, in places, wide, slow-moving rivers of bright yellow. The stench of sulfur rose from it, and already she could feel its heat, the temperature inside the carriage rapidly approaching that of a steam bath. She took off her hat, then her gloves, stuffing them into one of her coat pockets, then had to open her coat. Across from her, Anniska did the same; the guard remained stoically uniformed.

She soon wished she could shed the coat altogether, but there was no room to wriggle out of it, and so she sat and sweated and watched the red light reflect off the sheen of moisture on the faces of her companions.

Then, suddenly, they stopped. The carriage rocked as

Robinton and Falk jumped down. Robinton, no longer wearing his enchanted warmcoat, came to the side of the carriage. He opened the door and lowered the folding steps. "Miss," he said, and held out his hand to help her to the ground.

Mouth dry, and not all the sweat on her body from the heat of the Cauldron, she let him assist her. Once on the ground, she immediately took off her coat and held it out to Robinton. He took it without a word and tossed it back into the carriage as her guard and Anniska climbed down unaided.

Now, for the first time, she could hear the Cauldron as well as see and smell it, a deep rumbling vibration that shook her to her very bones.

Falk stood at the front of the carriage, watching her, also coatless, wearing his usual uniform of dark gray, silvered hair tinted a fiendish red by the Cauldron. The fiery lake's surface now lay just fifty feet or so below the broad, flat ledge, covered with crushed black rock where the road ended. Past Falk, Brenna saw a tower, built at the very edge of the precipice, with an outthrust platform near its top. Falk turned and gazed up at it avidly. "The Cauldron Observatory," he said, almost the first words he had spoken to her since they had begun this journey. "Our destination."

"Why have you brought me here?" Brenna demanded, remembering she wasn't supposed to know. "Were you so afraid I would run away again that you dared not leave me behind?"

Falk laughed. "No," he said, but he didn't answer her question. "Bring her," he instead commanded the guard, who seized her right arm and half-propelled, half-dragged her toward the tower.

As they neared it, she saw it was made of the same black volcanic rock as the gravel that crunched beneath her feet, gigantic blocks of it, more massive even than the limestone blocks of the Palace. A door of dull silvery metal, tinged red like everything else by the Cauldron's light, glistened despite the heat beneath a magic-betraying layer of frost.

Falk reached out his still-gloved hand and touched it, and with a slight flash of blue, it opened. Inside, magelights sprang to life, coldly illuminating the start of a winding staircase.

Up that staircase they went, Falk leading the way, Anniska behind him, then Brenna, then her guard. Robinton remained with the coach.

Though the tower was no higher than a wing of the Palace, the climb seemed endless to Brenna, as though the top were receding even as they approached it; but then, after an eternity but still all too soon, they suddenly reached the staircase's end. Falk opened another magically sealed door, and they stepped out onto the platform Brenna had first seen from below.

It was an alarming construction, for it had no guardrail of any sort. Brenna hung back, trying to stay close to the tower, but Falk made an impatient gesture and the guard dragged her forward to where the MageLord stood, what seemed to her dangerously close to the edge.

For a moment she entertained the fantasy of lunging at him and pushing him over the side, but the guard never released her arm, and even if he had, she knew she was just as likely to go over the edge herself; and now, looking down unwillingly, she saw that they were right over the Cauldron, at a place where one of the yellow-hot rivers of stone welled up, flowing a few dozen feet on the surface before plunging once more beneath the black crust. The heat struck her face like a blow, and she jerked back.

Falk, though, peered down avidly. He closed his eyes and spread his hands. "Ah, Brenna," he murmured. "You don't know what you're missing, having no magic. The power available here is . . . unbelievable. When a MageLord stands here, he feels he can do anything."

"You seem to think you can do anything no matter where you are . . . my lord," Brenna said. "Without regard for the law or the rights of others." Her own temerity surprised her; but after all, she thought, *What have I got to lose? He already means to kill me.*

Falk shot her a look, one eyebrow raised. "Without regard to the law? Brenna, I am a MageLord. The only law in this Kingdom is the will of the Twelve. We write the law, we administer the law, and if we choose, we can change the law. And as for the rights of others . . . sometimes the needs of the Kingdom are more important than the rights of any one individual. Here, tonight, is one of those times . . . and here, tonight, the needs of the Kingdom will finally be met." He flicked a finger, and a magelink globe popped into existence, floating in space ten feet in front of them, over the Cauldron. Falk flicked his hand again, and the magelink expanded, swelling until it was as wide as Falk was tall. He laughed. "So much energy," he said. "Enough to power the Great Barrier and the Lesser: all that energy constantly pouring into those two structures, and all the effect it has had here is to cause the Cauldron to crust over a little more than it otherwise would. Now . . ."

Suddenly, the magelink came to life, and Brenna gasped. She had seen magelinks used before, but they were small, and since they had been Falk's, they had typically shown the rather homely face of Brich.

But this . . . this was like a window, crystal-clear, so real she felt she could have stepped off of the platform and into the luxurious bedchamber it showed, right next to the huge canopied bed, hung with scarlet curtains . . .

. . . and then the image changed, moved, as the magelink at the other end drifted toward the bed, through the curtains.

She found herself looking down at the bed, the effect making her stagger. The guard's grip tightened on her arms.

Two men in the bed, one very young, her own age or younger, one older, perhaps fifty, lay spooned together in the bed beneath a sheet of pale blue satin. Brenna recognized the older man instantly, from dozens of official portraits, as King Kravon.

The younger man appeared to be feigning sleep. He lifted his head and glanced up toward the magelink, and nodded. Then he carefully disengaged from the King, who slept on unnoticing, and raised himself to a sitting position, the sheet falling from his naked body. He reached to the head of the bed and from somewhere . . . Brenna couldn't tell where . . . drew out a dagger. The image was so clear Brenna could even see his youthful face reflected in the glistening blade. Falk let go of her right arm, though his left kept its ironlike grip, and she heard his own dagger slither from its sheath.

Her heart raced so fast she thought she would faint. She couldn't take her eyes off the image, even as she felt the guard step back and Falk take his place. The MageLord suddenly let go of her arm and instead wrapped his left arm across her breasts, pinning her and pulling her close, his body pressing as tightly against her as though they were lovers like the men in the image.

Mother Northwind lied, or she's failed. Brenna's thoughts came in frightened bursts, like rabbits breaking from cover as hunters closed in, dashing back and forth in a vain attempt to escape the arrows picking them off one by one. *The King is going to die.* I'm *going to die . . .*

The young man leaned forward again, reaching toward the King's throat. Brenna could hear Falk's own quick breathing above her, could feel him trembling against her. He ground his hips into her buttocks and, with shuddering disgust, she felt his engorged manhood. Trapped between him and the Cauldron, she could do nothing but watch the King's death and await her own, as unstoppable, it seemed, as the rivers of lava below her.

But then, just as the knife approached the King's throat, and Falk's knife lifted toward her own, the boy stopped moving.

Falk's arm tightened so much she winced. "Do it," he whispered. Then, shouting, "Damn you, boy, do it!"

The boy drew the knife back as though about to make the fatal thrust, Falk's blade kissed her neck, and Brenna thought her heart would stop . . .

. . . and then the boy turned the knife and plunged it into his own throat, ripping it from side to side in one quick motion that opened an enormous gaping red mouth in his pale skin.

The King woke screaming as blood fountained across him. He rolled over and screamed again as he saw the boy above him, kneeling, the gush of blood already lessening. The boy's hands had fallen limp to his sides; the knife had dropped onto the pillows. His head was tilted back . . . too far back . . . and his eyes, wide, blue, already glazing over, stared up at the magelink . . .

. . . then he pitched forward and fell across the screaming, naked King, who, painted in red, scrambled out of the bed and out of the image coming from the magelink . . .

. . . which winked out of existence an instant later.

Falk had frozen in place. Brenna, beneath her horror, felt a surge of hope that she might yet live . . . if Falk didn't simply throw her into the Cauldron anyway in a fit of fury.

"No," Falk moaned. Then, "No!" he screamed, and then he *did* throw her, not toward the edge, but to the side. She spun away and fell, hitting the ground so hard the breath exploded from her lungs, and lay there, gaping, unable to breathe for a long, agonizing moment. Through her own pain she heard Falk's wordless howl of fury go on and on.

Mother Northwind, she thought.

Mother Northwind had known who the assassin was. She had *twisted* that poor boy . . . made him kill himself instead of the king. And before *that* he had been twisted by Falk, maybe not through magic, but through blackmail or threats or one of the many other ways a man like Falk could exert pressure on someone young and helpless.

And even though that had been all that had saved her own life, at that moment, as she gasped for air by the Cauldron that was the beating heart of the MageLords' domain, she hated both of them as much for what they had done to that poor naked boy as for what they had done to her.

CHAPTER 27

FALK BIT OFF HIS HOWL OF FURY. He glared at the place where the magelink had been, willing it back into existence, but saw nothing but flame-tinged clouds and swirling, blood-colored snow. A vast roar filled his ears, and his vision grayed. *Twenty years*, he thought, the words pushing through the roaring like the rivers of bright yellow rising to the black surface of the caldera below. *Twenty years preparing for the moment when I would hold the Heir, the King would die, the spell would be performed, the Keys would come to me . . . for twenty years I worked and waited, twenty years I plotted and schemed, twenty years . . .*

. . . and as quickly as one of the rivers of lava plunging out of sight beneath the black, stinking rock below, the moment had come, and gone . . . and all had failed.

The boy had killed himself, instead of the King. *The boy had killed himself.* Falk had never imagined such a possibility, never imagined the youngster he had groomed for this task through threats and bribes, seduction and carefully orchestrated rape, would take his own life at the climactic moment.

He had the knife at the King's throat. *He had the knife at the King's throat!*

And now . . .

Killing the King was no problem. There were a dozen ways Falk could kill the King or have him killed. But killing the King while Falk stood here at the Cauldron with the

Heir in his grasp and a mage ready to perform Tagaza's spell . . .

How much longer before he could make a second attempt?

That thought snapped him back from the confusion and horror of the moment. *So it's a setback*, he snapped at himself. *A major one. But it's not the end. I still have the Heir. I still know the spell. We'll return to the Palace, I'll conduct the investigation into the boy's death . . .*

. . . and assign a new bodyguard to the King . . .

He slammed his dagger back into its sheath, then turned and strode toward Brenna, who lay on her back, breathing as though it pained her. "Are you hurt?" he snapped.

"Why do . . . you care?" she snarled back, like a wounded, cornered animal. "You were . . . going to kill me. Like you were going . . . to kill . . . the King!" She struggled to a sitting position. "My father!"

Falk started. "*What* did you say?"

"King Kravon is my father. I'm the real Heir. That's why you 'fostered' me. That's why you brought me here. You were planning to kill me and grab the Keys and the power to destroy the Barriers the moment the King died!"

Falk knelt, grabbed Brenna by her shoulders, and hauled her to her feet. "*Who told you this?*" He shook her so hard her teeth clicked together. "*Who?*"

Brenna, with strength that surprised him, pushed his hands away from her. "Don't touch me! Who do you think? Mother Northwind."

"What? *Why?*" It made no sense. Mother Northwind wanted the Great Barrier lowered as much as he did. Why risk that by telling Brenna her part in it?

"Because Mother Northwind is not your ally!" Brenna shouted. "Who do you think those men on the dogsleds—the men you had murdered!—were taking us to? Who do you think twisted that poor boy's mind so he slit his own throat instead of killing the King like you'd planned? You thought you were using Mother Northwind all this time, and she's been the one using you!"

Falk stood very still. *Mother Northwind examined the boy to be certain he would do as he promised*, he thought . . . *and instead twisted him so that he failed*. It made perfect sense of what he had just witnessed—but no sense at all in so many other ways.

But she wants the Barrier down! he thought. *She brought Brenna to me and put Karl in the Palace. She's worked as long as I have to make this happen, so why wreck everything now?*

I'll be sure to ask her, just before I kill her, he thought savagely.

"Why are you telling me this?" he demanded. "If Mother Northwind is the one who warned you, why are you betraying her to me now? You must know what I will do to her when I return to the Palace. You could be lying. You could just be trying to sow discord between us, thinking that might save your life."

"Then who told me I was your intended sacrifice?" Brenna shouted back. "I'm telling you the truth. And I'm telling it to you because *I hate her as much as I hate you*. That witch is a monster, a worse monster than you. I hope you kill her!"

"If what you've told me is true, you can rest assured that I will," Falk said. He stepped closer to her. "But that will not help *you*. I hold no ill will toward you and I have made your life as comfortable as I could. But you are the key to the Plan I have worked toward for twenty years. I promise you that when the time comes, I will kill you cleanly and quickly, but you *will* die. There is no other way."

Brenna only glared at him.

Falk nodded to the guard, standing close at hand. "Put her back into the carriage," he said. "We're returning to the Palace." He turned to Anniska, who had not moved but had a slightly stunned expression. "You'll be coming to the Palace, too," he said. "I want you close at hand for when we try again."

"But, my lord, my own duties in Berriton—"

"Can go to the bottom of the Cauldron! Don't argue

with me, Anniska. Don't . . . *ever* . . . argue with me. You will do what I tell you, or you will have no duties in Berriton or anywhere else ever again, and I will find another for this task. Do you understand?"

Anniska's face, even in the ruddy glow of the Cauldron, turned noticeably paler. "I understand."

"Let's go." Falk turned and stalked into the tower and down the stairs to where the magecarriage waited. Robinton took one look at him and, knowing better than to speak, scrambled into his seat. As everyone else climbed aboard and the carriage started rolling away from the Cauldron, Falk stared straight ahead and thought black thoughts, thoughts that whirled through his mind like carrion crows above a battlefield, waiting to feed.

Mother Northwind would very soon learn what happened to a tool that broke in the hand of its user . . . and the very big difference between the hard magic he wielded, and the soft she had used for him—and now, fatally, *against* him.

News of the scandalous suicide of a boy in King Kravon's bed spread through the Palace like wildfire. Teran heard it first, in the guard barracks, and hurried back to Karl's quarters, relieving the night watch, then rushing in to wake Karl and tell him the news.

You couldn't keep something like that secret, not with servants having to clean up the blood, not with a body to dispose of, and especially not with Falk absent, Karl thought, staring out the window of his bedroom at the dark expanse of the lake. Had he been there, he might have succeeded in keeping the most salacious details, if not secret, at least obfuscated, turning the tale of a naked boy slitting his throat while in bed with the King to perhaps a deranged servant killing himself while the King slept alone. But with Falk gone north on his yearly inspection trip to the Cauldron, there was no one to hide anything.

And the impact of it?

None, Karl thought. The King was the King not because of any great abilities to lead, or any wonderful personal qualities, but simply because he held the Keys. Whatever he wanted to do, whatever whim he wanted to indulge, he could . . . and this might be the most titillating, but certainly not the first, example of that.

What kind of system is it that puts a wanton hedonist on the throne? Karl thought angrily. *By what right does he rule?*

Especially, by what right does he rule the Commoners? *Commoners like me*, he reminded himself. Why should thcy . . . *we* . . . be subject to a man like that, simply because we have no magic—and, for the most part, want nothing to do with it?

There must be a thousand men better suited to rule than King Kravon, Karl thought. *Shouldn't there be some way of finding one of* those *men to lead?*

Seditious thoughts, but thoughts, he realized now, that had been slowly working their way to the surface for a long time, ever since he was old enough to realize what kind of a man his putative father was, ever since he was old enough to realize what kind of a man *he* could choose to be when the power of the Kingship came to him . . . ever since he had begun to realize just how different life was for the Commoners who lived outside—not just outside the Lesser Barrier, but outside the webs of power and privilege woven by the Mageborn, and especially the Twelve. On every visit to the Commons, even though he had been carefully se- quested from the nastier parts of the city, he had prom- ised himself that he would build on the goodwill he was attempting to engender, that when he was King, things would be different.

Now he would never be King. But if Mother Northwind had told him the truth, he had far more power than he would have as King. He could actually *unravel* the Mageborn-spun web in which the Commoners were trapped like flies in a spider's larder, rip it apart like a cob- web in a gale and scatter it forever, never to be woven again.

Just hours before, he still hadn't been sure. But now, thinking of the dead Commoner boy in the King's bed, all the boys and girls and men and women who had suffered and bled and died at the capricious whims of MageLords and Mageborn, he *was* sure.

If he really were the Magebane, if he really could bring down the magical Barriers that protected Palace and Kingdom, and the insubstantial but even greater barriers that separated Commoners and Mageborn, he would do it . . .

. . . and pray to the SkyMage, if He existed, that whatever came after would be better than what had come before.

———

Mother Northwind heard the news of the boy's death from the servant who brought her breakfast—servants never had any qualms about gossiping with her, seeing her as just a harmless old lady from the countryside, a Healer, to be sure, which made her Mageborn, but so down to earth she might as well have been a Commoner.

When the servant had left, she sighed. *That poor boy*, she thought. *But I couldn't leave him alive to be punished by Falk. And at least I got word to the Cause about his family; they're safely out of it and away from Falk's clutches, as well.*

Falk would have seen the deed through his magelink. He would even now be rushing back to the Palace with Brenna in tow. Everything had happened just as she'd told Brenna it would. The girl knew now that her only hope lay with Mother Northwind. Karl knew his part, as well, and Mother Northwind was confident he would play it.

Falk's Plan had come crashing down around his ears, and though he no doubt had some scheme already forming to salvage it by arranging a new attack on the King, another trip to the Cauldron, he would never get the chance—because Mother Northwind's Plan was still very much intact.

She smiled and helped herself to a second boiled egg

from her breakfast tray. *Two days*, she thought. *Two days, and Brenna will be back in the Palace . . .*

. . . and the reign of the MageLords will end.

Davydd Verdsmitt, now permitted his own quarters, rather plainly furnished but far better than a cell, watched the attack on King Kravon as it transpired, through a magelink much like Lord Falk's own . . . except his did not depend on the life of the boy who killed himself. His was linked to an enchanted object, a gold ball that hung from the center of the canopy over the bed. Since a Common Cause sympathizer in the Royal household had placed that object there, he had spent far too many late nights watching what it showed him, watching the King entertain lovers, each panting, groaning encounter renewing his jealousy, renewing his rage at the man he had once loved who had denounced him.

Obviously my timing was bad, he had thought in the earlier hours of the King's encounter with the boy who killed himself. *Kravon reverted to his natural appetites once he did his duty and produced an heir. Maybe if I had waited, he would have returned to me. . . .*

But no. Kravon had burned that bridge early on, presenting himself publicly as a happily married man, renouncing Verdsmitt as a pitiable figure who thought he was in love with the King but whose love the King could not return. There could be no going back after that, no going back after Lord Athol had also denounced his son and apologized profusely and publicly for his "derangement."

And, certainly, there had been no going back after Davydd had faked his death.

He had thought he was almost over it, six years later when Mother Northwind had come to his door, but when she had offered him the opportunity to do something about it, to strike back at the King and the MageLords, all his anger had flared up again . . . and it had never subsided since.

And so he watched, night after night, as the King took lovers, but never took lovers of his own. He had had two or three in the years immediately after the King's rejection, but that, too, had ended with Mother Northwind's visit.

The boy who had tried to slay the King at Falk's behest, then had slain himself at Mother Northwind's, had been the youngest boy Kravon had ever bedded, almost as young as Kravon himself had been when he and Davydd . . .

Verdsmitt shook his head. Those days were more than thirty years gone. And soon the King would be gone, too.

Verdsmitt was able to watch the servants dragging away the dead body and stripping the bed of its blood-soaked sheets and mattress. He was able to watch right up until they also pulled down the blood-spattered curtains . . . and his enchanted golden bauble with them.

He swore. Then he realized exactly what had just happened, and swore louder.

Mother Northwind is too rutting clever for her own good, he thought savagely. His plan for killing the King, just like Falk's, had centered on the King's bed, the one location you could be certain he could be found at a particular time. His killing enchantments, like the enchanted bauble that had shown him what transpired there, were literally woven into the canopy; golden threads that that same Cause-linked servant had inserted after another Commoner servant had "accidentally" ripped a seam by stumbling against the cloth. But with the canopy gone . . .

So, too, was his weapon.

Falk's plan had failed, which meant Brenna would be returning to the Palace with Falk. Mother Northwind would be pulling strings, as she did so well, to get Brenna and Karl together. She would be counting on him to kill the King on cue . . . and he had just lost the ability to do so.

Verdsmitt's room was dark, now that the blue glow of the magelink had vanished. The fire had long since burned down to a few dimly glowing embers in the hearth, and his curtains were drawn.

But in his mind, Verdsmitt still saw images. He saw the

boy, in his last night of life, pleasuring Kravon with hands and lips and body. He remembered when he and Kravon had had the same enjoyment of each other. He felt the old rage, burning even hotter, and then, suddenly, everything became very clear.

Kravon had to die. Not for Mother Northwind's plan, but for what he had done to Verdsmitt. Verdsmitt's tools for killing him had just been stripped away. But the King still had to die.

And now Verdsmitt understood how it could be done . . . how it should have been done all along. The solution hung in his mind, perfect in every detail: especially the one detail that now, in retrospect, Verdsmitt realized had been the flaw in his original scheme.

He had been operating under the assumption that he would strike from a distance. He had been operating under the assumption that it was important that he survive.

But the best way to strike, the best way to kill the King, would be up close and personal, and his own survival, he suddenly realized, was not only unnecessary, it wasn't even something he desired.

The King would know, in that last moment, Verdsmitt thought, who was killing him, and why.

He may have thought he could not be with me in life, but I'll make damn sure he's with me in death.

Decision made, Verdsmitt took off his clothes in the dark, climbed into his empty bed, and slept a deep, untroubled sleep.

Chapter 28

AS THE AIRSHIP APPROACHED the top of the Barrier from the east, Anton wished more fervently than ever that the Professor was still alive.

The burner was roaring, a blue flame ten feet long reaching up into the envelope; the propeller was a blur, spinning at top speed as it had been for the last half hour while Anton watched the needle of the fuel gauge almost visibly declining. They had been climbing steadily almost since they left the Palace, and yet still the wall of cloud that marked the Anomaly rose higher than they had yet reached.

The wind streaming over the Anomaly from the west formed a layer of tattered cloud above them. If it had been at all a windy day it would have been impossible, Anton thought; they would have had to return to the Palace and try again some other time. But the chattering propeller could still give them headway against today's light breeze, and though fuel was low, they weren't out of it yet, and so they continued to rise. Now the gray wall of the Barrier was so close Anton thought he could have had a good chance of hitting it with a rock, if he'd had one close enough to throw, and he could feel the chill of it.

He watched the streaming cloud marking the very top of the Barrier coming closer and closer above them. They would hit a strong headwind at that level, he knew, and if it threw them too far to the east, they might run out of fuel

for the engine before they were able to regain the ground
lost.

"Gotta dump ballast," he muttered. "Pop through that,
get to the quieter air above it."

He glanced at Spurl, the Mageborn guard who had accompanied him. He'd hoped the man might at least take
instruction as they flew, but Spurl had spent the whole journey cowering in the bottom of the gondola, unwilling to
even look over the side. He sat there now, eyes closed,
moaning, rocking back and forth.

I wish Brenna were with me, Anton thought again.
Though she had no experience in flying an airship, at least
she had shown herself to have a cool head.

But Brenna was back at the Palace, and Anton was
heading the other way.

The ragged gray clouds streaming over the Barrier were
close above them. The envelope would enter them within
minutes, and almost certainly they would be thrown back
when that happened. He had to act now.

He scrambled over the legs of the guard. He didn't want
to repeat what he had done when he and Brenna were fleeing the manor and release all the ballast at once; if he did,
they might find themselves so high they'd not only be gasping for air, they'd pass out and could even asphyxiate before the airship dipped back into thicker air.

But releasing too little would be almost as disastrous.

He hesitated, then decided to follow the simplest course.
There were four rows of sandbags on each side of the gondola. He released two buckles on each side, letting half the
ballast fall.

Instantly the airship surged upward. Within seconds the
envelope was inside the streaming layer of cloud, and as
Anton had feared, they were pushed away from the Barrier
despite the propeller's best efforts; but they were rising so
rapidly that they were through that layer of cloud and wind
within half a minute, and above it the air was much calmer.
Almost at once they began to regain their lost ground.

Anton anxiously watched the fuel gauge. It seemed he

could almost see it dropping toward empty . . . but now they were over the Barrier itself. He could look straight down at that enormous wall of fog, and then suddenly he was looking down at the land outside the Barrier, terrain very much the same but completely uncultivated, wild prairie with grass so tall that even after three months of snow the fields were more brown than white.

Anton cut the burner. They wanted to descend now, not climb, and they quickly began to do so as the cold air sucked heat from the envelope. He searched the ground below them anxiously. His navigation had been iffy at best, and he wasn't entirely sure where they had crossed the Anomaly. But he hoped . . .

Ah! There, a smudge of smoke near the horizon, a dark stain on the snow-covered prairie. Elkbone, the town he and the Professor had left what seemed like a lifetime ago, though in fact it had been less than two weeks. He looked at Spurl, and smirked. The hand-picked minion who was supposed to enforce Anton's deliverance of Falk's reassuring lies to the poor deluded Commoners on this side of the Barrier was currently throwing up his guts over the side of the gondola.

Welcome to my world, Anton thought. *Let's see what survives of MageLord arrogance when the gentlemen of the press descend on us with flashbulbs popping.*

Anton had every reason to believe they would still be there. It hadn't been all that long, really, and since no railpath ran from Elkbone to Wavehaven, travel in winter was fraught with danger. Most of the reporters who had covered the launch had traveled here before the snow fell in the same caravan as he, the Professor, and the airship. They would be unlikely to go back until the weather warmed in spring.

They could send their words and images, though, thanks to the electromissive lines that had been strung along the road that would someday be a railpath, and that meant that whatever was said here would, before nightfall, be making news in Wavehaven. Two or three weeks later, when ships reached Hexton Down across the ocean, the President of the Union Republic would know of it. What he would do about it was out of Anton's hands.

What *wasn't* out of his hands was what *he* would do about it.

He would not leave Brenna at the mercy of Falk and Mother Northwind one minute longer than he had to.

The engines sputtered and the propeller stopped spinning as they swung low over a treed ridge just northeast of Elkbone. They'd obviously been spotted. People were streaming out of the town to meet them, pouring into the open field they were now drifting across. Anton watched the ground approaching and hoped the fools directly beneath him would be smart enough to move out of the way before several hundred pounds of gondola, burner, engines, propeller, and passengers landed on their heads.

At the last moment, with trees approaching and the ground still a little farther away than he would have liked, he pulled the ropes that opened the vents on the top of the envelope. Air rushed out, the envelope sagged, and with great finality, the gondola dropped the last few feet to the snow, hitting with a thump that Anton, holding on tightly, managed to weather standing up.

Spurl wasn't as prepared, nor as fortunate. He went sprawling, banging his head on the burner and opening his scalp. And so, as the crowd swarmed around the gondola, Anton climbed out to face them while Lord Falk's chosen emissary moaned and clutched his bloody skull in the bottom of the basket.

As he'd suspected, the reporters were there, shouted questions bombarding him so quickly he couldn't have answered them if he wanted to, flashes from bulky black imagers half-blinding him. He looked around rather desperately for someone official, and saw him: Ronal Ferkkisson, the Lord Mayor, a short, round man with a red face, pushing his way through the crowds with the help of a quartet of beefy policemen in green capes. "Clear the way, clear the way," the policemen growled as they approached, shoving people aside with oak truncheons. They managed to open a space next to the gondola for Ferkkisson, "Anton?" he said, peering up at him.

"Lord Mayor," Anton said.

"Where's Professor Carteri?"

"Dead, Your Honor," Anton said.

"Dead!" Ferkkisson shook his head. "I knew it was suicide to cross the Anomaly."

Um, hello, I'm *right here and very much alive,* Anton felt like saying, but didn't. "Your Honor, I have urgent news," he said. Then he raised his voice. "News that needs to get to the entire Republic!" he said loudly enough for all the reporters to hear.

Ferkkisson licked his lips. "News? What kind of news?"

"There are people on the other side of the Anomaly," Anton said. "A giant kingdom, hidden from us . . . until now."

Astonished murmurs and whispers ran through the crowd, followed by the hisses of people shushing each other so they could hear what he would say next.

Here goes, Anton thought. Taking a deep breath, he added, "They call themselves the MageLords."

That brought an enormous rush of sound, from gasps to catcalls to outright laughter. Reporters scribbled furiously in their notebooks, smirking. Anton remembered when he would have reacted the same, when "MageLords" had been nothing more to him than the villains in children's fairy tales.

"Can they do magic?" someone shouted.

"Can they make things disappear?" yelled someone else.

"Did they pull a rabbit out of a boot?" someone else called.

Anton hesitated, wondering how to convince them—

—and then Spurl took care of the problem for him.

The Royal guard looked like something out of a nightmare as he pulled himself to his full height inside the gondola. Blood had streamed down his face, masking his features in red, and then poured down his silver breastplate, giving him the look of someone who had survived, by the skin of his teeth, a horrifying beating. He stared around at the assembled people. They stared back.

And then, as one, the reporters with imagers raised them and started capturing pictures.

Brilliant white flashes exploded all around. Anton winced and turned his eyes away. But Spurl . . .

It was probably inevitable, Anton thought later, that a Mageborn guard would interpret flashing lights as a magical attack. And inevitable, too, that someone who had just discovered a terror of flying and a tendency to airsickness *and* had just hit his head would react so instinctively to that perceived attack.

Spurl screamed and thrust out his hands, palms up. A flash of blue hurled everyone within fifty feet of the gondola onto their backs as though struck by a giant fist. Men, women, and children sprawled into the snow. Bones broke as people slammed into each other. Blood ran from scalps and noses, staining the snow. Spurl looked beyond the fallen, moaning spectators to those outside the circle of the attack, who stood in frozen shock. He raised his hands again—

A rifle shot rang out, loud even above the screams of the people scrambling to their feet now and trying to flee.

Spurl jerked. Eyes wide, he stared down at the neat round hole in the middle of his breastplate. As blood pumped from the hole he gave Anton a bewildered glance . . . then his eyes rolled up in his head and he dropped like a stone into the bottom of the gondola, dead before he hit the wicker.

Anton felt something running down his cheek and wiped away a dribble of Spurl's blood. For a moment, everything had fallen still, the sudden violence freezing everyone in place; but now chaos erupted.

It was much, much later before Anton had the opportunity to continue his story, officially to the Lord Mayor, unofficially (and very much against Ferkkisson's wishes, but tough luck) to the reporters. After Spurl's display, he suddenly found it much easier to convince them all of the reality of the magical kingdom on the other side of the Barrier—and the threat that Kingdom would pose if Lord Falk succeeded in lowering the Barrier and moving into the Outside world.

The stories flew out along the electromissive wires long before Ferkkisson's official report was ready. Anton had watched the news cycle long enough to know what would happen. The stories would hit the papers. The government would have no comment because no official report had yet been received. When it did arrive, the government would be a day behind, playing catch-up as editorial writers demanded action against this new threat. *Maybe they'll build a whole fleet of airships*, Anton thought. *Wouldn't the Professor have been thrilled to see that?*

It would take weeks to get much in the way of military to the Anomaly; it was simply too remote. But Falk did not intend to act until after the snow was gone, Anton knew. And when he did emerge, he would find, not a small populace completely unprepared for his assault, but fully trained military armed with the same kind of modern weapons— and far more—that had just made short work of Falk's hand-selected emissary.

If you want to set up your nasty little magical dictatorship in our *world*, Anton thought savagely, *you're going to have to fight for it.*

But Anton didn't intend to sit around and wait. He told Ferkkisson he would take the airship west to Wavehaven, to give the governor there an eyewitness account of everything he had seen in Evrenfels. In response to that promise, Ferkkisson spared no expense outfitting the airship for the journey. It took a few days, but at the end of it, the fuel tank was full, the engine cleaned, tuned, and freshly oiled, the burner polished, the ballast replaced, the envelope mended, frayed ropes replaced, stores loaded. Spurl's blood had been mostly cleaned from the wicker, although a dark stain remained that Anton thought would never come out. And there were new additions, "in case of being forced down in the wilderness," Anton had explained. A pistol, a rifle, and plenty of ammunition for both; and, at his hip, a long hunting knife with a bone handle.

On a morning whose mild air held a hint of the spring to come, Anton shook Lord Mayor Ferkkisson's hand, waved to the crowd that had come out to see him off, posed for some final pictures, and then climbed into the gondola.

"Cast off!" he shouted to the men at the tie-down ropes, and as one, they released them. The gondola began to rise. Anton fired the burner, and lifted faster. He waved one last time to the crowd.

No doubt there was great consternation twenty minutes later when Anton fired up the propellers, seized the tiller—and steered, not west toward the distant mountains and the coast beyond, but east toward the Anomaly.

He hoped the Lord Mayor wouldn't have an apoplectic fit, but either way, Anton was heading back to where he really wanted and needed to be:

Wherever Brenna was.

For Brenna, the journey from the Cauldron back to the Palace was as silent as before . . . but the silence had a different quality. Falk's anger seemed to infuse the very air in the magecarriage. Anniska sat sunken in gloom, obviously regretting he ever become involved, but trapped without hope of escape now. The guard sat impassively as always, but Brenna thought even his face showed more strain than before: something in the set of the jaw and the frown lines between his bushy black eyebrows.

As for herself, she had far too much time to think, far too much time to see, over and over in her mind's eye, that horrible moment when the boy had slit his own throat, and far too much time to second-guess her decision, driven by anger and disgust, to tell Lord Falk how Mother Northwind had betrayed him.

Mother Northwind at least meant to keep her alive. Falk's Plan, if it were to succeed, required her death. Had she committed suicide as surely as the boy by telling him the truth?

Well, if I have, she thought, *at least I did so of my own free will!*

It seemed cold comfort, more bravado than bravery, as she remembered Falk holding her in a tight embrace at the very edge of the platform over the Cauldron, his body pressed against her in a travesty of affection. Falk had every intention of returning her to that spot, to stand once more above the heaving lake, and next time to, she supposed, to slice her throat as wide open as that boy's.

Maybe, she thought. *But not right away. I've escaped him once. I can do it again.*

But last time she had had Anton's help . . . and now he was Falk's twisted tool, and SkyMage-knew-where on the other side of the Barrier. It seemed doubtful he would ever return.

Mother Northwind still needs me, Brenna reminded herself. *And she may not be as easy to defeat as Falk seems to think. With the two of them battling, perhaps there will be an opportunity to . . .*

But her imagination failed her. She couldn't plan, because she couldn't even guess what awaited her at the Palace.

All she could do was try to remain ready, try to remain alert, try to remain . . .

. . . *angry*, she thought.

And with that thought, she found something to keep her occupied during the rest of the long journey back to the Palace. She sat in silence, and whenever her thoughts began sliding toward despair or self-pity, she turned them again to anger, anger at her supposed guardian, for whom she was nothing more than a vessel in which to capture the Keys, a vessel he would then smash and discard like a badly made pot to claim the Keys for himself; anger at Mother Northwind, manipulating, killing, twisting, so convinced of the righteousness of her cause that any evil she might commit could be excused; anger at King Kravon, lost in a hedonistic haze for decades, blind to the machinations going on all around him; and, finally and ultimately, anger at the Mageborn, convinced that their ability to manipulate the world through magic, an undeserved accident of birth, gave them the right to rule over and abuse the Commoners around them.

Mother Northwind is right, she thought. *She's a lying, manipulative witch, but it's time this whole damned Kingdom was done away with, and all the MageLords and Mageborn with it.*

But with that thought came one cold rivulet of doubt, cooling the fire of her fury.

In her righteous urge to punish Mother Northwind, had she ensured that the Kingdom would not only survive, but break through the Barrier and engulf the whole world?

Only two weeks ago she had been looking out of the window of her room at Falk's manor, wishing for the coming of Springfest and lamenting the fact that nothing ever happened.

As the carriage rolled on through the silent, snow-covered prairie north of New Cabora, she wished with all her heart she was back there.

———

Lord Falk's magecarriage rolled up to the Palace as the sun began to set behind the bloody shreds of clouds torn apart by a day of howling wind.

Prince Karl watched its approach from his window, staring as Lord Falk jumped down from the driver's seat and stalked up the steps and out of sight. Another man, thin and rather sickly looking, followed, and finally Brenna emerged with one of the bulkier examples of a guard close behind. She moved slowly, almost like an old woman, as though her journey to the Cauldron had aged her beyond her years.

Does she know? he wondered. *Does she know that she is the true Heir, and that I am the Magebane? Does she know everything Mother Northwind has schemed?*

If so, she was the only other person beside himself who knew the truth, and it suddenly seemed very important to him to talk to her, to have someone else he could turn to. She was apparently as crucial to the success of Mother Northwind's plan to end the rule of the MageLords as he was. Even though he had decided he shared Mother Northwind's aims, what if Brenna did not? What if she *wanted* to be the new Queen, perhaps even hoped to use her position to improve life for the Commoners? What right did he have to strip away that choice and opportunity?

I'll talk to her, he thought. *I'll talk to her* now. And he turned away from the window and strode through his rooms and into the corridor, where Teran stood watch.

"I need to talk to Brenna, Falk's ward," he said in a low voice, though no one else was near. "She's being taken to her quarters by a guard. I want you to relieve him and take her to the boathouse, instead. I'll be waiting there."

Teran nodded. "Yes, Your Highness." He gave a small grin. "Karl." He lowered his voice. "I've had word. My sister and mother are safe. Thank you."

"You're welcome, Teran." Karl returned the grin. "And I'm glad I can trust you again."

"I'm glad you can trust me again, too," Teran said. "I'll have Brenna at the boathouse within ten minutes."

Karl watched Teran go down the corridor. When his bodyguard was out of sight around the corner, he stepped out and went the other way, down the main stairs to the grand entrance hall of the Palace, down the front steps, through the ornamental garden. He waited by the boathouse, standing next to the same tethered rowboat he'd now used twice, and staring out over the water.

Five minutes later, Teran said behind him, "Your Highness?"

Karl turned. Brenna stood beside Teran, her face pale, her dark eyes bloodshot and deeply shadowed. "Your Highness," she said dully. "How may I serve you?"

Karl glanced at Teran. "Brenna and I are going to row

across the lake. Would you be so good as to meet us on the far side, at the usual place?"

"Of course, Your Highness," said Teran. As Karl stepped down into the rowboat and turned to help Brenna down with him, Teran started walking along the shore toward the bridge.

Karl put his back to the oars, but when they were far enough from the shore so he felt certain they could not be overheard, he shipped them and let the boat drift. "Your Highness," Brenna said cautiously. "To what do I owe the—"

"Mother Northwind," Karl said in a soft voice, "has recently spoken to me. Has she also spoken to you?"

Brenna went absolutely still, so still he thought she had stopped breathing. Then she said, "She has."

"And what did she tell you?"

Again that absolute stillness. "We spoke of . . . my childhood," Brenna said at last. "Her cottage is not far from Lord Falk's manor, where I grew up."

It seemed that if they were to break out of this careful courtly dance of noncommittal conversation, he would have to do it. "I see," he said. "And did she tell you the truth of your childhood . . . that you are the true Heir of King Kravon, not I?"

Another moment of stillness, then, "Your Highness, I—"

"I'm not Your Highness," Karl snapped. "You're mine. Now listen, we can drift here only a few more minutes. I know what Falk had planned for you, and that Mother Northwind thwarted it. But now I must know . . . do you know what *she* has planned for you? Do you know what she has planned for *us*?" He paused, took his own deep breath, and asked the most important question of all. "Do you know who—what—I am . . . what Mother Northwind, if she speaks truth, has made me?"

Brenna licked her lips. "Your Highness—"

"I told you, I'm a Commoner." And as he said that, out loud for the first time, he suddenly felt a sense of relief. *Yes*, he thought, *I am. And glad of it!*

"Your . . . Karl. She said that she had learned how to create a Magebane. Are you saying . . . you are it? Him?"

"So she has told me. And I must believe it, having twice seen magic . . . bounce . . . off of my person and rebound on the mage who cast it."

Brenna leaned forward suddenly and took his hands. "Then do it!" she said fiercely. "Do it now! Break the Keys! Now, at a time of *our* choosing, not Mother Northwind's!"

Karl felt a surge of hope, then, and relief that Brenna did not mean to hang onto the Kingdom whose rule she seemed to want no more than he did. He squeezed her hands, waiting for something to happen . . .

. . . but nothing did, except that his hands grew warm. "I don't know how," he said at last. "Mother Northwind hasn't told me everything . . . she's closemouthed, that one."

"She's a witch," Brenna snarled. "A horrible hag who talks about setting the Commoners free but who is every bit as willing as Falk or any other MageLord to use and discard them as it suits her purposes." She pulled her hands free—Karl felt a strange pang of regret as she did so—and sat back again. "But she has us where she wants us. We both want the MageLords cast down—or at least I do—"

"So do I," Karl said.

"—but she has not told us everything we need to know to make it happen. Which means we must await her pleasure." She suddenly clenched her fists and banged them hard against her knees. "I hate her!" she burst out. "As much as I hate Lord Falk."

Karl, glancing over his shoulder, saw that Teran had almost reached their intended landing spot. He turned back to Brenna. "Our conversation is almost over," he said urgently. "What do we do?"

"What can we do, but wait to be told what to do by Mother Northwind?" Brenna squeezed her eyes shut. "If she survives to tell us."

Karl stared at her. "What?"

She opened her eyes, and he was struck by how very

brown they were, a shining brown like polished wood. "I have told Falk that she has been working at cross-purposes to him. I think he must even now be confronting her in the Palace."

"Why?" Karl cried. "Why did you do that?"

"Because I hate her!" Brenna screamed at him, and then closed her eyes and hung her head. "And I let my hatred get the better of my reason." Her voice dropped so low he could hardly hear it. "I may have ruined everything. Handed the Kingdom to Falk, and signed my own death warrant. If he gets the better of Mother Northwind—"

And at that moment, as perfectly timed as if her line had been a cue in a Verdsmitt play, blue light flashed behind two of the windows at the eastern end of the Palace, and those windows exploded outward with a blast that echoed around the Lesser Barrier. An instant later the limestone facade covering the walls around those windows slid away like snow falling in an avalanche, peeling more of the facade with it as it fell, stripping one whole end of the palace down to bare wood. The rumbling of the facade's fall chased the echoes of the original blast around the Palace grounds, and dust rose up to obscure the gaping holes where the windows of Mother Northwind's rooms had been an instant before.

The blast seemed to have frightened every living thing in the Palace grounds into silence. Karl had been looking at the Palace already; Brenna had flinched, then spun around as the facade crumbled. Now she turned back to him. "He did it!" she gasped. "Falk has killed Mother Northwind!"

"And that means you're next!" Karl shot a look over his shoulder. Teran was gesturing frantically to them to get to shore. Karl grabbed the oars, gave a sharp tug with his left and backwatered with the right, and then began rowing as if in a race.

"Where are we going?" Brenna cried.

"Out of here," Karl panted. "Before Falk realizes you're gone and comes after you, too."

"But the Barrier—"

Karl said nothing, but kept rowing. Moments later he was floating just offshore from where Teran was. "Get in," he said.

"What?" Teran said. "No . . . there's been another attack . . . you've got to . . ."

"It wasn't aimed at me," Karl said. "It was aimed at Mother Northwind."

Teran's eyes widened. "Falk?"

"Who else? Now get in!"

Teran splashed off the shore and into the water, wading out and tumbling over the gunwale, almost upsetting the boat. Brenna fastidiously pulled her feet away as he splashed mud and water across the bottom boards.

The light was fading fast. Karl could hear shouting from the direction of the Palace, and glimpsed guards dashing through the pools of magelight, no doubt fearing some additional attack. Down by the boathouse, men were scrambling into another of the rowboats. *They've seen us*, Karl thought. Was that Falk himself, emerging through the massive front doors? Karl couldn't be sure in the uncertain light.

Karl drove the boat as far in among the reeds as he could. Teran jumped out and pulled it up farther, then held out his hand to help Karl and Brenna out of it. Karl took Brenna's hand, and together they staggered through the mud and pushed through the screen of bushes toward the shimmer of the Lesser Barrier and the drifted snow behind it. Teran hung back, watching the Palace. "That boat's coming fast."

"It doesn't matter now," Karl said. "We're leaving."

Brenna's eyes widened. "But . . . that's the Lesser Barrier. You can't—"

"Yes," Karl said. "I can."

With another boat heading their way Karl couldn't take time to explain, couldn't explain, didn't even know if what he hoped would happen would happen. All he knew was that if Falk had truly eliminated Mother Northwind, then

Brenna would die as soon as he could get her back to the Cauldron. And if Falk had discovered the truth about *him*, then his life was also forfeit: he might be impervious to magical attack, but he was pretty sure a crossbow bolt or dagger blade wouldn't care that he was the Magebane.

He might only be buying them a few days—maybe just a few hours—before Falk tracked them down, but that was better than nothing. He knew—or thought he knew—that he could pass through the Lesser Barrier. But could he take Brenna with him?

Could he take Teran?

Only one way to find out. He held tight to Brenna's hand, held his other hand out to Teran. "Take it," he said.

Teran refused it. "No," he said. "They won't have seen where you went. It's too dark. I'll get back in the boat, lead them away. Buy you some more time."

"Falk will kill you."

"Maybe. But I will have done my duty." Teran's face was grim in the dying light. "I swore to protect you, Your Highness."

"I'm not—"

"Whether you are or not, I swore an oath. An oath I have failed twice now. An oath I violated in spirit every time I reported to Falk about your actions and conversations." Teran stepped back. "Go, Your Highness. Let me do my duty."

Karl hesitated. Teran's voice hardened. "Karl, go! Take Brenna. Good luck. And . . . farewell." And then he turned and ran back through the bushes toward the boat, leaving Karl still reaching out with a futile hand to try to stop him.

"Farewell!" He called after his friend, then, tears stinging his eyes, turned to Brenna. "Hold on," he said. He grabbed her, pulled her tight to him in a lover's embrace, felt her stiffen—

—and with a twist and a thrust of his legs, hurled both of them at the Barrier.

Bursting into the cold air felt like plunging into an icy

bath. A moment later they were rolling together in the snow.

Karl scrambled to his feet, pulled Brenna up, then spun back toward the Barrier. In the fading light, he saw Teran rowing away, his boat a long dark streak on the pale water.

Then he grabbed Brenna's hand and led her at a run through the snow toward the yellow lights of New Cabora.

CHAPTER 29

BRENNA, stumbling through the snow in stocking feet, her boots having come off in the mud on the lakeshore, could barely grasp what was happening. Less than an hour had passed since the magecarriage had pulled up to the front of the Palace and Falk had jumped down and stalked inside. The appearance of the Prince, boarding the boat, his revelation that he, too, knew Mother Northwind's plan—then the explosion in the Palace, the frantic rowing across the lake, the mud, the loss of her boots, the Prince's embrace, the sudden shock of the wintry air, and now the cold tearing at her feet and face and hands . . . it had all happened with blinding speed.

She ran, despite the pain in her freezing feet, because she couldn't *not* run, not with the Prince pulling her along and the cold more of a threat than even Falk, left on the other side of the Barrier. *He really is the Magebane*, she thought. *Mother Northwind spoke the truth. He really can negate magic.*

But Mother Northwind might very well be dead in the rubble of her rooms back in the Palace, and her plan to bring down the MageLords with her. Which left only Falk, who would surely kill Prince Karl if he knew he was the Magebane, and would just as surely kill her when he had reconstituted his own Plan and could once more get her to the Cauldron.

Running seemed an eminently sensible thing to do,

except where could they run that Falk couldn't find them? He had already found the Prince once, and that was when he had been tucked away in the Common Cause's most secret safe house. Who would shelter them now?

In a dark alley on the other side of the park, Karl looked back at the way they had just come, and swore. Their footsteps were clear in the snow. "Stay to the cobblestones," he said. "Or Falk will track us with ease."

Brenna shivered. "I ca . . . can't. I l . . . lost my b . . . boots in the mud."

Karl glanced at her feet. "I know what that's like," he said. He straightened. "Then I'll carry you."

"What? No! You can't—"

"Piggy-back," he said. "I'm strong, Brenna. I can do it. It will save your feet . . . and save, us, too. If you cut your feet on the cobblestones and leave a trail of blood . . ."

Feeling self-conscious, Brenna climbed onto his back as he bent before her. He staggered a little as he straightened, but she could feel hard muscle in the shoulders she clung to and the hips she straddled, and though he moved slowly off into the darkness, he didn't falter.

Karl carried her through the streets, staying in the shadows, pulling her aside once into a doorway when someone passed the mouth of the alley they were in, silhouetted against the ghastly yellow illumination of one of New Cabora's gaslights. But few people were abroad, kept inside both by the cold and, she suspected, the recent crackdown in the city by Falk's forces.

Despite her being carried, her stockinged feet were almost numb by the time they reached their destination, an ordinary doorway in an ordinary alley like a dozen others they had traversed. Karl let her slide to the ground, and she winced as her feet landed in snow. *Not completely numb yet, then*, she thought.

Karl knocked, a complicated pattern. Nothing happened. He knocked again, varying the pattern. Still no response. Finally he put his mouth close to a closed eye-slot and said, so loudly her heart leaped in terror for fear someone would overhear, "Open, whoever is in there," he said. "It's Prince Karl. I seek the protection of the Common Cause."

The door opened so abruptly Karl almost stumbled through it—and almost onto the sword point that, catching the light from outside, seemed to hover in the darkness. "Get in," snarled a voice from the darkness.

Karl grabbed Brenna's hand and pulled her through the door. It slammed shut behind them and she heard the bolt shoot into place. In absolute—though blessedly warm—darkness, they crept forward. A second door suddenly opened, revealing a firelit room with a table and chairs. Beyond it Brenna glimpsed another room with beds and blankets, and beyond that, a kitchen.

The man who had admitted them waited until they were both inside, then came in behind them. The door clicked shut, and Brenna turned to see a man about Karl's height, bright blue eyes blazing above a barely-healed wound that had laid his cheekbone open, bared blade glinting red in the firelight. "Tell me why I shouldn't run you through here and now and save myself a hell of a lot of trouble," he growled.

"Vinthor?" Karl said. "I thought you were dead!"

"More than one secret way out of that farmhouse. I killed two guards in the kitchen, then got out while the getting was good. But I was the only one. Denson, Goodwife Beth—"

"Beth survived," Karl said. "She's in the Palace."

Vinthor's face paled, putting the cheek wound into stark relief. "Beth's alive? I thought . . ." He stiffened, face flushing again. "If that's a lie—"

"No lie," Karl said. "Vinthor, Brenna needs to sit down and warm herself. It's not as cold as the night you brought me here barefoot, but it's cold enough. Her feet . . ."

Vinthor hesitated, then sheathed his sword. "All right," he said gruffly. "I'll hear you out. Brenna, is it? Sit down and let me take a look."

Brenna sat gratefully by the fire. Her feet were beginning

to burn and itch with returning circulation. She felt embarrassed and self-conscious, having this strange man pull off her stockings and hold her naked feet in his callused hands, but his touch was gentle, and when he straightened, he said, "No frostbite. Not like yours."

"For which you called a Healer, who saved them," Karl said. "You didn't have to take that risk. I thank you for it."

"The Patron would not have thanked me if I hadn't." Vinthor gestured to the other chair at the table, and Karl took it. Vinthor remained standing.

"It is because of the Patron that I am here," Karl said. "And the Patron's grand plan."

Vinthor's eyes narrowed. "And what plan would that be? The Common Cause wants to shake off the yolk of the MageLords and let Commoners govern themselves. *You* are both Mageborn. Hell, you're the Heir, and will someday be the King. We tried to kill you."

"And, when I found my own way out through the Barrier . . . as I have again tonight . . . you were told to keep me alive," Karl said. "I didn't know why then. But I know now." He paused. "You call me Mageborn. I am not. I am a Commoner."

Vinthor snorted. "The Heir is a Commoner? Not bloody likely."

Karl nodded at Brenna. *Guess I've already decided to trust him*, she thought. She took a deep breath, then met Vinthor's gaze. "He's not the Heir," she said. "I am."

Vinthor's eyebrows shot up. He gave her a long, hard look, then said slowly, "And supposing I believe that, what does that make *him*?" He jerked a thumb at Karl.

"I'm the Magebane," Karl said.

Vinthor blinked, then barked a laugh. "The Magebane is a myth."

"Is it?" Karl said. "The Kingdom is real enough. The Great Barrier is there for a reason, too. Legend tells us the Commoners rose up against the MageLords in the Old Kingdom and drove them here. And legend also claims they only succeeded because of the Magebane." Karl spread his hands. "You've seen how unsuccessful your own attempts to fight the MageLords have been. Perhaps you need a Magebane, too."

"You?" Vinthor said.

"I walked through the Lesser Barrier," Karl said quietly. "Twice. And this time I brought Brenna with me."

Vinthor shot a look at Brenna. "Is that true?"

"It is," she said.

Vinthor studied her. "You say you're the Heir. But that must be something you've just learned. What were you before?"

"Lord Falk's ward," she said bitterly.

Vinthor's eyes widened. He glanced from her to Karl and back again. And then he sighed, pulled out a chair, and sat down with them at the table. "All right," he said. "Tell me."

When Falk jumped down from the magecarriage, stamped up the stairs of the Palace' and strode through the corridors toward Mother Northwind's quarters, he did not have immediate murder on his mind . . . but you would have been hard put to prove it from the reaction of the servants and Mageborn he passed, who took one look at him as he stalked through the hallways, pulling off his heavy outdoor coat, hat, and gloves as he walked, and scurried away like mice faced with an oncoming cat.

Falk was not yet fully prepared to accept Brenna's claim that Mother Northwind was working against him. The Healer had brought Brenna to him, installed Karl as the Prince, interrogated and influenced others for him for years. It seemed inconceivable that she had done so much to help him and then, at the very end of their long game, chose to sabotage his Plan instead.

And yet . . .

The boy in the King's bed had been on the verge of slaying the King, on the verge of at last releasing the Keys to Falk, when he had suddenly killed himself. No sane person, in full control of his own faculties, would have done such a thing . . .

. . . unless his mind had been twisted.

And Mother Northwind, though she might not have been the *only* soft mage in the Kingdom capable of such an act, was certainly the one who was *most* capable of it.

Mother Northwind had "examined" the assassin ahead of the act, giving her the opportunity to alter his mind as she saw fit. Throw in Brenna's claim that the dogsledders had been taking her and Anton to Mother Northwind, and he certainly had grounds for suspicion.

He wasn't convinced. Not yet.

But he was suspicious enough, and angry enough, after the failure of his Plan at the very moment of success, that he *could* be convinced . . . very easily.

He reached Mother Northwind's quarters, paused just long enough to toss his winter clothes on a chair outside, then pounded on the door twice with his gloved fist before seizing the doorknob and swinging the door inward.

Mother Northwind sat by the fire, knitting, for all the world as if she had never left her cottage. "Lord Falk," she said. "What a pleasant surprise."

"Is it?" Falk growled. He closed the door behind him, and took a look around. A maid, sweeping in the corner, froze like a startled rabbit as his gaze swung over to her. "Out," he said.

The girl looked at Mother Northwind. "Put your broom by the fire, Pilea," she said, and as the girl came over, Mother Northwind took her hand and gave it a pat. "It's all right," she said. "Go and fix some tea for us, and I'll ring when we want it."

Pilea glanced from her to Falk, gave a quick curtsy, then fled.

Falk glared at Mother Northwind. "The Plan failed," he said. "The boy killed *himself*, not the King."

Mother Northwind kept knitting. "I know," she said. "A terrible shame. Still, you have the Heir. You'll try again, I expect?"

"I expect I will," Falk said in a low, dangerous voice. "The question is, will someone sabotage my next attempt as well? I doubt I will get a third."

"Sabotage?" Mother Northwind raised her head and one eyebrow. "You suspect someone of sabotage?"

"Indeed I do," Falk spat. "You!"

"Me?" Mother Northwind's wizened face was the picture of innocence. "I have done everything in my power to help you achieve your goal for twenty years, Lord Falk. I'm hurt you would accuse me of doing otherwise now." She cocked her head to one side. "Why on Earth would you suspect *me*?

"You examined the boy to ensure he would go through with it. You said he would."

"I said he was *committed* to doing so," Mother Northwind said. "But I could not foresee that at the last moment he would change his mind. I know soft mages have a reputation for being fortune-tellers, but you know as well as I that the future is a book we can only read one page at a time."

Falk grunted. It was true; not even the most powerful mage could foretell the future. But he wasn't satisfied yet. "And then there is the matter of the dogsleds."

"The dogsleds?" Mother Northwind paused in her knitting and gave him a look obviously intended to make him feel slightly ridiculous; much to his annoyance, it did. "Do tell."

"The dogsleds," Falk grated, "that brought Brenna and Anton south after the airship came down on the shores of the Great Lake."

"Oh," Mother Northwind said. "What about them?" She began tucking her knitting away in the small wicker basket overflowing with multicolored yarn at her feet.

"Brenna says they belonged to you," Falk said softly. "She says you want her for your own purposes, not mine."

If Mother Northwind were surprised, she gave no sign of it, tucking her knitting needles into the basket and then closing its lid. "And what purpose could I possibly have that is not yours?" she said as she straightened. "Have I not helped you every step of the way? Brenna is frightened and lashing out in any way she can. She hopes to divide us." She spread her hands. "What possible use could I have for Brenna beyond the one we have both agreed to: to capture the Keys and with their help bring down the Barrier?"

"*Do* you wish to bring down the Barrier?" Falk said. "Or have you had some other purpose in mind all along?"

"What other purpose could that be?" Mother Northwind said. "Power? I'm too old to be interested in power, Lord Falk. I wouldn't live long enough to do anything with it." She went over the fireplace and pulled a tasseled rope hanging beside it. "If we are going to have a long chat, Lord Falk, I simply must have my tea."

Falk grimaced, but said nothing.

"I want the Barriers down, Lord Falk. I wouldn't have worked twenty years to achieve just that if I did not. And when the Barrier comes down, the MageLords will emerge," Mother Northwind continued. "How can it be otherwise? I do not care if you rule the whole world, Lord Falk . . . as long as the Barrier falls. And you alone know the way to make that happen. If I turn against you, the Barrier will not fall, and what would I then have been wasting my fading energies on for so long?"

"Tagaza worked at my side even longer," Falk growled. "He turned against me at the end. And he paid the price."

Mother Northwind's face took on an expression of false horror. "Is that a threat, Lord Falk?"

"Your powers are great, Mother Northwind," Falk said. "But they are soft. You must touch me to use them against me. Whereas I can summon power in an instant that will flay you to your bones. It is more than a threat, it is a promise. If I become convinced you have acted against me, you will die."

A servant entered, the same girl who had been sweeping in the corner when Falk first came in. She brought with her, on a polished wooden tray, a silver pot from which wafted the pungent scent of herbal tea. "Thank you, Pilea," Mother Northwind said. She patted the girl on her hand. "You're a good girl."

"Thank you, ma'am." The girl curtsied, turned, and walked past Falk on her way to the door.

Only luck saved him. On the corner of the mantelpiece stood a glass vase, surface shiny and bright as a mirror. In that surface, Falk caught, out of the corner of his eye, a hint of movement, enough to make him turn his head—which was just enough to bring into his peripheral vision the sight of the girl lunging at him with a dagger.

The dagger should have gone into his back. Instead, as he lurched to the side, it sliced along his right flank, laying a strip of fiery pain against his skin. As his doublet turned red, he roared and lashed out with his fist, but the girl moved faster than he would have thought possible and came back at him with the knife, though she was just enough off-balance that he managed to jerk his head out of the way as the blade lashed the air beneath his chin. Grabbing her wrist, he pulled her hard across his body with all his strength, flinging her away from him. She almost flew across the room, her head made a horrible crunching noise against the edge of a marble-topped table, and she fell to the carpeted floor, twitched, and lay still, blood pooling beneath her shattered skull.

Falk spun back toward Mother Northwind, seizing power from the MageFurnace as he turned, forming a spell in his mind. He released the spell. A wall of sun-bright blue flame slammed furniture to kindling against the far wall, crushed the plaster into dust, and blew out the far windows in glittering blizzards of glass. But of Mother Northwind there was no sign.

Falk strode to the gaping window openings and peered out, but no mangled body lay on the gravel path beneath or on the bushes below, and dust obscured his view a moment later as the facade collapsed, roaring, from the eastern wall.

Falk turned away. Perhaps the blast had reduced the old

woman to nothing more than red mist, scattering now on the winds . . . But he wouldn't have wanted to lay money on it.

Hand to his bleeding side, Falk went to the door and flung it open. Servants were running away from Mother Northwind's quarters and guards were running toward it, but Mother Northwind had vanished without a trace.

Bellowing orders at the approaching guards, Falk stalked away from the shattered room. If she lived, Mother Northwind could not leave the Palace grounds. He would find her. And then he would take great pleasure in personally crushing the life from her wizened old frame.

Mother Northwind had known from the moment Lord Falk entered the room that their alliance was at an end. Somehow, he had had a hint of the truth about who had sabotaged his attempt to seize the Keys. She could think of only one way that would have happened, and as they talked, he confirmed it. Brenna, the little fool. *Youth*, she thought bitterly. *You can't trust them to act wisely*. An older Heir would have kept her counsel once she realized Falk intended to kill her, would have realized that Mother Northwind had told her the truth and her own survival depended on doing what Mother Northwind told her.

But Brenna, little more than a child, had let her anger get the best of her and risked her own life—and now Mother Northwind's, too.

Well. Perhaps it was for the best. Mother Northwind had known that sooner or later this moment would come. She sparred with Falk, buying time, then reached up and pulled the rope to summon Pilea. She had long since primed all of the Commoners who served her here. Much like Falk could direct the mageservants in his manor, she could direct her human servants. All it took was a touch. She had issued her initial instructions as Pilea had left the room. When she returned, she would be bringing more than tea.

Pilea arrived, and set down the tea. Mother Northwind

patted the maid's hand and *twisted*, just a little. It took very little energy.

It would take a great deal more for her to do what she needed to do next, and so she sat absolutely still, summoning her inner resources—and waited.

Pilea walked past Falk, then with sudden, lightning speed, spun, drew the dagger she had procured after Mother Northwind had sent her out of the room the first time, and thrust it at Falk, her aim as expert as a trained assassin.

Somehow, Falk dodged the fatal blow, but he also took his eyes off Mother Northwind, and in that instant, she released the energy she had summoned . . . and vanished.

Even a soft mage had some hard magic to call on, and Mother Northwind had more than most, though unlike mages of Falk's caliber she could only apply it, as with her soft magic, by touch. But that was all right, because this magic was being applied to herself.

She wasn't truly invisible. Rather, she had changed the air close to her body so that the light from objects behind her flowed through it like water. If Falk had been looking closely, he would have seen a . . . distortion, a ripple in the air, moving from the chair where Mother Northwind had been toward the door.

But Lord Falk was too busy not getting killed. By the time he flung poor Pilea across the room, Mother Northwind was past him. She was at the door when he released that killing blast. And she was in the hallway before he realized she had vanished.

By the time he came to the doorway himself and strode away, bellowing, she was across the hall, and going down the servants' stairs. She could feel herself weakening. She had barely enough strength to hold the illusion until she had reached the hallway at the bottom of the stairs that ran the length of the Palace, the kitchens to her left and doors leading to other servants' stairs up to other parts of the Palace on her right. Then she had to let the magic go, staggering as she did so, collapsing onto a hard wooden bench.

For the first time, she felt afraid. Falk should have died in her room. But with him still alive, every square inch inside the Lesser Barrier would be turned upside down until she was found.

She had one trump card, though, literally up her sleeve, in a pocket where she carried another of the enchanted devices Verdsmitt had created to cut a hole through the Lesser Barrier. She had never expected to use it for herself, keeping it on her person only in case she needed to bring someone into the Palace grounds surreptitiously, but now it offered her only chance of escape.

She needed to get to the Lesser Barrier without being seen. How that would be accomplished needed some thought. She heaved herself up. She couldn't stay there, outside the kitchens. Sooner or later a servant would come by—probably sooner; and she could not count all of them as allies.

But some she *could.*

She had taken note long before of the location of the living quarters of those who personally served her. She got to her feet and, weary beyond belief and sorely missing her cane, made her slow way along the corridor that led to the room belonging to a maid named Malia, who would help her escape the Palace grounds . . . and, just maybe, help her salvage her Plan.

Besides, Mother Northwind thought, *Malia deserves to hear the truth of what happened to her sister Pilea . . .*

. . . well, as much of the truth as will serve.

The news that Lord Falk had apparently killed Mother Northwind raced through the Palace hard on the heels of the wall-shaking blast itself. Verdsmitt overheard it from servants talking in the hall outside his rooms, and felt a deep sense of shock, as though the blast that had taken Mother Northwind's life had ripped his own from its foundation.

But an instant later came a feeling of complete freedom.

Mother Northwind was dead. Her Plan had died with her. He no longer needed to kill the King on cue. He could kill the King whenever he felt like it . . .

. . . and he felt like it *now*.

Verdsmitt went to his battered old valise, kindly delivered to his room at Falk's orders after his "conversion" to Falk's cause, and tore open the lining. There, sewn in place, was a small leather pouch with something heavy in it. He ripped the pouch free, then opened its mouth and upended the contents into his palm. A ring glittered in the blue magelight, snakes of yellow-and-white gold twining round each other, each with the other's tail in its mouth. Ruby eyes glittered in the head of the yellow snake, emeralds in the head of the white.

Kravon had given Verdsmitt the ring as a token of undying affection, just two weeks before the Keys had come to Kravon and everything had changed. Six months later Verdsmitt had been denounced, "committed suicide," and vanished into his new life. But he had never thrown away the ring. And now . . . now it was his passport to the King's presence.

For the first time since he had come to the Palace, Verdsmitt stepped out into the hallway and headed toward the block of rooms at the Palace's rear: the quarters of the King.

———

Falk found Brich before he found Captain Fedric, and found out why when Brich, who had been searching for Falk even before the blast, said, before Falk could say anything, "Lord Falk, Prince Karl is gone again. And he's taken Brenna with him."

Falk, who had been on the verge of ordering a search for Mother Northwind, momentarily forgot all about her. "Gone? How?"

Brich swallowed, and glanced around. They were just inside the main entrance of the Palace, where more stairs swept up to the central rotunda whose domed roof suggested the shape of the dome that capped the Palace's center, though in fact there were several more floors above it—including the Spellchamber where Tagaza had been struck down.

It was a highly public space, and there were people even now rushing through it in both directions, the blast in the east wing having had much the same effect on the Palace as a boot kicking over an anthill. "Perhaps we should—"

"Perhaps you should answer my question," Falk snarled. He was far beyond caring what anyone else in the Palace heard or thought. "Were they both kidnapped? Did they ride across the bridge to the gate and some soon-to-be-headless idiot let them out? Tell me!"

Brich kept his own voice low, but complied. "They took a boat to the marshy place on the far side of the lake where we found the boats after Karl's first disappearance," he said. "They were seen, and guards went to investigate, but the light was failing. When they finally caught up with the boat . . . Karl and Brenna were gone."

"Then who was in the boat?" Falk said, but he already knew.

"Teran," Brich confirmed. "Karl's bodyguard."

"And Karl and Brenna?"

"Teran claimed they were hiding elsewhere on the grounds. But a search found their footprints . . . outside the Barrier."

"*What?*"

"They were very clear," Brich said. "Karl and Brenna went through the Barrier as though it weren't there, then ran into New Cabora."

Falk took a deep breath, pushing his fury and frustration and disbelief down, down, deep inside, until it was like fire hidden beneath a layer of ice. Now he could think. "Very well," he said. "There are two things we must do, Brich, and both are vital. One: I want the Palace and the Grounds searched for any sign of Mother Northwind."

Brich blinked. "My lord?"

"The blast you heard was my *attempt* to kill her," Falk said harshly. "Seconds after one of her ensorcelled servants attempted to kill me. I was near the door and did not see her leave, but nevertheless, I saw no sign that I succeeded in killing her. Search the rubble first for her body. If it is not found, then search every room of the Palace, every bush on the grounds. I do not believe she can pass through the Lesser Barrier—although from what you've just told me I can't be certain even of that.

"Second. We must find Karl and Brenna. They would not have been wearing winter clothing—"

"No, they were not," Brich confirmed. "Brenna's coat was in the boat, and she lost her boots in the mud. Wherever she is, she has no shoes."

"Then they cannot remain in the streets. They must find shelter. Begin a house-by-house search of New Cabora, starting with the streets closest to where they escaped. Use every available man. No doors are to be left unopened, no attics unsearched, no basements unplumbed. Any resistance is to be eliminated with overwhelming force. Is that clear?"

"Perfectly, Lord Falk."

"When Karl and Brenna are found, they are not to be harmed. Bring them to me."

"Yes, my lord."

"Next." This time Falk did take a moment to look around him, but no one had been foolish enough to stay anywhere close enough that they might be accused of overhearing. "The tragedy in the King's bedchamber . . . we have someone investigating?"

"Of course, my lord."

"Sathana?"

"Our best man," Brich said.

Falk nodded. "Tell him he is to personally guard the King, every night. Tell him that very shortly I will return north to complete my interrupted survey of the Cauldron. Tell him that I will check in with him every night by magelink . . . and that he is to be ready to carry out my orders."

"It will be done, my lord."

"Good." Falk's jaw clenched. "And as for Teran . . ."

"Yes, my lord?"

"I assume he is in a cell."

"Yes, my lord."

"Then leave him there. I'll deal with him later."

Brich started to turn away, then hesitated. "My lord?"

"What?" Falk snapped.

"Your side, my lord. You're bleeding . . ."

"You think I don't know it? It's just a scratch. I'll have a Healer attend to it when I have time. Now carry out my orders!"

Brich nodded and hurried away.

Falk itched to "deal with" Teran immediately, itched to make *someone* pay for all that had happened that day, but now that he had spoken to Brich, he instead returned to the hallway outside Mother Northwind's quarters. His winter clothing remained on the chair where he had dropped it. He looked inside. Servants were collecting debris and sweeping up dust. The girl who had tried to kill him had been covered by a sheet. But hers was still the only corpse in the room.

Well. Mother Northwind, alive or dead, would be found soon enough. Brenna concerned him far more. He would supervise *that* search himself. And when that was done, and she was once more in hand, then he would deal with Teran, and his bitch-mother and sister.

His side burned. A Healer first, he thought. And then . . .

He had been lenient with the Commoners last time Karl had vanished among them, confining his destruction to buildings.

He would not be so lenient again.

CHAPTER 30

ANTON, on his third crossing of the Anomaly, knew exactly what to expect and how to deal with it. By gaining enough altitude long before he came to that impossibly high wall, he was able to fly over it without getting caught up in the rush of wind at its top, or the downdraft that had driven the airship to the ground when he and the Professor had first cleared it, though he still felt a surge of speed as the cloud-capped top passed beneath him.

He had more confidence in his navigation now that he had successfully found Elkbone, and drawing on the careful bearings and notes taken on his way out of Evrenfels, he confidently turned the prow of the airship toward New Cabora. With the sun lowering behind him, and the propeller beating its steady rhythm in the cold air, he watched the snow-covered landscape beneath him fade from white to blue, pass into darkness, and then begin to gleam silver as the rising moon took over from the sun and spread its own ghostly light across the plains.

Here and there lights shone, the yellow glow of burning oil or tallow in Commoners' farms and villages, far less often the distinctive blue glow of magelights in homes belonging to Mageborn. His path did not take him over Falk's manor, but he passed another MageLord's estate at one point, the great house ablaze with light to rival the new electric-lit Crystal Castle in Hexton Down. There were several carriages drawn up in front of the house, some with horses, some without, and he thought he saw a footman glance up as he passed high overhead, no doubt puzzled by the throb of the propeller. But he himself was showing no lights, and he doubted the man saw anything.

Nor would he believe it if he did, Anton thought. *For everyone on this side of the Anomaly, this airship is as unbelievable as the existence of magic was to me.*

I suppose once you advance technology enough it's pretty hard to tell it apart from magic, really, he thought. *They both involve manipulating matter and energy. The methods differ, but not the results.*

He wondered what would really happen in a clash between the armies of Evrenfels, armed with primitive weapons but also with magic, and the forces of the Union Republic, with their cannons and steam-guns and armored crawlers. It had been a long age since the MageLords had last faced Commoners in combat. He suspected they might get a surprise.

But then he remembered uneasily that Falk had destroyed New Cabora City Hall single-handedly, and knew the surprise could cut both ways.

There is no place for magic in the modern world, Anton thought. *It will only bring chaos and bloodshed. . . .*

Unlike technology? an opposing thought intruded.

Anton had no answer.

These things were beyond him, anyway. He had done what he could to prepare his world for the possible emergence of Falk's army. Mother Northwind would have to look after the destruction of magic. His focus now had narrowed to one purpose—to save Brenna, pull her out of the web of intrigue that had trapped her, and take her far away from whatever happened here over the next days, weeks, or months.

If she will come with you, spoke that inner voice of doubt once more. And once more, he had no answer for it.

The sun had been down for four hours or more when at last he saw, dead ahead, a greater glow than any he had passed thus far. First he saw the blue magelights of the Palace, then the dimmer yellow glow of New Cabora's lanterns and gaslights; then he began to make out individual buildings, the Palace a marble jewel surrounded by dark foliage and the glitter of water, the city an untidy sprawl of smaller buildings at the edges leading to a few grander structures, several stories tall, at the center.

The wind was from the west, as it almost always was in these latitudes. Anton reached over and pulled back on the throttle levers, silencing the propeller. As its steady thrum subsided to a whisper and then to nothing, he lit the burner one more time, the roar filling his ears as hot gas filled the envelope and lifted him higher. Then, in silence, slowly descending, he drifted on the breeze toward New Cabora, using the rudder to turn the nose toward the open space at its center, the Square. He reached for the binoculars hung inside the gondola, not far from the rifle and handgun.

This time, he would not land without knowing exactly what he was getting himself into.

———

Vinthor listened to Karl and Brenna in silence. When they had, between them, told him everything they knew about the Patron—Mother Northwind—and her Plan, he got up suddenly and went into the back room without saying anything.

Karl glanced at Brenna. She still looked exhausted, but at least she had stopped shivering. She didn't meet his eyes, staring instead into the fire.

For himself, he felt . . . exhilarated, if he were honest. When he had so impetuously followed the two strangers out through the Barrier on the night of Verdsmitt's arrest, he had simply exchanged one captivity for another. But this time he was not a captive. This time, he was, at last, not only acting on his own, but acting with full knowledge of what he was doing, who he was, and who the players were in the intrigues that had swirled around him his whole life, oblivious though he had often been.

If Mother Northwind was dead, then many elements of her plan must be collapsing . . . but one thing remained: he was the Magebane, and he was with the Heir. Together they could, on the death of the King, bring down the whole corrupt edifice of MageLord rule.

The death of the King. Karl had shied away from thinking about that element of the plan, but it could not be denied. Just as Falk's plan had hung upon the failed attempt to assassinate the King, so Mother Northwind's must also rely upon the King's death at a moment of her choosing. Which must mean yet another assassin was waiting to strike. But who? And would that assassination proceed without Mother Northwind to give the order?

Mother Northwind had never explained exactly *how* his powers as the Magebane would work to destroy the Keys. But he remembered how they had passed through the Lesser Barrier together, moving from the warmth of a Palace night to the shocking cold of the Commons winter in an instant. The Barrier had made no impression upon either of them. While he held Brenna to him, she had been as impervious to magic as he.

If she should feel the call, he thought, *I will embrace her again, and we will see what happens.*

He rather wished he could embrace her anyway. *She's pretty*, he thought, glancing sideways at her profile, given a rosier glow by the firelight than her exhaustion and fear would have otherwise allowed. But then he laughed at himself. *You only just met*, he thought. *And the first thing you did was drag her across the lake, armed guards in pursuit, and throw her sock-footed into the snow. Not much to build a romance on!*

Vinthor came back. "I activated the magelink with the Patron," he said. "Mother Northwind is alive, but in hiding in the Palace. She hopes to escape from the grounds this very night. We are to meet her."

"Here?" Karl said.

"No. Falk's men are forming up to begin a building-by-building search of the city, starting in this area, close to where you emerged through the Barrier. They will certainly find this place. We need to get out of the city before they do."

"Horses?" Karl asked. "The old inn?"

"Burned after Jopps betrayed us," Vinthor said grimly, "though for whatever reason he doesn't seem to have told Falk about this little hidey-hole. No, we'll take a different way. Early each morning, wagons travel around the city to collect nightsoil. The man who runs the business is . . . or, at least, was . . . a member of the Common Cause. And some of his wagons have been modified to take passengers beneath a false floor.

"We'll get inside a couple of those wagons. They will make their rounds as usual, and leave the city before dawn to dump their loads. Once we are outside of the city, there are still safe houses I can get you to. Mother Northwind, if she escapes, will meet us at the wagons and ride out of the city with us."

Karl groaned. "You want us to escape the city by burying ourselves in shit?"

Vinthor's mouth quirked. "More or less." That hint of a smile faded. "But believe me, Your Highness, with Falk's men in the streets, if we stay here even another hour we'll be neck-deep in shit anyway."

"Anything," Brenna said suddenly. "Anything to get out of here. But I won't share a wagon with Mother Northwind. I won't let that hag near me!"

Vinthor started to speak, but Karl interjected. "If it is two to the wagon, I will lie with Mother Northwind . . ." He winced. "Um, so to speak. She can do nothing to me."

Is that true? he wondered suddenly. *I've assumed that the Magebane can be no more influenced by soft magic than hard . . . but is that really true?*

Better ask Mother Northwind. I'm sure *she'll tell you the truth.* He snorted.

"It's settled, then." Vinthor went into the room with the beds and came out with boots and a coat for Brenna. "Too big, both of them, but better than nothing," he said. "The man they belonged to is dead, so he won't begrudge your use of them. And they'll serve as a disguise, as well."

He looked at Karl. "There are other clothes in there," he said. "Get rid of your finery. Blacken your face with soot. If we're stopped, let me do the talking."

Karl nodded, and went into the other room. There were several sets of nondescript work clothes, black pants, flannel shirts, boots. He undressed and dressed again, found a coat that fit him, and, remembering what Vinthor had said, plunged one hand into the cold ashes of the fire and rubbed the black soot on his cheeks and forehead.

When he returned to the front room, Vinthor gave him a critical once-over, then nodded. "Best we can do."

"Wait," Karl said. "Is there a sword I can wear?"

Vinthor gave him the look of a man pitying an idiot. "Commoners don't wear swords. Not much point disguising yourself if you're going to carry a whopping piece of illegal steel on your hip, is there?"

Karl blinked. "Good point. A dagger, then?"

"Daggers we have."

Vinthor nodded and went to the wall, opening a cabinet to reveal several scabbarded blades. Karl picked two at random, one for himself, one for Brenna. As he held it out, belt and all, the girl's eyes widened, making her look very young for a moment; then her expression hardened. She took the dagger without a word, fastening it on beneath her coat.

Karl did the same. "All right," he said.

Vinthor led them out into the dark, snow-filled streets.

———

To get to the King's quarters, one climbed the broad staircase of green marble that swept up from the south side of the echoing, pillared rotunda. As Verdsmitt climbed it, he thought he heard Falk's voice, shouting something down by the main entrance, but he ignored it: the shouts weren't intended for him, and that was all that mattered.

On the broad platform at the top of the stairs stood four

pikemen, two on either side of the closed, gold-leafed double doors, their weapons glistening with the frost of enchantment, eyes reduced to glitters of light in the eye holes of face-covering helms.

Verdsmitt ignored them, focusing instead on the man who sat at a simple desk to one side, writing something on the single piece of parchment that was the only thing to mar the desk's dark, polished wood. "Davydd Verdsmitt to see the King," he said.

The man did not look up. "One does not gain a Royal audience merely by announcing one's presence," he said, his pen, one of the new Commoner-created kind with a built-in ink reservoir, scratching across the parchment. "Particularly not moments after a portion of the Palace has been damaged by a magical attack."

"King Kravon will want to see me," Verdsmitt said. "If you show him this."

He pulled his hand from his pocket, aware as he did so of a subtle shifting of weight on the part of the guards closest to him, and held up the ring.

The secretary put down his pen and leaned forward for a closer look. "Pretty," he said. "But why should the King care about your taste in jewelry?"

"Because it was also his, once upon a time," Verdsmitt said. "You might also mention a name: Calibon."

Verdsmitt had no idea how long this particular secretary had served the King, but he suspected no one at this level of the bureaucracy could have been unaware of some of the more sordid details of the King's personal history. The secretary did not do anything as gauche as raise an eyebrow, or even blink, but he did nod, and said, "Very well. I will pass your message to the King." He held out his hand. "I will show him the ring."

Verdsmitt's hand closed on it. "No," he said. "You just describe it to him. *I* will show him the ring. When I see him *in person*."

A brief pause. "Wait here," the secretary said. He picked up pen and parchment and turned, and a section of the wall behind him swung silently open. He disappeared through it, and it vanished into the marble once more.

Verdsmitt sat down in the chair the secretary had just vacated, and glanced over at the nearest pikeman, who continued to stare straight ahead as though he didn't exist. "Do you mind if I whistle?" he said, took the guard's silence for consent, and launched into one of the tunes written for one of his lesser-known comedies, *The Bride of Brethan*. He suspected he'd have time to get through the entire score before the secretary returned.

But he was equally confident the secretary *would* return.

After so many years, he would finally see Kravon again, face-to-face . . . one *very* final time.

When the call came from Vinthor to the Patron, Mother Northwind was waiting in Malia's empty bedchamber. She had been panting by the time she got there, and had dipped at last into her precious vials of restorative, downing one of the four. A good thing, too: as she swallowed the last of it, she heard the tumult of the guards racing through the servants' halls, doors slamming open as they searched room by room, and barely had time to summon up her coat of invisibility once more. Had she not taken the restorative, she wouldn't have been able to do it at all.

Had the guard who kicked open Malia's door and stepped into the tiny room with his sword drawn and a magelight globe floating above him lingered even half a minute longer, he would have seen his quarry appear out of thin air, pale and gasping; but he spared only a glance for the obviously empty room before racing down the corridor with his fellows.

To her relief, Mother Northwind had a good hour or more of much-needed rest, sitting quietly in the dark room. Then, much to her surprise, she felt the call from Vinthor.

His news reinvigorated her as much as the restorative and the rest. She gave him his instructions, closed the mage-

link, and smiled to herself for the twenty minutes more that
passed before Malia returned and found her there.

Malia, though relieved to see Mother Northwind was
not dead, as had been rumored, was still understandably
upset to hear that Falk had murdered her sister in a fit of
rage, but Mother Northwind did not have time to allow her
to grieve for very long before laying a sympathetic hand on
her arm and guiding her anger to a more productive purpose: helping Mother Northwind escape from the Palace.

It proved to be less of a challenge than she had feared.
The Palace was not a fortress, after all, but a glorified apartment and office building, with numerous entrances and ex-
its, some of them quite ... obscure. Mother Northwind's
quick rummage through Malia's mind revealed one known
to only a few. In fact, it was not officially an entrance at all.
Certainly it would not show up on any map of the building
or the grounds.

Most of the MageLords preferred to stay within the immediate vicinity of the Palace, but the Lesser Barrier was a
full two miles in diameter. Southeast of the Palace, a sheltered grove grew close to the Barrier. Screened by bushes
from passersby ... although almost no one ever did pass it
by ... it was a place where the Commoner servants who
lived in the Palace could slip for assignations forbidden by
their Mageborn masters. Malia had made much use of it, in
the company of the personal manservant of Lord Athol.

Ignoring the glimpses of those passionate encounters
she found in Malia's surface memories, Mother Northwind
focused on getting Malia to show her how she got to the
grove unobserved ... and so found out about the wood-
shored tunnel that led from a dark corner of the MageFurnace's blackened chamber to a trapdoor hidden beneath
dirt and leaves beneath the low-hanging branches of a
spruce.

With a little encouragement, Malia insisted on showing
Mother Northwind to that tunnel. The servants' hall gave
them access down to the MageFurnace level, where they
passed through a brick corridor that ran parallel to the

Furnace itself, the heat radiating from one wall so great that Mother Northwind, panting for air as she followed Malia, thought her fingers would blister if she touched it.

Blessedly the corridor was short, and they were soon climbing up through the cool tunnel, emerging into the quiet darkness beneath the spruce and then hurrying through the manicured grounds to the lovers' nest in the bushes.

Inside its confines, Mother Northwind turned to thank Malia, taking her hand in hers.

Five minutes later Malia suddenly started and looked around her, Mother Northwind forgotten, thinking her lover had just left and she had best hurry back to the Palace before she was missed. She returned the way she had come, and when the First Servant came to her room shortly thereafter, he found her sewing a ripped blouse by lantern light, unaware that Mother Northwind had vanished . . . or that her much-loved younger sister had died in the blast unleashed in Mother Northwind's chambers.

By the time Malia heard the news and dissolved into wailing sorrow, Mother Northwind, who had slipped through the Barrier without incident using the device Verdsmitt had enchanted, was already en route to the nightsoil collector's stable to join the Heir and the Magebane, the pieces of her Plan once more, she thought with satisfaction, firmly in her hands.

Tonight, she thought. *There is no need to wait longer. Tonight I will tell Verdsmitt to strike, the King will die, the Keys will come to Brenna, the Magebane will break them . . . and the rule of the MageLords ends.*

And then, she thought, pulling her cloak tighter around her against the cold blasts as she slipped like a gray ghost through the shadows of the alleyways, far from where Falk's guards were tearing houses apart in their search for Karl and Brenna, *then, I can finally rest.*

Falk, standing in a street of New Cabora that ended in the snow-drifted parkland surrounding the Lesser Barrier, watched yet another Commoner family being rousted out into the icy street, this one consisting of a young couple with two children, a wailing babe in arms and a small girl who clung to her blanket-wrapped father, silent and wide-eyed. The guards searched the tiny house with ruthless efficiency, overturning beds and tables, opening cupboards and dragging their contents onto the floor, thrusting spears into the attic through the thin plaster of the ceiling, ripping up floorboards. They were in and out in five minutes, leaving behind chaos and wreckage and the door hanging loose from one bent hinge, and moved on to the next. The young father gave Falk a look of pure hatred before taking his family back into the shattered remains of their home. Falk ignored it. The hatred of Commoners meant nothing to him. Finding Brenna was all that mattered.

They were moving rapidly through the city, but he was painfully aware that their quarry could have already fled ahead of them. He had sent men to guard all of the roads into and out of the city, but New Cabora, which sprawled four or five miles in every direction, did not have a wall, and so there was nothing to stop anyone from simply heading out into the prairie . . . nothing except for the winter cold itself.

Still, Mounted Rangers were patrolling the city's perimeter, and since neither Brenna nor the Prince were outfitted for or accustomed to the harsh realities of winter travel, Falk believed they would hide in the city instead of risking the open. But he could not be certain, and that uncertainty ate at him, driving him to periodically yell at the guards to move faster.

With speed came, of necessity, brutality, and it wasn't long before the first Commoner, bodily hurled from his home, clad only in a nightshirt, got to his feet with a scream of rage and charged at the guard who had manhandled him. The guard responded with a quick flick of his hand that hurled the man across the street with a flash of blue flame. The foolish Commoner hit the wall of the building opposite with a wet, crunching thud, blood spattered bricks and snow, and a naked corpse, nightshirt ignominiously twisted around its ruined head, slid to the ground and lay still.

It was the first corpse in the streets that night. It would not be the last.

And yet, three hours later, with half a dozen Commoners dead and a hundred Commoner homes and businesses left in near-ruins, no sign of the missing Heir and Prince had been found, and none of those questioned, no matter how thoroughly, had admitted to knowing anything about them.

Then, as the guards started down yet another street and the first doors on it were kicked open, a guard on horseback galloped up to Falk and reined his horse in sharply, its sides steaming and great clouds of vapor rising from its flaring nostrils. "A report, my lord," the guard panted. "A Commoner near the Square, late home from a tavern. Saw three people, two large men, one a much smaller boy or woman, slip into the nightsoil collector's stable. Couldn't imagine why anyone would go into any place that vile, he said."

"Was he sober?" Falk snapped.

"Sober enough by the time we started questioning him," the guard said.

Falk turned in his saddle. "Call off the search!" he cried. "Captain Fedric, to me."

Fedric shouted to his men to halt the search. Up and down the street the orders repeated. As some Commoners ran back into their houses and others farther up the street peered out of their doors with hope and relief plain on their faces, Falk ordered the captain to surround the nightsoil collector's establishment. "No one gets in or out," he said.

"Understood," Fedric said, and issued his orders.

Falk turned to the man who had brought him word of the sighting. "Take me there," he said.

CHAPTER 31

THE STREETS OF NEW CABORA WERE far from deserted this night, Anton realized as he moved the glasses back and forth across the approaching town. There were guards in the streets near the Palace, and one or two buildings seemed to be on fire, their smoke rising thicker and blacker than the moon-silvered smoke from the city's many chimneys. Here and there Anton glimpsed movement in open spaces, and, of course, he had no way of knowing what was happening in between the buildings where he could not see. Dogs seemed to be barking everywhere. Some of them were no doubt barking at the strange object in their sky, but anyone hearing them would surely think they were barking at the guards in the streets. They wouldn't look up. Why would they? Until very recently, there had been no possibility of anything being in the night sky but the moon, stars, and clouds.

He focused on what seemed to be the main locus of activity. The airship was drifting closer and closer, but also lower and lower, which in turn hid more and more of the streets behind the walls and roofs of buildings. But in an intersection he saw a man on horseback whose posture and bearing seemed familiar even without the binoculars. With them, there could be no doubt:

Lord Falk.

As he watched, another man on horseback galloped up and exchanged words with Falk. Falk, who had been sitting still, suddenly seemed galvanized, wheeling his horse, shouting something loudly enough that, though he couldn't make out the words, Anton heard a hint of the sound, two or three seconds later.

And then the guards began streaming through the streets.

Lower and lower Anton sank, closer and closer he drifted. He would have to make up his mind soon to either land in the Square or lift again and perhaps circle back. But that would take time, and setting off the burner and starting the propellers would announce his presence in a way Falk could not miss. And in the back of his mind, Anton couldn't help wondering just who it was Falk was searching for through the streets of New Cabora in the middle of the night. He wasn't privy to all the security concerns of someone in Falk's position, of course, but he could certainly think of one person Falk would turn out all the guard for.

Brenna.

Anton judged his rate of descent against the Square. He would make for it, he decided. He could abort his landing up until the very last moment. The night was still, and the airship silent. As he got closer, he might hear something that would confirm or deny his suspicion . . . if the damned dogs would shut up long enough . . . and then make a final decision.

The Square, still bordered mostly by crumbled ruins— the buildings Falk had singlehandedly destroyed, Anton remembered with a quiver of apprehension—slipped slowly toward him, growing larger and larger. A few blocks from it, a good two miles north of the Lesser Barrier and the bridge into the Palace, the guard had now formed a cordon around a nondescript building with a tall central chimney, and a lot of wagons drawn up around it.

I'll have to make my mind up within ten minutes, Anton thought. He aimed his glasses at the gathered guards, and waited to see what would happen.

———

Brenna had begun the day well north of Berriton, spent most of it riding in the tense silence of Falk's magecarriage, been dragged socked-footed through the Lesser Barrier and into the snow, and now, in borrowed boots and cloak, had hurried through the streets of New Cabora to the one place that, for all her interest in the city during her previous visits, she had somehow never thought to ask to be taken to: the stable of the nightsoil collector.

The place didn't smell as bad as she feared, but she suspected that was due mostly to her good fortune—such as it was—to be making her visit in midwinter rather than in high summer.

Silent wagons stood around them now, still some hours from being harnessed to horses. They were black, to slip as unobtrusively as possible through the dark streets—and to hide any unattractive stains, no doubt. In the back of each were sealed wooden barrels, empty now. It occurred to Brenna that one way to sneak out of the city would be to ride inside one of those barrels, but the thought sent a shiver of disgust through her.

Fortunately, that was not what was planned. Vinthor took them down the line of wagons on one side of the huge echoing space in which they stood, a long, narrow building with the wagons at one end and stables for the horses at the other. After one brief whinny and a few snuffles, the animals had accepted their presence, and now stood silent and sleeping.

Behind the stable area was a chamber containing a furnace, used not to provide magical energy—this was a strictly Commoner enterprise—but to burn some of the refuse that a second fleet of wagons in another long stable on the other side of the furnace collected each evening. That which could not be burned or salvaged made its own journey, to a tip a mile or so east of the city.

The nightsoil went several miles farther, as a matter of good public hygiene, to a noisome pit where it was buried by Commoner laborers. *A horrible job*, she thought, *but they're probably glad to get it. At least there they work for Commoners instead of Mageborn.*

Vinthor halted behind a wagon that appeared exactly the same as all the others to Brenna's tired eyes. "Help me," he said to Karl, and together they lifted down the empty barrels. Vinthor reached underneath the wagon and pulled or twisted something that made a loud click. Then he put his hand underneath the wagon's back end and lifted.

The floorboards, hinged at the front, raised to reveal a space swathed with sacking, just deep enough for someone—provided they didn't have a large belly or breasts, Brenna thought in horror—to lie in. "We'll smother!"

"No, you won't," Vinthor said shortly. "I've ridden in these myself. It's not pleasant, but it certainly isn't fatal." He looked around. "The night watchman is a Causer. And we'll need him to seal us in. But I haven't seen him since we entered."

Brenna peered around in the darkness. The only light came from a couple of lanterns in the central space between the wagons and the stable, and two more at the other end, one on either side of the big double doors that would swing open to let the wagons exit. Nothing moved in the gloom, but down in the stable, a horse stamped its foot and whinnied. As though that were a signal, all of the horses suddenly became restless, shifting in their stables, making loud snorting noises. Another horse whinnied, a shrill cry of challenge . . .

. . . and from outside the stable, that cry was answered.

Vinthor whirled at the sound. "Someone's outside!" he said. "I'll—"

Whatever he would do was lost in a huge, splintering bang as the double doors blew inward, hurtling through the air like fallen leaves caught in an autumn gale. One door crashed into the wagons on the far side of the stable, snapping the axle of one and bringing it thudding to the ground in a cloud of dust. The other skidded down the center of the wagonry. Karl and Brenna were beside the wagon with the false floor and thus out of its path, but Vinthor wasn't so lucky.

The door slammed into his feet, tossed him heels over head into the air, and then smashed into the last wagon in line, folding its rear wheel under it so that it crashed onto its side. The empty barrels it carried rolled across the floor with a noise like thunder, one ending its journey against Vinthor's unmoving body.

Karl and Brenna hadn't had time to do more than cower between the wagons. Karl recovered first, grabbing Brenna by the hand. "Come on," he shouted above the noise of the now screaming horses, and, pulling her after him, he ran toward the central space.

The stable doors were also open, though they hadn't been blasted inward; instead, perhaps to spare the horses, they had been forced outward, ripped off their hinges. Guards were entering from that end as well, and as Karl and Brenna emerged into the light of the lanterns, the one in the lead pointed and shouted.

His companion raised his hand and Brenna felt an icy chill as something like a rope of blue fire lashed out at them . . .

. . . touched Karl . . .

. . . and vanished, as the guard who had cast it was hurled from his horse, hitting one of the stable doors so hard it smashed open. The terrified horse inside reared, hooves flailing at the motionless body, and then raced into the stable, shouldering past the other guard and thundering toward Karl and Brenna.

Karl pulled Brenna out of its way and through a door into the furnace room. A wave of heat met them. They ran around the massive round brick structure. Karl eased open the door in the far wall and took a look into the refuse-collection side of the building, but slammed it shut again at once. "More guards!"

"Trapped!" Brenna said bitterly.

Karl bolted the door. "There must be another way out of here! Where do they tip in the garbage?"

"Outside?"

"But it doesn't come in here. There must be a lower level . . ." He cast around on the floor. "There!"

"There" was a trapdoor, with a big ring to pull it open.

Brenna was closest; she grabbed it and pulled with all her might, but it wouldn't budge. Karl joined forces with her. No luck.

Karl swore. "They'll be ripping the doors off the hinges any second!"

But Brenna wasn't looking at him. She'd looked past him, and saw, on the side of the rounded brick wall, a metal ladder . . . going up. She let her gaze follow it. It ended in another trapdoor. "There!" She pointed.

Karl spun, saw what she was looking at, and shouted, "Come on!"

He clambered up the ladder, and seized the bolt. It stuck, then flew open with an enormous crash. Karl flailed, almost fell, then caught a rung with his hand and pulled himself back onto the ladder again. Holding on with his left hand, he pushed the door open with his right, and peered up.

Above them towered the great central chimney. The ladder continued to its top. "Dead end!" Brenna said.

But both doors into the furnace room had suddenly turned white with frost, and Karl said, "Better up there than down here." He swung to one side. "You first."

Brenna hesitated. "I—"

"I'll be between you and their magic," he said.

The two doors groaned, folded like paper, and ripped away in a thunder of shattering masonry. Brenna jumped up the ladder as far as she could, then climbed.

Karl followed close on her heels, kicking the trapdoor closed behind them as guards burst into the furnace room. Brenna climbed as fast as she could, the ladder's rungs slippery in the grip of her borrowed gloves, her too large boots threatening to slip off her feet with every step. She didn't look down. Instead she kept her head up and headed for the black sky above her, even though she knew at this point it was only empty defiance.

But empty or not, defiance was all that was left to her. To climb was to defy Falk.

And so she climbed.

The guards in the furnace room wasted valuable time hurling magical lassoes at Karl, trying pull him from the ladder. He felt nothing, the insubstantial ropes of blue fire recoiling from him like snakes from a hot stove, lashing back at their casters, who fell out of sight in the room below. Their futile efforts allowed Karl and Brenna to get halfway up the ladder before anyone down below physically came after them.

But even as he watched Brenna's feet moving from rung to rung just above his head, he knew she had been right. This was a dead end. Once they reached the top of the chimney, their flight would be over. He would turn and try to fend off the guards climbing after them, but . . .

He'd already realized that he was not His Royal Highness to any of these men. They belonged to Falk. Probably Unbound, every one of them. They would laugh at him if he tried to order them to stand down.

Worse, though he was certain they would do everything in their power to avoid harming Brenna, who was vital to Falk's plans, they must know that *he* was dispensable.

Though they might not yet have thought of the term Magebane to apply to him, they had learned by now that they could not magic him off the ladder. But they could certainly still pull, shoot, or cut him from it.

And so he, too, climbed, to what he expected to be his last stand.

Down in the courtyard, he heard Falk shout.

"Don't harm the girl," Falk shouted. "I don't care about the boy, but keep *her* alive."

He'd watched with satisfaction as Brenna and the Prince had first emerged from the roof onto the chimney and begun to climb, since they were clearly going nowhere. But then he had seen the magical lassoes of his men slip away from the infuriatingly magic-impervious Prince, and his satisfaction turned to annoyance.

He studied the chimney. The distance from where he stood wasn't so great. And it would give him great satisfaction . . .

He dismounted, then reached up and pulled his crossbow from its holster alongside his saddle. He ignored the enchanted bolts in the quiver, instead drawing out one of the perfectly ordinary steel-tipped shafts. Deliberately he loaded and cocked, then raised the bow in his right hand, held his left arm across his body, and steadied the bow on it. He took careful aim . . .

By the time Mother Northwind reached the nightsoil collector's yard, she had had to call on her spell of invisibility several times to avoid the guards with which the streets of New Cabora seemed to be filled this cold, dark night. But avoid them she had . . .

. . . only to reach the place where she had anticipated joining with Vinthor, Brenna, and the Magebane and find it swarming with guards . . . and Falk himself, standing beside his horse, shouting orders.

She stood very still in the shadows, watching as the doors were blown in and guards rushed into the stables. She heard the horses screaming. Falk's attention was entirely on what was happening in front of him.

She felt mentally and physically exhausted, more exhausted than she could ever remember. She had already drunk a second of her restorative vials, half an hour before. That had been far too soon after her imbibing of the first vial, back in Malia's room. She would pay a terrible price when the restoratives wore off. But that didn't matter. She needed every possible ounce of energy now, and so she reached into her bag, took out the last two of the precious vials, and uncorked and downed them both, one after the other.

A roaring filled her head and for a moment the whole word seemed to recede, as though it would vanish forever . . . but then it came rushing back, and with it a new surge of energy, enough to do what had to be done.

Falk had long thought she worked to further his Plan. It was time, and past time, she made certain he instead worked to further hers.

Drawing invisibility around her once more, she stepped into the courtyard and stalked toward Falk.

———

Anton saw the blue flashes and heard the scream of torn metal, the rumble of falling masonry and the crash of wood against stone as the doors at both ends of the two long, narrow buildings that came together at base of the tall chimney were either blown inward or ripped outward. He was very close now, though still a hundred feet or so higher than the chimney. Soon he would have to light the burner to avoid hitting some of the city's taller buildings, looming ahead of him. The moment he did that, though, he would announce his presence. And right now, with Falk down there and obviously after someone inside those buildings, he preferred to silently watch.

Suddenly a trapdoor opened at the base of the chimney. Anton raised the binoculars and focused on it . . . and to his astonishment, saw Brenna emerge into the cold air. She began to climb the chimney, a young man behind her . . . the Prince!

But there's nowhere to go up there, he thought. *Unless . . .*

He studied the envelope speculatively. If he waited until he was almost on top of the chimney, started the propellers, could he hold steady enough and close enough to it to somehow get Brenna and the Prince aboard?

It would immediately betray him to Falk, but so what? What could he do from the ground?

Besides rip us from the sky with magic and hurl all of us to our deaths? Anton answered himself uneasily.

No, he thought. *Not with Brenna aboard. She's too valuable.*

To both of us.

He raised his glasses to take one last look at the scene below. There was Falk, off his horse now, standing beside it.

He blinked. For a moment, he'd thought he'd seen something crossing the dark cobblestones behind him . . . but it must have been a trick of the light.

And then he saw Falk reach for the crossbow slung on his saddle, crank it, load it, raise it, aim it at the climbing pair . . .

With a curse, Anton flung the glasses aside and grabbed up the loaded rifle. The air was still, the basket steady, and the Professor had made him practice his shooting long and hard before they crossed the Anomaly. Kneeling in the bottom of the gondola, he took careful aim . . .

. . . and pulled the trigger.

CHAPTER 32

THE FLAT, explosive crack of the rifle, a sound never before heard in Evrenfels, rang out across the city, echoing through the streets, bringing those few who had found an uneasy slumber upright and staring in their beds.

Brenna, nearing the top of the chimney, able to see nothing but the curved brick wall in front of her nose, flinched, but kept climbing, as did Karl, close beneath her.

Only Falk, looking almost directly at it, Mother Northwind, invisible behind him and at that very instant reaching up to touch him, and one or two of the guards actually saw the flash of yellow flame from the barrel of the rifle. It lit the underside of the airship's envelope and Anton's pale face for just an instant, suddenly revealing the presence of the flying machine and making the guards who saw it wonder how they could have failed to see it earlier.

Falk had no time to wonder anything of the sort, no time even to realize that Anton had returned, because before his eyes had finished registering the flash the spinning lead ball expelled by the rifle ripped through his throat in an explosion of blood and tissue, almost severing his head from his shoulders.

Falk's crossbow fired as his hand tightened reflexively, the bolt zipping past Karl and striking sparks off the curve of the chimney before ricocheting off into empty darkness.

Mother Northwind had just laid her hand on Falk's back, letting the invisibility fall away as she reached for his mind . . . but even as she touched it, that mind vanished, and in the same instant the rifle ball, barely slowed by its passage through Falk's neck and continuing on its sharply descending path, smashed her shoulder in a second spray of blood, spinning her around to fall facedown on the cobblestone.

Still not spent, the ball ricocheted off the cobblestones and followed the crossbow into darkness, terrifying a cowering Mageborn baker in his room an instant later by punching a hole through his window and burying itself in a the beam over his bed.

Mother Northwind, her mind a haze of pain and shock, realized she was bleeding badly. She gathered her waning strength together, tried to Heal herself . . .

. . . and failed. She had nothing left. Even the energy from her restoratives had fled, sucked away as her magic had been pulled from her into Falk's dying brain. All she could hope to do was staunch her own bleeding, buy herself a little more time, hold on until the guards found her and brought another Healer . . .

She managed to heave herself over onto her back, crying out with the pain and effort, then lay there, desperately trying to hold her torn tissues together with the last of her waning strength, staring up at the chimney.

She heard another sound new to her, then, a throbbing, chopping roar, as the propeller on the airship, now visible as a dim bulk almost directly on top of the chimney, came to life. The airship swung around and faced into the wind, descending as it did so, until the gondola touched the chimney. She watched as first Brenna, then Karl, climbed the rope ladder into the gondola . . . and watched as the frustrated guard just below Karl foolishly hurled magic upward, only to fall screaming as the blast intended to strike down the airship ripped him from the chimney and hurled him away. He disappeared behind the buildings, but the wet crunching sound he made when he struck the cobblestones carried clearly.

The next guard, smarter, reached for the crossbow at his

belt, and raised it . . . but Anton leaned out of the gondola with something small in his own hand. There was another flash of yellow light, another of those strange, sharp cracks, and the second guard fell from the ladder with most of his head missing.

There was no one else close enough to even attempt to stop the airship as its burner roared to life and it lifted into the night sky, illuminated from within like a giant blue lantern. It made a wide, sweeping turn, and then headed west . . .

. . . back to the Great Barrier.

The Magebane still lives, Mother Northwind thought. *Brenna still lives. My Plan still lives* . . .

. . . but if she did not get a Healer soon, *she* no longer would.

I will hold on, she vowed grimly. *I will hold on. The Barrier must fall. Falk is dead, but the MageLords still rule. I will not die until I see them overthrown!*

She closed her eyes, drew on every last bit of her fading inner strength, and concentrated on not bleeding to death, as, at last, she heard boots pounding across the cobblestones toward her and Falk.

———

Brenna couldn't believe it when the airship suddenly appeared above her, even closer than it had been that day on the hillside above Falk's manor when it had first roared over her head. Its propeller chopping the air, it turned. The gondola bumped up against the chimney. A moment later a rope ladder appeared over the side, and she saw Anton's face, ghostly in the dim light from the city streets. "Get in!" he cried. The rope ladder danced just to the right of the metal one she'd climbed; she managed to snag it with one hand, then held on to it while keeping her feet on the last few rungs of the metal ladder before transferring herself entirely to the rope one. The gondola sank a few feet as she climbed aboard. Karl, as always, was right behind her. He was just clambering over the edge when blue light flashed.

Someone screamed down below, but whatever the spell had been, it had left them untouched.

Anton, pulling up the rope ladder, yelped, dropped the ladder again, and from his belt grabbed a strange metal object, a short tube projecting from some kind of handle. He pointed it over the side, and there was a flash of light accompanied by an enormously loud bang that made Brenna flinch and clap her hands over her ears. Then Anton spun back into the gondola and cranked the lever that fired the burner. Yellow-and-blue flame exploded upward into the envelope, the heat searing her face, and almost at once they began to rise. Letting the burner roar, Anton reached for another lever, and the propeller at the back of the gondola began to spin twice as fast, adding its own throbbing beat to the noise in the gondola and making it quite impossible to talk.

Not that Brenna had anything to say. She huddled in the gondola, knees pulled to her chest, arm wrapped around them, and shook . . . in reaction to everything that had just happened, because she was cold, because the strain in her arms and legs had been relieved, because . . .

She didn't know all the reasons. But she trembled just the same.

Karl crawled over to her, put his arm around her shoulder. "Are you all right?"

"Yes," she said. Then, "No." And suddenly she found herself weeping, and turned and buried her head in Karl's shoulder.

Karl felt a bit like weeping himself, but he held Brenna close, trying to warm her trembling body and provide what comfort he could . . . all the while aware of Anton watching the two of them with a stony face. He wanted to assure the Outsider that this wasn't what it looked like, that he and Brenna weren't . . .

. . . but then he thought, *To hell with that*, and put his other arm around her for good measure.

So, Anton thought, looking at Karl embracing the weeping Brenna. *It's like that. I should have let Falk kill him.*

He almost meant it.

Well, time enough for him to beat Karl to a pulp later. The important thing now was to get all three of them out of this accursed Kingdom and into the safety of the Outside.

Through the cold, clear night, with only a light westerly breeze to fight, the airship flew steadily toward the Anomaly.

Davydd Verdsmitt had been confident the King would agree to see *anyone* who arrived at his doorstep with that ring. He wasn't disappointed—although the secretary certainly seemed to be, giving Verdsmitt a sour look as he ushered him through the big doors into the inner sanctum of the King's sanctuary.

Verdsmitt had never been there. Few MageLords had, Falk and Lord Athol . . . Verdsmitt never allowed himself to think of the Prime Adviser as his father . . . being the obvious exceptions. The King was reclusive, disengaged, hedonistic . . . it was no secret to anyone that he had frittered most of his reign away on his own pleasures, leaving the sordid business of the actual running of the kingdom to Athol, Falk, and the rest of the Council.

Not that the Kingdom would have been any better off to have Kravon fully engaged with it, Verdsmitt thought bitterly.

He'd loved Kravon once. Now he hated him. But he suspected even if the love had continued and they had remained together, he would not be blind to Kravon's deficiencies. Kravon could be funny and charming; he could have been a professional clavierist had he not been the Heir, and his artistic ability with pen and ink and brush and paint was every bit as notable. But he was totally unsuited to running the Kingdom ... or even his own household, a task he left to men like the secretary.

Had he kept me by his side, I could have helped him, Verdsmitt thought. *Together we could have reformed the Kingdom, brought the Commoners properly into the government, made it a fairer and freer land ...*

... but instead, it's rotten, from the core on out, and the only thing to do is throw it, Palace and Barriers and MageLords and all, onto the garbage heap of history.

Whether what he intended to do would accomplish that, he didn't know. He knew Brenna and the Prince were probably together somewhere. Would they know what to do when the moment came? He couldn't count on it.

But this was his chance. There would be no other. And really, he thought as he walked down a long white-walled hallway carpeted in thick red plush that swallowed the sound of his footsteps, so that it almost seemed he glided magically toward the audience chamber, what did it matter to him one way or the other? He would have had his revenge.

He had already died once, as Calibon, son of Lord Athol. Now he would die a second time, as Davydd Verdsmitt, the most notable playwright of his age.

His lip quirked. It almost made him regret his impending death, thinking what a juicy ending it would make to his autobiography, which he would now never have the opportunity to write.

He had reached the gilded door of the audience room. The secretary, face as pinched as though he'd eaten a chokecherry, opened the door and ushered him in.

The small room was comfortably furnished with a fireplace, two chairs, and a table between them on which sat a steaming silver teapot, two dainty white cups trimmed with gold, and a plate of round pink objects that Verdsmitt could tell just by looking were mostly sugar.

Two Royal guards stood at attention on either side of the fireplace, rather like overgrown bookends.

"You may wait here," the secretary said, pointing Verdsmitt to one of the chairs. "His Majesty will attend you presently. Please help yourself to refreshments."

The secretary went out, closing the doors behind him. The two guards ignored him. He sighed and reached for one of the pink trifles, expecting a long wait; but in fact he had barely popped the dainty trifle into his mouth (and it was every bit as sweet as he had expected) before King Kravon entered the room through a door opposite the one through which Verdsmitt had come.

Aware of the guards, Verdsmitt got to his feet and bowed his head. "Your Majesty," he said. "Thank you for seeing me."

Kravon looked very different from the boy Verdsmitt remembered. Years of soft living and pleasure had taken their toll. While Verdsmitt, hardened by life on the stage and in the Commons, remained almost as slim as he had been at sixteen, Kravon had . . . expanded. His stomach strained at the buttons of his scarlet waistcoat, his calves bulged in white tights above soft black indoor boots. The golden belt he wore seemed barely big enough to contain his ample belly. He had three chins, his hair was mostly gone, and what little was left was liberally streaked with gray.

He looked twenty years older than Verdsmitt, twenty years older than he should have looked, and Verdsmitt felt a renewed surge of hatred at the way he had let himself deteriorate, as though the bulging middle-aged man in front of him had somehow murdered the boy he had once loved.

But, no—that boy had *voluntarily* turned into this loathsome creature.

In a small corner of his mind, Verdsmitt wondered at the depth of his hatred, after so many years, wondered why it seemed so fresh and ever-renewing, as though it didn't spring from himself alone, but from somewhere outside . . .

. . . but that small, questioning voice drowned in new waves of gut-wrenching loathing.

It was all he could do not to kill the King there and then,

but he wanted Kravon to *know* who was killing him. He would wait just a few moments longer.

"Yes, yes," the King said, waving his hand airily. "Sit down, sit down." He plopped himself into the other chair and Verdsmitt resumed his place in his own. "Stelp told me of this ring you carry. Show it to me."

"Of course, Your Majesty." Verdsmitt reached inside his own plain black vest and drew out the ring from the inner pocket. He handed it to Kravon.

The King, who had filled the empty moment by stuffing one of the pink trifles into his mouth, took it. " 'Straordinary," he mumbled, mouth full. "Fellow this belonged to is dead. Thought this went to the bottom of the lake with him. Where did you find it?"

"I didn't 'find' it, Kravon," Verdsmitt said, and his deliberate familiarity made the King's head jerk up as though hearing his voice for the first time. "I've always had it . . . since the day you gave it to me, and pledged we would be together forever . . . just weeks before you renounced and denounced me and left me to ridicule and ruin."

The King's eyes widened. "Calibon?" he breathed. "Sky-Mage, it is you!" And then he turned white. "Guards!" he shouted, shoving his chair back, stumbling to his feet. "Arrest—"

It's a pity we didn't get to chat more, Verdsmitt thought in that last instant, as the guards, moving, to his eyes, as slowly as insects caught in tree sap, began to draw their swords and lurch toward him. *It would have been nice to know what he thought of my plays.*

Ah, well.

He reached out with his will. Kravon screamed as the ring in his fist turned searingly cold, but he had barely begun to open his fingers before he and everything else were blotted out in an enormous explosion of blue fire.

———

Anton, looking west, saw the flash reflected on the bottom of the envelope above him, and on the gleaming surfaces of the brass-bound burner and propeller controls. He shot a look over his shoulder, but could see nothing amiss.

Down in the bottom of the gondola, Brenna didn't even notice the flash. But she felt the magical blast that had just killed the King deep in her bones—deeper, in fact, in the very pit of her soul, a searing wave of agony that ripped through her like wildfire through dry grass. She stiffened, her head snapping back against the wicker of the gondola, breath whooshing out of her in one wordless cry of pain and terror, turning instantly to a cloud of white in the icy air.

Karl, holding her, felt her shudder in his arms, saw her head jerk back, saw her breath explode out of her . . . and not resume. "She's not breathing!" he screamed. "She's not—"

He could think of nothing else to do. He pulled her rigid body closer, put his mouth on hers to share his breath with her . . .

Anton heard Brenna's grunting cry, then Karl's shout. He tied off the tiller, surged around it to help Brenna . . .

. . . and skidded to a stop so suddenly his feet slid out from under him and he fell hard on his rear end. He barely noticed.

Karl and Brenna were locked in a kiss, both unmoving, and around them the air glowed blue.

The glow waxed second by second, brighter and brighter. Streamers of blue flame, burning nothing, poured across the night sky toward the airship, passing through the wicker of the gondola, through the envelope, through *him*, he realized with horror as he looked down, pouring soundlessly, faster and faster, into Brenna, into Karl . . .

Anton had to shield his eyes, unable to face the light, now as bright as the sun and getting brighter. He closed his eyes but still the light blinded him, turned and pressed his head into his gloved hands and could still see it, threw his whole arm across his eyes and *could still see it* . . .

. . . and then, like a candle being snuffed, it vanished.

Anton raised watering eyes. The yellow glow of the

steering lantern now seemed only a feeble spark, but it was enough for him to see Brenna and Karl, still locked together . . . and then to see Karl jerk straight and push himself away from Brenna, gasping for air. Brenna slumped to the bottom of the gondola and fell over on her side, limp and lifeless as a rag doll.

"No!" Anton cried, and lunged forward. He pushed the stunned and unprotesting Karl out of the way and rolled Brenna over onto her back. She still wasn't breathing, but when he put his fingers to her neck he could feel her pulse, slow, weak, weakening . . .

He pulled her head back, pinched her nostrils, began giving her his own breath as Karl had begun to do moments, or ages, before. In . . . out . . . turning to watch the rise and fall of her chest . . .

. . . and then, suddenly, she coughed, gulped air, and started to choke.

He rolled her over on her side just as she spewed watery, yellowish, foul-smelling liquid across the bottom of the gondola. Karl scrambled back further to avoid it; Anton ignored it, but rolled her onto her back again . . . and was rewarded with her eyes opening. She blinked at him. "Anton?" she asked. "Are we safely away from the manor?" And then she frowned. "No . . . that was a long time ago . . . I . . ." She closed her eyes. "I'm confused," she mumbled, and then she slept, but now her breathing was normal and her color was good, and Anton leaned back from her with relief.

Karl seemed to be slowly coming around, as well. "What . . . what happened?" he said. "Brenna . . . I tried to help her breathe, and then . . . light . . ." He shook his head. "I don't . . ." And then his eyes widened. "Or . . ." He scrambled up, looked behind them at the fading yellow glow of New Cabora. "We have to go back."

Anton gaped at him. "Are you crazy? They tried to kill you!"

"*Falk* tried to kill us," Karl said. "Falk's dead. You shot him yourself."

"Mother Northwind isn't," Anton said.

Karl shook his head. "Mother Northwind has no use for us anymore," he said. "What she wanted us to do, we just did."

It was Anton's turn to stare. "You mean . . . that was the Keys? The King died, the Keys came to Brenna, and you . . . ?"

"Do you have any other explanation?" Karl demanded.

Anton barked a laugh. "I didn't even believe in magic two weeks ago. Of course I don't have an explanation."

"Take us back," Karl insisted again. "We don't have to land if there's danger. They can't do anything to us up here, even with magic, not while I'm aboard . . . take us back. We have to know."

Anton glanced at Brenna. "All right," he said. "We'll go back." He returned to the wheel, untied it, and spun it to bring the lumbering airship slowly around to head east again. He killed the engine, so they once more drifted with the wind. "Running short on fuel," he explained. "And better for sneaking up on things."

He aimed the airship's prow toward the yellow glow of New Cabora. "I hope you know what you're doing."

———

Mother Northwind, holding onto life with all of her dwindling strength as the guards above her called for a Healer, did not see the blue flash that signaled the death of the King. But moments later, as the Keys attempted to transfer to the Heir, only to encounter the magic-killing force of the Magebane, she felt the surge of magic all around her as the intricate web of power built by the long-gone architects of Evrenfels was ripped apart.

Magic poured out of the guards, the MageLords in the Palace, the Mageborn in the enclave within the Barrier and the gated neighborhoods in New Cabora, in the Colleges in Berriton, in towns and villages all over the Kingdom. Mother Northwind could feel that magic rushing toward Brenna, as the Keys, as they had been designed to do, reached out for all the available power, attempting to accomplish a task suddenly made impossible.

A guard had been kneeling over her, holding a cloth to her shattered shoulder, trying to staunch the blood. He stiffened, gave an audible groan, and fell forward across her body, a heavy weight that made it even harder to breathe than it had been . . .

. . . but, she realized as she heard the clatter of armored Mageborn guards fainting throughout the Square, she wouldn't need to breathe much longer.

She had always thought soft magic would survive the destruction of the Keys, and perhaps it would; she could still feel inside her the power she used to twist men's minds into doing her will.

But Healing had always been intertwined with hard magic. Realigning bones, relieving pressure on nerves, excising tumors—all were exercises in the manipulation of matter and energy, just as the Lesser and Great Barrier were, however much smaller in scale.

And so, too, was the stopping of bleeding.

As she felt both her magic and her lifeblood pouring out of her, as a final, fading roar filled her ears, Mother Northwind's last thought was for the Minik.

I wish I could be there when they discover the Wall of Tears is gone, she thought. *I wish . . .*

It was her last wish, and her last thought.

CHAPTER 33

LITTLE RAIN TRUDGED THROUGH THE SNOW on unsteady feet. The wife of his brother Black Spruce had given birth to twin boys that day, and the celebration had gone on long into the night. His own wife would be worried about him, and he'd probably feel badly about that when he was sober. But for now he whistled the tune to the bawdy sea chantey Black Spruce's Minik-na friend Thissen had brought back to the village from his recent trip to Wavehaven. He'd brought many other things with him in his fine new wagon, including some rich, strong Minik-na beer, which they had all enjoyed liberally and long.

It was a fine, moonlit night. Little Rain was only about halfway home, with still twenty minutes' walk ahead of him, when it became urgently necessary for him to stop for a few minutes. He stepped off the path and faced east, toward the immovable fog of the Wall of Tears. He had just unbuttoned and begun to relieve himself when, between one blink and the next, the wall of fog that had stood unchanged for his entire life collapsed, rushing downward and vanishing into fading shreds that blew away eastward.

Though his people had long since settled in southern-style houses and no longer moved from place to place as they once had, the valley he had been crossing had been a Minik winter campground for many centuries. And there, clear in the moonlight, not more than a mile away, he could see low round huts of the traditional kind, smoke rising from them into the clear, cold air.

He started forward, realized as cold stabbed at him that he had not buttoned himself, and sealed his clothing with trembling fingers as he stumbled forward through the snow, first walking, then trotting, then running.

And so it was that Little Rain became the first Minik to enter the Hidden Kingdom of Evrenfels in eight hundred years; and so it was that the Great Sundering of the Minik ended.

His wife eventually forgave him for not coming home at all that night.

In the streets of New Cabora, the fallen guards began to stir. Most of the Commoners knew nothing of what had happened; asleep in their beds or cowering in their houses if they were close to those neighborhoods Falk's guards had swept through.

But other Commoners were abroad, agents of the Common Cause watching the guards and looking for an opportunity to strike at them. At the corner of Tanner Avenue and Palace View Road, a young guard named Tilden jerked awake and staggered to his feet even as two men rushed him from the shadows, bared blades gleaming. He flung up his hand to cast a spell that would solidify the air in front of them . . . and belatedly realized he didn't know how.

Or rather, he remembered doing it, but now it seemed, somehow, impossible.

As did breathing a moment later, as one of the Commoner blades found his heart.

Most of the guards fared better. Bereft of magic though they quickly understood themselves to be, they still had armor, weapons, and horses. Rallying, they gathered their dead, Falk and Mother Northwind included, and galloped back to the gate.

Except there was no gate, and no need for one. The Lesser Barrier was gone. Already flowers were withering in the cold and ice forming on the edges of the lake that had not seen ice for eight hundred years. The Palace seethed like an overturned anthill, guards rushing out of it to defend it against any attack from the Commons, weeping Mageborn charging madly and uselessly about.

The Council met in emergency session, without Falk, without any representative of the King, and without the Commoner, who had apparently vanished into thin air. The First Healer was there, but so shocked by the disappearance of his power that he didn't seem to hear a word that was said. None of the Councillors had been privy to the secrets of the Unbound and so had no explanation for what had happened. Brich might have enlightened them, had he not been beaten to death during the mass escape of prisoners from the no-longer-magically sealed cells in Falk's prison.

Still, the members of the Council knew that the King was dead, the Heir had vanished, magic had failed, and all that stood between them and a Commoner uprising were the guards ringing the Palace with steel.

They all agreed that the Commoner servants had to be locked up, and since the only space secure enough for that was the chamber of the MageFurnace, that was where they were put. Guards were set on them, but a few found themselves out of sight of those guards long enough to slip out through the tunnel Mother Northwind had followed earlier that night. Those that did rushed into New Cabora, the Barrier no longer there to stop them, and spread the word to friends and family all over town.

Among those who escaped Falk's cells was Goodwife Beth, who had found that the forgettings laid upon her by Mother Northwind had unraveled with the old woman's death. She remembered everything she had ever known about Mother Northwind and the Common Cause, and that meant she knew exactly who to talk to in New Cabora.

Soon crowds of Commoners were moving through the streets, some armed with swords, some with daggers, some with nothing more than crude clubs. All of them were headed toward the Palace, where most of the Mageborn had already fled, to cower behind the guards grimly determined to make a last, desperate stand.

All those details Karl found out much, much later. What he *saw*, as Anton steered the airship over New Cabora, were armed mobs heading purposefully toward the Palace, still surrounded by snow-free ground but no longer protected by the Lesser Barrier. Around it, Anton's glasses showed him—and when he first put them to his eyes and the tiny figures below seemed to leap toward him, just as in the magniseer in his room, he thought Anton must have been lying about the lack of magic in the Outside—the guards were drawn up in a defensive perimeter, crouched with crossbows behind makeshift barricades made of furniture from the Palace.

"It's going to be a bloodbath," Anton shouted as they roared over City Square, the noise of the propeller and occasional blast from the burner turning heads below, heads which promptly displayed the tiny black circles of open mouths as their owners tracked the flying contraption's progress.

"Not if I can help it," Karl said. "Can you land me between the Commoners and the guard, there at the front of the Palace?" He pointed. Commoners were at one end of the ceremonial gardens, the guards at the other. The Commoners were clearly leery of the crossbows, but he could see bows among them, too. It would only take one shot to set off a conflagration of violence.

"I wish I had magic to make my voice louder," Karl said. "I want both sides to hear me."

Anton grinned. "It's not magic, but maybe it'll do." He tied off the wheel, then dived into a chest near the still-sleeping Brenna, pulling out a cone-shaped object, open at both ends. "Talk into the small end," he said. "We use it to yell instructions to the ground crew . . . when we have one."

Karl took it a little gingerly. "Set us down."

Anton nodded. He hadn't fired the burner for several

minutes, and already they were descending. Now he judged the angles carefully, aimed toward the middle of the garden, and with the judicious release of air from the envelope at the last moment, settled them gently onto the frost-blasted flowers.

The appearance of the airship had brought a stunned silence to guards and Commoners alike. Karl took advantage of that silence.

"People of Evrenfels!" he shouted, the megaphone expanding his voice so that it echoed back from the high marble walls of the Palace. "You know me! I am Prince Karl, Heir to the Throne of Evrenfels . . . and with the death of King Kravon, your new King!"

That brought a roar of approval from the guards, but silence from the Commoners . . . not at all what he'd hoped for. "Common people of New Cabora," he shouted in their direction. "Will you send me a representative so that I may address your grievances?"

Anton eyed him. "Eight hundred years of grievances?" he said softly.

Karl lowered the megaphone. "I'm doing the best I can," he growled. "If you have a better idea, I'd like to hear it."

Anton shrugged. "A famous statesman once said talking to avoid war is far better than warring to avoid talk. Good luck."

"Thank you." Karl lifted the megaphone again. "Will you send me a representative?" he shouted. "Someone from the Common Cause, perhaps?"

There was a commotion, someone . . . no, two someones, pushing their way through the crowd. Karl felt a surge of relief as they reached the front and he saw them clearly for the first time: Goodwife Beth, supporting none other than Vinthor. One of Vinthor's legs was crudely splinted and blood stained the white bandage wound around it, and a second bandage around his head, but he was alive. In the moment the door had banged into him in the stable, Karl had been certain he'd been killed.

Vinthor turned and surveyed the crowd. "I am City Leader of the Common Cause and had the direct ear of the Patron," he shouted. "And this is Goodwife Beth . . ."

Even under the circumstances, that name brought snickers from those who knew the Verdsmitt play.

". . . who was Leader of the Common Cause for all of southern Evrenfels, and a personal friend of the Patron." That silenced the snickerers. "All those within the Cause will confirm this."

There was a murmur in the crowd as, apparently, they did just that.

"Does anyone object?"

No one did, and with Beth's help, Vinthor turned and made his long, slow way to the airship. "He won't be able to climb in with a broken leg," Anton said as Vinthor approached.

"He won't have to." Karl vaulted over the side of the gondola and went to help his former captor. He held out an arm. Vinthor looked at him for a moment, as though weighing carefully what he was about to do, then nodded his thanks, released Beth's arm, and took Karl's instead. He allowed the Prince to lead both him and Beth to one of the curved wooden benches scattered around the now-dying garden.

They sat together. "We've got to keep the guards and Commoners from massacring each other," Karl said softly, being very careful to do nothing that might appear threatening to anyone watching. "Do you agree?"

"I agree," Vinthor said.

"And I," Beth said. "But it will not be easy. There is a lot of hatred among the Commoners."

"I know," Karl said.

Vinthor studied him. "So you really are the Magebane."

Karl nodded. "So it appears."

"And, in truth, a Commoner yourself."

Karl nodded again.

"But we can't tell anyone that."

"I don't think it would be wise." Karl glanced back at

the guards. "The Commoners might applaud me, but the MageLords ... Vinthor, I know the Common Cause won't like it, but we need them. We have to have stability while we redesign the Kingdom. And more than that ..." Karl glanced back at Anton, who was watching them from the gondola. "The Kingdom is no longer hidden. Only the army and guards can keep it from falling prey to whatever forces may converge on it from the Outside world. We need the MageLords working for the Kingdom if the Kingdom is to survive at all."

"I don't disagree." Vinthor glanced over his shoulder at the gathered Commoners. "But ultimately, Your Majesty," he said, his use of the title verging on the sarcastic, "you *cannot* govern this Kingdom as it has always been governed. The MageLords claim they have the right to rule us because they have magic and we do not. But now there is no magic. And you cannot expect the Commoners to simply forget the ways in which the MageLords have abused their power over the centuries."

"We can't let the Commoners take revenge," Karl said.

"It's already too late for that," Beth said. "Far fewer guards came out of New Cabora tonight than first went into it. Many scores have already been settled."

Something in her voice caught Karl's attention beyond the words she had spoken. "And would our old friend Jopps be among the dead?" he asked softly.

Beth said nothing.

Vinthor glanced at her, then said, "Never mind the city. Even if you restore control here, out in the country what the villagers do to the MageLords' manors is beyond your or mine or anyone else's control."

"True," Karl said. "But if we are to restore stability anywhere, we must have it somewhere. And here is where we are. We can start here and now to reshape the Kingdom." He put his hand on his chest. "I must remain King for the MageLords' sake. But we need a representative from the Commoners. If you could provide me with a list of names, I could formally appoint ..."

Vinthor shook his head. "No. We need someone chosen by the Commoners to represent them . . . and we have that person."

"You?" Karl said.

"Not I," Vinthor said. "I have made enemies as well as friends during my years with the Common Cause. No. I'm speaking of the Commoner."

"The Council Commoner?" Karl raised an eyebrow. "But he's—"

"The Commoner with the most knowledge about how the Kingdom is governed," Vinthor said. "And someone chosen by the Commoners specifically to advise the King." He gave Karl a hard look. "In exchange for defusing the passions of the Commoners of New Cabora and sparing lives on both sides, I want the Commoner . . . Janson Ironsmith is his name; did you even know that? . . . named your Prime Adviser. I want all the other Councillors thrown out of office, and a new Council, half Commoners and half Mageborn. If magic is truly gone, eventually that distinction will fade."

"If the Kingdom survives at all," Karl said. He looked at the crowd of silently watching Commoners, hundreds of breath plumes rising into the dark sky, glowing red in the light of the fires burning all around the Palace. "Very well," he said. "You have my word. Do you know where the Commoner . . . Ironsmith . . . is?"

"I do," Beth said. "He fled the Palace the moment the magic failed. He is in a safe place in the city."

"Then I should meet with him. But not here." He glanced at the Palace. "There. *If* I can convince my own guards to let me back into it."

Vinthor glanced back at the Commoner crowd on the lakeshore. "Then I had better go talk to *them*."

"*We* had better, my love," said Beth. She held out his hand and pulled him to his feet. "*We* had better."

Karl began the long walk through the ceremonial gardens to the Palace. But he stopped at the gondola of the airship on his way. "With luck, we'll avoid civil war," he said to Anton. "Go back to your own people, tell them what happened." He gave the Outsider a hard look. "Will they invade?"

"I don't know," Anton said. "It's very difficult to get a large force this far inland. You have a few weeks' grace, at least. I'd recommend sending a formal delegation to Elkbone. I'll let the Lord Mayor know you're coming."

Karl nodded. "Do that. And if no formal delegation comes . . ." His lips tightened. "Then the Kingdom of Evrenfels no longer exists and only chaos remains. Take control and welcome."

Anton nodded again.

"Now get out of here," Karl said. "Before someone decides to put a few crossbow bolts into you or your flying machine . . . or both. Take Brenna. Take her someplace safe. And tell her . . ." He looked down into the gondola at the sleeping girl, remembering the warmth of her body against his. "Tell her . . ." He paused. "Tell her I said good-bye," he finished finally.

"I will," Anton said quietly.

Karl turned away and resumed walking toward the Palace and the waiting ranks of guards. His heart leaped with relief and renewed hope as he saw, among the blue uniforms, Teran's face. *At least I have one ally there.*

Behind him he heard the roar of the burner and, a moment later, the throbbing of the propeller; but as the airship lifted from the ground and flew away into the unknown west, he didn't turn to watch it go.

———

Brenna opened her eyes.

For a moment she didn't know where she was. Her head lay on something soft, but not a pillow—more like a rolled-up coat; the blanket that covered her was rough and scratchy; and her bed seemed to have turned into a wicker basket.

Above her a tongue of fire roared into leaping, flickering life, lighting up the inside of a vast blue loaf-shape, and as though it had also lit up the inside of her mind, she suddenly remembered everything . . . everything up until the moment when pain had struck her like a hammer blow and the world had been swallowed by blinding blue light.

She tensed, but there was no pain now beyond the ordinary discomforts of cramped limbs and a distended bladder. She sat up.

Anton stood at the tiller of the airship on the other side of the burner, his face haggard with exhaustion in the gray light before dawn. Behind him, a few late stars still burned, and the propeller spun and bellowed its steady, thrumming roar. "Anton?" Brenna said, her voice sounding more like a frog's croak in her ears.

Anton's eyes, which had been focused on the horizon, jerked down toward her, and the utter relief and joy on his face as he saw her warmed her more than the blanket or the still-roaring burner.

He pushed a lever to cut off the burner, tied off the tiller, and came around to her, falling to his knees beside her and gathering her to him in a hug that also seemed to contain more than the usual amount of warmth. She hugged him back, closing her eyes and laying her head on his shoulder for a long moment.

He showed no signs of letting go, and she had no real complaints about that, but nevertheless after a moment she pushed him away. "What happened?" she said. "Where's Karl?"

"Back at the Palace, trying to keep the ex-Mageborn and Commoners from murdering each other," he said.

"Ex-Mageborn?" Brenna remembered the pain, the blue light. "It worked?"

"It worked," Anton said softly. "We should be crossing the Anomaly now. And . . . well, take a look." He helped her to her feet, and she peered over the edge of the gondola.

The prairie below them was unmarked snow . . . but there was a line of drifts and ice, straight as though laid down with a ruler, stretching away as far as she could see to north and south.

The Great Barrier had vanished. The Hidden Kingdom was hidden no longer.

She felt dizzy, though it had nothing to do with her long sleep. She had thought she'd believed what Mother Northwind had told her, but now she realized she hadn't, not really. Even seeing magic bounce off of Karl hadn't fully brought home to her what they were trying to do. But this . . .

The Barrier, which had stood for eight centuries, had disappeared as though it had never existed, taking magic with it. The world would never be the same again. A world in which she flew in an airship across the long-sealed borders of Evrenfels was completely different than the one in which she had always lived . . . and very nearly died.

There were children's stories of visitors from other worlds, sometimes said to lie among the stars, sometimes deep under the Earth, sometimes . . . she smiled weakly . . . from outside the Great Barrier. She had never expected one of those stories to come true . . . never expected that she would be both the one who met the visitor from another world, and an otherworldly visitor herself.

The line of the vanished Barrier was behind them. She was Outside. She was flying, a thing no one from the Kingdom had ever believed possible. And she was with a young man who had grown up and lived all his life out here.

It was all true, and all strange, and though she felt a little dizzy as the implications rushed at her, it was also utterly exhilarating.

Anton had seized her arm when he saw her waver; now she tucked her arm inside his and leaned her head against his shoulder again. "A whole new world," she said. "Will you show it to me?"

"There's nothing I'd like better," he said. He leaned down and kissed her, a soft, lingering kiss that warmed her so thoroughly she thought she would never be cold again.

Behind them the sun broke the horizon in a blaze of orange fire. Below them, the prairie snow spread out all around, unbroken. Ahead of them, the land and sky still lay in shadow . . .

. . . but a shadow that would soon be lit by the sun.

The kiss ended. Brenna let out her breath in a contented sigh, and snuggled against Anton, whose arms tightened around her.

Long ago, her Commoner nursemaid had told her that with every sunrise a new world was born.

Brenna, gazing down from the airship, watched that saying come true.